G000136611

Devil On
My Shoulder

Devil On My Shoulder

Janet Mary Tomson

PIATKUS

In Memory of Orlando,
and for Karinda who loved him.

Copyright © 1996 by Janet Mary Tomson

First published in Great Britain in 1996 by
Judy Piatkus (Publishers) Ltd of
5 Windmill Street, London W1

**The moral right of the author
has been asserted**

*A catalogue record for this book is available
from the British Library*

ISBN 0–7499–0343–0

Set in 11 on 12pt Times by
Phoenix Photosetting, Chatham, Kent
Printed and bound in Great Britain by
Mackays of Chatham PLC, Chatham, Kent

Chapter 1

Ireland
March 1642

'Bless you, child, 'tis nothing to be feared of. You've had the sign, that's all. 'Tis your springtime, your growing up.'

Sorcha O'Neill nodded doubtfully at her mother and tried to keep the disbelief from her eyes. That very morning, before daylight had penetrated the cracks in their hut where the rotting door met the splintered frame, she had turned in her bed and felt a strange dampness in the straw beneath her. For a terrible moment she thought: Dear Jesus, I've wet meself; then hearing the rain falling with such unrelenting force, she guessed that the cracks in the walls had widened again and water was flooding up and across the floor. The sight of the thin, brown blood on her fingers made her jolt with shock.

Sorcha lay still, her heartbeat whooshing in her head. She should not have washed her hair yesterday. Washing your hair on a Friday was a sin and now she was being punished. She closed her eyes and waited to see what would happen. There was no pain, only a dull ache at the base of her belly. Into the gloom she prayed: Holy Mary, mother of God, please don't let me die in agony. Don't let me go to hell. She wondered how long it would take to die.

When her father finally dragged himself from the couch and blundered off to scavenge dead fish and driftwood from the shores of the river, she confessed her terrible secret to her mother.

Dervla O'Neill gave the semblance of a laugh. 'It means that you're a woman now. The gods have given you the sign. Tomorrow we'll light a fire and sprinkle the last of the salt onto it, and drip those few drops of honey into the flames. When the time comes we'll ask the gods to guide you safe through the dangers of

1

birthing.' Dervla tilted her head to one side and pushed a dank strand of hair away from her furrowed cheek. Her skin had a dusty, parched quality and was the same colour as the coarse grey apron that covered her tattered skirt.

'But don't you be doing nothin' foolish with the boys.' She gave her daughter a warning look.

Sorcha shook her head. She dared not ask what sort of thing, guessing it had something to do with the ugly, dangly worm that hung between boys' legs. At night sometimes, her father would climb over her mother and grunt and push at her. At such times, Sorcha froze in her narrow couch, hoping they would not suspect that she heard them. It was such a shameful ritual, dark and terrible. Then, her mother's belly would always swell, and after the passing of three seasons, she would undergo the ordeal of birthing. Invariably this was followed by the brief presence of a brother or sister, drawing a few, sad, painful breaths, before being consigned back to the earth gods.

Looking out at the dreary March morning, her mother said: 'Spring is the rebirth, the season of hope. You must always have faith.'

Sorcha believed in the power of the gods well enough, for hardly a day passed when she did not witness some new proof as to their power to give or to take away. Soon now, the mysteries would be revealed to her. But today, she felt so weary that the idea of hope and rebirth was impossible to sustain.

'We'll go to the Mass, too, say a prayer for you. If we can find a coin, we'll light a candle. Now, go and fetch some water and clean yourself.'

Comforted by the prospect of having so many gods on her side, Sorcha took the pail and set out to fetch water from the ditch that skirted the end of the lane. Yesterday it had been little more than a shallow, smelly trickle. Today it was racing with glistening yellow-brown water.

The alley which ran between the two rows of tumbledown shacks was thick with mud. As she made her way down towards the ditch, slipping and sliding, mud squelched between her toes. She had draped an extra piece of sacking over her shoulders to keep the rain off, but it was too small to cover her head and her brown hair turned black as the long strands plastered across her face. Her thick eyelashes were soon heavy with water, giving her

2

a strange, sparkly look. 'You've eyes of true Celtic blue,' her father sometimes said, when the drink was upon him.

As she dipped the pail into the tumbling water, Sorcha thought about what was happening inside of her, this sign from the gods that she was now a woman. She felt taut with a sense of expectation, that something momentous was bound to follow . . . yet when she considered the women about her, they offered little inspiration. All, like her mother, were drained, used up, old before their years. Whatever the secret of womanhood might be, it seemed to have by-passed these women of Dublin. In a moment of rebellion she thought: It's not going to happen to me.

Back inside the hut she wiped herself clean with a piece of rag, then started to make a soup with some stinking fish her father had brought home the evening before. The scales had a strange, rainbow hue that belied the ugliness of the decaying flesh. Sorcha's insides contracted with a mixture of nausea and hunger and she knew that however bad the smell, she would still eat the fish.

A moment later Kathy O'Connell from next door barged her way into the hut, a baby bouncing on her hip. 'Bejasus, Dervla, we're moving out; all of us. Your man's on his way back. We're going to fight the English.'

'Where? I don't . . .'

Kathy O'Connell shook her head impatiently. 'Don't be asking me. 'Tis your man that knows all the answers. He says the English are coming to take the castle at Carrickmain. There's been a call to arms. Everyone round here is going.'

'But it's miles away!'

'Not so far, I think. Four miles straight.'

Sorcha drew back into the corner, afraid that Kathy might see her and stop. Already her pulse was racing with a mixture of excitement and fear.

Her mother asked: 'But what are we going to do there?'

Even as she spoke, Ciaran O'Neill pushed his way past the woman in the doorway. He was breathing heavily, his own Celtic blue eyes bright with excitement. He answered for her. 'Get your scarf, woman, there's no time to be wasting. King Charlie's boys are invading our shores. We won't stop until the very last Englishman is dead.'

To Sorcha, who had never before left the confines of her native

3

city, the journey to Carrickmain seemed long and fraught with danger. She had a heavy load to carry and the roads were rutted deep beneath the puddles. Soon the jagged stones cut into her feet and added to her general sense of unease.

All along the route there were signs to watch out for – a mangy dog with three legs, two crows in an oak. Only her mother could interpret what they meant, but she was saying nothing. Dervla's mouth was drawn tight, and now and then she rested her hand in the small of her back as if to help herself along. As she glanced round to check that her daughter was following, the swell of her belly protruded against the greasy rag of her skirts. She was near her time.

'Come along, child. We must get there before night.'

Sorcha's father walked with the men. As she watched, Ciaran stopped in his tracks, waving his hands about. She knew that he was arguing some point of belief. Short, wiry of build, eyes aflame with zeal, he raised his voice loud so that all could hear. The enemy were coming to take their land and they must fight to the last man to rid Ireland of the cursed English. This was why they must fly to the defence of Carrickmain.

After a few hours they reached their destination. The castle stood guard on the road to Dun Laoghaire. Massive and forbidding, it looked out across the dense hills of Dalkey, Killeny and Ballybrack where patriots hid in the sheltering woods. It reminded Sorcha of an ogre, motionless, terrifying. As they drew near, she instinctively did not want to go inside. This was a bad place where evil spirits waited for the likes of poor families such as her own.

The rest of the party crossed the moat in a continuous stream like Noah's beasts into the towering Ark. There were some two hundred of them. Left alone, Sorcha had no choice but to follow.

They found themselves in a deserted square yard. Some dilapidated buildings flanked the walls and the earth beneath their feet was pitted with broken stones. High walls surrounded the courtyard and from the battlements a few men greeted their arrival. They looked gaunt, skinny – hardly human – and Sorcha had a powerful feeling that these were demons waiting to feast upon her flesh. It was hard to distinguish their shaggy heads from the thick furs they wore for protection because both were caked with mud. They alone held the fort against the unseen enemy.

4

When the men came down from the ramparts they spoke in Gaelic and Sorcha realised that they were ordinary mortals like herself. One even winked at her, and a surge of pleasure mingled with disapproval gave her a sudden sense of power.

In one corner of the courtyard stood a tower from which it seemed the whole of Ireland could be seen. In the distance was Dublin Bay and beyond that, Wales.

They made camp on the damp earth, clearing the stones, setting their belongings about them. There was no cover and little food. Sorcha was sent to collect kindling for a fire. At the thought of warmth and having something to do, she jumped to her feet, anxious to obey.

'Stay within sight,' her mother warned.

Brashly she ventured back out across the moat to gather sticks from beneath the canopy of oaks. It was strangely silent. All the time she tried to gauge whether she could outrun any attacker back to the safety of the fortress. She did not know which was worse, fear of the foreign soldiers, or of the hungry spirits of the woods. With every second, panic rose until the very hordes of hell seemed to be stalking in her wake. Suddenly she could hold back no longer. With a gasp of terror she began to race, sticks falling from her arms, becoming entangled in her legs, stumbling, fuelling her own nightmare.

Once inside the castle gates, she stopped, panting with relief. It took minutes to get her breath back. She looked up hopefully at the sky. What cloud there was moved fast away to the west. There was too much wind to permit more rain and yet the southwesterly brought its own discomfort.

'Help me,' said her mother. They busied themselves building the fire. It took many attempts to light it, for the gusts blew out the infant flame time and again, but finally the courtyard was muffled in smoke billowing and guttering at the whim of the wind.

Sorcha's father returned with a sheep's haunch. He and the menfolk had raided the neighbourhood. Her tongue could already taste the smokey meat, feel the texture of the flesh. She had good teeth and could chew the toughest carcase. Her mother stripped, tore and then skewered the meat over the fire. It took forever to cook and she tasted it a thousand times before the juices finally trickled over her tongue.

5

They slept in the open and from time to time one of the band roused themselves to stoke the blaze, for by night it was bitterly cold. Strange animal noises echoed across the forest, hungry, merciless. Once darkness fell, Sorcha was grateful for the safety of the castle, snuggling into her mother for warmth.

The next day Dervla O'Neill rose with the first, fragile grey of morning light. 'Come.' She took her daughter outside the walls.

'Where are we going?'

She did not reply.

Outside it was silent. The distant trees seemed to be waiting for their approach but Dervla strode ahead with purpose. After crossing the damp chill of the surrounding pasture, they moved into the woodland.

'Where are we?'

'Glendruid.' Her mother's tension, her stealth made the girl refrain from asking more.

The woods became increasingly dense, darkening. A long way off a dog, or maybe a wolf, howled. Malicious, disembodied eyes spied on them. Sorcha held on tight to her mother's sleeve on the pretext of helping her along but in reality afraid to be lost.

Of a sudden they came to a clearing. Grass grew short and pale beneath the trees, splashed by dappled sunlight. In the very centre, rising stern and ancient as life itself, was a stone. Dervla put her hand to her lips. From the folds of her shawl she produced the last of the mutton, reverently laid it in offering at the base of the column, then fell to her knees. Her forehead touched the ground. The stone was so black and awesome it might surely strike her dead. So much power poured forth from the grained and gritty surface.

Dervla began to chant, a strange toneless sound older than the Gaelic. She was oblivious to everything. Not knowing what else to do, Sorcha clasped her hands together in an attitude of prayer, willing God, any god to protect her. To these woodland spirits belonged the power of life and death since long before the coming of the Cross.

After an age her mother rose and bowed to the stone then rested her lips against it. She nodded to the girl and reluctantly she followed suit, feeling the gritty coldness against her mouth. Now the stone owned her. Perhaps it would keep her there for ever.

They turned and Sorcha gripped hard to her mother's arm expecting at any moment to be pulled back by some invisible force. She was almost running in her haste to escape but nothing barred the way. Dervla said not a word and her daughter asked no questions. The magic of the stone was too potent, too frightening to give a name.

They remained at the castle for several days. At one point, foreign soldiers came.

'There's nothing to fear,' said Ciaran O'Neill. 'They are no more than a raiding party, too few to cause trouble.' He spoke with such authority that Sorcha felt no fear.

Everyone climbed to the battlements to look down at the men below. Sorcha knew that they were English. It was not just the thick protective buff coats and high leather boots, the deep-brimmed felt hats; there was another, indefinable something to do with height, pallor, the uniform brown of their hair. Encouraged by their scant numbers, the besieged peasants shouted insults. Sorcha rushed down to the courtyard to arm herself with broken masonry then joined in the fun, throwing stones. How they laughed when the soldiers ran away.

The enemy knew that there were too many inside the castle so they set up camp outside and waited. Inside the Irish waited too, aimlessly. Some of their men amused themselves by taking pot shots at the besiegers. An occasional scream told of their success. All the while Sorcha's mother maintained a calm expectancy as if she awaited some answer to her prayer.

One morning there was something different. Ciaran O'Neill put it into words: 'The enemy have brought up reinforcements. Today will see it happen.'

Sorcha did not ask what, because she did not want to hear the answer. She wandered instead to a point high on the castle walls where there was a view of the pasture below. It was like a tableau – diminutive men, horses, tents, a pattern of life frozen in activity, framed by a stockade of trees. Occasionally a voice drifted up to her, and she strained her ears to understand. She'd heard the English spoken often enough in the streets of Dublin; in the shops where she sometimes went to stare – though never to venture inside; in the kitchens where her mother had once worked for an English lord who owned the land as far as the eye could see. She understood sufficient to know that these men intended to stay.

In the field below were pinpoints of orange where camp fires flared and smoked, scattered like sparks from an ember. The rain eased and men peered hopefully from beneath buff coats and blankets, shaking off the crystal beads that dripped from their hats and sleeves. They called to each other in the heathen English, laughing, certain. Sorcha was suddenly afraid.

Her eyes focused on a thatched wooden cabin where a group of soldiers gathered. They seemed better dressed than the rest. In the early morning sun some had removed their coats and wore embroidered jerkins. Their shirts were soft and full-sleeved, and their hair and beards were recently washed and trimmed. Sorcha thought of her father's shaggy head and her confidence ebbed.

In their midst somebody gave orders and she wondered if he was their Commander. Her father said that his name was Sir Simon Harcourt and she tried the alien name on her tongue. Even as the thought came to her, there was a flash and an echoing report from a firepiece. Simultaneously the same man jerked back as if he had been surprised by the noise then, slowly and gracefully, he fell to the ground. Others bent over him. She watched in fascination. Never before had she seen a man die. It looked painless, easy.

Within seconds everything changed. Outside the walls soldiers ran in all directions. One young man hardly past youth took up the call and sprang to the saddle. His buff coat flapped open and his long waving hair, darker than many of his companions', streamed in the sudden uplifting of a breeze. Round his hat he had an orange sash and in his hand he carried a standard raised high above his head. 'Revenge!' he screamed. 'Give no quarter!'

Like washing roused to wakefulness by a frisky wind, other standards began to ripple across the valley and the whole army surged forward as one.

Inside the walls, men scrambled everywhere to find an advantageous position. Through the narrow slits of the keep, over the castellated walls, musket-shot, cannonballs and arrows raced each other down the valley, knocking the advancing army aside. The discordant noise of men, horses, guns, fear and pain, hurt Sorcha's ears. Within moments nothing could be seen beyond a blanket of smoke that formed an outer wall between the Irish and the enemy. It was sulphurous, suffocating, and she ran to find somewhere safe to hide. Suddenly she wanted her mother.

'Here, girl, find anything you can to stuff the cannon with – stones or turf will do.' She hardly looked at the man but raced to do his bidding. Now that she had a role her panic faded. There was now a breech in the castle wall. Cavalrymen poured through it with speed and ease. As one fell so five more took his place. In a sudden frenzy she gathered up lumps of masonry and ran back to the soldier.

'More!'

As she turned away there was a report so loud that for a second she could hear nothing more. Looking back, she saw that the cannon was now a black smoking wreck, its nose buried into the bank, the wheels of the carriage blown jaggedly apart. The soldier, what was left of him, lay raggedly on the ground. He had no head.

She ran. She did not stop until she was deep down a passageway, crushed into the narrowest crevice. Slowly the sounds of battle returned but they were different now. Uppermost was the hated heathen tongue, jubilant, crazy. Somewhere in the midst of the castle other sounds froze her blood.

One hope sustained her. Her mother knew magic. She would ask the totem at Glendruid to strike them all dead. But Dervla O'Neill was not here. She was out there, somewhere in the seething inferno of the courtyard.

Suddenly someone *was* there, dragging her out of her niche, towering above her, holding her fast. In the darkness she could feel the fabric of his buff coat, smell a powerful blend of gunpowder and horses. Sheer terror overwhelmed her. He held her so tight that gasp as she might, she could not draw enough air into her desperate lungs. Dimly she saw his face, long, young, cleareyed. In his hand he held a sword. He was going to kill her.

Struggling to face the unthinkable, Sorcha sank beneath a blackening wave of fear, and darkness claimed her.

Chapter 2

For two days, Ensign Robert Hammond sheltered with his troops beneath the dripping canopy of leaves outside Carrickmain. Rain dripped relentlessly, splashing onto his hat, soaking his long dark hair and forming a steady cascade past his eyes. From time to time he shook his head to send the spray flying in an arc off the brim. An icy trickle seeped down his neck and his buff coat weighed heavy on his back.

Some of the regiment were more fortunate. The Commander and certain chosen officers had located a thatched cabin and passed the night inside, but many of the foot soldiers were camped in the open forming a miserable, untidy circle around Carrickmain Castle.

Robert struggled to be stoical in the face of such discomfort. This was his first experience of action. He was not sure what to expect but knew that he had to put up a good show, live up to the high hopes of his uncle, Captain Thomas Hammond and his god-father, the Earl of Essex.

Last evening, reinforcements had finally arrived from Dublin. Like all those present, Robert offered up a prayer in the hope of being spared in the battle to come. He could not conceive that he might die. There was still so much to experience, not least the proposed marriage to Mary Hampden. At the thought of this marriage settlement a glimmer of satisfaction warmed him. Within the next two months, he would reach his majority. Soon he would be wed. John Hampden, his future father-in-law, was held in such high esteem – a man who had defied the King and refused to pay ship money for the illegal raising of a navy.

Robert felt a mixture of pride and unease. Whilst revering the

King's person, he had his own misgivings about recent events. Yet he personally would never have the courage to defy King Charles – better to get on with the job in hand and leave affairs of state to others. Anyway, God willing, it would soon be settled.

Cold morning light filtered across the horizon and the word was passed: 'It's on.' Lieutenant Hammond tightened his grip on the butt of the pistol. This was no time to be thinking of home. Using what shelter there was, he picked his way across to where the officers stood.

Over the past two days the enemy had amused themselves by taking pot shots at them. There had been casualties. Now it was time to turn the tables.

As Robert drew near to the cabin, Sir Simon Harcourt, Commander of the King's forces, stepped out into the damp morning. 'You all know what you have to do,' he said. Heads nodded.

As the officers made to disperse, a shot rang out. Robert saw the blurred flash and almost simultaneously, Sir Simon leaped back as if he had been prodded by some heavy, invisible object. He staggered several paces and fell to the muddy ground. Robert jumped from his horse and was the first to reach him. A darkening puddle of blood oozed from a ragged wound in his chest. Dear God, Robert thought.

Sir Simon started to struggle to his feet and Robert took his weight, helping him towards the cabin but the injured man's legs gave way and he slumped back. 'Go on!' He nodded in the direction of Carrickmain. 'God go with you.'

The young Ensign hesitated a moment then swung back into the saddle, the awful image of the gaping wound still before his eyes. Anger replaced the shock.

'Revenge! Give no quarter!' He raised his pennant and spurred his mare forward, charging towards the castle gateway. His action was like touch paper, a moment of stillness and then the angry booming of men as they advanced. Pikemen alternated with musketeers, the one offering cover to the other as they struggled noisily up the slope towards the castle walls.

Answering fire rained down on them but sheer force of numbers bore them on. Meanwhile, their own cannon were concentrating fire on the outer wall. Although in the lead, Robert had difficulty in seeing as the pall of smoke closed around him. His chest began to tighten from the suffocating fumes. The cloud cleared momentarily and he saw that a breach had been made in the wall.

'This way!' Taking his chance he cantered forward, other cavalrymen close behind him.

The noise was deafening. Every man present was shouting, whether from fear, excitement or the pain of savage wounds. The thunder of cannon, the firecracker reports of muskets, the terrified whinnying of horses created a hell on earth.

There was no time to think. He aimed his pistol and brought down one of the Irish rebels. The man seemed to fall in slow motion, his half-raised arm continuing its arc and then gently falling away. Although Robert could not distinguish the sound, he watched the man's mouth open wide, the eyes grow large with surprise and the sudden spasm of pain claim him as he fell. It was the first man that he had killed.

He could not dwell on this sobering moment. Thrusting his pistol into his belt, he drew his sword the better to strike down more rebels who, now that the castle was entered, fought like demons. It all seemed unreal, the ducking, driving forward, meeting fear-crazed eyes.

He became aware of another sound, higher-pitched, hysterical. There were women in large numbers within the castle walls. Even as he registered the fact, he saw a girl pass a loaded musket to a rebel crouched beneath a buttress. At that very instant Robert's horse gave a scream of surprise. She staggered, nearly unseating him. For an eternity she seemed to be trying to stay on her legs but they finally gave way beneath her. Robert leaped from the saddle to avoid being crushed as she fell. Sadness sent him cold. He was fond of the mare.

On foot he felt defenceless. He raised his sword and drove it hard into the man beneath the buttress. The Irishman spat at him in some heathen tongue. His hair was a startling red and his pale eyes were pinpoints of hatred. It took strength to withdraw the weapon and the man grunted as the blade finally slipped away. It dripped warm and crimson onto the rocky pathway. Robert felt an insane desire to apologise.

A sea of army banners filled the courtyard. The damp ensigns of the night before now fluttered victorious in the breeze. From the east the sun illuminated the carnage. The castle was full of English victors, breathless, exhilarated.

Robert halted, panting, waiting for the order to cease fighting. It did not come. Foot soldiers advanced along corridors and parapets, into the cluster of tents in the courtyard, down into the bowels of the castle dragging wretched human dross into the open.

The noise changed. Excitement echoed in the shouts of the raiders. Terror rent the air as women and children were pulled from huts and crannies. Robert was transfixed with disbelief. There, before public gaze, men tore the tattered clothes from their female victims and entered them unashamed, one, two, maybe up to six of them, immune to their victims' screams. When a woman was too bloodied to be of use she was despatched by the cutting of her throat, the disembowelling of her swollen belly. The surviving officers looked on.

'For pity's sake, call a halt!' Robert could no longer contain his disgust.

The Captain standing nearest shook his head. 'Never try to do what you cannot achieve. Their blood is up. Deprive them of this and you'll have a riot on your hands.'

'But the women, children . . .' Even as he watched, a small child, little more than a babe was carried aloft, skewered on a broadsword, a terrible trophy held high for all to see. 'For God's sake!' Robert cried again.

Another officer shook his head warningly. 'These are Irish. Vermin. Leave one man alive and you've left yourself an enemy for tomorrow. Spare one woman and you'll have another brat before the year is out. Show mercy to a child and it will stab you in the back when next you meet. You're too soft, my dear Robin. Your tender heart does you credit but serves you badly.'

Robert turned away and with the flat of his sword began to knock soldiers aside. Quickly he despatched a wretched woman whose breast had already been sliced off in the bloodlust. He gagged on his own disgust.

Pushing blindly down a narrow passageway, intent on getting the stench of blood from his nostrils, he stumbled against an object pressed hard into the wall. At his touch it whimpered. He dragged the creature up to reveal a child. Her shoulders were hunched against assault and her clenched fists hugged her chest to

13

defend herself. The eyes that met Robert's were large, vivid blue, terrified. Her mouth opened but no sound emerged and for a second she swooned against him. He guessed that she was about twelve or thirteen years of age.

As her eyes flickered open he raised his hand to his lips, cautioning her to silence. Suddenly the path was blocked by three infantrymen. They had the wild, sated look of drunks. As one their eyes homed in on the girl.

'We'll see to her,' one of them said. He licked his lips and reached for her.

'No, you don't.' Robert pushed his protégée behind him and formed a barrier with his body. The plunderers jostled uneasily.

'You've no right. Anything we find is ours. Hilty here hasn't had a go yet.'

The man referred to as Hilty looked shamefaced but could not resist trying to peer past Robert to get a sight of his proposed reward.

'The man who touches this child is dead.'

'Want her for yourself, do you?'

Robert brought the blade of his sword down hard across the man's chest, sending him crashing back into his companions. Before they could extricate themselves, the point of the blade rested against the neck of the spokesman. 'Go now or say your prayers.'

Grumbling, they scrambled up and retreated the way they had come. Robert closed his eyes to draw strength. As he turned back the child was staring at him. She was very still, her thick brown hair tumbling across her shoulders, her mouth set, her expression defying him to move. In her hand she held a dagger.

The words of the Captain echoed in his brain. This was an enemy, an Irish peasant brat, a nothing. For a moment he thought: Shall I kill her? Then he saw a single tear hover on the brink of her eye before making its silent way down her cheek. He held his hand out for the knife and as her fist tightened he grabbed it and gave it a single flick. The blade flew from her grasp.

'Hush now.' He did not know if she understood but as he held her close he felt the taut fear gradually subside.

'What the devil have you got there?' It was his friend, Captain

14

Berry. When Robert did not reply, he said: 'You can't take her home, you know, like some stray dog.'

'I found a puppy once, gave it to my mother. Now it's dead.'

'Time to find her another one?'

'Perhaps.'

The Captain sighed. 'Remember what I warned.'

'I heard you but I cannot set her loose in this hell. You know what her fate would be.'

Round and about they were clearing the dead from the castle. The English casualties were buried in graves hastily dug at the bottom of the curtain wall. Where possible they were identified so that their kin should know of their going. The Irish dead were piled outside and upwind. There were no Irish living.

Robert took the child to a hut that had the night before housed the rebels. There he deposited her on the floor and raised her chin to try and make her look at him but she refused to meet his gaze. Her blue eyes were like crystals in her mud-smeared face.

'Be sensible, child. If you go out there you will die. I will try to protect you. Do you understand?' By way of reply she kicked him hard on the legs.

'You she-cat!' He slapped her hard across the face. 'Stay there, damn you, but if you are gone when I get back I won't have the bother of you.' He limped out, swearing, rubbing his shins.

Outside he paused and watched the systematic searching of the castle. His own dilemma preoccupied him. What should he do with her? Perhaps when they got back to Dublin he could give her away? Even as he thought of it he knew that Dublin was awash with orphans and abandoned brats. Maybe he should simply take her outside and set her free like a caged linnet? That way she had a chance but . . . He knew that he could not.

His fellow officers began to tease him, making lewd jokes. He was offended by their coarseness and hoped the girl had run away. That would solve the problem.

When he returned to sleep however she was still there, crouched in a corner. In his hand he carried a lump of mutton, just in case. He held it out. For a while she simply stared at him then her hunger got the better of her and she grabbed it, shrinking back once more against the wall. He watched her eat.

'There's nothing to fear. I'll take you to England. You'll be

15

safe.' His monologue was greeted with silence. Beneath the grime he could tell that she was pretty.

'What is your name?' He spoke slowly. When she did not reply he said: 'I am Robert Hammond. Do you understand?'

She swallowed the last piece of meat and wiped her mouth on her hand. Her eyes burned with suspicion. 'What is your name?' he repeated more gently.

'Dublin.'

'Dublin? That's your name?'

She looked away from him.

'Is that where you come from?'

She gave a little shrug and her glance darted around the room, whether looking for more food or for escape he wasn't sure.

'What shall I call you then?'

'Dublin.'

Robert shrugged. 'If that's what you say then so it shall be. Well, Dublin, you can curl up there like the little mouse you are. Tomorrow we'll be on the move. When, with God's blessing, we reach England, I'll take you to my home.'

For the first time in two days he pulled off his heavy square-toed boots and draped the sopping woollen socks over them to dry. Seeing that he was undressing, the girl moved further back into the corner. Terror showed on her face.

He shook his head and sighed. 'There is nothing to fear. I intend to sleep. I don't despoil children.'

'Dublin,' she answered.

'So be it.' He sank to his knees and began to pray aloud, thanking God for delivering him safely from the battle and assuring his Lord that he acted with good intent. As he opened his eyes, it was to see the child make the sign of the cross.

'You understand the act of prayer if not the meaning,' he said. 'But you'll have to stop those Popish ways.'

Gratefully he fell onto the straw and pulled his blanket about him. The air was cold, damp. In the corner the child did not have the benefit of a cover and he thought that he could hear her shivering, tiny movements, spasms of cold. With a sigh he sat up again and pulled the blanket off.

'Here. Take this.'

She did not respond so he took it across to her. In the gloom he could make out her skinny form, sense her fear. Bending down he gently placed the cover over her. At the feel of his hand she whimpered and he patted her reassuringly on the arm. Her helplessness did strange things to his heart.

Lying uncovered on the straw, he said into the dark: 'Don't you fear now. As God is my witness, I give you my word that I'll take care of you.' Even as he said it, he felt that he had made a pact with the Almighty.

Chapter 3
England
March 1642

Charles Stuart, King of Great Britain and Ireland, awoke with a start from a dream. It was a confusing mixture of images, but the whole was overlaid with a sense of menace. He had imagined himself walking naked through Newmarket. All around people stared and sniggered, laughing at his slight stature, his limp. When he tried to explain, they made mock of his stutter. He felt vulnerable, humiliated. His last memory before waking with a jolt, was of his dear Henrietta with the children around her. As they faded away from view he heard her say that he had nice eyes.

The King's heart beat faster than was comfortable and he sought for some familiar object in the room to bring him solace. These days he was never in the same place long enough to feel at home. Little by little the pieces fell into place, dozens of them, and the picture that formed left him with an unrelieved sense of gloom.

It was now nearly three months since he had left London, abandoning the traitorous capital for the countryside. In that time he had moved from Hampton Court to Windsor, then Royston and Newmarket, trying to find some way of bringing his rebellious Parliament to heel. In the meantime his dear Henrietta and his nephew Rupert, had set sail for the Low Countries, hoping to raise support and arms. Charles consoled himself. His brave little wife would stand no nonsense. Frail she might be, but she had the heart of a lion. She was even prepared to barter the royal jewels to ensure that Charles kept his crown. He missed her.

Everywhere there seemed to be dissent, and in spite of the King's certainty that God would defend his right to govern as he saw fit, things did not augur well. In fact, the only area where he and his Parliament were in any agreement at all, was over the need to do something about Ireland.

Reports came almost daily of barbarities carried out against the English settlers. Rapes, murders, drownings, even crucifixion. Charles shuddered at the images. He could not stand unpleasantness and the thought of nails hammered through the palm of the hand kept coming back to haunt him. He tried in vain to push the vision away. The violence had to be stopped.

Even more delicate was the rumour that some of the Irish Catholics were actually fighting in their King's defence – thus adding fuel to the suspicion that Charles was sympathetic to Catholicism. He sniffed into the silence. Just because his dear wife was a Catholic did not mean that he was other than true to the Protestant faith. In fact, he had always prided himself on his tolerance, but sadly such noble sentiments were lost on some of his court. He had to act quickly, but how? And with what resources?

The thought of the army brought Charles to another crisis in his life. Under John Pym's influence, Parliament had tried to persuade him to surrender command of his troops. The idea was preposterous, yet when he refused to sign their Militia Bill, they had issued an Ordinance of their own, intending to take the army out of his hands with or without his consent. If he wanted that control back, he would have to fight for it.

As usual it was a question of money. To be realistic, he and Parliament agreed that they needed a million pounds to settle the Irish question, but how to raise it was a different matter. They had hit upon the idea of taking ten million acres of rebel land and offering it as a reward for financing the war, and as a result, some troops had been despatched, although not enough. Now all they could do was to wait and see.

Charles sighed as he remembered the great list of complaints that had been formally laid at his feet. Even good subjects, like Lord Falkland and Edward Hyde, seemed unable to grasp the fact that as King, and one who ruled by Divine Right, he was certainly not going to make concessions to his Parliament. Meanwhile he wondered whatever he should say to keep the various factions at bay.

There was some comfort. His son Charles was travelling with him and they had enjoyed a measure of entertainment, hunting, music, the occasional game of cards. The King allowed himself the luxury of thinking for a moment on more pleasant times. The groom of the bedchamber then came to assist him to dress, preparatory to his devotions, and he made a kingly effort to throw off his worries, but the gloom remained.

Later in the day two messengers arrived from Westminster. Charles was less than pleased. The Earl of Pembroke and the Earl of Holland made no secret of their sympathy for the Parliament. Charles wondered what they had come for this time.

'Gentlemen.' He offered his hand to be kissed and went through the formalities, although with a marked coolness in his manner that they could not fail to notice. 'What news of the war?'

'Little as yet, Sire.' Lord Pembroke hesitated. 'Until we can agree some measure of compromise, it is difficult to pursue it with the vigour it requires.' Again he paused then took the plunge. 'If Your Majesty could see his way to agreeing that the Parliament should have a free hand to organise the military, if only for a short while . . .'

'By God!' Charles threw down his gloves in a dramatic gesture. 'Never will I agree to this! Never! Not for one hour!' As his pulse-rate slowed to a canter, he made up his mind once and for all. He would raise his own army, independent of the traitors at Westminster. Once he was strong enough, he would take back Ireland, negotiate with all and sundry and put his rebellious Parliament in its place. The noble visitors, sensing that they were wasting their time, bowed low and withdrew.

'Sire?' The King's plottings were interrupted by his gentleman usher who brought him a beaker of cordial.

'These are distracted times,' Charles observed, sipping listlessly at the beverage.

'Sire.' The man made a show of picking up the royal gauntlets from the floor and removing a few, invisible hairs before placing them upon the table. To break the silence, the usher asked: 'Is there any news of Ireland?'

'Ireland.' The King sighed and gazed into space, trying to visualise what the whole country looked like. In his mind's eye, he conjured up one hazy image – people, scenery, politics. He had no idea if it was accurate. As the usher went down on one knee, preparatory to taking the goblet from the royal hand, Charles said: 'Yes, Ireland. I wonder what is going on there?'

Chapter 4

The morning after the raid at Carrickmain, the English made ready to depart.

Inside Sorcha's head there was a void, numbing, terrible. She dared not let her thoughts loose. Clasped firmly at the wrist by the foreign soldier, she was dragged across the drawbridge of the castle, where broken masonry thrust, raw and jagged as newly snapped bones. Ahead lay weary miles across fields and up tracks towards the coast. And after that? She dreaded to think.

As they stumbled along she recited to herself, drawing comfort from the sound of her words, a haven of Gaelic in the hubbub of English voices: 'I must not think. Don't think. I must go home. I must find Mam. I must go back to Dublin. Dublin. Dublin.'

'Dublin.' Trudging along the muddy paths, his boots ankledeep in the ooze, the soldier nodded his head as if he understood. His eyes were large and brown and clear, marred only by the smudges of fatigue shadowing his cheekbones. 'That's your name, isn't that right?'

Sorcha stared at him with hatred, her own toes curling in the soupy mire. A cruel wind from the Irish Sea pierced her skimpy gown. The soldier was stupid, abysmally stupid. All the English would be like this. Stupid – and dangerous. She glared at him with fear-darkened eyes.

As she repeated her litany, another soldier wandered up and looked at her as if she were some peepshow. 'She doesn't understand,' he observed. 'If you're set on taking her with you, you'd best make her realise that once we board ship, she won't be seeing Dublin again.'

'I think it's her name.'

21

The soldier shrugged and lost interest. Sorcha thought that she must have misunderstood. Of course she would see Dublin again. She had to get back there. She must!

Along the broad estuary of the Liffey, there was little to bring comfort. The solitary ship tied alongside the jetty had a bedraggled look, with slime and flaking paint disfiguring her once vivid prow. A fifth-rater, intended to house not more than sixty men including the crew, now some ninety wearied soldiers began to clamber aboard her. The long, low prow of the *Expectation* dipped down as if she would happily submit to her destiny and glide to a watery grave.

Until the very instant when the gangplank was cast back onto the quay, and the thick fibre rope dragged up onto the deck, a fragile flame of hope sustained Sorcha. No matter how many people had perished in the doomed castle, surely her mother had survived? And if she had, then Dervla would come to rescue her, there was no doubt about that.

She sought comfort in her mother's power. Dervla knew so much. She was favoured of the gods. Always she had survived sickness, birthings, even the perils of imps causing bridges to wash away or roofs to cave in. Her mother was immortal. Besides, Sorcha needed her.

Shivering on the slippery deck, crushed up against her captor, craning to see among the mêlée of people on the quayside, she thought about Dervla's prayers, the offering left at the pillar in Glendruid. It was inconceivable that it could have failed. If only she had been told her mother's secrets . . .

'Mother!' Her frantic voice barely touched the wind as the ketch tugged away from its mooring and swung around into the black inferno of waves. Nothing now stood between her and certain death, except the person of Robert Hammond, and she felt only fear for this alien, heathen soldier who had slain her fellow countrymen and carried her away. At that moment she died a death.

Yet some inner sense of preservation remained. It warned her not to enlighten her captor that she understood his ugly language. When the chance came, she would escape. But the ship drifted ever further away from the Irish shores. Soon her homeland disappeared and a vast soup of blue-black waves tossed them this way and that. With terrible certainty, Sorcha knew that there was no escape. Her mother's gods had failed. Jesus the Saviour had failed. Neither had been able to save them. The English and their gods were insurmountable.

For twenty-four hours they buffeted their way across the Irish Sea during which time Sorcha was achingly, vilely sick. Her stomach felt bruised and even when her guts were empty, the nausea remained. Never had she felt so cold or so wretched, and yet the very misery kept the agony of her loss at bay.

The ghosts of her murdered companions sent witches to raise the wind. Their revenge fell as much upon herself as on the miserable soldiers who crouched on the deck, enveloped by the icy waves that crashed over the vessel, spewing up their insides.

Only Robert Hammond seemed immune from the sickness. Bracing himself between two stanchions, he held her tight against his chest. It was useless to struggle. Even as she pulled away, the boat turned tail and pitched her back against him, taunting her like a rat on a string.

'Shush, shush.' He smoothed her head as if she were some favoured dog, rocking her in time with the dipping of the boat. His fingers caressed behind her ear and sent a ripple of treacherous magic through her aching frame. Glancing covertly at him she took in his wide, straight back, his handsome, long, aristocratic face. Such fine features, so well defined. For a moment fear was suspended in contemplation of this beautiful man. Something told her that here indeed was a living god, immune to the worst that the elements could throw at him.

Thus reassured, and prostrated by sickness, she finally allowed herself to be sheltered in his arms, too ill to care whether she lived or died.

'There, child, it will soon be over.' He cuddled her to him, tucking her into the shelter of his buff coat. Some long-forgotten babe within her warmed to the gentle strength of his body. She could still smell the gunpowder on him, the rich aroma of horses. Perversely the smells excited her. In some fearful, unnamed way, his maleness stirred a new sense of danger, one that she might bring upon herself. But he was her only hope in this alien world. Her grip around his neck tightened and her knees closed about him. At last she slept.

It was morning when they came ashore.

'Where are we?' Sorcha wailed in Gaelic, addressing no one in particular. The fear was back.

Robert Hammond shook his head, not understanding her question, then, as if some inner sense translated it for him, he said: 'We're in England now, and this is Chester. We have a long journey before we reach home.'

She gave no sign that she understood.

For a while they simply stood on the quay, waiting for the land to stop behaving like the sea. Gradually the nausea subsided and when nothing bad came to taunt her, Sorcha began to look around. For the moment any danger was forgotten. She had seen nothing like this place before.

The town was shielded from attack by massive stone walls, along the top of which guards patrolled at a leisurely pace. They passed through the town gate, walking along purpose-built roads of blocks and cobbles. Sorcha looked with wonder on the rows of fine stone buildings. Compared to Dublin . . . She quickly shut out the thought of her native city, acknowledging instead that even in her dreams she had not imagined that such places as this existed.

Robert continued to lead her by the wrist. They found their way to some sort of market where he was soon in negotiation with a stringy-looking fellow with the bandiest legs she had ever seen. She could not help but compare the healthy good looks of her captor to the gaunt, skinny ugliness of the trader. For a moment, she forgot where she was, intrigued by the performance that took place between the two men. Robert appeared to offer a price, the man shaking his head and countering; Robert then threw up his hands in disbelief, making a shocked, scoffing noise in his throat. Once he threatened to walk away but soon the man called him back and after much low-toned discussion, a bargain was struck. Robert handed over some coins. He had purchased a horse.

Sorcha looked with amazement on the mare that had changed hands. It was a fine animal, a bay, with a star beneath her forelock which marked her out as of special value. Compared with the Irish horses Sorcha had seen, this was a queen amongst beasts. Epona. She thought of the goddess of horses and wondered if the deity resided within this beautiful creature. A sense of reverence overcame her.

Glancing up at the soldier, she saw that his eyes were shining with victory. Catching her look, he said: 'There. I got him down to three pounds. She's a true bargain.' He patted the horse on the neck and Sorcha was infected by his excitement.

The hubbub of voices intruded again, suddenly reminding her that not one of those about her was Irish. At the thought of what they might do to her, she moved closer to her captor then almost at the same time she wondered at his intention in stealing her away. Immediately her worst fears were back.

There was no escape. Only he stood between her and the fate she had so narrowly escaped at Carrickmain. As the thought of events at the castle crowded in upon her, she began to cry, huge wracking sobs for her mother and father whose going she had not shared. A wild abandon dragged great groans of misery from her very soul. When her captor shook her arm to stem the tears she screamed at him.

'Devil's piss!'

His face darkened between surprise and anger and he shook her harder.

'Enough, child. You cannot know what you say.'

She spat at him, calling up words used by her father when talking of the English. 'Son of a whore!'

He struck her then, hard across the shoulders. The first stinging pain let loose the deluge of her anger and she began to beat him back, swearing in English and Gaelic, pummelling him wherever she could reach, until she was swept under by the tide of her anguish. In Gaelic she screamed: 'I want to go home, to Dublin!'

'Dublin.' He pulled her close, constraining her arms to contain her anger, rocking her against him.

The small crowd that had gathered to watch the spectacle lost interest and drifted away.

'Hush, child.' For a while he was silent then he said: 'I had no idea you were such a wild thing. I do not think my mother will appreciate your presence. I shall take you instead to my Aunt Jane.'

They travelled for several days, Sorcha perched on the pillion behind her new master. The horse had a smooth, steady gait and fatigue eventually lulled her into a dreamlike state. As her cheek came to rest against his buff coat, she gave up all thoughts of resistance, again acknowledging that her gods had failed. This man and his religion were the victors. She vowed there and then to learn as much about them as she could.

On the first evening, they stopped at a hostelry where Robert took a private room. The innkeeper raised his eyebrows as he surveyed them. Reading his thoughts, Sorcha blushed and wondered if he would intervene to save her, but his face was florid, indifferent and she knew that there was no point in appealing to him for help.

Robert led the way, trudging up the wooden steps, bending his head to avoid the heavy wooden beams that crossed the low, upper corridor. Stinging wisps of woodsmoke, mingled with the smell of roasting meat, teased Sorcha's nostrils.

Alone in the room with him, she stood woodenly as he unpacked his kit, struggled out of his coat and boots then tested out the mattress on the bed. In spite of her fear, her curiosity got the better of her. She had never been in such a room before, draught-free, panelled with wood that was rich and varnished. Even the floor was made of smooth wooden planks. Her eyes were drawn to a small square window, set in the thick stone of the wall and covered with diamond-shaped glass. Never had she been in a room with a glazed window before.

A movement from the soldier brought her back to her ordeal. She longed for it to be over. It was no more than she deserved, deserting her family while they lay dead at home. Pressing her fists to her mouth, she looked to him for mercy. But he turned away from her and bending down, dragged a truckle bed from beneath the large couch at the centre of the room.

'You sleep there.'

She lay down as she was, stiff and fearful, no longer having anyone to pray to. As the man made another movement, she closed her eyes and waited, but he made no attempt to touch her. Peeping beneath one eyelid, she saw him kneel beside the couch. She watched, curious, wondering about his all-powerful God. As his lips moved in prayer, her own followed suit.

As he went to get up she quickly closed her eyes again and tensed herself for his approach. Instead she heard the groan of the couch as he lowered himself onto it.

Late into the night, when she was certain that he slept, she

26

crept out and tried the door. It would not budge. As he grunted and turned over she froze, then fumbled her way back to her little nest. It seemed that Fate meant her to stay here. She slept.

To Sorcha's dismay, they travelled to another coastline and there boarded a pinnace. 'No!' She began to object but Hammond hoisted her up under his arm and carried her aboard.

'There is nothing to fear. This crossing will not take more than a couple of hours.'

Although the ship was smaller than the one on which they had crossed the Irish Sea, it seemed to glide effortlessly across the strait of water. Gone were the heavings and tossings that had tormented her on that last journey. Seated on a wooden bench, a gentle breeze deflecting the warmth of the sun, Sorcha reasoned that her kin must have forgiven her, for the punishing wind had abated. The vessel drifted swiftly in the direction of the distant coast.

As far as she could see, a backbone of undulating hills swept up from the sea, continued for some miles and then dipped gradually back into the water. As they drew near, it was to a heavily wooded coastline and sweeping bays. She wondered where they were.

'Where are we going?' she asked in Gaelic but he did not answer, so she tried again. 'Where?'

At her hesitant use of the English word, he smiled encouragement. 'The Isle of Wight. My aunt lives there. I shall ask her to take you into her service.'

As he continued to talk, Sorcha gave up the struggle to understand. There was kindness in his voice and in spite of its foreign sound, the tone was pleasing to her ear. In fact, tired as she was, as she studied him covertly through the blanket of hair that shaded one side of her face, she could not help but admit that he was pleasing altogether. Like herself his hair was dark, but as hers was straight and tangled and reached past her waist, his was combed and waved softly to his shoulders. He stood tall and straight-backed, his body slim but broad at the shoulder. His legs, encased in soft leather boots, were muscular. Some strange excitement made her heart beat faster. Most of all, his eyes, light brown and deepset above his prominent cheekbones, had a compassionate glint that warmed her battered being.

27

It was getting dark when they landed but he pushed on as if anxious to reach his destination. The roads were in worse condition than on the mainland and the journey was hampered by the inordinate number of gates that had to be opened. Some were manned by small children, running out in the hope of a penny. At other places, the soldier descended himself or, after about the sixth time, he lowered Dublin and bade her let them through. By now she had recovered some of her spirit and stomped sulkily to open each gate, glowering at him as she did so. On one occasion the mare trotted through and threatened to leave her behind. Sudden panic overwhelmed her and she gave out a savage screech, running desperately after him. With a sigh he reined in and hoisted her up again.

'There's no fear that I shall lose you, child. I do believe you are some sort of punishment to me. God alone knows what my aunt will say.'

They continued to pass through deserted countryside, past occasional thatched cottages, in front of some tottering wooden huts, through meadows and across streams. Sorcha had no idea how far they had travelled, or in which direction. Clinging on behind her soldier, astride the great mare, she let her cheek rest against his shoulder and tried to pretend that they were crossing Ireland and just ahead they would come to the welcome spread of her Dublin home.

It was dark when they finally came to a halt before the silhouette of a huge stone house, square and solid against the distant line of black hills.

As they jogged across the courtyard, they seemed to be swallowed up by its presence, but there was no time for fear. The latch of the door lifted and a solitary woman stepped out into the night. She held a torch aloft, shading her eyes the better to see.

'Who's there? Robert, is it you?' She descended quickly towards them and held out her hands in greeting. 'I cannot believe it! We heard that you were in Ireland. Whatever brings you so far from home?' Her expression changed to alarm but he shook his head to assure her that all was well.

'You will not believe it. I have indeed just returned from Ireland.' He slipped from the mare pulling Sorcha with him as he did so. 'While I was there I acquired more than I bargained for.'

Sorcha looked away from the lady who was studying her with

28

interest. She was short, plump, rounded like a suety pudding and her expression was mild and not unfriendly.

Robert said: 'I intended to travel direct to Chertsey but – well, you know how my mother feels about the Irish, and this girl – I was wondering if . . .'

He pushed Sorcha forward, and for a terrible moment she thought that he was going to abandon her. She pressed hard back against him and began to scream.

Robert shook his head and raised his shoulders helplessly, looking at his aunt. 'This, will you believe, is Dublin. Her parents were killed in battle. I came upon her and could not leave her to her fate, so . . .' Again he seemed lost for words, finally saying: 'I realise now I am asking too much. If you will give us shelter for the night, on the morrow I will take her to the Justices and pay for her to be taken in.'

At this, Sorcha gripped harder to his jacket, frozen rigid by the thought that he would leave.

Aunt Jane Dingley shook her head at the endearing foolishness of this, her favourite nephew. 'You are an ass, Robert. Only you would be so tender.' Turning to Sorcha, she held out her hands again. 'Come, little one. Come along inside. I will look after you.'

Sorcha shook her head, defying the woman to come closer with a scowl.

'Come along, child.' Robert pushed her encouragingly. She still held him firmly in her grasp.

In the face of his determination, she reluctantly acquiesced, allowing herself to be led inside, still hanging onto his sleeve. If he tried to leave her, then she consoled herself with the knowledge that she could run at least as fast as he could. He would not get away so easily.

Once inside, they passed through a hallway and into a fine, lofty room. When the door was safely closed, Sorcha cautiously released her hold on her saviour and to her relief, he remained close by. Reassured when he sat down, she began to look about her.

The panelled walls glowed hazel-brown from the application of beeswax and elbow power, and the table that dissected the hall gave off the same smooth dark gleam in the flickering incandescence. At the centre a pewter salver radiated a distorted reflection of the many faces that lined the walls, each in a wooden frame. It was like being studied by an army of motionless ghosts and Sorcha hid her eyes with her hands, wondering if these spirits of the dead were the source of Robert's power . . .

Mistress Dingley pulled her close and nestled her against her bosom.

'Poor child. She is sore afraid.'

They talked for a long while and Sorcha peeped out to see if the faces on the wall had moved, but their expressions remained the same. Mistress Dingley smelled of thyme and lavender. Something of the musky scent from her bodice set Sorcha sneezing.

The woman said: 'Pray God she is not infected with the sweats!'

Robert pulled his burden back to his side. 'No, Aunt. The child is well enough. Only dirt ails her.'

Sorcha looked down surreptitiously at her stained hands and blackened feet, her muddied skirts. In contrast to the perfumed elegance of Aunt Jane, she felt suddenly as nothing. Scratching her nose on her sleeve, she edged closer to Robert for reassurance. His male, horsey smell was like a balm.

Mistress Dingley rang a bell and before long they were taken to the table and fed. Aunt Jane waited upon her nephew with obvious pleasure.

'I thank God for sending you hither. Sir John is much away in London, and my sons no longer live at home. Sometimes I find it lonely.'

'If you need a mission in life, Aunt, you would do well to turn this savage into a Christian.' Robert drained his cup and nodded to Sorcha that she should eat. She scowled at him, stung by his words, outraged at the implication of what he had said. She knew well enough about being a Christian – the Mass and the candles and the prayers, the exhortations to be good like the Virgin, the punishments meted out to her when she failed. She did not need to be turned into a Christian; she'd already been one!

'Go along, eat.'

At his second bidding she lunged forward to tear some bread from the loaf on the table and dipped it into the broth in the bowl set before her. She wondered what a 'savage' might be.

Her action in cramming the food into her mouth caused nephew and aunt to laugh and her face grew hot with shame. She cared little for what the woman thought, but to her confusion, the man's opinion was everything.

At last they made ready to leave the table. Just as they got to the door, Mistress Dingley grasped Sorcha firmly by the arm and began to pull her away.

'Come along, child, it is time we got you out of this filthy rag.'

'No!' Realising that she was to be taken away from her rescuer, she struggled to break free. As the woman's hand tightened on her arm, she began to scream, but immediately a serving woman grasped her other arm and together the two women dragged her across the yard to the wash-house, where they began to strip off her solitary garment.

Her only thought was to get away. She managed to bite the drudge and in return received a hearty cuff across the face. Now they had a firm grip on her and struggle as she would, she could not prevent them from dousing her with water from a large stone ewer, then rubbing her all over with hard yellow soap. The maidservant began to scrub her hair with iron fingers. All the while Sorcha cursed them in Gaelic, calling on Robert to help her.

Finally, jug after jug of water was poured over her until she stung with the cold. Her skin shone red and angry.

They clothed her in a shift, then a gown, more splendid than anything she had ever known. The material of the shift against her skin did not chafe, and the gown was of soft wool, grey, with coloured stitching at the neck and cuffs. 'It's old, but it will do,' Robert's aunt pronounced. Stunned by the finery of her new clothing, she submitted to their ministrations and meekly followed them back to the house.

Mistress Dingley took her to sleep in her own chamber, pushing home the bolt so that she should not leave without being heard.

The room was square and dark and like the one at the inn, draughtproof, but despite the rich hangings and high panelled ceiling, it felt like a prison. Aunt Jane's voice was kind though firm and finally, fatigue and wonder at the feather mattress on the little truckle bed, soothed Sorcha into sleep.

She dreamed of being cornered in the dark deep recess of a castle. Gaunt, merciless wraiths came ever closer, their hands reaching out to tear at her clothing. Somewhere nearby her mother screamed.

She awoke to darkness, shouting for her protector. Driven by fear, she flew from the bed and tried to draw back the bolt on the chamber door, but it would not budge. Her very survival depended upon escape and when Aunt Jane touched her shoulder, she began to kick and bite in order to get free.

'Aunt Jane, are you safe?'

Hearing Robert's voice, Sorcha called to him to save her. He said: 'Dublin, be calm.'

It was Jane Dingley who unbolted the door and allowed her to flee into his arms. He swept her up and held her close, smoothing her hair.

'Hush, child. You are safe here.'

Indeed, in his arms, she felt safe. Rocking her gently he fingered her newly-washed hair and she felt a sudden pride in her cleanliness. She frowned round at Mistress Hammond, defying her to come close, but to her distress, Robert prised himself free and handed her back. 'Go now.'

'No!'

He accompanied them into the chamber and stood close as his aunt tucked her back into the bed. Sorcha allowed her to do so, only because she held tight to Robert's hand. His presence calmed her fears, and when she finally awoke it was with the memory of his lips against her hair. Whether it was real or a dream she did not know.

In the morning, Sorcha was aroused at five of the clock and put immediately to work. Her first duty was to go with Jennet, the skivvy, to draw water from the well. Jennet, garrulous, pleased to have an assistant, kept up a running commentary as she led the way down passages and across yards. In silence, Sorcha followed behind.

Cautiously she stepped outside into this new world, wondering what she would find. The early sun shone kindly on the landscape, warming her skin, giving her an immediate sense of wellbeing. Gaining courage, she looked about her.

Even in the broad light of day, the house still seemed very large. Red and grey, solid as Carrickmain, it nestled snugly in a dip between the gently rolling downs. At the thought of

32

Carrickmain, Sorcha shuddered. She remembered that first feeling of fear when they had come upon the fortress. That instinct had been right. She should have been guided by it, insisted that they did not stay, only no one would have listened to her. This house, however, gave out a warm, confident air. It made her feel safe.

Away to the north was a distant village.

'That's Shorrel,' said Jennet, following her gaze. 'And this 'ere's Wolverton.' She indicated the house and its sprawling grounds.

Sorcha gave no sign that she understood. Jennet gazed at her unabashed and in her turn, Sorcha studied her new companion whilst pretending not to do so. The girl was about her own age or a little older, plump, grey-eyed, fair-haired. She stared back with a matter-of-fact air, as one who would not be surprised by anything. Sorcha knew that she was a poor girl, and her poverty was reassuring. For the first time she felt that here was someone familiar, someone not unlike herself. She turned her attention again to their surroundings.

All about them the hills were splashed with rambling stands of trees, an occasional hedged enclosure and a multitude of sheep. It was a huge tapestry with something new in every quarter. The background chatter of geese and the gentle moaning of cattle was comforting, familiar.

As she watched, the sunshine turned the remote cliffs pink and the sea was distantly visible to the south, in shades from slate grey to aquamarine.

'C'mon.' Jennet poked her and together they drew up the cold, clear water from the well, struggling back across the yard under the weight of the large leather buckets.

Breakfast was at eight and following Jennet's lead, Sorcha helped to spread the table with mutton, tongue and bread. A pile of about a dozen wooden trenchers and a collection of tankards, some pewter and horn cups, and some leather, were placed ready to hand. Then they fetched ale in heavy stone jugs from the brewhouse across the yard. The ground was muddy, but for the first time in her life, Sorcha's feet were encased in a pair of ancient shoes that had once belonged to Mistress Dingley. They felt strange, constricting, and she would rather have gone barefoot as nature intended, but she endured the discomfort, for only gentle-

33

women wore shoes. The knowledge sent a tremor of pride along her spine.

Before they could eat, there were prayers and a sermon. It seemed to go on for ever but she tried to pay attention, anxious to win the favour of this English God who was clearly so powerful.

By the time they were permitted to take food from the table, she was ravenous, pushing her way through the assembled workers to get her share.

'Hey, no need for that!'

She ignored the protests, haunted by the too-recent memories of an empty belly.

After breakfast the day began in earnest, with sweeping and scrubbing and polishing. There were rugs upon some floors and reeds on others. Having endured the humiliating scrubbing of the night before, Sorcha was not, for once plagued by flea-bites. Last night, after washing her hair, Mistress Dingley's maid had ignored her protests and dragged a comb through the under-growth of knots. At the time it had hurt and she had protested loudly, but now her hair was neatly coiled and pinned beneath a white cap. Again, she felt like a gentlewoman. Suddenly everything seemed possible.

As she worked, plans to run away formed in her head. In her mind's eye she could see herself boarding a ship, galloping across the English countryside, riding out the waves over the Irish Sea. But then the memories of the outward journey came back. Without Robert Hammond to protect her, such a flight would be a nightmare. In any case, what would she find when she got back?

Everything was in a state of suspension. In one of those rare moments of revelation, it struck her that her old life had ended at Carrickmain and now she was somebody new, a puppet, waiting for these English to pull the strings.

Because of her unwillingness to speak other than Gaelic, it was assumed that she had no understanding and for the moment it suited her purpose to keep it so. She understood well enough, and who knew what a dumb girl might hear?

On a practical level, she easily understood the vocabulary of the house. Jennet, now her special friend, boosted her sense of importance, clearly intrigued by Sorcha's past.

'Do you really come from across the sea? You speak some foreign lingo? You got any brothers and sisters?'

At first, Sorcha decided to remain silent with her, as with all the others, but gradually curiosity got the better of her and it dawned on her that if she did not ask, there might be some things that she would never learn.

'Master Robert?' She tried his name awkwardly, when they were sent out to find watercress in the stream. His name buzzed for ever in her brain, but it sounded strange spoken out loud.

'What of him?' Jennet looked surprised but did not comment on her speech.

When Sorcha did not reply, her friend shrugged then eyed her curiously. 'You sweet on him?'

She did not know what Jennet meant but her embarrassment at having spoken his name caused her to blush.

'You ARE!' The skivvy gave a shriek of laughter. 'Well, no good you hopin', Dublin. He's affianced.'

Sorcha frowned as Jennet added: 'He's been betrothed this twelvemonth. To one of the Hampdens.'

Still Sorcha did not understand and by way of explanation her companion circled her finger with an imaginary ring. 'The Hampdens are important folk. Mr Hampden nearly went to prison because he wouldn't pay the King his ship money. Then the King tried to have him arrested but he ran away. He's a hero.'

None of this was of interest except the gloomy realisation that Robert was spoken for by some other woman.

'Pretty?' Sorcha asked, meaning the girl.

'Who? His betrothed?' Jennet shrugged. 'Don't much matter if she is or not. Her father's rich and powerful. That's what counts.' Giving her a quizzical look, Jennet added: 'Don't you think along those lines. That can only lead to grief. You be a sensible girl and remember your place. Even if you are an Irisher there's some feller would have you, you're that pretty.'

Sorcha stopped listening. If Robert was in the clutches of some other woman, then she had discovered her mission in life. It was to release him.

'Dublin!' She jumped. Jennet pushed her, in the act of stuffing waterweed into the cress bucket.

'Mistress'll be that mad,' she warned, then with a secret smile: 'She'll not take kindly to you having such thoughts about her nephew either. Best keep quiet.'

Sorcha nodded and kept her thoughts to herself.

35

Chapter 5

By the time they had been at Wolverton for about a week, Sorcha was beginning to feel quite at home. Now and then, tormenting thoughts about the past tried to threaten her sense of safety but she fought resolutely to drive them away. At other times, equally disturbing fears about the future goaded her but these too, she refused to consider. For the present, today was all that mattered.

One evening she was summoned, along with several other servants, to carry hot water up to the chamber where Robert Hammond slept. The knowledge that she was about to see his private sanctum caused a tightening around her heart, but she tried to suppress it. This was a house where it seemed that women were admired only if they were modest, hardworking, and knew their place. Sorcha tried hard to be demure and industrious, but where Robert was concerned, her feelings were new and raw, and dangerously exciting.

Robert's chamber faced the back of the house and looked across the broad swathe of fields that ended at the distant sea. Inside, it was much like Aunt Jane's, dark, panelled, cosy. His bed was tumbled, and clean linen lay across a blanket chest. There was such an intimacy about these objects that she immediately lost the battle for control of her thoughts.

In a vain attempt to avoid them, as she passed the window she gazed out at the view. By screwing up her eyes until the hazy mist looked like distant hills, she could almost imagine that she was back in Ireland. For several moments she was lost in contemplation and when she eventually looked round, the rest of the servants had already left. Hastily she hurried out to catch up with them, fearing that she might receive a clip round the ear.

Being the smallest, by the time she made her second journey, she was the last to reach the chamber and the others had already departed again. A large, shallow tub had been placed on the floor near to the fire and filled with water.

She panted in through the door struggling not to splash the scalding water onto her skirts. Her arms ached with the weight of the heavy pan. Glancing up, the first thing she saw was Robert, now naked, seated in the bath. She jerked to a halt and a few drops of water overflowed onto her bare feet.

Her cry made him look up. 'Dublin, be careful.' He beckoned her across and ignoring her stinging toes she scurried over with the kettle, trying not to look at him.

'Put it there.' He indicated with his head. She felt suddenly very hot and however she tried, could not keep her eyes away from the whiteness of his skin, the way his long back curved in a gentle arc and the muscles moved along his torso. As he raised his arm, a cluster of brown hair sprang gently, like grass disturbed by a careless foot.

'Good girl. Here, come and soap my back.' He held the cake of soap out to her and she took it warily. It was too large to hold comfortably and threatened to slip out of her hands. Her heart pounded and she was captivated yet shamed by the sight of his body. As he nodded encouragement and turned his back towards her, she began timidly to rub the wet soap across his shoulders. She could feel his magic, emanating from his skin and passing through her fingers, along her veins, into her very soul.

The skin became slippery as cautiously her fingers moved over him. Oblivious to everything, he stretched and gave himself up to these ministrations.

She began to work harder, soaping across his shoulders and down his back to the water line, where the white of his buttocks flattened out against the hard bottom of the bath, then down his forearms and finally up along his neck and into his hair. He was relaxed as a child, his head thrown back and eyes closed, clearly enjoying the service, unashamed of his nakedness.

Glancing covertly down, she saw for a second the bobbing cylinder of his manhood and stopped short.

'Come on then, soap my hair.'

Startled back to the present, she followed his signals, washing the thick brown locks, feeling the shape of his scalp beneath her fingers. Remembering her own rough treatment at the hands of Mistress Dingley's maid, she was gentle and he gave a little murmur of pleasure. Now, as he leaned back she could see his private parts clearly, the way the hair snaked down across his belly and spread between his legs, the soft pouch of his balls. She felt something approaching fear, but it was spiced with excitement. A moment later she realised that he had opened his eyes and was watching her. He sat forward and said: 'Enough, now. Get that kettle and rinse me off.'

Blushing at her shameful curiosity, she picked up the pan with shaking hands, mixed the water with cold from the ewer and anointed him in a cascade of suds. When he was rinsed clean, she handed him the cloth that lay near the fire and he stood up, wrapping it about him as he went.

'You may go now.'

She kept her eyes averted, ashamed of what he must have seen in her expression, but try as she would she could not rid herself of the thrill of seeing his body, its maleness, its healthy innocence.

Laboriously she began to ladle the water from the bath and back into the containers, then descended to the kitchen with the first kettleful. The other servants went back to complete the job.

That night she could not sleep, tossing from side to side, remembering how she had lain beside him in the hut at Carrickmain and in the room at the inn. Suddenly it seemed a long time ago. Then she had been a frightened child, seeking comfort. Now she wanted him to hold her again, to experience his warmth, his closeness, but in a different way. She realised with shock that she wanted to touch his cock and quickly fell to prayer to drive out the thought. The feeling did not go away.

The next morning she arose late, her legs like lead and eyes heavy as shot. Scurrying out into the courtyard, it was to find Robert's horse saddled and his belongings packed into panniers flung across the back of a second animal. Until then, she had had no inkling that he might leave.

'What about me?' Nobody heard. Pain and fear crowded her heart. She knew with a terrible certainty that because of her wickedness the night before, he was leaving her behind.

They all gathered to say goodbye to him, the servants and of course Aunt Jane. She was crying although she fought to restrain her tears.

38

All the time Sorcha held her breath, waiting for him to say: 'Come along, Dublin,' but he did not. By now he had put on his hat and gauntlets. The orange ribbon round the brim of his hat flickered in the breeze and she wondered bitterly if it was a favour given to him by some girl, perhaps his betrothed. He took his horse's reins from the groom.

Sorcha was about to run and plead with him, when he turned towards her.

'Here.'

Her face tight with misery, she took one step forward. Still holding the mare's rein, he bent towards her and ran his gloved finger along her cheek. The movement was tender, as to a favoured bitch. When he spoke, it was slowly and distinctly – one might speak so to someone deaf or witless. 'I shall be back. You stay here. Be sure now, to obey my aunt. Try your best to be a good, Christian maid. This is where you are safe. You understand?'

She started to shake her head but he placed his finger against her lips to still any entreaties.

'I will be back one day. Serve my aunt well.'

She reached out to touch him but already he had his foot in the stirrup and within seconds he was mounted and moving across the courtyard.

'God's speed, Robin.' They echoed their farewells.

'Robert!' For the first time she called his name aloud and with a smile he nodded towards her. He had not heard. Today was 30 April, her fourteenth birthday. Moments later he was gone.

As soon as Robert left Wolverton, Sorcha knew that she had to follow. The stinging pain of his desertion made no difference. Even if he did not want her, she still had to go. From now on she would follow him to the ends of the earth.

She knew that he was going home to Chertsey, to the mother he had first promised to take her to and then changed his mind. She had no idea where that might be, or how to get there. Neither did she know how long he intended to stay. With a start she thought that perhaps, after his visit, he might return to Ireland. At the prospect, her soul wept with longing for her home.

After a while she put such painful thoughts aside. Her hopes would never come true if she were to stay and mope helplessly, here at Wolverton. Chertsey should not be impossible to find. Anyway, the one thing she knew for certain was that she could not remain without him. Even if he had bewitched her, which she strongly suspected, she did not know how to break the spell.

Soulfully, Sorcha stirred a skillet over the smoking logs. In spite of her assumed confidence, inside she began to quake. There was so much that she did not know about this foreign land.

After the first night at Wolverton she had been consigned to a pallet in the scullery, sleeping beside Jennet. Although far less grand than Aunt Jane's chamber, it had the advantage of backing onto the kitchen wall, where the great fire warmed the bricks. Being on the ground floor, it now also made escape that much easier.

As usual, they retired to sleep some time after nine. Fortunately Jennet had a habit of dropping off the moment her head touched the straw. She was a heavy sleeper so that Sorcha did not have to wait long before the porcine grunts told her that her neighbour was lost to the world. Carefully she eased herself off the pallet and started to creep away.

Once she had left the safety of the bed, the route across the uneven slabs of the kitchens and through the echoing confines of the hall filled her with panic. At any moment someone would discover her and give chase. The fear of being caught stirred black memories of Carrickmain and she fought desperately to subdue them.

Once outside she started to run, making off across the fields towards the northern, wooded slopes. Instinct told her which way to go. Somehow she had to find a boat and cross back to the mainland of England.

But outside, it was an alien world. As she ran, she repeated: 'Dear God, protect me.' Her prayers were now to Robert's god. Although he was called Jesus, and Robert professed to be a Christian, it seemed that he had nothing but contempt for her own religious belief. Popery, he called it; superstition. She did not understand the difference but, in order to please him, she no longer crossed herself, or made reference to the Blessed Virgin. Of the other gods who lived in the trees and the rivers, some instinct told her to keep quiet. It was all a mystery.

As Sorcha travelled, she whispered to herself to obliterate other sounds, ominous stalking noises that filled the night, praying that Robert's deity had dominion over the beasts of darkness. If she was spared, by daybreak she would find somewhere to hide, perhaps a barn or a bothy.

The undergrowth was growing denser, more tangled. There was a large moon, but frequently black, threatening clouds hid it from view, leaving her struggling in the morass. She started off wearing Aunt Jane's shoes but her heels were rubbed raw, and anyway it was easier to feel her way with bare toes.

Having climbed up and up, the land seemed to level out, then tumble again along a chalky ridge. As she slipped and slid downwards, she thought she could see the first hint of dawn and a mixture of relief and anxiety spurred her on. She must find somewhere to hide.

Back in bramble-strewn woodland, she forced her way along, aiming for a lighter tunnel, glimpsed ahead through the trees. It looked like some sort of track, or path. As she hastened towards the welcoming light, a sudden, vicious fire exploded around her ankle. She went to lift her foot but nothing happened. Stabbing blades of pain radiated out from her left leg. With a cry she fell backwards into the ferns and the last thing she saw as she hit the ground, was the hungry jaws of a trap snapped shut about her foot.

Chapter 6

York
1 May, 1642

King Charles was sunk in an abyss of low spirits. In spite of his prayers and best endeavours, his plans continued to go disastrously wrong.

On 22 April, he had sent his second son, James, with a party of lords and gentlemen, on a well-schemed visit to Hull. Charles had heard that the Governor there, Sir John Hotham, was not passionate in his support for the Parliament, and urged on by Queen Henrietta's letters, he hoped to secure the port of Hull for himself. That way, the troops raised by his wife and Prince Rupert on the Continent could be brought into England. Once they arrived, Charles would march on his traitorous, capital and teach its citizens a lesson.

That was the plan. Dear Henrietta believed totally in his ability to accomplish it. Rupert, with his usual blunt manner, could see no problem. In the face of their confidence, unpleasant twitches of anxiety stirred in the King's vitals. He sighed.

Stage one of his design had gone smoothly enough, and young Prince James was courteously received by Hotham and installed within the city. Charles then moved to stage two. He and a troop of horse rode north to Hull on the pretext of visiting his son. Once inside the walls, he was confident that he would have no trouble in persuading the Governor to surrender the port to himself, the rightful ruler, but he had not allowed for the divided sympathies therein.

To his chagrin, the royal party were stopped at the gate while discussion took place within. For a while things hung in the balance. Governor Hotham eventually appeared on the city wall, and with much wailing and supplication, begged the King to desist from asking for entry. Some of the Royalists urged the towns-people to throw their Governor off the ramparts and open the gates themselves. They teetered on the brink of revolt, but to Charles's dismay the gates remained closed. Governor Hotham obeyed Parliament's orders and refused to let his sovereign inside. The King then had the ignominy of having to retreat.

Now the news of his attempt had reached Parliament, and he had received yet another condemning set of demands. Outrage welled up in his injured breast but he resisted the first, angry urge to write back. Even now he must think carefully of his position. He did not know how best to answer.

There was nobody close to him in whom he could confide. He guessed that if Rupert were here, he would see it all clearly. Unlike the royal advisors, Rupert had no doubts at all about the concept of Divine Right. He would suggest a short, sharp rebuke to the rebels, a few well-chosen threats. Charles warmed inside, wishing that such confidence, nay, even arrogance, was his, then he brushed the weakness aside as unbecoming in a monarch, but the feeling remained.

Young Prince Charles, heir to the throne, already worshipped his dashing cousin. The King drew comfort from the hope that one day his son would emulate his hero. In truth, Rupert seemed blessed with most of God's gifts, a brooding, dark-browed face that set female hearts fluttering, a well-muscled body packed into six feet four of manly grace, and yet at the same time something of the aesthete about him, poetic, enquiring, inventive. Charles sighed again. If only . . . In spite of his youth, Rupert, fruit of Charles's dear sister Anne's abundant womb, had supreme confidence. When he was present, his certainty always boosted the King's own courage. With such an adviser at his side, anything seemed possible. But for now he felt paralysed by a crippling sense of uncertainty. He prayed for his nephew's speedy return.

For a long while he stared at the lattice of his chamber. The sun behind the glass reflected his own image back to him, but he did not study it, for the sight of a small, thin, middle-aged man offered small comfort. He turned to the desk where papers lay in abundance, waiting for his attention. On the top, Henrietta's writing, bold, emanating her buoyant sense of enthusiasm, beckoned him.

Today, 1st May was Charles's wedding anniversary. At the

thought, he was overwhelmed by a sense of loneliness. Desperately he wanted Henrietta back, here at his side. She of all his circle was the only one who truly understood him. Such a dear, sweet, clever companion. Even greater than Rupert, her presence was Charles's inspiration. Unkingly tears began to trickle down his slender cheeks, soaking his beard. *'Henrietta, come back quickly and tell me what to do.*

Chapter 7

Caulbourne Village, Isle of Wight

Caleb Gosden stood on the village green. Watching. From habit he stood apart from the human flurry of activity, his back shielded by the hedge surrounding the churchyard.

The Church called this day the Feast of St John the Baptist, but Caleb knew otherwise. It was 1 May, and in defiance of the dictates of the law, the great Pole of male virility had been erected in the centre of the Green.

As he watched, mummers acted out their cautionary tale and young men galloped on hobby horses, whooping and engaging in mock battles. Girls had garlands about their necks and flowers in their hair. That morning, each house had been decked with May blossom, and as the day progressed, people bared their arms to welcome the late spring sun. Soon the dancing would begin.

Caleb gazed at his shadow foreshortened on the grass. It was distorted and he thought grimly that it made him look normal. He reached up and touched his hunched shoulder.

'Come on, Caleb. Come and play.'

Throwing off the dark thoughts, he took his fiddle and began to bow tirelessly, while the dancers jumped and circled. As the sweet melodies flowed from his fingers and through the strings of his fiddle, his soul was lifted. It seemed as if a Power outside himself had taken possession of him and carried him along on a higher plane of feeling. When the dancers finally sank exhausted onto the grass, people cheered and touched him on the arm. His soul came back to earth and he knew that they avoided touching his shoulder.

Nearby, his brother John – tall, copper-haired and four years

45

his senior – stood with his arm around his young wife. Anne Gosden was big with her third child.

I have lived for twenty-one summers, thought Caleb, and each year this festival has taken place. It belonged to a time long before the coming of Christ. These days, arguments ran high about the rights and wrongs of every aspect of their worship, but today's celebration paid service to another religion, barely acknowledged and yet as much a part of daily life as the Sunday service.

He glanced up at the smokey, sun-streaked sky and his thoughts closed him off from the boisterous crowd about him. As soon as darkness fell the young ones would divide into couples and make for the woods. Their parents would smile, indulgent, nostalgic. They would defend what happened as harmless fun. Tradition. Only those who were betrothed would go the whole way. The others would kiss and fondle and no harm done. Caleb shied away from the images.

Few times in his adult life had he lain with a woman, and those memories were tinged with bitterness. On the first occasion he had been barely sixteen and he and John had been to Newport with sheep to sell at the Michaelmas Fair.

They had drunk too much ale in the tavern and at some point a doxy had come to sit on his knee. At first he had been amused by her artlessness.

'You're handsome, young 'un. Look at they great blue eyes in among yer thatch.' She had ruffled his hair and then kissed him. She seemed old to him, probably not much more than the age he was now, but her bodice was open and he had slipped his hand inside to feel her breasts.

'C'mon.' She had taken his hand and led the way out of the tavern and down an alleyway to a small, smelly lean-to. Untying the strings of his breeches and leaning back against the wall she had lifted her skirts and pulled him to her. He remembered the urgency of his need. He seemed to have been inside her for only a moment before it was all over, and she had chuckled.

'I'd 'spected you'd be different but yer prick's like all the rest.'

His face had burned with humiliation.

'How much?'

'A brass farthin', seein' as how I feels sorry for ye.'

He had flung some coins at her and escaped back outside, now sober and smarting. The smarting had continued in another sense, for by next day and for weeks afterwards he had been sore and itchy until he was forced to seek out the cunning man of Watchingwell who had given him some herbal ointments. Mercifully the discomfort had gone away.

'Come and eat, Caleb.'

Coming back to the present, he realised that his mother was speaking, her fading green eyes upon him. 'How are you, Mam?' He took her arm and together they joined the queue for food, piled high on the tables around the Green.

Lizzie Gosden was over sixty now, her red hair peppered, her shoulders bowed. Since her husband's death, she had a lost, hopeless look. Sometimes Caleb resented her protective manner but he guessed that it gave her a purpose in life.

'I can't leave this earth till I've seen thee wed,' she would often say.

'Then you'll live for ever.'

She would sigh with exasperation. 'You think the maids don't want you on account of your shoulder, but you're wrong. I've seen the way they look at you. That face of yours would charm a princess. Who else is there with eyes like that, blue as the heavens and fringed black as night . . .' As he went to protest, she continued: 'It's your tongue what frightens them away. Always thinking about things what don't concern ordinary folk.'

It would be his turn to argue then. 'They do concern us, Mam. Every man should be accountable for himself.'

'Hush, not now. We're here to enjoy ourselves.'

His plate piled high with boar and rabbit, pigeon and venison, he sank onto the grass and soaked up the juices with a hunk of rye bread. Belching quietly he licked his fingers and thought fleetingly of the morrow when most of the village sheep would come into his care. From then on he would take to the downland for most of the summer with only his dogs for company. He fancied he heard the dull metallic chink of sheep bells and the call of an ascending lark.

Over the weeks he had repaired his hut on the hill. Firewood was stacked by the wall and the wooden hurdles that enfolded the sheep at night were all mended. With some jars of ale and cheeses to see him through, tomorrow he would begin another summer's solitary watch.

47

He became aware of the heightened tension around him, the raised voices, the too-loud giggles from the girls and the horse-play among the men. This evening, only the very young and the very old would lie alone. His mother Lizzie would sleep alone and he, Caleb . . .

Two young women were eyeing him, nudging each other and whispering. They turned their heads in unison as if to confirm some theory, then simultaneously began to giggle. Finally one of them called out: 'Hey, Caleb, you free tonight?'

His chest tightened as he recognised their taunting but outwardly he remained calm.

'Nothing's free. And you can't afford me.'

They sniggered then the second girl asked: 'Is it true you've got horns on yer head? Yer hair's that thick we can't see.'

'Is it true you've got hooves instead of feet?' giggled the other.

'I've only got one horn and you can both feel it if you like to take turns.' He pretended an amusement he did not feel. Both girls laughed out loud but the joke had gone as far as he would let it.

Getting up, he was about to make his way back across the Green when he noticed a group of men approaching. He knew immediately that it meant trouble. The village Constable, the Overseer of the Poor, the Inspector of Highways and two yeoman farmers flanked the austere personage of the Reverend Hopton Sydenham, newly-appointed rector of the Parish.

Those who noticed them stopped what they were doing and gazed apprehensively at the approaching party. The others, oblivious, continued to dance and drink and chatter. One by one they joined the abstainers until the last person froze to a halt. As a man, the villagers took a step back, with the exception of Caleb who stood his ground.

He had unwittingly become the spokesman and it was to him that the minister addressed his remarks.

'Are you not aware that by God's good majesty this pagan ceremony is banned?'

Caleb eyed him, challenging. His earlier self-consciousness was forgotten. Taking his time, he spoke slowly and loudly enough for everyone to hear. 'Parson, this is a village celebration. It started long before Scots Jamie laid claim to the English throne. It went on long before our religion was chopped and changed by his son and the Bishops. You may rightly think you have a say in what we do in church, but this celebration belongs to the village. It is for us to decide. Now kindly allow us to enjoy ourselves as we see fit.'

The atmosphere was charged as the people visibly drew back, looking from Caleb to the Minister. The Reverend Sydenham coloured and his jowls shook with indignation.

'Shepherd, your disrespect will not go unnoticed. I have it within my power, and the power of these gentlemen here, to order the removal of this maypole. I give you one chance to cooperate and if you don't, then the Constable will decide what to do with you, all of you.' He encompassed the rest of the villagers in his menacing statement.

'Caleb, please!' Lizzie pulled his arm. ''Tis almost dark. Let's just go home.'

Her son shook her off and keeping his eyes on the minister, he bent down to pick up his fiddle. Slowly and deliberately he started to play.

For a moment everyone remained frozen, then from the back of the crowd a young woman stepped forward and began clumsily to dance. As one, everybody present turned to regard her. She was both poor and plain and her movements were jarringly at odds with the rhythm of the music, but the shepherd turned towards her and played with exaggerated care.

Somebody started to laugh. 'Look at that, the dummy's dancing. She can't hear a thing but she's dancing like a good 'un.'

The tension was broken. Groups of people began to laugh too, then joining hands they started to circle and twist. The Constable and his entourage looked on blankly. Only the minister spluttered and grew more choleric.

'This won't be forgotten,' he finally shouted.

'By the time you've decided what to do it will all be over,' Caleb reminded him. 'Why not join in?' Looking at the rest of the delegation he said: 'There's many a wench to spare and if your conscience won't let you join the frolics in the woods, then you can go home and pray.'

'Caleb!' Lizzie was again tugging at his sleeve. 'They'll punish you if you don't stop.'

He merely smiled then turned his attention to the girl who had started the dancing.

'How are you, Sara?' He communicated to her with his hands and in reply she smiled at him, her plump cheeks suddenly strawberry red. With a wry grin Caleb patted her on the shoulder and, ignoring the discomposed officials, he took his leave, walking back across the Green to Sheepwash Cottage.

As its name implied, the cottage was situated by the sheepwash and for Caleb as for all the villagers, sheep were central to their lives. Given a choice he would still have stayed with shepherding. It was all he had ever known or wanted, the solitude, the oneness with nature. No man could look for more.

As he reached the cottage he called to the dogs. In response they jumped and whined, looking for his approval. They were mother and son. Fly, the bitch, was in her eighth year, her coat greyed and her limbs growing stiff. She pranced briefly in answer to his call before sitting down again at his side. Tyke, the pup, leaped and yelped vigorously. He was just a year old and understood his master's signals now, learning from both man and bitch, but his impetuous nature still often got the better of him.

It was a great expense to keep two dogs but Caleb reasoned that it was better to train his own than to wait until the old bitch died and then have the task of finding a good replacement. As he saw it they were the tools of his trade and nothing but the best would do. In any case, working dogs were a novelty, and he enjoyed the curiosity their skills aroused.

The events taking place in the village had disturbed him more than he had realised. Inside the cottage he wandered about the tiny room. The minister and his posturing was now forgotten but he saw through the doorway that couples were still following the old tradition, taking a sweetheart if only for one night, to steal to the woods. Once again he was fighting down his own loneliness. You don't need to be alone, he told himself, but as he thought of the village girls who were available to him he knew that he would find no comfort there.

Pouring himself more ale he went back outside to look across at the candle-lit Green. The youngsters were gradually slipping away into the gloom. Rest was impossible so he decided to go and check his hut one last time. He collected shears and knives, candles for his lantern and the ointments he used for his lambs. With a blanket, his change of clothes and the dogs at his heels he set off for the downs above West Over.

With Fly close by and Tyke now bounding ahead, he strode out towards the downland which, as the sun set, made a misty grey backdrop to the village.

The Parish of Caulbourne spread over several miles but the village was compact, mainly nestling along the bourne that gave it its name. One church, a few holdings, a handful of cottages, a cluster of wooden hovels, a blacksmith's forge and a wheelwright's shop, two mills along the stream and two manor houses a mile apart, made up the community. Thinking about it, Caleb thought that he would stay there until he died.

By now he was taking the path through the woods and ahead he could see the lighter patch where he would emerge onto the open downland. He whistled sharply to Tyke who had scared a rabbit and was about to give chase. The wildlife in the wood belonged to the Manor of West Over, and to be caught taking a coney or a partridge would mean a fine or a beating and perhaps prison.

The dog came momentarily to heel then edged his way ahead and down into the undergrowth. Immersed in thought, Caleb reached the open down before he realised that Tyke was missing. He whistled but the pup did not come. Cursing silently he turned back, now calling him by name. He heard him bark in reply off to his right.

'*Come!*' The order was peremptory and the dog appeared briefly, only to return the way he had come still barking and whining.

With a sigh Caleb followed him down a track, the faithful Fly at his heel. Dimly he could see Tyke crouching flat then springing up, bobbing his head and barking at a dark object on the ground.

'Away.' Now that Tyke had his master's attention he obediently came to stand behind the shepherd, circling in the excitement of the find.

Caleb lowered his bundle onto the leafmould and let out a whistle of surprise from between closed teeth as he bent down to investigate. Lying beneath a hazel tree, one leg bent and the other stretched out as if still in the act of running, was the unconscious form of a young woman.

Chapter 8

Dimly, Sorcha became aware of two sensations. Somebody was shaking her shoulder and at the same time, her left foot was on fire. She opened her eyes then immediately forgot the pain, the cold, everything. A black silhouetted figure was bending over her. Dear Jesu, she was back at Carrickmain!

'Lie still.'

The stranger had an odd country lilt to his voice. In the near-dark she could only discern the outline of his head, thick dark hair, the profile of a straight nose and wide brow. Cringing back into the bracken she waited, helpless to defend herself. The agony in her foot began to claim her again and she almost welcomed death.

'Who are you?' he asked.

'I want to go home,' she whimpered in Gaelic, any semblance of courage deserting her.

The man sat back on his heels, studying her intently.

In English she said: 'Help me.'

Getting no other answer he bent closer to study the trapped foot, shaking his head in dismay.

'Hush, now. This will hurt but it has to be done.'

With strong fingers he wrenched the evil teeth of the trap apart. A new inferno of pain engulfed her and she began to sob.

'Hush, girl, it's over now. I'll take you somewhere safe.'

At the thought that he should carry her away, Sorcha began to edge back, dragging herself painfully along on her behind. She could not prevent little murmurs of agony escaping her lips with each jarring movement of the injured limb. Again she wished that she could die.

'You won't get far like that.' Ignoring her protests the man wrapped a blanket about her, hauled her up and started to carry her off. The pain in her foot was too great, the terror too paralysing for her to resist.

They came to a hut, a small, square wooden construction, roofed over with turf and nestled in a hollow where two gently sloping hills met. He ducked inside and laid her on a pile of reeds, arranged like a couch along the inner wall.

'Right now, let's see.'

She lay rigid, waiting for him to do his worst, but he turned away from her and lit a candle, driving it into the fine tilth of the earth, then delved into the leather pannier he carried over his shoulder. After some rummaging he produced a jar of thick tarry balm.

'This works on sheep. Pray God it will work on you.' As he talked, he cleaned the ragged holes punched by the trap and began to coat them with the salve. 'I'm Caleb Gosden. A shepherd. And the local freak.'

From the light of the single tallow candle, Sorcha saw his jaw tighten as he spoke. His eyes were hard, an almost black-blue in the smokey gloom. Then he seemed to throw off some troublesome thought, saying: 'What's your name, girl? You aren't from round here.'

Sorcha hesitated. Her instinct was to say nothing, but she feared the silence more than his questions. 'Dublin. Dublin O'Neill.'

'That's a rare name. You a Papist?'

She did not reply.

'If you are, you'd best be careful. They hang people for less.' He finished what he was doing and wrapped her ankle in a sheet of clean cloth. Surreptitiously she pulled her skirts down as far as she could, shamed by the man's attentions to her legs.

Seemingly unaware, he gently positioned the injured foot on the ground. 'Good job I keep things at hand for my flock.'

Dublin thought perhaps it was meant to be a joke for he smiled briefly, but there was little joy in it. In repose, his face had a closed, distant look, but it could not mask the fine shape of his features. He scrambled up and it was then that she saw that he stood hunched to one side, his right shoulder drawn up, his right hand hanging awkwardly at his side.

'I'm going to leave you while I get some things. You'll be safe enough. No one comes this far.'

The throbbing in Dublin's leg began to ease to a dull ache and then a muffled sensation about her ankle. All the fears and troubles of the past day suddenly pulled her down and she was unutterably tired. Just now it didn't matter who came, or what happened. The only thing she wanted was to sleep. Robert and the security of his protection beckoned like some distant beacon, underlining the loneliness of her present predicament. As the shepherd ducked back out of the hut and left her alone, she willed her master to think of her, to come back and seek her out. *Robert, I love you.*

Dublin awoke to the distant bustling of a spring dawn. Inside the hut it was still dark, but a shaft of light dissecting the bothy told of the arrival of a sunny day. For a while she lay still, gently testing the ankle. It felt stiff and throbbed in reponse to her tentative movement. Carefully she dragged herself up, remembering the shepherd. Immediately her fears were back. She wondered where he was and what he intended to do.

Somehow she dragged herself as far as the doorway and peered cautiously out. There was no sign of him and for a few seconds she sat getting her breath, allowing the surge of pain in her leg to subside. Turning back she noticed a pile of clothing just inside the door. On top there was an old-fashioned kirtle which she lifted up and examined. Beneath it lay a well-darned shift and some odd pieces of rag. She realised the shepherd must have fetched them for her.

Looking down at her own skirt and bodice, she realised then how muddy they were. For a moment she hesitated, unwilling to part with the finery of Aunt Jane's garments, afraid to accept anything from the ill-formed stranger, but then, after glancing quickly outside again, she struggled out of her own clothes and into the others. The kirtle was much too big but she gathered it in at the waist and secured it with the laces from her own skirt. Immediately she felt better.

Around her there seemed to be everything that she could reasonably need – a leather bucket filled with water, bread and cheese, a stone crock with some ale, kindling, logs and flint for a fire. With the merest hesitation she helped herself to food, realising how hungry she was, then, when she had gathered her strength, she crawled outside and began to lay a fire in the hollow outside the hut.

The sun was well over to the west before the peace of the downland was disturbed by the persistent sound of bleating. With a start, Sorcha's eyes flew open. She realised that she must have fallen asleep again and lay still, her heart pounding, listening as the unending wave of noise grew louder. Struggling up, she hopped to the doorway and peered out. There below her, a very large flock of sheep moved in a pale, undulating mass, scrambling and jostling their way up the slope towards her. Out to the left two dogs dived and leaped, urging the flock on. To the right, a slim, dark-clad figure prodded the nearest animals with a crook.

The flock stopped a short distance away and began to graze. She noticed that the rams had flowers entwined in their horns. The dogs were now down on their haunches, positioned one at each side to contain the flock. Meanwhile the shepherd bounded up the slope and came towards her, stopping uncertainly as he saw her in the doorway.

To break the silence, she said: 'It's a lot of sheep you have.'

'Aye. Today's the day they come into my protection. May the second, every year. It's a village celebration.'

He was looking at her, his expression impossible to read. She felt embarrassed by his candid stare but did not know what was expected of her. Eventually she pointed to the fire.

With a nod, he brushed past her, going into the hut. Moments later he emerged carrying some rye bread and sheep's cheese for an evening meal.

Dublin continued to stand awkwardly by the fire, her weight on one foot, uncertain as to whether she should sit down or withdraw. She felt that she owed him some explanation but did not know what to say.

The shepherd indicated the food. With relief she sank to the ground and following his example, hungrily tore off pieces of bread and gnawed at the hard, discoloured cheese. Her appetite matched his own.

When he had finished eating, and drunk sufficient ale to quench his thirst, he sat back and regarded her. Sorcha lowered her gaze and felt her cheeks growing hot.

'I thank you for the clothes,' she said, indicating the green kirtle she now wore.

He inclined his head.

'Are they belonging to your wife?'

'Does it matter who they belong to?'

'No.' She blushed again, as if he had caught her out in some indelicacy.

He seemed to relent. 'They belonged to Sara Bush's mother. She's dead now. Sara's my neighbour in the village. She's a good friend.'

Dublin did not know what to conclude from the last remark. She guessed that the girl was probably his sweetheart. All the time her stomach churned with anxiety, knowing that she should be away from here, following Robert across the sea.

'What brings you here?' he asked.

'I was brought by my master.' She glanced up at him briefly. 'I have to get back to England.'

'What for?'

'To find my master.'

'How did you lose him?' For a moment his face registered humour.

She shook her head, not knowing how to explain.

'Well, you can't wander around the countryside on your own.' For a while he looked away, preoccupied, then he said: 'It's best you don't go into the village. There would be too many questions. Once the Constable finds out you're here, you'll find yourself packed off to your own Parish.'

'I do not have one.' His prediction only added to her sense of fear.

'Where do you come from, then?'

'Ireland. I was – taken.'

The shepherd looked surprised. 'Well, where did you stay last, before I found you?'

'At a fine house, with my master.'

From his expression, she guessed that he did not believe her. Aloud, he said: 'Then you'd best go back there.'

'*No!*' She was embarrassed by the force of her objection. 'If I do, they won't be letting me go again,' she said hurriedly. 'I've got to get to England. I must find my master.'

She saw his mouth tighten into a hard line, as if she had said something which offended him. He stood up, brushing crumbs

56

from his lap. As he made to move off and check the flock, he said: 'Well, you can't stay here.'

'Please. For just a day or so. Till I can walk.' She suddenly felt very afraid. Moving closer to him, she added, 'It won't be for long. As soon as I'm well . . .'

All the time he was shaking his head.

'Please.' In her desperation she reached out and touched his hand. Quickly he shook her off, turning away. She could see a nerve twitching in his jaw. She wondered why he should resent her so.

He stood for while as if wrestling with some huge problem, then without looking at her, he said: 'You can stay for tonight, but after that you'll have to go.'

She went to express her gratitude, but already he was striding away from her, a solitary, prickly figure, scrambling back to his flock. The thought of his tender care the night before only added to her confusion. I don't understand him, she thought to herself. I really don't understand him.

Dublin spent a second night inside the shepherd's hut. In spite of her injury and the need for rest, she lay awake, tormenting herself with a confused jumble of thoughts.

While part of her did not want to leave this fragile safety, some other, deeper fear, had her poised for flight, all the while aware that a few yards away was a strange, humpty-backed man, who at any moment might come and eat her up, or turn her into a hare, or worse.

During the daytime, in spite of his cold manner, it was not so bad. When the sun was up, notwithstanding his deformity, the shepherd was clearly an ordinary mortal. Only his changing moods and sudden ill-humour unnerved her. But at night it was different. Who knew what he might turn into? In the dark, she crossed herself.

In the early hours of the morning it started to rain. Now guilt began to torment her at the thought of him sleeping outside. He was hardly likely to let her stay if it meant being soaked himself. She heard him cough and her heart jolted. She ought to invite him in but she was too scared. The minutes crawled by, and as the first hint of grey entered the hut, she could bear it no longer.

Dragging herself painfully up, she went to the entrance, but peering nervously outside, it was to find that he had already gone to attend to the sheepfolds. In the dawn light she could hear the animals stirring restlessly. Wearily she sank back into the reeds and pulled the blanket about her. Her foot pained and the thought of leaving was worse than the prospect of staying.

'Get up!'

The voice was terse, and Dublin jerked awake. For a moment she did not know where she was, and stared around without recognition, then seeing the shepherd, she pulled her blanket closer about her. Clearly she had fallen back to sleep.

'It's morning. Time you were on your way.'

She did not reply but scrambled awkwardly to her feet, afraid of his resentment, still wiping the sleep from her eyes. Edging past him, she ducked outside and headed for the bushes. While she was relieving herself, perched awkwardly to keep the weight off her injured foot, she wondered what was to become of her. Again she wished that she could curl up somewhere and quietly die.

Hobbling back towards the bothy, Dublin saw that the shepherd had already lit the fire. As she watched, he peeled off his shirt and held it out to the flames. After a moment a waft of steam began to rise.

She gazed spellbound at his torso, turned away from her. The thick belt that held up his breeches, pulled the material tight across his buttocks and she felt herself bewitched by the muscular curve of his thighs and legs. But it was upwards that her gaze was drawn, up across the smooth, naked back that ended where his thick, curling hair hung in damp locks down his neck. Muscles moved smoothly under his creamy skin. His left shoulder was finely proportioned, the biceps of his arm flexing as he waved the shirt backwards and forwards in front of the flame. His right shoulder was raised higher, tucked in towards his neck, as if he was deliberately hunching himself up. His right arm was thinner than the left and he moved it awkwardly. Suddenly Dublin felt overwhelmed by sadness at the sight of his marred beauty – and something more.

At that moment he swung round and espying her, he glared angrily. 'Get away!' he swore, and she stumbled back, her eyes still upon him. She felt something akin to the shame that had claimed her when she had been caught out seeing Robert's nakedness – two men, both vulnerable, exposed to her prying eyes. Tripping, she fell and her ankle screamed its hurt.

The shepherd's face turned scarlet and in spite of her own pain, she felt his crushing humiliation.

'I didn't mean to offend you.' She scrambled painfully up again.

The man clenched his fists and she saw that his hands were trembling. 'Just get your things together and be gone.'

Dublin lowered her eyes and closed her arms about herself for comfort. Swallowing hard, she said: 'I cannot walk. How can I get to the mainland if I cannot walk?' When he did not reply she added: 'Perhaps I could help with the sheep, just till I'm healed. I don't mind sleeping outside.'

He looked at her, his mouth tight. 'I don't want you here.'

The vehemence of his voice was like a slap. 'I – I wouldn't be a burden.' To her own surprise, she added: 'I feel safe here.'

He snorted derisively. 'You think because I'm humpty-backed I'm safe?' He gave a mirthless laugh. 'Don't you know I have the Devil sitting on my shoulder? Ask around the village and they'll tell you.'

Dublin shook her head. 'I wasn't meaning that. I just don't think you'd do me harm.'

Caleb's shoulders sagged. 'This is no place for a woman.'

To her shame she began to weep. The tears brimmed over and streaked her cheeks. 'I wouldn't be a burden,' she repeated.

He had struggled into his still-damp shirt and was now tucking it into his breeches. Dublin held her breath, waiting for him to pronounce sentence. Her very future depended on it.

With his back to her he said: 'I can't make allowance for you. I've got my own way of living and if it doesn't suit then you'll have to go.'

She nodded her head, the relief a torrent, ready to promise anything, as long as she could rest up and get well. Only then could she seek Robert out. 'Shall I be making you breakfast?' she offered.

'No. Just keep out of my way.'

As soon as he left the camp, Dublin put the blankets outside to air over some gorsebushes. The shower had faded away and a comforting sun bathed the gentle slope of the hills in warmth and light. Taking water from the pail inside the door, she began to prepare a meal with the mutton and turnips that hung inside the hut. She had little experience of cooking, but the memory of her mother's routine came clearly to her. As she worked, Dublin felt very close to her mother, as if she was taking up the mantle that

Dervla O'Neill had so long worn. It gave her a comforting sense of continuity.

When Caleb returned at sundown, Dublin immediately set about dishing up a bowl of the stew, holding it out in supplication.

He took it wordlessly and sank crosslegged onto the ground. Warblers quarrelled in the gorsebushes and a cartwheel of a sun gently slid beneath the skyline. The shepherd nodded to her to take a bowl for herself, and before eating, he offered up a prayer: 'Thank Thee, Father, for Thy bounty. A blessing on our village, I pray Thee.'

Dublin wondered if his God was the same as Robert's. She opened her mouth to ask him but then thought better of it, mouthing an 'amen' instead. As soon as he started to eat, she followed his example.

They ate in silence, she with her fingers and he stabbing the chunks of mutton with his knife. The sounds of their chewing punctuated the unspoken tension. When he had finished, he put his bowl on the ground before him and nodded his approval. She let out her breath in relief and tentatively asked: 'Shall I be fetching some ale?'

He accepted the jug and drank long and slow, now relaxing. When his thirst was sated he wiped his lips on the back of his hand. 'How's your foot?'

'It hurts.'

'Let me see.'

She hesitated but he was already unwrapping the cloth about her ankle. She tried not to look. She did not want to see the wound, or gaze upon his bent form, hunched over her leg. He was very close to her and she noticed the ring that hung from his ear. His ear was a nice shape.

'There's pus in the wound. The leg's hot.' His hand moved up her calf and she caught her breath but he ignored her. 'I'll bathe it with hot water, then put more salve on it.'

There was nothing to do but give herself up to his ministrations. She gasped with pain as he dabbed at the teethmarks in her ankle. 'Sorry, girl I'll try not to hurt thee.'

This man, gentle, caring for her, bore little resemblance to the angry shepherd who had sworn at her that morning. She wondered which one he really was.

When he had finished and bound the leg again, he stood up. 'I'll enclose the sheep and then 'twill be time to sleep.' Gruffly he added: 'You lie right inside the hut and I'll stay near the door. That way if there's any trouble I won't disturb you.'

'What sort of trouble?' Dublin imagined the Justices coming to take her away. They would surely beat her then lock her up. Being a stranger, they might even hang her for a spy. Whatever happened, she would never find Robert. Her hand closed over her mouth to keep the fear from erupting.

He said: 'I only meant trouble with the sheep. You needn't fear, I'll be close by.'

She nodded and her confusion at the thought of sleeping next to him dissipated her other worries.

For an eternity, Dublin waited for his return. Her foot hurt but she did not dare to lie on the bed of reeds which was rightfully his.

As he ducked inside the hut he looked surprised to see her standing there. 'Get to sleep,' he said.

Without undressing, she sank down onto the bedding and pulled the blanket tight up to her chin. Now that it was night again, all her fears were back. She found it difficult to breathe, trying to hear above her racing blood for the least movement. Even if the man did come towards her, she knew that she would not be able to run fast enough to get away. She thought of his shoulder. Surely God must be punishing him for some reason? The knowledge only added to her fear. At all costs she must not touch his deformity – if she did so, then surely she too would be bewitched.

Caleb was stretched out on the bare earth, lying with his back to her. The hut felt cold. The yard that separated them seemed to have some magic power, trying to pull Dublin closer to the warmth of his body, but she fought the magnet, protecting herself by thinking of Robert.

But before she could find him, she had to get well, then discover a way of getting off this island and finding her way to – where? She still did not know where Chertsey might be. If she asked, would somebody tell her, but who? Quickly she shut the difficulties out for they were too much to cope with. In the meantime she would have to endure the days here, cooped up with this dour, distant misfit. Again the tears began to flow.

Chapter 9

As the days passed, Caleb and Dublin fell into an uneasy truce. Nothing more was said about her leaving although the uncertainty hung over her like some threatened ordeal, having to be faced, and made worse by the living of it over and again.

Then her spirits rose. One afternoon, she saw the shepherd coming across the top of the down carrying two lambs. The sun was behind him and his silhoutte bobbed blackly as he strode in her direction. As the wind plucked at his shirt, disguising the misformed shoulder, she thought how fit and athletic he looked. Her chest tightened. For once there was an air of excitement about him, a willingness to come into her company.

'Here. Here's a job for you. These two are lateborn and their dam has died.' He plonked them down on unsteady legs. 'Twins are a rare thing. Put them in the hut and I'll fetch another ewe. Do you know how to draw milk from the udder?'

She nodded.

'Right. Then draw some off and set these two to feed. I can't afford to lose them.'

'Poor little things.' She rubbed her fingers over the ribby coats, wondering at the pinkness of the skin showing through. As she glanced up, she found Caleb watching her and for a second she caught the intent, gentle expression on his face. Immediately it hardened.

'Just feed them,' he said gruffly, and then was gone again. She was left wondering what it was about her that made him angry. The failing, for failing it must be, gnawed at her like hunger.

When the ewe had been brought and hobbled, Caleb went off again about his own business. Left alone, Dublin gripped a bucket between her knees and managed to draw off enough milk to offer to the lambs. At first she dipped one finger in the bucket, encouraging each infant to suck, then gradually she persuaded them to lick the warm liquid off her hands, and finally to take it direct from the pail.

At supper, Caleb nodded his approval. 'You have a way with you.'

She flushed with pleasure.

Drinking deeply of his ale, he said: 'There is a difficulty ahead. On the fifteenth of May I castrate the lambs.'

She looked at him questioningly.

'Sara comes to help me. She's a deaf girl from the village.'

'Your neighbour.' Dublin felt her pulse quicken at the thought of anyone coming near.

Caleb added: 'Sara's as good as any man, and it gives her the chance to earn a few pence. The village don't like it, they don't think it's seemly.' He shrugged. 'After the first summer they wouldn't speak to me but then they began to see the advantage. After all, it leaves another man free to get on with other, pressing tasks and besides, Sara is good.' He looked up at her as if expecting her to challenge his claim. When she didn't, he continued: 'She delivers the stones fresh to each housewife on the day they are cut. There's nothing like them, fried golden brown and served with parsley.' He pulled a wry face. 'In any case, why should they worry? Sara's a dummy. She's not likely to wed.'

So she wasn't his sweetheart. Dublin tried to create another image in her mind of Sara Bush. 'When will she come?' she asked.

'Tomorrow.'

'Couldn't you do it later?' Dublin wanted to know.

Caleb shook his head. 'It has to be done when the moon is on the wane.'

'Why?' She felt upset by the proposed change of routine, and had not realised how used she had become to their way of life.

'Because that's how it is. 'Twould be bad luck to do it at any other time.'

'Then could I not help instead?' She sat up on her knees and looked hopefully at him.

Again he shook his head. 'Do you know how to cut the codde? Or pull the stones with your teeth? I've got eighty-four lambs to

63

cut and it's got to be quick. If you don't do it proper you'll cause infection.'

'Is she your sweetheart?' she asked after a while.

'Don't be so foolish.' He stretched his shoulders and scrambled to his feet. 'Best that you get to sleep. We'll have an early start.'

By first light the sky was cloudless and there was a soothing breeze as a sun the colour of barley sugar began to unfold over the distant horizon. Standing in the doorway of the bothy, Caleb called to Dublin.

'See, here comes Sara now.'

She was just in time to see a sturdy figure skirting the dense outgrowth of scrub and furze below them at the base of the down. Dublin watched her for several moments, her unhurried, dogged movements, now and then tugging at her skirts which were held captive by the army of thorns through which she forced her path. The girl looked round and motherly.

'There's nothing to fear.' Caleb broke into her thoughts. 'I'll do the explaining, but you can trust her – as you do me.' He flushed.

'How can you explain to her?' Dublin asked.

'When she was a child we invented our own language. I'm the only person who can really talk to her. I can make myself understood as plain as I can to you.'

'You can?'

'Without someone to talk to, she's cut off from everything.'

'Then what does she do when you aren't there?'

He had not thought of that before.

By now Sara Bush was only a few hundred yards away and they both observed her progress in silence. Caleb waved and in response the girl increased her pace, the smile on her face soon visible in the rapidly increasing daylight.

Her expression changed to surprise as she saw Dublin. For several moments she gazed wide-eyed at the visitor, then slowly turned her attention to Caleb.

He took the girl's hands in greeting and nodded towards Dublin, then began a series of complex gestures with his fingers.

'What are you saying?' Dublin's voice was anxious and she felt excluded.

64

'I told her you were in trouble and I am protecting you until you can move on.'

'And what did she say?'

'Nothing. She accepts what I say.'

'Can we really trust her not to give me away?'

'I've already told you. Yes.'

Dublin became aware of Sara's candid stare, and she noticed that Caleb's face coloured. It dawned on her that their living arrangements were bound to arouse curiosity. She wanted to explain to the girl but had no means of doing so except through the shepherd, and she could not voice what she was thinking. Instead she simply nodded her head in greeting, but Sara's attention was on the man again.

'You must say nothing,' he signed to her. 'Trust me.'

She looked at Dublin, her face expressionless, then lowered her eyes and blinked, as if some hurt had befallen her.

Aloud, Caleb called to Dublin: 'We'll be back before sundown. Have a meal ready for us.'

'Can I not come with you? See how it's done?'

He shrugged. 'If you wish.'

Sara and Caleb walked in silence and Dublin tagged along behind, limping in her effort to keep up. She could see that there was a certain comfort in the familiarity with which he treated the dumb girl, and she felt a moment of envy, wondering what it was about herself that made him so hostile. As she watched, he touched Sara's arm to point out a bird, poised momentarily on the sheep track before making its hawk-like flight back to the copse down in the valley.

'Cuckoo,' he mouthed the eponymous sound and Sara responded with a half-smile but her expression remained troubled and he raised his eyebrows.

Sara signed briefly and Caleb nodded.

'What did she say?'

'That you are beautiful.' He sounded dismissive.

'What did you say?'

'That you are at risk. That she must tell no one that you are here. Now, are you going to keep asking questions all day?'

Dublin fell behind, chastened by his ill-humour. After a few minutes they reached the sheepfolds where the ewes and gimmers – the young female sheep – were quickly released to graze nearby. A few fortunate rams joined them. Caleb and Sara then turned their attention to the second pen.

The ram lambs were soon part of a regular chain, grabbed and upturned by the shepherd, the tender bag between their back legs sliced open and the soft, fertile contents sucked out. At Caleb's side, Sara collected the fresh offerings, placing them on clean linen in a wicker basket and then deftly applied a protective lotion of herb tansy chopped in butter, to the oozing wounds. Within moments the emasculated lambs were back on their feet and grazing abstractedly as they sought to regain their composure.

Dublin watched Caleb, crouched forward, working rhythmically. There was a calmness about him, a certainty. He had tended her ankle so, with the same assurance, inspiring confidence. Under the carefully sewn folds of his shirt the disfiguring shoulder was barely visible. His face, for once relaxed, looked undeniably handsome, his brow furrowed against the sun. His eyes were such an intense blue, shrewd, intelligent. Dublin felt confused. After a while, she made an excuse to leave, saying that she should start the meal. In reality she felt excluded from the companionship between the pair. It made her feel increasingly lonely. Wandering back towards the bothy, she was weighed down by an undefined sadness.

At last the workers returned. Sara's basket was covered with clean cloth, and Caleb walked at her side, his leather sack slung across his shoulder. He immediately poured himself a large measure of ale, glad to wash away the residue of his activities, rinsing his face and mouth in cool spring water collected by Dublin in the leather bucket. She was pleased to be of service to him, feeling a strange rivalry with the dumb girl.

Silently she dished up two bowls of the now familiar mutton which was seasoned with some wild garlic she had found in the copse.

'Are you not eating?' he asked, signalling to Sara to be seated and sinking to the ground himself.

'We don't have sufficient dishes.' Dublin could not stop herself from glancing accusingly at the visitor.

'You can share my bowl.'

She sank down beside him and took a mouthful of the stew. She had an odd sense of having scored some victory over the other girl.

66

When they finished eating it was time for Sara to leave.

'Thank you for your work. Eat well of the sweetbreads. Take care on your route.'

Caleb patted her plump shoulder and Sara lowered her eyes. Clutching the now heavy basket, she glanced at Dublin before turning and starting her journey home. As Dublin watched, Caleb stared a long while after her until she was diminished by distance to the size of a jackdaw.

With a sigh he turned back.

'She likes you.' Dublin blushed as she said it.

'I'm like a brother to her.'

'I don't mean like that.'

He raised his eyebrows, and under his scrutiny her cheeks grew hotter. Immediately she saw his brow darken. 'You women are a curse. You think of nothing but foolishness.'

'I only meant . . .'

'I know what you meant. Leave me in peace, woman. It's time you thought of leaving.'

Dublin stared in confusion at his back. He turned and watched the diminishing figure of Sara with a concentration that defied her to speak. She did not know what to think. One minute he was friendly and the next, for no good reason, his temper would flare up and he would be fuming and silent. Now she could almost feel the resentment emanating from his tense body.

'Where are you going?' she asked as he finally turned back.

'To check the folds.'

'Can I help?' She did not want to be alone.

He shrugged, his face now expressionless, and she followed him round in silence as he tested poles and re-tied lashes to keep the hurdles in place. When he was satisfied, he nodded curtly to her and started back. She found herself hobbling in order to keep up.

Conversation was impossible. The question of her staying hung in the air like a thundercloud, black and ominous. Although her foot had well-nigh healed, and she desperately wanted to seek Robert out, the prospect of setting off alone made her quake. Perhaps in a few more days, or a week or two, she would be truly well.

To break the oppressive silence she said: 'Your friend Sara seems of good heart.'

'She is.'

'Does she live alone?'

He looked round at her as if about to protest but then shrugged, letting whatever it was that troubled him, pass. He started to talk. 'Sara's quite alone. Her father was a soldier, billeted here in '25, a Scotsman, come with his regiment to be shipped abroad.'

He slowed his pace to let Dublin catch up before continuing his tale. 'Whatever happened I don't know, but the Scotsmen weren't needed. There was no money to send them home and nobody knew what to do with them, so they shipped them over here, to the Island.'

They reached the bothy and Caleb sank down outside, picking abstractedly at the spiky grass. Dublin watched his strong brown fingers, remembering the feel of them against her foot.

He said: 'I can just recall him. He spoke some heathen tongue and had hair red as a rooster. He must have been here nigh on a year then suddenly they found money from somewhere and the Scots were called back. Our man left, leaving Emmy Bush . . .' He did not finish the sentence.

Dublin bowed her head in respect for Emmy Bush and her shame. Caleb continued: 'When Sara was born her mother neglected her something shameful.' His face was hard, sharing that suffering. Glancing at Dublin he said: 'I think she thought Sara was a punishment for her wickedness. When she realised the child was deaf, she treated her even worse.' His eyes blinked fast as at some remembered sadness. In a low voice he added: 'I can't abide cruelty.'

'You've been kind to her.'

Caleb shrugged. He drew in his breath and Dublin expected some further explanation, but instead he said: 'As long as you stay with me you respect my way of doing things.'

'I do.' Her relief was tangible.

After an age, he added: 'I believe that there is no difference between prince and pauper. All men are equal in the eyes of God – and that means you and me and Sara Bush.'

Dublin nodded. The idea was so new that it hit her like a bolt of light.

'And I believe that God is in us all. He is not the property of the Bishops, or the King. He doesn't need a minister or a priest to teach us His will. It is in everyone, here.' He touched his chest.

'Are you a Dissenter?'

'I am myself. I believe what I believe. I don't need the Church to tell me what to think. You too should think for yourself.'

Dublin was beginning to feel out of her depth. So much had happened to her in the past few months that she had no idea who she was, or what she believed. She badly needed a god to protect her.

'Are people afraid of you?' she asked, to change the subject.

'You think they should be?'

She was amazed at how blue his eyes seemed beneath their black lashes. Suddenly blushing, she looked away.

'No – I . . . Are you afraid of the Devil?'

Caleb shrugged. 'I fear evil. And I fear tauntings and cruelty to man or beast.'

'Do you think the Devil made you . . .' she nodded towards his shoulder '. . . like that?'

His jaw tightened. After too long he said: 'It is what others think that matters. If they believe that, then that is how it is.' After a pause he asked her: 'Is that what you believe?'

'No.' She shook her head. 'I think – it was an accident. It's nothing really, it doesn't matter,' she finished lamely. She could think of nothing more convincing to say.

He stood up and with a curt, 'Goodnight,' entered the hut and threw himself down on his bed so that she had to climb over him to reach her own.

He did not move and lying silently in the dark, with him between herself and the doorway, she listened to the soporific regularity of his breathing. For a while, when he had been talking, she had felt closer to him than at any time since he had brought her here. She tried to work out how long ago that had been – three, four weeks? At the mention of his shoulder, he had changed back to his normal self, cold, resenting her presence. She suddenly wanted to cry.

Dublin rolled over to face the wall. Hunchback, outcast, Devil-worshipper, angel face, Samaritan – the names came one after the other and they all seemed to fit him. She sighed and rolled back again studying his black, prostrate outline. Whatever he might be, she was now very aware that she had underestimated him, and the knowledge filled her with new and previously unexperienced sensations. Not all of them were unpleasant.

* * *

69

Mercifully, Dublin's leg was all but healed. Although there was still some puffiness around her ankle, and crusty brown scabs covered each puncture hole, it no longer pained her and she could walk normally.

As the days passed she began to feel more confident. Although not very forthcoming, Caleb seemed to accept her presence and she began to venture further from the bothy to collect water and kindling, mushrooms, spinach and wild thyme, to make tasty meals. She reasoned that as long as she made herself useful, he would have no reason to send her away.

There was also a plethora of sheep's wool strewn along the needle-sharp banks of gorse and painstakingly she collected it up, making a rough spindle from a piece of wood. This activity kept her busy during the day and she hoped that by presenting the spun yarn to the shepherd, she would in some small way be paying for her keep. She did not wish to be beholden to him.

Whenever she was away from the hut, the fear of discovery haunted her and she took great care to stay within the shelter of the bushes. One day at the end of the month however, she was shocked to see a well-built young man making his way towards Caleb's hut. Heart beating fast, Dublin scrabbled into a hollow in the furze and crouched low, trying to ignore the razor-sharp grazes along her arms and legs. As she watched, the stranger went into the hut, then after several moments came out again and set off towards the distant flock of grazing sheep. Dublin stayed there waiting, expecting the man to return, but he did not. At last, after what seemed like hours, with the sun beating mercilessly upon her, she crawled out and scurried back to the hut. After the heat of the June sunshine, the darkness of the bothy was like a balm. Dublin went to fetch herself a drink of ale and picking up the crock, realised that the stranger had already helped himself to some. The thought of his presence in their hut, touching Caleb's things, intruding, filled her with fear.

When the shepherd returned that evening, she told him what she had seen.

'It was my brother John. He came with bad news for himself, but good news for us. Shortly I'll be leaving for the annual shearing. Normally John comes to oversee the lambs that are left behind, but this year there is a sickness among his horses. He cannot leave them, so he has asked Sara to come instead.'

Dublin felt a curious mixture of relief because the visitor was Caleb's kin, and a sense of exclusion because she was an outsider and had not even known until that moment that he had a brother. She wanted to know more about him, be accepted here, and felt a sudden envy for Sara who was a local girl and therefore belonged. She experienced a sense of indignation that the dumb girl was coming back.

'How long is she coming for?'

'Probably two weeks. If the weather is good, the shearing should be finished by mid-June.'

Eyeing Caleb, she observed: 'Your brother does not favour you.'

'He is like my father was. I – I am like no one. Perhaps I have the Devil's face.' He pulled a quizzical expression but she did not respond.

As she dished up the stew, she said: 'Do we need to have Sara here? I can guard the lambs myself if that's all it takes.'

Caleb ignored the bowl she was offering to him. 'Two things seem to have escaped your notice,' he said. 'First, this is my hut, my flock and I decide who comes here. Secondly, even if I conceded, there would be questions in the village as to who was guarding the flock.' Suddenly catching her arm he forced her to look at him. 'You are not mistress here.'

Dublin's face flushed with anger until tears glistened in her eyes but she said nothing. After a moment he released her and took the bowl. But she could not hold back her sense of affront. 'Why are you so horrible to me?'

'I'm not. I just want some peace.'

'Then I'll go in the morning.'

He did not reply and his silence increased her panic.

'It's what you want,' she prodded, hoping for some denial.

Now he swung round and she was frightened by the anger in her eyes. 'How would you know what I want? You, you have no idea. All you can do is torment me. Just get out of my sight!'

Dublin's heart began to drown in a sea of fear. His dismissive gesture, the intensity of his pent-up rage, paralysed her. She retreated early to the bed and took refuge in pretending to sleep, and although she listened long into the night, the shepherd did not come to bed. When she found the courage to look outside in the morning, he had already gone.

71

She stood surveying the empty landscape, aching inside. Soon Sara would be arriving. She had no wish to be here, to witness the quiet togetherness of Caleb and his dumb companion. It only underlined the fact that there was something wrong with Dublin, something that made men angry, made them abandon her. Remembering the way he had spat out his words, she knew that he must hate her. There was nothing for it; she would go now, before either of them came to the hut.

She went through the familiar routine of collecting wood and water, seeking out mushrooms to put with the evening meal – only she would not be there to eat it. When she had struggled back from the stream, and laid a fire, there seemed to be nothing else to delay her.

Reverently she placed the ball of spun wool on Caleb's bed, a modest thank you for the grudging hospitality. Back outside she looked down across the valley, wondering which way to go. The only thing to do was to aim for lower ground, follow the distant track, and hope it led to the river. From there, perhaps, she would be able to find a boat to take her to England.

Still she delayed, then far below her she saw the distinctive shape of Sara, picking her way up the hill. Empty-handed, Dublin started the descent by another path.

Tears blinded her as she walked. She wanted Robert now, with such longing that she began to run, hoping to find a boat and be carried miraculously into his arms. He was so strong, so comforting. In a strange way she felt that she had grown up during the past weeks. It would no longer be necessary for him to look after her, like the child she had been at Carrickmain. Now she would look after him. Her tears stopped as she imagined caring for him, the intimacy, the privacy of a room where she would hold her arms out to him and welcome him to her. Somewhere deep between her legs, she ached, wanting to be touched, pressed into, until the emptiness inside her was filled.

'Got you!' Her fantasy was shattered as a man stepped from the hazel coppice through which she passed, and grabbed hold of her arm.

A scream formed on her lips but she did not utter it. The shock was too great. The man was huge, big-bellied, and his florid face was alight with satisfaction.

'Let me go!'

72

He smirked. 'Seems like the rumour's right, then – you're a foreigner, a Papist spy.'

'I'm not so. Please . . .'

'No good "Pleasing", young woman. I'm Constable of this Parish. It's my duty to take you in. I reckon you'd best start saying your prayers.'

Dublin struggled but there was no escape. As she stumbled along beside her captor, she tried not to think of what would happen next. Whatever it was, it would not be pleasant.

Chapter 10

It was with a sense of liberation that Robert left his aunt's home in the Isle of Wight and set out for the family home at Chertsey. Riding across country he tried to imagine what his mother would have said if he had brought Dublin back with him. Although a kind woman, he knew that she would not have welcomed such a harum-scarum. He smiled briefly to himself, thinking of the wild, abandoned creature, swearing and screaming her way across England. No, his mother would *not* have been amused.

Perversely, the more he thought about Dublin, the more he came to miss hér. Although it was not in his nature to court unconventional behaviour, there was something exciting about such straightforward savagery. The child seemed to have adopted him as slavishly as a favourite hound. He had a lunatic image of her barking and biting in his defence, wild, fox-like. The vision was dangerously stirring. But no, he had done the right thing. Anyway, he must think of his position. What would the Hampdens say? Now he was at a crossroads in his career and more than ever it was important to keep on the right side of his influential, future father-in-law.

Thinking of Dublin's small, arresting face, the fierce independence of her expression, his loins stirred and a measure of guilt began to torment him. Other people might not understand his honourable motives in rescuing the child from certain death. He could not quite admit it to himself, but he was not absolutely sure about his own motives either. Anyway, now he could forget about her. As soon as he got home, there would be plenty to distract him.

The Hammond house was situated in Chertsey Beomond, Surrey. Known as Abbey House, as the name implied it stood on the site of an old monastery. Only a few foundations remained to show where the original building had been. Robert loved the house, its deep gables and latticed windows, the warm orange of the bricks. Inside there were quiet corners and cool parlours where as a boy he had hid from prying eyes, and outside there were always sheltered spots in the gardens. Beans and artichokes grew among the flower beds and in summer, the scent of box mingled with thyme and lemon balm.

In addition to his mother, Elizabeth, the house was occupied by his brother John and his new wife Margaret, daughter of the Duke of Warwick. John had made a good match, but then, Mary Hampden, although the sixth daugher of her illustrious father, would be an excellent match too. He passed the rest of the journey in contemplation of his bright future.

When Robert finally reached home, there was a reassuring joy in the welcome.

'Robert, my dearest boy! I thank God that He has brought you back safe from that heathen place.'

He swept his mother off her feet, swinging her around and she laughed her objection. At her words, he thought again of Dublin. No, she could never belong here.

There was much news to catch up on. Robert told them of Carrickmain, omitting to mention his strange trophy. Neither did he enlighten his mother that he had made a detour via the Isle of Wight. Her sharp wits would soon wheedle out of him the true purpose of his journey.

'Well, what do you plan to do now?' John asked, as they sat long over supper.

Robert shrugged, eyeing his brother with affection. When their father had died, Robert had been only ten and it was John who had taken on the burden of the estate. Here John would stay and it was a comfort to know that there would always be Hammonds at Abbey House.

For Robert, a different future beckoned, but for the moment he had no clear idea of what it would be. He said: 'I could do with a few days' rest. After that, I shall go to visit Mary, see how the wind blows in London.'

John frowned. 'I hear that the King has gone north. It seems that there is no sign of an amicable settlement with the Parliament.'

75

'So I believe. I might find myself following him. I suppose, given time, it will work out as God intends.' He yawned.

His brother put his cup aside. 'Best get you to bed, brother. We can talk again on the morrow.'

At Abbey House, Robert soon settled into a routine. He accompanied John on his daily tour of the Manor, appreciating the familiar. Always there was plenty to discuss and do, trying out a mare here, weighing a fleece there, planning new boundaries for the fields, and which crops to plant where. Mostly their talk was about the estate but sometimes it turned to the discontent in the country. They did not always see eye to eye.

'There is talk of civil war,' said John as the brothers worked to construct a new grain store. 'Such an idea is madness.'

Robert felt inclined to agree, but for the moment everything seemed in limbo. He wanted it settled, peace between King and Parliament, so that his own career in the Army could move forward. As long as the King was in this undecided state, Robert did not know where he belonged. In the meantime, there was plenty to do on the estate. In spite of his best intentions, he delayed leaving.

Early summer gave way to July. On about the fifth day, two visitors arrived at the house. This was not an unusual occurrence, for callers were frequent, but on this occasion it was clear from their demeanour that they came on serious business.

Announcing them, Elizabeth Hammond confirmed their grave mission. 'John, Robert, leave what you do and come to the hall. Your uncles are here. They wish to speak with you both.'

Inside, the two uncles and their nephews embraced. When the greetings were over, they seated themselves around the table. The elder of the two uncles opened the discussion. He was a big man, as old as the century and his resemblance to John was immediately evident.

'Well, nephews, I fear that matters have come to a head. Things have gone too far now to go back. The time is fast coming to take sides.'

John sat with his head bent, listening. There was a slight frown on his face as he sifted what he had been told. Robert felt his pulse quicken. After a moment his Uncle Thomas added: 'War is coming. I am here to levy soldiers for the Parliament.'

At this John shook his head. 'Uncle, I am not a soldier.'

'An army needs money too.'

'I'm not rich.'

The second visitor moved impatiently and John turned his attention towards him. 'And what think you, Uncle Henry?'

Henry Hammond was slow to answer and then picked his words carefully. There was a gentleness to his expression which Robert warmed to. This was the man to whom he bore the closest resemblance, the man who, upon the death of Robert's father, had been his guide and mentor for much of his young life.

At last Henry spoke. 'What Thomas asks is dangerous. It is treason. You cannot take up arms against King Charles.' He caught his breath and struggled for the right words. 'This matter cannot be resolved by force. Somehow a compromise has to be reached. Any other course of action spells disaster.'

'Compromise?' Thomas snorted in disagreement. 'This struggle has been going on for an eternity. The King won't listen to reason.' He looked back at John. 'Everyone has tried to excuse him, to blame his ministers, to say it is the Queen's fault, that the Church is in the wrong . . .' He glanced quickly at Henry and added: 'The Parliament are recruiting their own men. Only a show of force will convince the King that he has to take his people seriously.' He leaned back and took a large gulp of ale. 'The country is in turmoil,' he went on. 'No one knows which way the Scots will jump and the King tries to play them like a fish on a hook. The Irish are as like as not to support him – don't you realise he may import men from the bogs to suppress us, his own citizens?'

Robert's face grew hot, as if his uncle spoke of his own, personal act of treason.

'The ports are closed,' Thomas said heavily. 'Trade is at a standstill. There is only one way. I am here to recruit men for the Parliament. If you cannot raise money then you can give me men.'

Still John looked troubled. 'I've few enough good men to work the land as it is. I have no wish to be involved in this.'

Henry was nodding his head in agreement and Thomas darkened. 'Curse it, man! Everyone is involved. If you do not act then you are still taking sides.'

Henry said: 'If you have to choose, John, then I pray you will remember your duty to your King. As a minister of the Church I must remind you that he is God's representative.'

John looked from one to the other. 'And Robert? Will you be fighting over him too? He's the professional soldier.'

Thomas turned to his younger nephew as if he were the sensible one, a man who would see reason. 'Robert, the time has come for a decision. You will have heard that the King has left London. He is holding court in York. It is almost as if he has declared a second kingdom away from the capital.'

Robert hesitated. 'I have been thinking of going to join him.'

There was a pause then Thomas said: 'Well, I have thrown in my lot with the Parliament. I am commissioned to raise a regiment of foot.' He looked to Robert for a reaction. 'You may not have heard, but your godfather has elected to serve the Parliament at Westminster and disobeyed the King's order to go to York. The King has called him a traitor.' Seeing Robert's surprise, he drove home his advantage. 'The Earl of Essex has heard good reports of your conduct in Ireland and agrees that I should offer you a captaincy, under Sir John Hotham, at Hull.'

'An act of treachery!' Henry intervened, his voice trembling with emotion. 'The Earl of Essex is my patron but his conduct in this matter pains me. Robert, pray you do not follow his example. My brother is asking you to join a pack of rebels.'

In the face of their joint plea, Robert struggled to make sense of the choices. 'It pains me to think of disservice to the King,' he started.

Henry nodded in agreement and seeing his hope, Robert felt a moment of compassion for his gentle uncle, but he continued: 'Yet I have been disturbed by the way events are unfolding. I, too, have not been able to see a peaceful outcome so what you tell me puts a different light on matters.'

'Robert, do not think of deserting your King!'

He turned sad eyes on Henry. 'I would not take up arms against the King, but if needs be I will show my sword against those who misuse him. Once his ministers are discredited then we shall be able to deal with him fairly.'

'King, ministers – that is the same thing. Boy, you talk treason!'

Robert turned from the anguished face back to Thomas Hammond. 'You say my godfather approves?'

There was a note of triumph in Thomas's voice. 'The Earl of Essex is, with God's blessing, now Commander of the Parliament's land forces. He requests your service.'

Robert looked from one to the other, weighing up all that he had heard.

Thomas continued: 'You may not know, but the King went to Hull. There he attempted to gain entry to the city but Sir John Hotham refused him. His Majesty had no choice but to retreat. As you will realise, if he had gained control of the port it would have enabled him to bring in supplies – and foreign troops. The Queen is busy recruiting French mercenaries, and for what other purpose than to crush any dissent we, the King's subjects, may show?'

'What of John Hampden?'

'He is even now recruiting his own regiment.'

With a decisive grunt Robert said: 'Then that is how it must be. I thank you, Uncle, and will be honoured to accept this captaincy.'

He glanced guiltily at Henry. The minister's face was hard with grief. His Uncle Thomas looked satisfied with his morning's work.

The older man said: 'The troops are raw, untrained. There will have to be musters and you will need to march them watchfully. Be prepared for desertions and make the punishments harsh.'

'I have always believed that reward is more effective than coercion.'

Thomas shrugged. 'Well, watch out for Hotham. He blows with the wind. I have a suspicion that his loyalty will last only as long as it suits his person.'

'I will bear that in mind.'

Turning to Henry, Robert said: 'Uncle, I truly regret . . .' Henry Hammond shook his head, too choked by emotion to speak. Robert sighed. There was nothing more to say.

When he and John were alone, he looked to his brother for his verdict. John raised his eyebrows and threw up his hands in a gesture of resignation. 'Never, never did I think it would come to this.'

Robert lowered his eyes. Traitorous thoughts of adventure crowded into his mind, but at what cost? Aloud, he said: 'Let us always be friends, brother. I imagine that throughout the land, there are other kin divided by this grand quarrel.' He looked up and held his brother's gaze. 'This moment surely marks a turning point in our history.'

Chapter 11

Dublin was half-dragged, half-carried down into Caulbourne Village by the Constable, and from there deposited across a horse and taken into Newport.

'Let me go!' she screamed at her captor but he ignored her. She could see that he was pleased with himself, and unlikely to let this moment of glory pass him by.

When they arrived in the town, Dublin was taken to the Audit House. Standing frightened and alone in the dusty hall, she found herself facing a Justice who had been called in especially because of the nature of the case.

She eyed him with stark terror. The man was stockily built and sat with his portly belly supported by his arms. Now and then he rocked backwards and forwards as if to redistribute the inordinate amount of weight he was carrying. His mouth was small and pouting and he eyed her with a hungry interest that made her feel sick inside.

The Constable cleared his throat. 'Stand up straight now. Show proper respect for Sir William Meux. You've caused him inconvenience, having to come here.'

Dublin bowed her head in despair. Tears began to trickle down her cheeks.

Sir William leaned towards her. 'Well, young woman. It seems you are in grave trouble. What are you doing here?'

Dublin shook her head. She did not know what to say. She wished that Caleb was here, appreciating now the shepherd's assurance, his gift with words. He would help her, know how to explain.

'You have been hiding out. Who from?'

She was trembling so much that she could hardly speak but

she knew that she must say something in her own defence. 'No one. Really, sir, I was trying to get to the mainland, to find my master.'

'And who might that be?'

'Lieutenant Hammond.' She blushed as she said his name.

'You're a soldier's whore?'

'No!'

Sir William leaned further forward, eyeing her. His belly bulged alarmingly and his manner was conspiratorial. 'You're not English. Who are you spying for? Come on, now. It will go easier for you if you say.'

Dublin shook her head 'I'm not so. Truly I'm not. I don't know what you mean.'

Her interrogator sat back again. He licked his plump lips. 'Caleb Gosden, the shepherd – you've been indecent with him?'

'No!' She gazed at him, shocked. 'He – he helped me when my leg was hurt, in a trap.'

'You were trespassing?'

'I was not!' She turned to the Constable, begging for some understanding, but his face was impassive. 'Please, I want to get back to England.'

'I'm sure you do.' Sir William sat back smugly. 'Come on now, who are you working for?'

Again Dublin shook her head. It was hopeless. She looked up to find the Justice gazing at her breasts, and her face grew hot.

'Were you sent here to get information?'

'No.' Nothing that he asked made sense.

'There is only one way to treat spies . . .'

'Please, sir, I'm not a spy. I was brought here from Ireland.'

'Brought here? Against your will?'

'Yes – no!'

'Then by whom?'

'My master. He rescued me.'

Sir William snorted impatiently. 'Well, enough of that for the moment.' He leaned forward again, his piggy eyes bright with lust. 'This shepherd now, did he force you? How often did he enter you?' He lowered his voice. 'Was it straightforward – or did he make you do other things?'

Dublin did not know what he was talking about. She appealed

to the Constable for some explanation and he looked uncomfortable.

'You aren't a virgin,' persisted Sir William. It was a statement rather than a question.

'Yes, sir, I am.' Dublin willed him to believe her.

With a glance at Barnabus Holbrooke, the Constable, Sir William said: 'Perhaps we should check.'

'I don't think so, begging your pardon, sir. I think that should be for the court to decide.'

Sir William pouted, clearly disappointed. With a sigh, he said: 'Well, I haven't got any more time to waste here. For the moment charge her with vagrancy and put her in the Bridewell. I'll be on the Bench when the court next sits. I'll decide what happens then. In the meantime, a few days locked away won't do her any harm.'

He leered at Dublin as he got up and she drew back towards the Constable, unnerved by what she saw in the Justice's eyes.

As Sir William left the room, Barnabus Holbrooke took Dublin by the arm. 'Come along, girl. I'll get you something to eat and drink, then you'd better think hard about your case. Whatever else they try you for, you'd better pray it isn't spying. If it is, they'll have your life for it, for sure.'

As soon as Sara came to guard the sheep, Caleb called the dogs and prepared to leave for the village.

'Did you see Dublin?' he asked, wondering what the girl was up to. His anger of yesterday was fast evaporating, to be replaced by regret.

Picturing her, his stomach knotted with hopelessness. He was a fool. The girl was vulnerable, in danger. He had a sudden, crazy thought of rescuing her by making her his wife. She might be young, but he was sure she was of marriageable age, and that way no one could send her away. The more he dwelt on it, the more he thought that it wasn't so foolish, but . . . He sighed. Just now, he was so hungry for sex he couldn't think straight. Best to sort things out with her first, put things right after last night's harsh words, then they could think about the future.

'You'll take care of Dublin for me? Guard her well?'

Sara nodded and her face was serious, sad. Caleb gave her a pat on the arm. 'Good girl. I'll see you in a week or two.'

He started off with the flock, making a detour back to his hut. His hands tingled with uncertainty. For once he had no words to describe what he felt.

As he drew near to the bothy, it was clear that Dublin was not there. The sound of the sheep alone would have brought her hurrying out – unless she still slept. At the thought of her lying on the reeds, rolling onto her back, her legs parted to accept him, his cock pressed hard against his breeches. He cursed his need.

'Dublin – are you there?' The dogs stood guard with the sheep while he ducked into the hut. The first thing he saw was the ball of wool. Frowning he picked it up, wondering if Sara had brought it for some reason.

Going back outside he scanned the landscape but could see no one, so with regret he set off down the slope.

He was so deep in thought that it took him by surprise when he looked up to see the first of the villagers coming to meet him. This was a special day and anyone who was not working would take time out to greet the flock. They represented much of the village wealth and were revered as such.

Tomorrow they would begin the daunting task of washing every sheep in the stream outside his cottage. The village would be deafened by bleating and much of the green would soon be awash as the struggling animals splashed water far and wide. He looked heavenwards. Praise be to God, there was not a cloud on the horizon.

All being well the clipping could then start in three days' time – weather always permitting. The important thing was that the fleeces should be dry. The teams of clippers would arrive and Caleb would work alongside them. He reckoned he could manage eighty sheep a day, but for once he would not have Sara at his side to sharpen his spare shears with the heavy whetstone and put tar on any torn skin to keep fly-strike at bay. He'd have to make do with someone else which would probably slow him down, but it couldn't be helped.

For tonight he would sleep in his own bed. While it always pleased him to see his mother with whom he shared the cottage, this was one time he would have given anything to be back on the scratchy straw of his bothy. Tonight he could have settled things with Dublin. His imagination overtook him as he thought of taking the girl, gently, offering her the chance of marriage and safety. In return he would have the comfort he so greatly needed. He tried not to think of what he would do if she refused him.

When work started, everything went according to plan. Day after day the sun shone benignly on the village. Everyone was involved in the shearing; clipping, rolling fleeces, dabbing, even the youngest stirring the tarpot. Food arrived punctually from farmhouse and cottage, and with every moment of respite, Caleb thought of Dublin.

The last evening was traditional. The big barn was decked with the posies of flowers given by the village maids to every shearer. They stood in colourful clumps along the tables, holding the communal supper. Everyone was at ease. Now the only worry was that the weather would break and the naked sheep would be unable to withstand the sudden cold or rain. The fleeces had been weighed and stored on slats in the barns ready for the time when the woolman came to take his pick. Some would go to the local market and some would be used by the villagers themselves. Caleb already had his bellwether's fleece, coming from the biggest castrated male in the flock. This was his annual entitlement and he always handed it to his mother to supplement her income. Perhaps this year, he would give it to Dublin . . .

Benches were set out on the Green beneath the late evening sun, and a piper had been hired especially for the occasion. Caleb's fiddle was nearby, hidden beneath an old piece of sacking.

Almost immediately he was called upon to accompany the piper. With a pretence at reluctance he scrambled to his feet, smiling in spite of himself at the enthusiastic anticipation from his friends and neighbours. He played, as always, with his soul – all the pent-up feelings he denied release, now escaping through the bow and out into the night. This time there was a jubilation in the sound. Tomorrow he would be back on the hills, back with Dublin. He did not care if people noticed the difference in him. He felt wild, abandoned. He even flirted with the village maid who had given him his shearer's posy.

In the mêlée, he recognised one of the girls who had taunted him on May Day.

'Where you sleeping tonight?' she asked, coquettish, thrusting out her chest at him.

'I can't wait till tonight. Come on.'

The girl's eyebrows shot up in surprise as he took her hand and together they slipped away to the privacy of the copse.

He did not speak to her. Pulling her hard against him he lifted her skirts and pushed her legs apart.

'Oi, hang on.' She started to protest, but he ignored her, dragging her breasts from her gown. She tried to struggle free.

'Caleb!'

He could feel her misgivings. This wasn't what she had expected, but he did not care.

'Shut up.' He sucked hard on her nipples, his fingers biting into her buttocks as he lifted her up, shoving so hard into her that she gasped.

Then he drove ferociously inside her, ridding himself of his anger.

'You're hurting me!'

His seed exploded into her and he let her slip away. Tomorrow night he would take Dublin, gently, holding back, making each touch, each moment, something to remember.

'You're a pig!'

'No, a ram.'

He fastened his breeches while she stood watching, her arms hugged around herself, her breasts still exposed. Going to her, he tucked them back into her bodice, ignoring the already insistent pushing of his cock.

'You're a good girl.' He dropped some coins into her bodice.

Mollified, she took his arm and they went back to the celebrations. Once on the Green, he parted from her. He had had too much wine and it was an effort to drag himself away now and check that all was well with his flock. All he wanted to do was sleep.

As he was about to get up, he noticed Barnabus Holbrooke the Constable, and two of the local yeomen coming in his direction. He nodded to them, but the stern expression on all three faces froze his smile instantly.

'There's trouble?' he asked, immediately thinking of the flock.

'William Caleb Gosden,' the Constable stepped forward and his grave mien had Caleb immediately on his feet. 'A serious charge has been made against you. You have been hiding a fugitive.'

Caleb's blood pounded. 'I don't deny it,' he said, 'but you must hear the whole story.'

The Constable lowered his eyes before continuing. 'You are accused of having carnal knowledge of a girl who calls herself Dublin O'Neill, not of this Parish.'

'No!' Caleb was shaking his head. 'It isn't so. If you let me tell my story it will be clear to you.'

'No time for that now. You are to appear before the Justice of the Peace on the morrow. Let him be the judge of your case.'

Chapter 12

Being midsummer, the petty court was held in the open air. A number of notables and clerks were present, plus a smattering of clergy, but the bulk of the audience was made up of ordinary people, who felt like a day's free entertainment.

A raised dais had been erected across from the Audit House, which was so shaky that the vibration of passing wagons threatened to cause its collapse. A number of officials stood on the platform, and sitting in the middle were three Justices. In front of them, a circle had been penned off to hold the accused.

Dublin was placed with several other female offenders to the right of the rostrum. Her head felt muzzy and the babble of voices cut her off from her surroundings. Looking helplessly around her at the sea of alien faces, she had never felt so alone. Then suddenly she saw Caleb. Her heart leaped and she called his name, but her voice was drowned in the hubbub. He looked strained and then, with shock, she realised that he too was a prisoner. Catching sight of her, he nodded.

'Caleb.' Desperately she wanted to reach him, draw comfort from his assurance, but he was as remote as the moon.

Now the sessions started and Dublin's palms began to sweat as she listened to the cases of those ahead of her. No one seemed to know exactly what the charge would be, and guilt or innocence largely depended on how many people could be persuaded to speak up on each side. Except for Caleb, Dublin had no one to speak for her.

Disputes over land and livestock, the theft of a butter churn, two cases of swearing on the Sabbath, one of being drunk in the marketplace, one of playing dice on the roadside, were heard. They were resolved with either fines, beatings, or the payment of compensation.

Finally, as she watched, Caleb was pushed into the lone circle in front of the magistrates.

'William Caleb Gosden,' – for such a formal occasion he was addressed by his full name – 'you are charged with hiding a fugitive, suspected of being an Irish insurgent, and having carnal knowledge of her. How do you plead?'

Dublin drew in her breath as she listened to the shameful accusations.

'I do not.' Caleb straightened himself and looked directly at his accusers. 'When I found her, the girl was injured. I nursed her back to health.' He seemed calm, self-possessed. 'She is just a poor maid.'

'A maid? You know about the state of her virginity from personal experience?' Sir William Meux, one of the three justices, smirked with amusement.

'I found her bleeding, her leg in a trap.' Caleb ignored the insinuation.

'You knew that she was a runaway?'

'I knew that she was hurt.'

The officials shuffled impatiently. A second man took up the questioning. 'You are not answering the question, shepherd. This woman would seem to be illegally on our shores. We must get at the truth.'

Caleb thought for a moment before saying carefully: 'She's nought but a child. She knows nothing of spying.'

'You did not think it your duty to hand her over to the Constable, to be returned where she belongs?'

'She was scared. I kept her safe.'

'Be careful, shepherd. If you kept her against her will, that is a serious matter.'

'Ask her.'

Sir William Meux took up the questioning again. 'Have you had carnal knowledge of this woman?'

Dublin's face began to burn. She glanced from under her brows at Caleb and saw the anger on his face.

'I have not.'

Meux sat back with satisfaction. 'In that case she must be

88

examined, to see if she is still a virgin. I will represent the court at the examination.'

'No!' Caleb had to be restrained by his captors.

'Then tell the truth.'

He hesitated. Dublin lowered her eyes, crushed by shame. After a moment, Caleb said: 'We are to be wed.'

'She is your betrothed?'

He inclined his head.

'Then you are saying that you have poked her, but with her consent, as your intended wife?' Meux's disappointment was evident.

Dublin could not believe what Caleb was saying. There was no question that she could marry him, and in any case, he did not even like her!

The shepherd addressed the magistrates. 'What passes between my bethrothed and myself is of no concern to this court.'

There was laughter round about and spurred on by the response, Meux continued: 'What of the other wench, the dummy who comes to your hut – how many times have you tupped with her?'

'Never!'

Dublin could see that Caleb's anger was growing. It was all he could do not to leap forward and land his fist into the bloated, dissolute face before him.

'If you lie, shepherd, you will find yourself in hell.'

'I never lie.'

The Justices seemed to be considering all that they had heard. Finally Sir William Meux spoke on their behalf. He spread his hands on his podgy knees and said: 'It seems to us that you have been guilty of several offences here. You have kept a fugitive hidden, with or without her consent; you have committed fornication with that same girl, again, with or without her consent; but it also seems to me that you have little respect, shepherd. You stand too straight.' Here he paused before adding: 'For a humpty-back, that is.' This was greeted with a burst of laughter. When it died down, Sir William continued: 'I don't think you respect the King's law. Before I sentence you, is there anything you wish to say?'

Caleb thought quickly. He suffocated all his feelings so that he could concentrate on helping the girl and himself.

'My lords,' he finally said. 'I do respect the law of the land, as long as it is just. I must say in my defence that I have committed no crime out of malice. I want it to be known that I intend to marry Dublin O'Neill as soon as is humanly possible. For her part, she became lost, and it was then I who made the decisions on her behalf. You should set her free.'

Sir William leaned back again and smiled. 'Well said, shepherd. I wish you happiness in your marriage.'

Caleb nodded cautiously.

Sir William continued: 'As far as the offences go, we fine you one crown for keeping the girl illegally with you.'

There was a murmur amongst the crowd and people began to shuffle about as they assumed that the case was closed. As Caleb was about to step back, Sir William added: 'And I sentence you to twelve lashes and eight hours in the pillory for your lack of respect. That should teach you a little more humility. Case finished.'

Dublin began to scream. As Caleb was hustled away by the Constables she tried to reach him, but she was held fast and in her turn, was pushed in front of the interrogators.

She barely heard anything that was said to her, wishing only to escape to safety with the one person she knew.

After the charge was read, Sir Robert Dillington, the second magistrate, said: 'If we are to believe your affianced, you are a girl of good reputation. But more serious is the question as to how you came to be here. If you cannot answer that satisfactorily, then I feel it is our duty to send you to the Quarter Sessions at Winchester. These are dangerous times. We cannot afford to be lax about such charges. Do you understand me, girl? You must speak for your own sake.'

'Sir.' Dublin tried. In a tumble she began to tell the story of Carrickmain, of being rescued and brought back to England. She was just about to explain about Robert leaving her in the care of his aunt when the third magistrate intervened.

'What is your name, child?'

Dublin repeated it.

He raised his eyebrows. 'Were you really baptised with the name of a city?'

She lowered her eyes, suddenly afraid at being found out in a lie. 'No, sir. My given name is Sorcha, Sorcha O'Neill. But everything else I have told you is true, as God is my witness.'

'What was the name of your rescuer?'

Her cheeks grew red. 'Lieutenant Robert Hammond, sir, a very noble gentleman.'

The magistrate turned to his fellows and a whispered discussion followed. Dublin felt her knees beginning to fail her. She tried to pray but there was no one she could trust to hear her plea for help.

Turning back to the assembled crowd, the third magistrate addressed the gathering. 'There is no case to answer here. Robert Hammond is my wife's nephew. It is true that he did bring an orphan child into her protection. The girl ran away.'

Looking down at Dublin he said: 'You have had a lucky escape, girl. If I had not been at home this week, and offered to sit on the Bench, you would have found yourself in serious trouble. As it is, you will be returned into my wife's care – although you do not deserve it. Make sure that you repay her charity.' With a glance at his fellow magistrates for confirmation he then announced, 'Case dismissed.'

'What about Caleb?' Dublin appealed to the men to reconsider but already they had turned away and her plea went unheard.

Caleb spent a nightmarish time housed in the Bridewell. He had little money on him, just enough to persuade his gaoler to bring him a beaker of ale and a quarterloaf. Although his appetite was small, his thirst was insistent and kept him awake. All the time he agonised about what had become of Dublin.

Crowded about him, other petty felons shifted this way and that, bemoaning their ill-luck. In a moment of pity he gave half his bread and a few sips of ale to an old man who had no money and had been sentenced for vagrancy. On the morrow he was to be whipped to the Parish boundary and sent on his way.

'God bless you, Crookback. You have more sympathy than the Parish elders. All they want is to get rid of me. That way I won't be their problem.'

Caleb did not reply and for once even the reference to his shoulder went unnoticed. At this moment he could spare little sympathy for anyone for he was stunned by the severity of his own sentence. Being put in the stocks he could have understood, humiliating as the experience would have been, but the pillory was a different matter.

Not long after daylight he was fetched from the cramped cell and bundled along the street to St Thomas's Square. Already the sickly stench from the butchers' shambles and the rancid waft of decay from the neighbouring fishmongers offended his sense of smell. Only a few yards away, the pillory stood as a permanent warning to the citizens, whether it was in use or not.

The panic rose in him, not only because he was afraid of the beating, or even the taunting that would be his for the next eight hours, but because of the certain knowledge that before subjecting him to his fate, the shirt would be torn from his back, exposing his shame to the world.

Angrily he began to struggle, but his captors held him fast. 'Steady, man, take your punishment as you should.'

There was nothing that he could say.

With pounding heart and tears of shame threatening to spill down his cheeks, Caleb was forced forward as the shirt was torn away, then his head and hands were pushed through the three holes that would hold him fast. The top of the pillory was slammed shut and he was captive. Although of medium height, he had to stand almost on tiptoe to prevent the rough wood beneath his throat from choking him.

A few people stood in front of him, gazing with vacant, unresponsive eyes at his anguished face. Behind him he could hear the whispers and giggles as his back was exposed for all to see.

The first lash was totally unexpected and landed with sufficient force to cut deep into his shoulder. He let out a groan of surprise as much as pain. As the second lash landed over the first, the newly-opened raw wound caused an agony such as he had rarely known. He bit back the cry and braced himself for the third. There was a pause before it came and he knew that the whipper was playing with him, tormenting him to the full. Whether from malice or because it was so ordained, he did not know or care. The man would earn six pence for this.

When the fourth blow landed, by some fluke the lash whipped around his neck and up under the crossbar of the pillory, the tip stinging his cheek. He turned his head aside to avoid a repetition as he steeled himself to receive the fifth which landed almost simultaneously, low down on his back.

The crowd were counting now, each stroke accompanied by a

higher-pitched call. '*Six, seven, eight . . .*' Finally the last stroke wound itself around his bloody torso and he sagged momentarily until the cruel bite of the pillory against his throat and wrists forced him to stand upright once more.

Before long his mangled back was tormented by flies settling on the congealing blood. The sun, toasting hot since it first appeared over the skyline, now seared into his ravaged skin. He became increasingly desperate to drive away the probing insects but his hands were held fast.

The ache in his arms grew in intensity and his legs threatened to sag beneath him until his whole body was one unbearable ache.

'Humpty-back, humpty-back, jig about like a jumping jack!' The inane chorus was taken up by the children and a lump of caked dung hit him in the face. This was closely followed by an assortment of filth, then a jagged stone caught him just above the eye. Blood soon blinded him and he hung his head as best he could to protect his face from further bombardment.

This served only to anger the crowd.

'Pin him up by the ears,' someone shouted.

'Nail him to the post.'

The threat was real. In the past Caleb had seen felons nailed into position by the lobes of their ears to prevent them from moving their heads, thus providing better targets. In his worst nightmare he had never envisaged such a fate for himself.

By now the temperature had soared to unbearable heights. This had the effect of drawing the crowds away to the shelter of the taverns. Caleb remained at the mercy of the scorching sun. His thirst, already desperate before he had started his ordeal, now drove him to unbelievable depths of despair.

'Please, a drink,' he begged of the few remaining spectators, his pride now deserting him. 'For pity's sake, give me a drink.'

'For a penny I'll piss on you, shepherd, cool you down a bit.' The oaf who jested slapped his thighs with glee at his cleverness and his companions joined in.

'Get the horse to pee on him, really cool him down.'

He had no idea how long he had been there. Mercifully, the Square was now almost deserted but this did nothing to slake the torment of his thirst. He was aware now that he was moaning but he could not stop. His misery was so great that he could no long suffer in silence.

In his agony he thanked God that his family were not there to witness his shame and humiliation.

Everything was blurred now and strange flashing lights and bursts of darkness alternated in his head. He continued to mumble words of comfort to himself.

The next thing he knew, someone was supporting him under the chin and holding a tankard of ale to his cracked lips. Desperately he struggled to fill his mouth with the life-saving liquid. It trickled down his chin and chest, cool and heaven-sent.

With difficulty he managed to swallow. It felt as if there were boulders in his throat but gradually the pain eased and he drained every last drop. His eyes were closed by blood that had dripped from the cut on his brow and congealed in the heat. He tried to utter his thanks but no words would come.

A few moments later somebody was wiping his face clean with a cool, damp cloth. The sensation was one of pure pleasure. It was only then that his eyes focused on his saviour and to his amazement he found Sara standing before him. The expression on her face was of such anxiety that he tried a reassuring smile but he did not seem to have the strength to move the muscles of his face.

An occasional missile still came in his direction, now striking Sara on her plump back but she seemed unaware of it. With gentle strokes she was cleaning his face with a piece of rag and he longed only to give himself up to her care.

Finally they came to take him down. As the bar of the pillory was lifted he slid down the length of the upright, coming to rest at the foot of this hateful instrument of punishment. His arms screamed their outrage and his back was one agony from the cuts and the prolonged exposure to the sun.

As he tried to struggle up, Sara was there to help him and he had no choice but to lean on her. They made their clumsy way out of town.

'What has become of Dublin?'

He forced the signs from his numbed fingers and with a flicker of her eyes Sara replied: 'Her story was believed. She has been taken back to the Dingleys, at Wolverton. They are her guardians.'

He was overwhelmed by a sense of bitter irony. The idea of

rescuing her, of marriage, suddenly seemed obscenely stupid. She had no need of his protection. When would he ever learn?

They made their way back along Deadman's Lane where the invading French had once been ambushed, and Caleb was aware of the curious gazes as he leaned helplessly on his neighbour. He wanted only to be away from prying eyes. The man at the tollgate grinned but Caleb did not have the strength to strike the smirk from his face. As if reading his thoughts, Sara squeezed his arm, encouraging him forward and up the Castle Hill.

Finally they stopped in the shadow of Carisbrooke fortress and Sara produced a pot of salve which she began gently to apply to his lacerated back. He mumbled a protest that she should shame him further by having contact with the hated deformity, but the ointment was so soothing and he reminded himself it was only Sara and submitted to her care. Under the gentle caressing of her fingers he fell asleep there on the grass and when he awoke it was night-time. Sara was sitting by his side as if to guard him and he gave her hand a fraternal squeeze.

'I thank thee.' He mouthed the words in the shaft of moonlight that embraced them and struggled to his feet. Immediately she stood up and followed behind.

It was a slow journey back to Caulbourne, with many stops. As Caleb travelled, little by little the enormity of the day came back to him. His mind was a jumble of thoughts; the indignities he had suffered, the pain his mother would feel if she knew, and most of all, the outrage of his sentence.

He asked himself how it was that the Justices, whose power came from the King, had the power of life or death over him? Caleb had committed neither crime nor sin. The King and the Bishops – jointly they ruled his life as if he were no better than a cur. He vowed there and then that never again would any man – or woman – have dominion over him.

Chapter 13

Dublin arrived back at Wolverton to find herself something of a celebrity. One by one the servants crept out to stare at her, hoping to glean some snippet of gossip about her adventures, but it was Jennet who satisfied their curiosity, asking outright about the weeks spent living wild on the hills with Caulbourne's firebrand shepherd.

'Is it true you're bethrothed?' Jennet lowered her voice. 'Have you – you know?' She nudged her friend and giggled.

'No, I haven't.' Dublin sought refuge in being distant, superior, but Jennet was undaunted.

'What's he like, then? They say he's bewitched. Did you see his – his hump?'

Thinking of Caleb's face, the harsh shell of indifference behind which he hid his pain, Dublin felt suddenly angry. 'There's nothing wrong with his back.'

Jennet shrugged off the snub. 'Love is blind,' she teased, then quickly added: 'He's handsome, though. I wish he'd kidnapped me.' There was a faraway look in her eye, spiced with excitement at the thought of being captured by this dangerous, Devil-touched shepherd.

Something about Jennet's expression stirred a discontent in Dublin. She gave vent to this disturbing emotion by responding with disdain. 'You're welcome to him. He's that bad-tempered.'

Jennet changed tack. 'Why did you run away? Were you scared?'

'What of?'

The skivvy sighed in frustration. 'Well, there must have been some reason. *Tell* us about it!'

Dublin remained silent. She felt so many conflicting emotions. Part of her was ashamed that she had deserted Caleb, left him to take the blame for sheltering her. The power of his personality, his way with words, his gentleness when she was sick, stirred up such confusion. But there was another part of her that felt that she had been bewitched, held captive by some supernatural force. Only now was she free. This was an easier alternative to cope with.

She merely said, 'It was an accident.'

To Dublin's dismay, Mistress Dingley seemed to have thoughts of her own.

'Have you no idea what anguish you caused us, child? We feared you had been abducted, murdered. It was wicked of you to go off without permission, and as for living with that shepherd . . .!'

'I did not –'

'Enough! You have caused such a scandal. The quicker you wed, the quicker it will all be forgotten.'

'Wed?' Dublin had never seen Mistress Jane look so forbidding. 'But I can't wed with him, ma'am. I –'

'Will you be silent! It is too late to change your mind now. You should be grateful to my husband, too. Sir John has personally spoken to the minister and he agrees that in the circumstances, you will not be made to do a public penance.'

'But I've done nothing wrong!'

'*How dare you!*' Jane Dingley slapped her hard across the cheek. Dublin's eyes watered and she felt herself drowning in a sea of misunderstanding. Her mistress continued: 'Fornicating with that man was a vile sin, even if he did promise you marriage.' Softening slightly, she asked: 'How could you be so artless?'

Dublin shook her head, needing to explain herself, but wanting also to defend Caleb. In spite of the blow, she could not hold her tongue. 'But I didn't, he didn't. And I never agreed to marry him, neither!'

'Whether you did or not is no matter. People think you are his harlot, so you are going to marry him now. We'll not have any more nonsense.'

Everything was a nightmare. In the ensuing silence, Aunt Jane appeared to think that she had settled matters and Dublin did not

97

offer any further objections. Instead she asked: 'Do you have news of my master?' Her face coloured as she dared to voice her thoughts.

For a moment the older woman frowned, then realising to whom Dublin referred, she said: 'If you mean my nephew, he is no doubt with his regiment. Not that it is any concern of yours. Don't you be so cheeky now. You can go and help Jennet clean the buttery. And no talking! Tonight you will forgo supper and pray for forgiveness for your wickedness.'

Dublin remembered similar punishments at home. She thought wryly that the English God and the Catholic one seemed to have the same idea. The differences were still a mystery to her.

But first and foremost, she must think about the future. There was nothing for it. Dublin knew that she had to get away. Stay here and she would be forced into marriage with Caleb Gosden. As she worked industriously, pretending a preoccupation that defied Jennet to ask more questions, she had a terrible vision of Caleb's face taut with anger. True, he had told the Justices that they were betrothed, but Dublin knew that he did not even like her. She could not imagine what had possessed him to say such a thing and now she wondered what weapons they would use to force him to keep his promise. At the idea of being his unwanted bride, seeing his cold, resentful face, listening to his sharp tongue, her spirits sank. Then there was that other, dark, intimate side to marriage. She would rather take her chances by running away! At the thought of what she was running to, her spirits lifted again. Somehow, she would find Robert, and once they were together, everything would be well.

For the next few days, Dublin bided her time, meekly carrying out her domestic duties, feigning remorse for her recent misbehaviour. As the Sabbath approached however, two fears battled for possession of her thoughts. She feared that when they reached the church, the minister would indeed single her out for public reprimand, and her second dread was that Caleb would be in the congregation. She could not face him. This thought made up her mind.

On Saturday night, when she was certain that everybody slept, Dublin crept from the house. Memories of her last flight came back to haunt her, only this time it was worse, because if she were to be caught again the punishment would be extreme indeed. There would be no third chance.

As soon as she was free, she began to run in the opposite direction to that she had taken before. Towards the north-east was the town of Newport, and at the centre was the quay. She had heard that boats tied up daily there to unload cargo. It should not be too difficult to hide aboard one of them then let herself be carried to the mainland. Once safely away, it would surely be possible to find news of someone as famous and noble as Robert Hammond. She only had to find the place called Chertsey.

The journey to Newport took her through dense woodland. Fortunately the night was clear and the moon was large enough to afford some light. At the same time, the interminable noises of the forest had her in a frenzy of fear. It seemed that at any moment she would be grabbed by malevolent hands and dragged back to her doom . . . but apart from badgers and the occasional deer, the journey proved uneventful.

As the first light crept up from the sea away to the east, Dublin found herself walking through the streets of Newport. She strode out purposefully, hoping that by looking determined, no one would question why she was abroad.

At last she found the river. She hid behind some stacks of timber, awaiting transport across to the dockyard at Portsmouth. As yet there were few people abroad but all the time it was growing lighter. If she did not act soon, she would be seen. A little way further downriver, a merchant vessel was moored to the bank. Even as she watched, two seamen were loading piles of fleeces into the hold. As they both disappeared from view, Dublin took her chance. Scurrying quickly up the plank she sank down behind a pile of coiled rope, tucking herself up small to avoid discovery.

The men emerged from the hold, deep in conversation. They did not notice her. The moment they were ashore she leaped up and peered down into the hold. Already it was half-full of fleeces. Quickly, Dublin scrambled down and secreted herself in the furthest corner, pulling the stinking wool over her. There she stayed, while the men returned several more times, flinging more cargo down on top of her. Finally a hatch was pulled across and she found herself in suffocating darkness. Up above she could hear the sound of sails being raised, ropes untied and before long the ship began to pull out into the river.

Still lying amid the greasy pelts, she offered up a prayer. So far so good. In an hour, two at the most, they should reach the opposite coast. Once there she would seek out her master. In the meantime, to escape from the cloying stench of the fleeces, she closed her eyes and dwelt on the pleasures to come.

The merchant ship, *Fortunate*, pulled out of the narrow channel between the East and West Cow, and turned towards the fast-ascending sun. It then bobbed its way through Spithead, hugging the south coast. The ship was well-named, for a fortuitous combination of wind and tide sped her along at a good twenty knots. If all went well, it should be possible to ride the tides and within a few days reach their destination.

As the hours passed, Dublin went from impatience to panic. Scrambling to her feet, she tried to reach up to the hold and peer through a crack in the wooden hatch, but she was too short. Laboriously she piled fleeces under the opening and perched precariously on them, pulling herself up so that she was level with the slats. But there was nothing to see, only skyline, or was it more sea?

Hunger and thirst began to plague her. It reached such an intensity that there was no choice but to give herself up. Whatever the seamen did, it could not be worse than the present torment. Dublin began to call out, at first tentatively, then with increasing desperation, but the wind was high and noisy, and in the depths of the hold, her voice was lost. When no one came, she curled into a ball and sobbed hopelessly.

Inside the hold, water oozed down the wooden struts and dripped into a narrow channel that ran the length of the enclosure. Painstakingly she began to lick it up, drop by drop, finally slaking her thirst to the point where it again became bearable, but food there was none.

Day or night, it was the same, by turns stuffy and cold, but always dark. At some point she must have fallen asleep for the next thing she knew, a shaft of light was pouring into the hold. She blinked painfully, and quickly scuttled out of sight.

Immediately it dawned on her that her pile of fleeces would alert the crew to her presence. Simultaneously, she realised that once the cargo was unloaded, there would be no way of scaling the sides and pulling herself to safety. She had a sudden, terrible image of being trapped below for ever, until one day, months ahead, her skeleton would be discovered. The only hope was to make a dash for it now, scrambling up and hoping to avoid capture.

For a moment the huge silhouettes of sailors loomed over the entrance to the hold, then there was a shout from somewhere in the distance and both men disappeared. Quick as lightning, Dublin scrambled onto the fleeces, leaped to grab the edge of the hatchway and hauled herself up, wincing at the rough splintering pressure on her palms. She hoisted her legs over the hatch and began to run, not knowing which way she should go, but it did not matter. If she found herself on the seaward side, she would dive over the edge, and somehow stay afloat long enough to reach the sea wall.

As it was, she chose the port side, and within seconds was racing down the gangplank and making for the jumble of buildings ahead of her. She did not stop running until she knew herself to be completely away.

As her heart began to slow its excruciating pace, she took stock of her situation. The land about her was flat, barely rising from a wide estuary that seemed to stretch for miles. As it narrowed there was a confusion of dwellings, some of wood, a few stone-built, and the majority little more than lean-tos. These straggled around what was clearly a city wall.

The people who filled the narrow alley where she stood were alien to her – mostly seamen, some with straw-yellow hair, a few burned pitch black. All around a babble of noise pervaded the air; the language was surely not English, certainly not Gaelic. She wondered if she might be across the sea in France.

Then as she watched, a boat moored nearby began to discharge its cargo of passengers. They came ashore in dozens, some carrying muskets, then a group of pikemen. When each man was on land, the slow business of unloading horses, then cannon followed. For a moment the sight of so many English soldiers took her back to Carrickmain. She froze into a space between some large bales, quaking at the thought of discovery.

At that moment she became aware of someone watching her, a seafaring man, barefoot, bare-headed, his skin like cowhide. Now her heart increased its pace again; it was the patter of fear. Quickly she slid from her hiding place and began to hurry away.

Dublin walked for perhaps an hour, passing through the city gates without incident. All the time her thirst and hunger wracked her. Finally she could bear it no longer. Bending down, she scooped a handful of brackish liquid from a rut in the pathway and raised it to her lips.

'Don't you drink that!'

The prized liquid was dashed away and Dublin looked appalled at her assailant. A scrawny young woman stood on the path, hugging a baby to her side. Her face was badly marked by smallpox, and several of her teeth were missing which gave her a hollow, gaping look.

'It'll kill you, that. 'Tis filth.'

'Please!' Dublin began to cry. She was so desperate and weary. As the salt tears reached her lips she drew them greedily into her mouth.

'You poor thing. Come along o' me. I've got a pail o' water in my place.'

Hopelessly Dublin trailed behind. The woman led her down a side turning, even narrower than the alley she had just travelled.

Dimly Dublin wondered if she was about to be murdered. She had nothing worthy of stealing, except the clothes she stood up in, but compared to the rags that clothed the other woman, they were like riches.

'This is where we live. Come and have a sup of water. I'm afraid there's nothing else.'

Dublin shook her head to show that it didn't matter. Her mouth was too parched to speak. She fairly fell on the pail and scooped handful after handful of water over her tongue. The relief was total.

'There, now. We've no food, neither. I was hoping to earn a crust by unloading at the docks.'

Dublin said nothing until her Samaritan asked: 'Where are you from?'

It was too difficult to explain so she merely said: 'I've lost my master, become separated from him. I've got to find him. You don't know Lieutenant Robert Hammond?'

The woman shook her head. 'There's plenty o' strangers round here. We're more or less besieged.' Wiping her sleeve across her face she added: 'My man has been arrested for vagrancy. He's done nothing wrong but I can't afford the fine to get him out.' She glanced up at the sun, as if gauging the time. 'I ought to go. If I can get work on the fortifications, I might earn a crust or two, then I'll be able to take him a bite to eat.'

Dublin felt that she should go too, but she did not know where. This place bore little resemblance to the island she had so recently left. It reminded her more of her home city, but she did not pursue the comparison. Meanwhile, her new friend appeared to be fast losing interest in her.

'Is this a village?' Dublin asked. 'Are we anywhere near Chertsey?'

The woman raised her eyebrows in surprise. 'Why, girl, don't you know where you are?' As Dublin shook her head, she added: 'I don't know where Chertsey is. Never heard of it.' She scrutinised Dublin anew. 'Don't you really know where you are? Well, that out there,' she pointed at the wide swathe of water, 'that's the River Humber – and this here is the city of Hull.'

Chapter 14

Dublin wandered lost and alone through the streets of the town called Hull. In spite of the bright sunshine it was a cold day, with a sharp wind blowing off the river. She began to feel sick and shivery, weighed down by the hopelessness of her situation.

She had no clear sense of direction and so many problems beset her, the most urgent being the need for food. Since leaving Wolverton at least a week ago, she had barely eaten. Her appetite, so insistent in the hold of the merchant ship, was now replaced by dull gnawing worms in the pit of her stomach and she feared that she would never be able to swallow real food again.

The second need was for shelter. Trying to think clearly, she guessed that the sensible thing was to approach a tavern, see if there was work. That way, both roof and rations might come her way, although at the thought of labour she wilted, having little energy even to drag herself along the narrow streets.

Then there was another worry, even more alarming and one about which she could do nothing. As soon as she opened her mouth, her accent gave her away and suspicion would again fall upon her. Perhaps it would be wise to pretend to be dumb, like Caleb's Sara. Instantly she rejected the idea, not wanting to think about Sara, so at home in the company of the shepherd. The thought of being at the bothy with the sheep, and their moody master, now seemed like an Eden.

Starbursts of black light began to blur her vision. She stopped to gather her flagging energy, gazing out across the light-bathed countryside. In the distance, a troop of soldiers had set up camp and were digging a series of trenches and fortifications. Dublin wondered why they were there. If their siege was intended to be serious, it was not very effective, for all the while travellers were taking to the river, and like herself, entering the town unchecked. Now and then a few cannon shot rang out from the besieging army, but it was desultory.

With a sigh she turned back into the town, wondering whether to crawl into a niche somewhere and quietly wait to die, but as she rounded a corner, a tavern stood directly across the street. Swallowing down her fear she crossed over and pushed open the door.

Inside it was hot and smokey. The floor was littered with straw and the air was pungent with the smell of stale beer, overlaid with sweat and piss. The orange glow from the fire sought out dark, low-ceilinged corners where one or two customers slaked their thirst, but the place was in the main deserted. Dublin hesitated for a moment then, seeing the innkeeper eyeing her, she dredged up her flagging courage and walked across to him.

'I'm looking for work. Anything.'

'Are you now?' he frowned, looking her up and down, a big man, coarse, threatening. She was aware of her expensive but dirty gown, her mud-stained feet and tangled hair. She had neither washed, nor combed her hair for days.

'I've been a-journeying. I'm travelstained.'

'So I see. What business brings you here, then?'

'I . . .' Tiredness and hunger made it difficult for her to think. She had no convincing answer. 'I got on the wrong ship.' It sounded weak, even to herself.

She could see the suspicion in his eyes and glanced towards the door, wondering whether to run for it, but there was nowhere to go. She was nearly dropping with fatigue.

The innkeeper began to circle her, looking her up and down. 'You know that the Army have their headquarters here, don't you? That's why you come knocking at my door. Well, if you're bent on finding something out, you can ask them direct.' He grabbed her arm. 'You must think I'm simple-minded. Just you come with me. The officers can decide what to do with you.'

Dublin did not resist. Whatever they did with her, as long as they allowed her to eat and sleep, she did not care. Her captor dragged her up the stairway and stopped outside one of the upper chambers, knocking on the door. A moment later a tall, sandy-haired man poked his head out, regarding them both with surprise.

'Begging your pardon, sir, but this woman has come asking for work. She's foreign – Irish, I think. I thought she might be up to no good.'

'I thank ye.' The soldier nodded to his host, then to Dublin he said: 'Inside,' and stood back to let her pass. The landlord pushed her into the room and the door closed behind her.

'Right, lass. What's going on, then? If ye're come frae the King, ye're in the wrong place – or was it the Governor ye wanted tae see?'

Dublin shrugged. Her inquisitor had a strange accent, at times so pronounced that she had difficulty in understanding him. 'You're not English,' she said, in her own defence.

'As it happens, I'm Scots. And I'll lay odds ye're Irish. Do ye come spying out the territory for the King?'

'No!' She felt confused and hopeless. 'I'm only wanting work, and food.' She glanced at the table where meats and bread had been laid out. Following her gaze, her captor seemed to relent and indicated that she should help herself.

'My name is Sir John Meldrum. I imagine that means nothing to ye, but I'm here to ensure that the will of Parliament is maintained in this city.'

Dublin stuffed her mouth full of beef. She wanted to swallow it in great chunks but her stomach was already protesting. Unbidden she sat down, feeling decidedly ill. Her stomach hurt and she feared that she was going to vomit.

'Are ye sick, lassie?' There was compassion in the Scots voice.

'I . . .' She couldn't get the words out. Seeing her distress, the soldier lifted her legs onto the settle and eased her into a more comfortable position. 'Just you rest a wee while.'

His kindness was the life-line that she needed. Unable to hang on any longer, she closed her eyes and slept.

When she finally came to, it was dark outside. In the soldier's room, three candles played tag with the shadows. Dublin opened and closed her eyes at intervals, gradually piecing together her predicament.

'Well now, ye've had a long rest.'

He was still there, Sir John Meldrum, waiting for her. In silence he poured some ale and physically lifted her into a sitting position. 'Just you sip this now, then we'll have a wee talk.'

Released by his kindness, Dublin poured out her story, the flight from Carrickmain, her sojourn at Wolverton, the escape to Caleb's hut, the time in court, and this, her nightmare journey to Hull.

When she had finished, Sir John blew out his breath as if he had just endured a route march. 'I see. What was the name of your soldier again?'

'Hammond, sir. Lieutenant Robert Hammond.' She looked at him hopefully.

He pulled the corners of his mouth down and shrugged, shaking his head. 'I can scarce credit what you say, lassie. It all sounds too far-fetched.'

'It's true, sir. Surely it is!'

For a long while he studied her, chewing the corner of his red moustache, his eyebrows working up and down like ducks bobbing on water. Then he let his breath out and shifted his position. She guessed that he had reached a decision.

'There is a Captain Hammond here in Hull. I think his name is Robert, but I cannot believe you found your way here by accident.'

She didn't say anything. The thought that after all she had endured, Robert might be nearby, had her stunned like a rabbit, waiting for a weasel to decide its fate.

'Right.' He stood up. 'You come with me. We'll find this Captain Hammond. See if he knows anything about you.'

Hastily she got to her feet, steadying herself against the table as dizziness threatened, then followed close behind as he led her outside.

They walked for about a quarter of an hour, along narrow streets, little more than alleyways. Overhead occasional lanterns flickered, making the gaps between the fragile flames seem even darker. Beneath their feet, the route was uneven, and piles of rubbish littered the footways making each step a hazard. Finally the vista broadened out as they came to a row of well-built houses down near the river.

'We've conscripted these for military use,' her captor announced.

Going in through a door, Dublin waited while Sir John

107

conferred with two soldiers on duty. In unison they turned to stare at her, their expressions impossible to read. In confusion, she ducked back behind Sir John, afraid of their knowing eyes.

'C'mon.' He jerked his head towards the stairs and she scurried up behind him until they reached the second floor. There he stopped before a door and rapped smartly on it.

Dublin's heart thumped, both from exertion and anxiety. Inside the room she heard footsteps. Somebody fiddled with a bolt, pulling it back, then the latch lifted – and there he was!

'Hammond. Are ye settling in well?' Sir John made no reference to Dublin and she hid behind him, too overcome with emotion to show herself.

'Sir John. This is a surprise.'

The sound of Robert's voice was soothing as honey to a sore throat. It bathed her tiredness and lifted her spirits but as soon as he saw her, she feared that he would be angry. She scooted into the room in Sir John's wake, taking advantage of the gloom and keeping to the shadows.

Sir John sank onto the settle near the fire and accepted a glass of sack. Dublin cowered back into the dark, keeping her face averted, trying not to draw attention to herself.

Sir John put his goblet down on the hearth. 'Well now, we have a bit of a mystery. See what we have here.' He turned in Dublin's direction. 'My landlord thinks he's caught a wee spy, and she claims to know you.'

Dublin did not look up. Robert came closer and she heard him draw in his breath.

'May God preserve us!'

Slowly she raised her eyes to meet his. He was staring at her with disbelief, perhaps even horror. Her insides turned to water. He stepped back and she could see that he was shaken.

'I don't believe it.'

Sir John raised his eyebrows. 'Well, Captain, I was hoping for some explanation.'

Robert shook his head. 'There is no explanation. I left this child hundreds of miles away, on the Isle of Wight with my aunt.'

'So she tells me. What I'm wondering is how she managed to find you.'

Again Robert shook his head. 'Really, sir, I have no idea. It isn't possible. With the exception of my family at Chertsey and

108

the Earl of Essex, nobody knows that I am here.' He glared suspiciously at Dublin. 'How did you get here?'

She found it hard to speak, eventually saying: 'I came here by accident.' His anger stung her like a slap across the face.

It was clear that Robert did not believe her. Her sudden arrival had unnerved him to the point that he had turned ashen. In a panic Dublin thought that the good fortune in finding him was in danger of turning against her.

'I got on the wrong boat,' she said, willing him to understand. 'I thought it was going back to where we started out, but it came here.' Memories of her flight from Wolverton and her unplanned arrival in Hull flooded in upon her.

The two men looked at each other questioningly. Dublin caught a glimpse of her master's light-brown eyes, before quickly closing her own. Robert! With a sudden burst of elation, she knew that despite his anger, some god had smiled on her, bringing her back to where she belonged.

The conversation drifted over her as the young Captain recounted his time in Ireland and the all-too-brief sojourn at Wolverton. Hopefully, Dublin listened for some sign that he had missed her, regretted leaving her behind, but there was none. He finished by saying: 'God alone knows how she managed to follow me here.'

'Or why she should do so.' There was suspicion in the Scotsman's voice. He leaned closer to his companion and whispered: 'Are ye certain she's nae a spy?'

'Not a spy. I found her in the aftermath of battle. She was in danger of having her throat slit. By no means could she have planned it, and yet . . .' He seemed to struggle for some explanation, finally saying: 'I feel as if the girl's bewitched me. I cannot seem to get away from her.'

Dublin blushed painfully.

Sir John asked: 'What do you wish me to do with her?'

Robert looked directly at her, his brows drawn together, defying her to speak. To his senior officer, he said: 'What would you suggest?'

'Well now,' Sir John began to list the alternatives. 'I could put her in prison for vagrancy; or set her to work on the city wall; or have her sent back on the next ship going south; or charge her with espionage; or give her a spell in the stocks; or . . .'

109

She lowered her eyes, a supplicant, waiting for them to decide her fate. Robert said: 'I think she'd better stay with me.'

Her spirits soared again. *Thank you, God, thank you!*

The two men continued to talk. Now that her future was decided, Dublin felt once more the heavy weight of exhaustion. Unbidden, she crept closer to the fire and sank first onto her haunches, then onto her bottom, and finally curled up in a tight ball, sleep hovering pleasantly around her. Snippets of conversation drifted in and out of her head.

Sir John was talking again. 'There's things I think ye should know, Hammond, but . . .' He glanced across at the fireplace. She heard Robert's footsteps come closer and screwed her eyes up tight, feigning sleep.

In a low voice, he replied, 'There's nothing to fear, she's sleeping.' He returned to join Sir John and the trickle of liquid told that they had replenished their goblets.

After an appreciative silence, Sir John said, 'I'll speak honestly with ye. This siege is not what it seems. Some weeks ago our garrison took a ship in the estuary, a wee ketch, the *Providence*, purporting to be for the Crown. All those aboard had fled by the time it was boarded, except for one, a supposed Frenchman whom we handed over to the Governor. He turned out to be none other than Sir George Digby, come expressly from the King to persuade Hotham to hand the port over to the Royalists.'

Robert made a grunting sound to show that he understood the seriousness of events and Meldrum continued, 'When the story got out, the Governor of course denied that he had even considered such a betrayal, but subsequent events throw his story into doubt.' He lowered his voice. 'It is our belief that the troops out there on the barricades are merely for show, so that Hotham can surrender the city to them without losing face. I was sent to join this garrison, expressly to assist in the routing of these supposed invaders. I can tell ye it's come as something of a shock to them to be actually challenged and they've put up little resistance. Every day more drift away frae the barricades and it's my guess within a week or so they'll all be gone.'

Still feigning sleep, Dublin thought that the half-hearted siege around Hull now made sense.

'Where does this leave the Governor?' she heard Robert say.

'Unblemished, but not without suspicion.' Meldrum stood up,

putting his beaker aside. 'This wee skirmish is as good as over but there'll be more to come. Ye'll need to get your men fighting fit and at the same time we must work on the city defences.' He hesitated. 'I need to trust you.'

'I am a man of honour, a true Englishman.'

'I am glad to hear it.'

Robert poured out another measure of sack and held it out to Meldrum.

'Ye'll need to give the Governor some encouragement,' his companion said obliquely, accepting the drink and relaxing back into the chair. 'Now, what of your runaway?'

Robert shook his head. 'I don't know, sir. I guess I shall have to keep her with me. There's work a'plenty. Perhaps she can go into the kitchens.'

Dublin felt both relief and affront almost simultaneously. Dismissing the thought of the kitchens, she allowed herself a moment of elation in the knowledge that she was not to be sent away.

'Well, make it clear to all about that she has your protection. The Irish are not welcome anywhere.' Sir John drained his drink.

Dublin was assailed by a sense of fear. Memories of her ordeal at the petty court were too recent.

'She'll come in useful,' Sir John ventured. 'Do your laundry, cook for you – you can't beat having your own comforts . . .' His silence implied something more and Dublin felt herself grow hot, whether from hope or fear she was not sure. She resisted the urge to move and perhaps remind the two men of her presence.

Her patron said: 'I've no inclination for small, savage girls. If I take pleasure it will be with a full-grown woman, and one that's willing.'

'Perhaps I should introduce you to Sweet Lips.'

'A whore?'

'You could say that.' Sir John gave a dry chuckle. 'She's the toast of Hull, and a sight more popular than the Governor.'

Robert demurred. 'My taste does not run to harlots.'

Just as Dublin was savouring the last remark, Sir John asked, 'Are ye wed?'

'I'm betrothed to Mary Hampden, one of John Hampden's daughters.'

'A fine man.' Meldrum sounded impressed.

The two officers stood up and Robert said, 'I'll walk a way with you, get some fresh air.' He glanced across at the hearth before picking up his hat, adding, 'The lassie'll likely stay asleep.' Together they went quietly out into the passageway.

Dublin lay still, trying to piece together her thoughts. After a while she climbed unsteadily from her sleeping place. The room began to spin and she rested back against the wall-panelling until the dizziness subsided. Peering out through the window, her gaze followed the broad curve of the river. It moved slowly but inexorably and there was something comforting in the certainty of it. Dublin considered anew her position, drawing hope from the thought that there must be some divine reason why Robert had rescued her, of all others, from the ruins of Carrickmain.

A sudden optimism came to her. This Mary Hampden was miles away. Dublin had no inkling as to what Robert felt for his betrothed, although it was clear that he admired her father. However, the lady was not here like Dublin was, to tend him every day, bring him food and clean linen, nurse him if he were sick.

Mary Hampden's weapons might be wealth and position, but Dublin was here and she was not.

Grey ribbons of cloud cast zig-zag shadows across the river. Like the Humber, Dublin was drifting. It would take something very serious indeed to stop the tide that brought her and Robert daily together. Surely love must be more potent than wealth? She smiled.

To her mortification, on Robert's return Dublin found herself dismissed from his bedchamber.

'I don't know how you managed to follow me,' he accused again, indicating that she should get up and accompany his own manservant to other quarters. 'You must have unnatural powers.'

'I—'

'No arguments!'

She said nothing, too crushed by his suspicion to fight back. Before leaving the chamber she put her hand to her forehead, feigning faintness, but his heart was hard. 'Go along with you now, you'll be quite safe.'

Reluctantly she climbed the increasingly steep and narrow steps, following old Obidiah Strange until she found herself in a cubbyhole nearly under the eaves of the inn.

'You'll be all right, young 'un.' Obidiah patted her arm. 'Given the master quite a turn, you 'ave, turnin' up like this.'

Dublin bent her head to squeeze under the rafters. Through the tiles she could see pinpoints of light in a smooth cobalt sky. She sank down on a pile of straw, thoughtfully provided, and reviewed her situation. After the initial affront, she comforted herself with the thought that at least she had not been consigned to the area where the rest of the kitchen staff bedded down, and allowed herself some foolish hope that perhaps it was merely propriety that had forced Robert to dismiss her from his presence. In the fullness of time it might be possible, under cover of darkness, to creep back there and . . . Such wild imaginings had her out of her depth, thinking the unthinkable. With a sigh she fashioned a nest from her bedding and settled down to dream.

Regular food and ale soon did much to restore Dublin to health, yet in spite of her triumph in sharing Robert's accommodation, she rarely saw him. When he was not at a muster he and the military worked all the daylight hours to secure the town. He was tireless. Some nights he stayed over at the Army headquarters and on other evenings he did not return until the small hours. All the time Dublin waited for some sign, some chance to make herself indispensable.

It soon became clear that her duties were manifold. Collecting firewood, clearing and replacing reeds on the many floors, cleaning and skinning carcases for food and pelts, washing pots, working in the brewhouse. Her role was not, as she had hoped, confined to caring for Robert Hammond.

Whenever possible she escaped from the inn on the pretext of finding more logs and kindling. This was a chance to explore and, if she was very fortunate, to catch a glimpse of Robert somewhere in the town.

She stopped to watch the pikemen on the wide expanse of scrubland. By numbers they formed and re-formed, going through their drill. On the command they moved and turned as one, the sea of staves glittering in the sunlight. They wore no uniform as such but each man had about his waist an orange sash denoting that he served the Earl of Essex. Dublin remembered the orange band that had adorned Robert's hat at Carrickmain, realising it was his godfather, not his sweetheart whom he honoured. She felt foolishly pleased.

Junior officers screamed commands while columns of cavalry rode in mock attack. As long as the ranks did not break, the pikemen were well-nigh impregnable. In battle, a charge of cavalry would be thrown into disarray when they came face to face with a wall of angry points.

Further afield, rows of musketeers went through the interminable rota of tasks required to load, aim, fire and retreat. Here and there officers rode among them but strain her eyes as she would, there was no sign of Robert.

The officers were busy trying to lick their recruits into some sort of shape. Some men had volunteered for service but others, like Obidiah Strange, had been recruited by their masters and had little experience of weaponry or parades. The vast majority of troops however, had been emptied from the gaols, accepting this precarious freedom as better than life in the cesspits of the prisons. As a fighting force they had little to recommend them and were as much a danger to their own side as to the enemy. Dublin thought of the woman who had offered her water when first she entered Hull and wondered if her own man was part of this motley array.

The men marched and drilled until they near dropped. It seemed to be the aim that fear of disobedience should outweigh any reluctance to fight. Verbal battering and physical blows rained on the slow or inattentive. All the time preachers read to them from the Bible and extolled the virtues of clean living and obedience.

Dublin stayed as long as she dared, but there being no sign of Robert, she picked up a few sticks and made her way back to the inn.

That evening Robert went to dine at the house of a family of quality. Dublin laid out clean linen then stood by hopefully as he prepared to wash.

'Here, take my boots down and clean them well.'

Reluctantly she left his presence. The memory of him bathing on his last evening at Wolverton filled her thoughts. She cleaned the boots as quickly as she could, hastening back in the hope that she might be able to help him, but when she returned he was already dressed. He looked so handsome that she thought her

114

heart might burst with love, and tormented herself with the thought that the family where he dined must have a pretty daughter.

'I shall be late returning. Don't wait up for me.'

As soon as he left, she crept back up to his room. Everything here was a part of him, his clothing, his prayer book, even his saddle bag. She smoothed the supple leather, resting her cheek against it, breathing in the smell of him.

Guiltily she peeped inside the bag and found some papers. Pulling them out, she unfolded them and spread them on the table, looking at the puzzling symbols. Her ignorance weighed heavy upon her, thinking that a fit wife for my lord would need to have her letters. She wondered if they were love missives from his betrothed and had to fight the desire to screw them up and consign them to the fire. With a sigh she folded them up and returned them to the pannier.

Gloomily she sank onto the big wooden chair near the fire and drained the sack left in his goblet, then poured herself some more. She felt abandoned, worthless. The sack made her head fuzzy and in defiant mood she wondered whether to climb into his bed and stay there. What would he do then? But the idea was too dangerous and she could not think it through. The rebellion passed and instead a knot of pain weighed her down. Goblets and trenchers remained, unwashed, on the table. If he were to chide her for her slovenliness, she would run away.

The evening dragged on for ever and try as she might, her thoughts would not turn from the image of Robert in fine company, paying court to a beautiful girl. Tormented beyond endurance, she finally began to launder his dirty linen in the washing basin where he had washed himself. She handled the lace lovingly, caressing the garments as if they were his own skin.

'What are you doing here?'

Dublin jumped guiltily as he came in, wondering if he thought she had come to steal something. 'I thought you might be needing me.' Her face flushed scarlet.

'All I need is sleep.'

Dublin scrutinised him for tell-tale signs of elation, wondering if he had this very evening kissed a beautiful girl. He merely looked tired.

115

'You dined well?' she asked, trying to regain her composure.

'Well enough. Come here.' Her heart doubled its beat and she moved closer, holding her breath.

'Pull my boots off and get me a flagon.'

She knelt and heaved at the long leather boots, her hand resting momentarily against the muscular bulge of his calf. Reluctantly she stood up then poured out the ale, pushing it sullenly at him.

'Does something ail you? You looked devilish sulky.'

'Nothing.'

He pulled a dismissive face. 'You sound tired. Get you to bed – and shut the door properly on your way out.'

Miserably she stomped up the stairs to her room, thankful for the privacy even though the summer temperature made the niche as hot as the bread-oven.

She yearned to escape her pain by sleeping, but sleep would not come. Hurt and longing swallowed her up. She wanted only to be close to him and he would not allow it. What was she to do? What *could* she do? There must be some magic, some power. For a moment she thought of Glendruid, wondering if nearby there was a secret place where she could make a sacrifice. But such thoughts were dangerous, condemned by these Christians in their interminable sermons. Robert certainly would not approve – that is, if he knew . . . She shook her head. So far, praying to Robert's God had yielded little reward, other than to bring her into his presence and then torment her. The old religion was best. She knew then that she would pay any price to make him love her.

116

Chapter 15

Rods of grey, August rain drove angrily across the concourse of Nottingham Castle. King Charles stared forlornly through strands of bedraggled white feathers that had earlier risen so erect from his hatband. Now, battered beyond recovery, he brushed them aside with a damp glove and straightened himself in the saddle. To his dismay, his hands were shaking. The stench of the tanneries wafted up to him and he wrinkled his nose with disgust. This place felt wrong for his mighty purpose.

The faithful had gathered, but not in such numbers that could lift his spirits. Banners trembled across the concourse but they looked dejected and in spite of the fanfares and drumbeats, there was no backbone to the occasion. Charles had not, in his worst nightmares, thought that it would come to this.

He wondered why he had allowed himself to be persuaded to come here. His courtiers pinned such hopes upon Nottingham, looking for support from the surrounding lords. He comforted himself with the thought that when the Queen arrived, she would be able to sail reinforcements directly up the river from the Humber estuary. *Henrietta, hurry home!*

Silently the King began to recite his speech, trying to recall the umpteen amendments that had come to him over the past days. Now he wished that he had phrased it differently, been more flamboyant. He agonised as to how his herald would deliver it – would he get all the nuances right? Charles wondered, even now, if he should not read it himself, but the knotting in his stomach warned that when he came to open his mouth, the traitorous stutter would claim him.

At the signal, he rode forward and nodded to announce that it was time to hear the proclamation.

All about him, faces were turned towards his messenger. The man started off in good voice, but soon he began to hesitate, then stumble over the fine lines that Charles had so painstakingly penned. The man glanced apologetically towards his sovereign and Charles guessed that his crossings-out were making it difficult to follow.

The King felt near to despair. Why were so few people responding to the call? Harvest-time it might be, but surely his subjects could see that defending their monarch was more important than reaping the fields?

Closing his mind to the shortcomings of this most solemn occasion, he wondered how soon before he could return to London and his palace at Whitehall. He missed its stateliness, his paintings.

The Royal Standard was slowly raised. It fluttered and jumped and Charles had a fearful image that it was trying to run away. One by one, the assembled battalions began their parade. People cheered thinly. Charles raised his hat, nearly losing it in the vicious August wind.

Turning the stallion to face his army, and offering up a prayer for God's blessing, the King thought: Can I really be at war?

Chapter 16

News that King Charles had formally declared war on his Parliament was greeted in Hull, as elsewhere, with sober misgivings. Already the people lived in a besieged city and the troops behaved as if hostilities had long since started, but things were now clearly much worse.

Renewed efforts were poured into making the port safe. When the inner fortifications were finished to the army's satisfaction, a second phase of work started, but this time it met with opposition.

Many people had already risked their lives in order to stay in the jumble of houses that stood without the city walls, but now the army, the city's defenders, began to knock them down. Reluctantly the inhabitants resigned themselves to the fact that in time of conflict, it was the duty of every loyal citizen to deprive the enemy of a place to hide, even if it cost him his own fireside.

At the army quarters Dublin continued to work in the kitchens, consoling herself with every small service that she could provide for the man she loved. Now indeed, he was under great pressure and she rarely saw him. When she did it was a precious moment, to be dwelt upon at length in the endless hours of toil. She had risked much to be here, nursed such dreams of reunion with him, but the reality was drudgery and only the barest recognition.

Valiantly, she did not give up. 'You look fatigued, master. Would you want a bath?'

'A ewer of water, then leave me.'

She went over each phrase many times, wondering how he had interpreted her words, pondering on his tone of voice, looking always for some hint that maybe he was softening towards her.

When the news that war was declared reached them, the

distance that Robert so determinedly maintained was for once relaxed. Bringing water to his chamber, Dublin found him explaining the situation to Obidiah. She stayed to listen.

'. . . and as you know, His Majesty suffers from an impediment of speech.'

Without thinking, Dublin interrupted. 'Why would God so afflict the man who is His divine representative on earth?'

Robert stared at her with a mixture of surprise and disapproval. It was clear that the thought had not occurred to him before. Finally he said, 'Who can understand these things? The King is of modest stature and hampered by a limp. Others have been similarly afflicted, Richard Crookback, for example. But there, Charles was not born to be King.'

She looked at him in surprise and he continued: 'His brother Henry was heir to the throne before the fever took him. My own grandfather was physician to Prince Henry's father, King James. Prince Henry was my brother John's godfather.'

Dublin pondered on the information, trying to work out the complex connections, but above all weighed down by the realisation that the Hammonds were next to being royalty. There could be no place for a peasant girl in such a family. Rebellion stirred in her heart.

She asked: 'Do you believe that there is no difference between pauper and prince?'

Robert looked at her with shock. 'Of course there is a difference! That is a dangerous thing to say. Who put such a thought into your head?'

She did not know how best to answer. 'I – I just wondered.'

Still staring at her, Robert looked doubly suspicious. After far too long, he said, 'Dublin, I have risked much to have you here. There are others who still believe you to be an agent of the enemy. When you talk like that, you voice evil ideas. Don't let me down.'

'I wouldn't. Never.' She shook her head vehemently, wishing she could unsay the offending remark. Slowly Robert relaxed and turned back to Obidiah.

To cover her confusion, Dublin began to clear the table, but all the time, she remembered Caleb Gosden's words – 'I believe there is no difference between prince and pauper.' He must be wrong, and yet it was no use denying it. In her heart she knew that Caleb was right and the difference of opinion with Robert frightened her. The fact remained that like Caleb, the King was beset by physical imperfection – only Caleb had a magical power with words and the King was denied even that. She remembered the passion in Caleb's voice, the zeal in his vivid blue eyes. Something approaching nostalgia touched her at the thought of the sun-baked hills of the island.

Robert was still talking. 'In any event, I hear that a storm blew up and the Royal Standard blew down. That seems to me to be a good omen!' He gave an amused grunt. 'This war will not last long.'

When Obidiah left, Dublin busied herself about the room, clearing trenchers, picking up wet woollen stockings, hoping not to be dismissed. Robert seated himself at the table, the silence punctuated by the rhythmic scratching of his quill.

Finding a tear in his shirt, Dublin settled on the stool in the corner and stitched industriously, now and then glancing across to feast her eyes on him. Occasionally she stopped to stoke the fire or renew a candle. This was a treat indeed, just being here. She tried to pretend that she was his wife – except that when bedtime came . . .

'Is there anything else I can do for you, Master?'

He put the quill aside and stretched his shoulders. He was within touching distance and she stepped closer.

Her yearning made her bold. 'Would you wish me to rub your shoulders?'

He sat back and looked at her. 'Why did you say what you did earlier? I have tried to instil into you good Christian virtues. It pains me to hear you mouthing dissent.'

She wondered how to make amends. 'If I was a prince, or a pauper, I would still serve you.'

He gave a sudden laugh. 'You're a good girl, Dublin. As it happens, you can do something for me.'

She felt her mouth go dry. 'Of course.'

'Send down for Obidiah, will you? I want him to take these letters tonight, and find someone travelling south.'

Her heart lurched and she could feel her face stiffen, biting her lip to hold back the disappointment, but already he was writing again.

Angrily she left the room and thundered down the stairs. Obidiah was sitting in the tavern with a group of older men.

'Master wants you.'

121

Obi drained his ale and stood up. 'He drives himself hard,' he said to the assembled company. 'All work and no play, that one.'

There seemed no point in going back upstairs. Instead Dublin wandered out into the damp night air. Everything was still and calm. Inside she churned with discontent. She wondered if Robert was at fault for giving himself so totally to the war, or was it her, wanting something no honest girl should even think of? She felt heavy, hopeless.

Moments later, Obi came out clutching the messages and hurried in the direction of the river. It was after midnight.

Dublin tried to throw off her dark thoughts, wondering how other people viewed the news of war, but soon Robert was back in her mind again.

Surely it was wrong to think of her own needs when such serious events were taking place? She had no answers to any of these questions but one thing seemed certain – they would not be leaving Hull for a very long time. In the meantime, she would do whatever it took, anything, to win her master's heart and make him hers.

Chapter 17

The pain and humiliation of the pillory left Caleb Gosden in a state of simmering melancholy. On returning to Caulbourne, he retreated immediately and alone, to the hills.

Every now and then his anger bubbled up – outrage with the Justices and their phony charges, fury with the Irish girl who was no better than a flibbertigibbet. He wondered how he could have been so misguided as not to recognise that she had no sense of loyalty or gratitude. Wrath burned inside him, eating away at his pride, making him want to lash out at whoever came near. He rued the day that he had taken pity on Dublin O'Neill and rescued her from the trap.

Back on the downs was the only place that he could find peace, and yet the hut was filled with Dublin's presence. Angrily he turned out all the bedding, trying to get rid of the smell of herbs that reminded him so potently of her. The perfume clung persistently.

During his enforced stay in Newport, his old dog, Fly, had taken sick and died. He missed her sorely, blaming Dublin for this, too. If he had been present, perhaps he could have nursed the bitch back to health. The Devil was in that girl, causing mayhem wherever she went.

His summer passed in an unrelieved cloud of anger. It took his back a long time to heal, the combination of the whip and the sun leaving him with raw wounds, but the deepest cuts were within. When Sara came to call, offering her services to help salve the sheep against lice, he dismissed her curtly, unable to tolerate any reminder of his ordeal. Her sad, accepting face both angered and wounded him. It was so easy to hurt her and he despised both the dumb girl and himself, but he could not behave otherwise.

Time for the tupping already drew near. Some shepherds set their rams to work at Michaelmas but Caleb held back so that the lambs born next spring would benefit from the March grass. He therefore loosed the males on 18 October, St Luke's Day, remembering the old rhyme: 'On St Luke's Day, let the tup have his play.' A good, lusty ram would cover as many as fifty ewes.

In the meantime, he carried on alone with the task he disliked most, greasing each sheep with salve to ward off lice and scab. It was a thankless job, laborious, and even if he worked flat out all day, he could not grease more than seven ewes, soaking every staple in the protective mixture of tar and molten tallow. Always he aimed to complete the task before mid-October, to protect his flock against bad weather. This year he would be hard put to finish and secretly he cursed his stubbornness in sending Sara away.

Meanwhile, ovine copulation went on all about him. Brooding, Caleb tried not to dwell on this random, passionless intercourse, but it stirred his hunger until he burned with restless lust. He remembered the slut from the shearing and a sense of hopelessness weighed him down. Rubbing his fingers deep into the shaggy fleeces, he thought that man was forever a slave to his cock, driven by need, his finer feelings overridden by lechery.

When the salving was complete, and the rams exhausted, it was time to return the flock to the village, the pregnant ewes to overwinter there, and the others to be slaughtered and their meat salted for the long cold months ahead.

Caleb had no wish to return to the life of the community. He was restless, wanting he knew not what. The confines of the village could not contain him. The sheep, which had once been enough to keep him fulfilled, now served little purpose. This year he had no misgivings about the annual slaughter, glad only to be relieved of his burdens. Instead of the hundreds, Caleb would have only his own three pregnant females to tend over the winter months. When the time came however, he also kept back the two lambs that Dublin had hand-reared, convincing himself that they were too small to be killed, not worth the price of their carcasses.

Relieved of his responsibilities, he wandered through the village, walking with his head bent, defying neighbours to come near, but as he passed the fulling mill, the girl he had taken on the last night of the shearing came hurrying after him. He increased his pace, ignoring her calls, until she began running to catch up.

'I've been looking out for you.' She scurried along at his side, glancing into his face to assess his mood. He remained silent.

'I've got to talk to you. I'm – you know . . .'

He jerked to a standstill, his brow darkening. 'What are you saying?'

'You know. You've got me in trouble.'

He snorted. 'Me? Or who else?' He began to run through the names of every unwed man in the village.

She dropped back in the face of his derision, calling: 'I'll have to tell the minister.'

He swung round on her, finding a focus for his simmering discontent. 'You tell him, sweetheart. You tell him you slept with the Devil, how I forced you – or perhaps you've been visited, like the Virgin.'

'You're a blasphemer, that's what you are!' She stamped her foot and her lips formed into an angry pout. As Caleb kept walking, she called after him: 'Anyways, they'll know it's yourn when it comes out bent and twisted!'

In his desire to get away from her, he went into the alehouse. Inside, the first person he saw was his brother John.

'Caleb! You're back, brother. How are you?'

Caleb fought down his ill-humour. The girl's accusation had disturbed him, in part because he had no wish for notoriety, but mostly because he did not want his seed to grow in her vulgar belly.

'Are you all right, brother?' John was looking at him with concern.

'How's Mam?' he asked, evading the question.

'Well enough. She'll be glad to have you back. Have you heard the news?' And John began to bring him up to date with village events, then he turned his attention to wider matters. 'You know war's been declared? We've come out for the Parliament here, but there's some that don't agree. The ports have been holding out for the King. I hear the Solent's been blockaded, and Sir William Meux and Mr Weston and Mr Leigh have all been sent to be examined by the Parliament, as delinquents.'

'Meux?' For the first time, Caleb showed some interest. 'There's been fighting?'

'There has been. The Governor's wife and all her brood have been driven out of the castle. We've got a new Governor now,

Lord Pembroke. He's for the Parliament. I reckon they'll be recruiting men afore long. There's bound to be a showdown.'

Caleb felt a sudden surge of excitement. 'Who will they recruit?'

'Why, anyone that's fit and willing.' John hesitated. 'Which side do you favour?'

Caleb regarded him; in spite of his general gloom, he felt a wave of affection for his handsome brother. 'I can't abide the way things are. There has to be changes. The King stands for the old order. Me, I've got to go with Parliament, no matter where it leads.'

John looked troubled. 'I don't know. I fear things could get out of hand. Better what you know than stepping into the dark.'

Caleb shrugged and downed his ale. 'You thinking of volunteering, then?'

John shook his head. 'Anne would never allow it. We need every penny I can raise, for the young 'uns. Still, I suppose there will be a demand for good horses. I might make my fortune.'

'Would you spare a horse for me?'

John regarded him with a mixture of dismay and disbelief. 'You aren't serious? You wouldn't think to go and fight?'

'Why not, brother? What good reason is there to stay?'

'This is home.'

'Then every reason to defend it.' Slamming his beaker down on the bench, Caleb patted John's arm and took his leave, thoughts of war and travel racing in his blood.

He started to head for home but then could not face his mother's gentle intrusion. Instead he decided to call on Sara. He felt unhappy about the deaf girl. She had been good to him and in return he had snubbed her. To salve his conscience, he thought he would take a quick look at her roof, see if he could patch some of the thatch before winter set in. That way she'd be dry at least.

As he slipped down the narrow passageway to her house, he wondered whether to confide in her that he was considering leaving. At the moment it was only a thought but at least she wouldn't tell anyone. Now he considered it, there were a lot of things he had shared only with Sara. He pushed open her door and stepped inside, his eyes needing a moment to adjust to the gloom. When they did, the sight that greeted him caused him to suspend breathing.

Sara stood in the centre of the room, her head bowed, rubbing her scalp with her fingers. A stream of water trickled from her long brown hair to the floor and then across the room in his direction. She was naked.

Caleb could not take his eyes from her body. In his mind's eye he saw a short, dumpy, shapeless girl, older than her years, plain-faced, her bulky body clothed in rough cloth. Before him was a small, rounded girl, her skin pale and shimmering in the rivulets of water. It was her breasts that held his attention. As she leaned forward, tipping a cup of water over her hair, her breasts hung down, full, rounded, pink-nippled. His prick leaped but another part of him was entranced by the sheer beauty of her. Her waist, normally bound round with a piece of rough rope, was slender, curving in, between her beautiful, heavy dugs and her rounded bottom. His eyes roved appreciatively across her buttocks, following the near perfect shape down across her thighs and legs to her feet. He swallowed.

At that moment Sara turned her head and jumped with alarm. Her arms closed across her breasts, and her cunny. She looked helpless, vulnerable, and beautiful. The face he had always regarded as plain, was refined by the tumbling strands of wet hair.

'Sara, have no fear.' He signed to her and bent to pick up her skirt which lay crumpled on the floor. Flushing scarlet she took it from him and turned her back, struggling into it. As she fastened the strings, he reached out and turned her to him, looking down at her breasts, touching them. 'You are beautiful.'

She stood still, neither responding to his touch nor moving away. After a moment he bent forward to kiss her shoulder, finding his way down to one of her large nipples. Gently he licked it and she flinched.

'Forgive me.' He recovered her bodice from the ground and wrapped it about her, holding her now protectively by the shoulders. She was trembling beneath his touch.

When she was clothed, he took her hands and began to tell her about the war. All the time he saw her naked body, its beauty. He was bursting with the need to fuck her.

'If I go – will you come with me?'

She looked at him, surprise and alarm showing in her blue-grey eyes. Meeting her gaze, he reached out again and uncovered her breasts, unable to help himself. She stepped back but he gathered

127

her to him, pushing his knee between her legs to force them apart, lowering her onto the reeds and pushing her skirt up so that he could get into her. She tried to close her legs but he was insistent. 'Let me,' he said, uselessly, against her ear. He kissed her lobe and her temple, forcing himself up between the tender folds of skin, thrusting when he was in position.

For the first time in his life he heard her make a sound, a gasp of pain and fear. He caught her wrists to stop her from pulling back and rode her as gently as his need would allow, until relief came in a juddering, soul-soothing rush. Spent and breathless, he lay where he was until his prick slipped out of her.

When he sat up, he saw that Sara was silently crying and he pulled her up, rocking her against him. 'Hush, sweetheart, hush now.'

Sitting back, he cupped her face in his hands and forced her to look at him. Very carefully he formed the words on his lips. 'Forgive me if I hurt you, but there's nothing to fear. I am going to make you my wife.'

'I'm glad you've seen sense at last, chosen a decent girl, but I wish you'd do it proper, get wed in the church.' Caleb's mother was sewing a skirt from woollen cloth, spun and woven in the village, in readiness for a harsh winter.

'We don't need the church to make us man and wife,' he answered. 'We'll do it like it always used to be done, plight our troth and set up home. That's all the blessing we need.'

'Well, when is Sara moving in?' Lizzie sniffed, resigning herself to the inevitable. She had long since learned that it was no use arguing with Caleb, but for good measure she added: 'You could have had any lass, but none of 'em's gonna risk damnation, not being properly wed. Poor Sara, she don't know no different.'

Caleb let the monologue go over his head. The thought of two women fussing over him made him want to flee, never to return to this stifling village.

Doubts assailed him at every turn. Caleb feared that his sexual intrusion into Sara's life had been unwelcome and might continue to be so. In the foolish, perfect romance of his dreams, he wanted a woman to whom he could give pleasure, as much as to take it.

He also feared that Annie Colenutt, the slut from the shearing, would still make trouble. If she were publicly to accuse him of fornication, he might well find himself again before the court.

Above all, while he craved sexual release, he did not want to be married, but when he looked at his betrothed, her gentle, plain, trusting face, he knew that he was trapped.

On the day of the ceremony, Caleb allowed his hair and beard to be trimmed, washed himself all over, self-consciously rubbed his torso with the musky smell of rosemary, and wore the best of his clothes. The smell of the herb stirred his loins, reminding him . . . but he shut the thought of Dublin O'Neill firmly from his mind. This was Sara's day. He would try to be decent about it.

On the green swathe of grass before the sheepwash, they made their pledge, one to the other. As Caleb formed the words, slowly on his lips, Sara followed suit, her silent covenant binding her to him. She wore a new skirt and bodice, purchased by her betrothed. The borrowed slippers on her feet made her mince and totter. A lace collar loaned by Caleb's sister-in-law was about her throat, and more lace adorned her cuffs.

A cluster of village maids came to embrace her and wish her well. In normal circumstances they would have shunned her, sniggering behind her back, but something about the shepherd's action changed their demeanour.

Sara's hair was dressed with flowers and bound about her head. It made her face look rounder and her plump shoulders sloped, disappearing beneath the cloth of her bodice. Caleb thought about her breasts, trying to find some enthusiasm for this deed.

He caught sight of Annie Colenutt and his heart jolted. Was she going to make trouble? He noticed then that she stood next to Elijah Wavell, the cooper, whose wife was hardly cold in the ground. Seeing Caleb looking at her, Annie linked her arm with the widower's and turned away. Old Elijah was well set up, a very good catch for a labourer's slattern of a daughter. Caleb's relief was tangible.

Turning to his bride, they toasted each other with mead, then he slipped a ring onto her finger, fashioned from copper by the smith. Sara raised her eyes to him and her face was aglow with love. Gently, sadly, he kissed her.

Lizzie Gosden had provided a spread at the sheepwash, and friends and family gathered to toast the newlyweds with last year's elderberry. Conversation was difficult and one-sided because of the bride's handicap, but Caleb kept her at his side, defying the guests to ignore her.

After they had supped, Lizzie prepared to go with her eldest son and his wife, leaving the cottage free for one night, for the bride and groom to consummate their union in privacy. Before they left, the womenfolk helped Sara to undress and placed her in one of Lizzie's shifts, broadcasting herbs across the linen for good luck and fecundity. Her hair was combed out and spread across the bolster.

'Go to it, brother.' John patted Caleb's arm. 'She's a good sort, Sara.'

'Good, yes.'

John raised his eyebrows. 'Does she not rouse you to . . .'

'She's a good friend.'

'Then why . . .' John backed away, his discomfort showing. 'She'll serve you well,' he said, by way of farewell.

Alone at last, Caleb remained in the downstairs room, drinking more elderberry, looking around at the familiar walls, the single shelf with its trenchers and beakers. This was now his house, rather than his mother's. He did not want to belong here.

Upstairs, his bride waited for him. He wondered if some temporary magic had blinded him into believing that Sara was beautiful. Beneath her garments, could she really be transformed into the paragon he had seen that day? He tried to tell himself that it didn't matter. Next to his own kin, she was the nearest, dearest person he knew. But the thought of beauty, passion, self-possession, stirred him, not goodness and virtue.

When he felt sufficiently fuddled, he stumbled his way up the stairs and stripped off his breeches, fumbling his way under the covers. Sara lay on her back, tense, not moving. He began to fondle her breasts, trying to find some excitement but a blanket of gloom pervaded his mood. As if he was someone else, he observed the reluctant swelling of his cock, fingered the girl's crutch, slipping his fingers inside to try and make her moist. She was dry and wooden as a board.

Dragging himself on top of her he forced his way inside, moving almost with disinterest, drowning in his own sense of loss. When he came, it was without joy. He knew that he had hurt her and despised himself for his selfishness. A good husband, a good friend, would have made it right for her.

In the night he woke to find himself aroused again. Sleepily he turned, and feeling another presence, wondered for a moment where he was. Suddenly he was aware that Sara had turned towards him. In the darkness he could feel her hesitation, sense her longing to please him. His heart beat faster.

Reaching out he took her hand and guided it to his prick. Gently she smoothed him, caressing until he moaned with pleasure. He found her mouth and explored it with his tongue.

As he went to move on top of her she drew back and he guessed that she was bruised and sore. Instead he pressed himself between her legs, making no attempt to get inside her. Compliantly she moved against him, held him close. The sound of her panting was like music. A sudden sense of joy bathed him.

'Sara,' he said into her silence. 'I'm such a fool. Believe me, girl, I'll always take care of you.' In the darkness, she placed her fingers against his lips and held him close.

It was 23 October, in the year of Our Lord 1642. A day he would always remember.

Chapter 18

It was 23 October, in the year of Our Lord 1642, a day he would always remember.

King Charles felt the exhaustion that spread across the plâteau of Edgehill like a winter fog. Night was approaching and not a man present, friend or foe, was spared the horror. The animal cries of sick and wounded haunted the air. Thousands lay dead. The King was cold, shocked, miserable.

Charles had not anticipated that it would turn out like this. With men rallying daily to his Standard, and with the advantage of high ground and Right on his side, victory had seemed certain. Charles had supported the decision not to try and outrun Lord Essex to London, but to stay and fight. Now everything was confusion. Not really wishing to know, he asked: 'How stand things, nephew?'

Prince Rupert was bright-eyed with fatigue. Charles thought his nephew had conducted himself with great bravery but wished he would temper it with a little more caution. The Prince's cavalry charge had scattered the enemy like chaff, but once started, it had proved impossible to stop. Instead of turning and finishing the job, Rupert's horsemen pursued the enemy off the field and then fell upon Lord Essex's baggage train. Meanwhile, the Parliamentarians rallied their forces and inflicted savage casualties on Charles's poor, brave infantry, many armed only with cudgels. Tears brimmed over the King's eyes and dried cold on his cheeks.

Rupert said: 'We wait tonight, and see what tomorrow will bring.' He sighed. 'Lord Essex should have accepted my challenge to settle the matter by mortal combat.'

Charles glanced at the young man's long, dark face. There was such magnetism about him. The enemy spread lies about Rupert's occult powers – 'Robert the Devil', they called him, but his nephew's real power lay in his untiring enthusiasm and his inborn hunger for adventure. It was a pity he upset so many of the older courtiers.

'We must waste no time,' the lad said now. 'London awaits us. We must press on!'

The King secretly thought that many Royalists would rather not take London at all, if it meant setting this young firebrand free to sack and pillage it. The boy did not really understand how an English nobleman thought. Charles felt all the more tired in the face of his nephew's unflagging drive, and resigned himself to staying another night with his men.

During the battle there had been moments of sacrifice and glory. Charles's loyal friend, Sir Edward Verney, had given his life in an unsuccessful attempt to protect the Royal Standard, then when dusk fell and it seemed lost for ever, a Royalist Captain, unknown to the King and bearing the name John Smith, rode among the enemy, crying: 'They shall have me with it, if they carry it away!' and recaptured the banner. It was a brave deed. A pinpoint of warmth touched Charles's heavy heart.

The other comfort was news that his sons Charles and James were safe. At the outbreak of fighting, he had ordered their retreat, but in so doing they had narrowly missed capture. Young Charles, in spite of his eleven years, had been all for joining the battle and it was only with difficulty that he had been dissuaded and carted off to a barn for safety. Charles felt proud of his valiant firstborn.

For this at least, he could offer up thanks. Kneeling on the damp rug by the bed in his tent, he closed his eyes. It was hard to know where to begin – whether to give thanks or ask for forgiveness. He remembered Lord Astley's prayer as that noble man rode into battle: '*O Lord! Thou knowest how busy I must be this day: if I forget Thee, do not Thou forget me.*' Lord Astley had been spared. King Charles wondered: in all the turmoil, had the Lord forgotten the needs of His royal subject?

Chapter 19

In Hull, it was the end of October before news of Edgehill reached the garrison. Dublin was in the act of dishing up boiled onions for supper when the messenger was announced.

For a few minutes he and the Captain were in quiet conversation. She strained her ears to hear what was being said, infected by Robert's growing exitement. As soon as the man withdrew, her master turned towards her, his face flushed with pleasure.

'Praise be to God!' He jumped to his feet and let out a whoop of joy, suddenly grasping her by the waist, swinging her around.

'Whatever is it?' She was so taken aback that she gasped aloud.

'See, Dublin, the King has been taken prisoner and they say his nephew, Prince Rupert, has been slain! The war is as good as over!'

She was caught up in his excitement, but another, more pressing joy enveloped her at the feel of his hands about her waist, the pressure of his chest against hers. She longed to link her arms about his neck and hold him fast.

'What will happen now?' she asked unsteadily.

At that moment he seemed to realise what he was doing and hastily set her back on her feet. His face was red although whether from exhilaration or embarrassment, she was not sure. He clasped his hands together as if still congratulating himself and said: 'Now the King will *have* to negotiate. Soon we shall all go home.'

Disappointment that he had let her go coupled with uncertainty about what the news meant for her, crowded into Dublin's mind. She asked: 'Shall I go with you?'

'Well . . .' Already she could see that he was back on his guard, distancing himself. He said: 'Pour me some sack – and some for yourself. This is a celebration.'

She noticed that as he took the goblet, his hand was trembling. He sank onto the big wooden chair near the fire and drained the draught then poured himself another.

'We shall have to think about your future,' he said, his voice now formal, a master addressing his servant. 'It isn't right that you should trail around the countryside in my wake.'

The words and their tone crushed her heart. 'But you'll still need a servant.'

'I have Obidiah.'

She flushed scarlet at the transparency of her feelings, the clear message of rejection that he gave in return. Whether it was the drink, or the so recent nearness of him, she found herself losing control.

'Why? Why can I not stay with you? What are you afraid of?' She did not want to hear the answer but asked the question anyway. She could see that he was growing increasingly uncomfortable.

'Mind your tongue, girl.' He hesitated. 'You cannot stay because I am a soldier, not a nursemaid.'

His tone, pompous, upright, suddenly made her see red. 'I don't need you to look after me! Rather I should look after you.' Suddenly near to tears she asked: 'Why did you bother to rescue me?'

'What a foolish question. I rescued you to save your life. As a Christian I . . .'

She snorted impatiently. 'What was the real reason? Why me?' She knew that she had gone too far, burned her boats. For some reason she suddenly thought of Caleb Gosden's angry face. In spite of herself she cried: 'Why doesn't anybody really want me?'

Her master remained silent. Carefully he put his goblet on the table and leaned back in the chair. His back was half to her. When he spoke his voice was so low that she could hardly hear. 'You are a foolish girl, but an honest one – by which I mean that you are open, innocent. You do not hide your feelings with a pretence at indifference or politeness. There is nothing of the harlot about you. I find that disturbing.'

She remained silent, unsure if he was chiding her. After an intolerable time he said: 'Yes, I find you disturbing. It is not right.'

135

He was saying that she was in some way to blame, only she did not understand how or why. Aloud she said: 'I don't mean to offend you. I only want to stay.' She was in danger of pleading now, any semblance of dignity cast aside.

He sighed and got to his feet, addressing the fire. 'I try to think of you as a child, but you are not. You are wellnigh a woman.' Turning to face her, she saw that his eyes were dark with sadness. 'I shall only make you unhappy.'

In spite of the warnings, the message he was giving filled her with overwhelming emotion. With a tremor of joy she thought: he *does* like me. Only his honour, his duty to that spoiled creature, Mary Hampden, holds him back.

'I . . .'

'Don't say anything.' He stared back to the fireplace, his shoulders rising and falling with the weight of his dilemma. 'I am only saying what has to be said.'

'But . . .'

He swivelled round and grasped her by the shoulders, looking into her eyes. For a moment she could see into his soul. 'Believe me, Dublin O'Neill, you are like no one I have ever encountered. But I am bad tidings for you. And you for me. *Believe me.*'

For an eternity he simply looked at her, then slowly, almost sadly, he bent forward and his lips found hers. Dublin closed her eyes and was baptised in the gentle pressure of his embrace.

'I love you,' she said.

'Hush. Save your love for someone more worthy.'

'Please, don't send me away.'

Still holding her gaze, and with barely a movement, he shook his head, then he released her. 'You must give me your promise. We must never speak of this again. Go now.'

This was a day that she would always remember.

Dublin lay abed, tormented by wild emotions, longing for Robert and his presence. At one moment she was swept along on a crest of joy because he was not indifferent to her. In its wake came a slough of despair because she was only a servant and unworthy of his love. Tossing on the scratchy straw, she felt herself to be as helpless as the *Expectation*, bobbing on the sea of life, buffeted by waves, driven offcourse by gales – only now, at this moment, the harbour of love was distantly visible. Pray God that she would soon reach that port!

It dawned on her that after all, her prayers had been answered. Had he not hinted that he loved her? Knowing that the gods were on her side was the reassurance that she needed. Her heart overflowing with love, she snuggled down into the straw and tried to sleep. No matter what happened in the future, things could never be the same again.

When she finally dragged herself from her couch and came face to face with him the next morning however, it was to find that nothing had changed.

'Some ale and bread, quick, Dublin, then I must be away.' Robert spoke as master to servant, distant, indifferent. She glared at him, stung by his betrayal. He did not meet her eyes. Then, when he had gone, she comforted herself with the thought that only his honour held him back. The day would surely come when he would not be able to fight the strong feelings that bound them together. It was meant to be. Be patient. Be patient.

Meanwhile, a different version of events at Edgehill reached the garrison that same morning. It seemed that the King, not Essex, had the victory, Prince Rupert was very much alive. As the household were poring over the significance of this, yet another message arrived, penned personally by Sir John Meldrum who had been present at the fray. He informed them that some seven hundred souls had perished on each side. There was no clear victory, only a bloody battle with both armies claiming the advantage. Winter was approaching, the King was heading for Oxford, not London. An end to the war was nowhere in sight.

Robert announced the news in the presence of Obidiah. Still he did not look in Dublin's direction. 'I wish you both to know that for the present, we shall be staying here.' His eyes flickered towards her but he quickly moved away again.

Whilst she felt relief that they were to stay, she knew with sinking heart that there would be no alteration in their roles. 'We must not speak of it again,' he had said. The only difference was that she had seen behind the mask, knew that behind the formal exterior, was a man who was not indifferent to her. This small pearl of comfort sustained her.

Winter was fast approaching and the job of fortifying the city was hastily resumed. Robert threw himself into his work and

Dublin found a new fulfilment in her role, taking pleasure in seeing to his needs. She reasoned that if she could keep him fed, his room warm and his linen clean, then her time was not spent in vain. Once he was free of the obligation to Mary Hampden . . .

In the meantime, the loyalty of Sir John Hotham still gave cause for concern. His son, Captain John, was caught out corresponding with the Royalist Earl of Newcastle, voicing the need for an early end to hostilities. Then in February of '43 young Hotham met with Queen Henrietta on her return from the Continent, on the pretext of arranging an exchange of prisoners. The Queen then travelled unmolested from Bridlington to York. Young Hotham was suspected of negotiating the safe conduct of the royal party. Neither he nor his father made any attempt to intercept their supposed enemies. Among the Parliamentarians, fear for Hull's safety was rife.

Robert scribed this information and charged Dublin with taking his letter to a messenger in the town. Once outside the tavern, she stopped to look at the mysterious symbols on the missive. As she handed it over to the man, she asked: 'Whose address does this bear?'

He glanced at it. 'A Mr Hampden, at Westminster.'

Mary's father! No doubt the lines would include some sentiment for the girl herself – '*Give my fondest thoughts to my betrothed . . .*' Dublin burned with resentment and wished that she had thrown the letter into the bushes. Before long however, she came to regret her thought.

Supplies of food and fuel were running short and the population of Hull began to lose heart. Without a firm stand from the Governor, it seemed inevitable that the town would surrender to the monarch.

In Robert's chamber he pored over maps in the fading light, working until his eyes were sore. Dublin brought him a good hot posset to refresh his weary mind.

For once he smiled as he accepted the bowl. Her heart prickled with pleasure and she busied herself by brushing crumbs from the table while he sipped the thick frothy liquid.

After a while he said, 'I hear that at Mr Hampden's request, Mr Pym has personally written to Governor Hotham asking him to be patient until Parliament can send money.'

Dublin waited. Often he used her as an echo for his thoughts, bouncing ideas off her as one might a ball from a wall, to see how it came back. The name of Mr Pym was a familiar one.

He continued, 'I am glad I wrote to Colonel Hampden. A man like Governor Hotham is likely to go to the highest bidder, but a letter from someone as exalted as Pym will keep him loyal for a while longer, at least.' After a moment he added: 'If Hull falls to the King, I could lose my head.'

Remembering her wish to destroy the letter, Dublin's heart jolted. Seeing her shocked face, Robert shook his head. 'Fear not, child. I believe God has other plans for me before I leave this earth.'

'I'm not a child, and I wouldn't want to live if you died.'

He shook his head, smiling as at a youngster's foolishness. 'You have a long life ahead of you too. God must have had some purpose in saving you at Carrickmain.'

'It was you who saved me.'

He moved back. 'I did. But I am the instrument of His will.' She could tell that he was growing ill at ease with the intimacy of the conversation. He became brusque. 'Come along now, I still have work to do.'

Reluctantly she picked up the empty bowl and left the room. In her heart she felt that her jealousy had nearly cost him his life. Never again would she disobey him, no matter what it cost.

Spring came early that year of 1643. The weather was mild and fresh, a symbol of hope, but any hope of negotiating a treaty with the King was finally abandoned. Only outright victory would now do. Old Obidiah came to seek Dublin out.

'We'em leaving here, Missy.'

She waited, stunned by the news, unable to work out what it meant for her.

'Master's been given a commission. Lord Essex hisself has offered him a captaincy. He's to serve in the Regiment of Cuirassiers.'

'Cuirassiers?'

'Cavalrymen. Heavy cavalry. Part of my Lord's bodyguard.' The old man tutted with pleasure at the thought. 'Each man wears plate armour and a closed helmet. They look just like lobsters.' He gave a little chuckle, then with unexpected intuition added:

'Master'll be safe as a fortress. That armour weighs heavy but it can stop a pistol-shot at point blank range. No need to worry about him.'

Dublin flushed, suspecting that the old man read her thoughts. She asked: 'Do we return south?'

'Aye. With God's blessing we might see our kin.'

'Are we all going?'

'We are.'

At the thought of leaving the familiarity of Hull, anxiety welled up in her. Once away from here she might be consigned to the service of some other family member, while Robert continued to risk his life in the conflict. The thought of being separated from him filled her with pain, and to her shame she began to snivel like a gutter rat.

'Now then, young Dublin, no need to distress yourself.' Obidiah gave her an awkward pat on the arm.

'You'll be pleased to see your wife,' she said in an effort to stop crying.

'I will. I reckon the Captain'll be glad to get home too.'

'Where does his betrothed reside?' Whatever the answer, she knew it would twist a sword in her heart.

'Her folks come from Great Hampden, somewhere in Buckingham, though I heard they was in London. Her father's a fine man.'

She struggled with her jealousy.

After a moment he said: 'I reckon she'll be glad to have him back.'

Until this moment Dublin had not thought that Mary Hampden might have feelings for her betrothed. The realisation that her rival was a real woman, with passions and perhaps good looks and wit, threw her into confusion.

'Cheer up, gal. You look like you said a prayer and found the Devil listening.' Obidiah went to leave but not before adding: 'Reckon you're getting to be quite a young woman. We should have a word with the Captain. It's time he found you a soldier boy of your own.'

'I don't want a soldier boy!'

He smiled. 'Never mind, we'll be out of this place in a few days.'

On the evening before they left, Dublin packed everything into bundles and piled it ready at the door to be loaded into the baggage train. She felt empty, desolate. Suddenly this house and its dusty rooms seemed like the perfect home.

The latch clicked open and Robert came in from a last-minute sortie, to check that all was ready. He struggled out of his buff coat and flung it along the bench then sat down in the only chair.

'This time tomorrow we shall be on our way.'

She tried to read something into the remark but it sounded matter of fact. She asked: 'Do you go to Chertsey?'

He shook his head. 'We are charged to join Lord Essex straight away at Reading.'

The name meant nothing to her. Instead she wanted to ask if by 'we' he meant her as well. She sought in vain for the right question and then blurted out: 'Shall I still be your servant?'

He rested one leg across his knee and leaned back. She could not look at him. After an eternity he said: 'This is a war. Who can tell what will happen: I have something for you.'

Her heart quickened at the thought of a keepsake and she looked up to meet his intelligent brown eyes. The kindness in them weakened her waning resolve and she could hardly restrain herself from going to him. Swallowing hard, she waited to see what he would give her, then he said: 'Down in the passageway, with the baggage. I have found you a tent.'

A stab of disappointment greeted his words. She had hoped for some stone or bauble to wear on her bodice, a statement of his devotion.

'You don't look pleased.'

'I thank you.'

He smiled. 'It might sound a strange gift but from now on we will be nomads, and a safe, dry place to sleep is the best present there is.'

'I thank you,' she repeated.

'Right. Get you to bed then. We must be early on the road.' Still the forlorn hope remained that on this, their last night, he might keep her with him but already he was on his feet and waiting for her to leave. With heavy heart she went for the last time to her attic bed.

Chapter 20

The journey south from Hull was long and tedious. Bad roads, bad weather and uncertainty added to the general misery of the Parliamentary troops. The party was as slow as the slowest ox-cart, and all the while the talk was of skirmishes and ambush and the big showdown to come when they reached Reading.

As Dublin walked the weary miles with the baggage train, she was ever aware of the dangers. When they set out, soldiers were to the fore and rear of them, but the luggage convoy grew increasingly sluggish and soon it was left further and further behind.

When her feet grew too sore to carry her, Dublin clambered onto the overloaded wagon, squeezing herself into the tiniest of spaces, but the jolting and swaying was such that walking was the lesser of two evils. Meanwhile, at any time a Royalist force might find them out and scatter their troops, pillaging their supplies and doing unspeakable things to the women. The spectre of Carrickmain haunted her every unguarded moment.

Each night scouts went ahead to find good quarters. Sometimes there was a village where they might stay. At other times they slept in the open with only sentries for protection. On these occasions Dublin felt a cocoon of comfort, sheltering in the tent that was Robert's parting gift. It was like wrapping his love around her.

The first taste of conflict came when she least expected it. One day, as evening was drawing in, the convoy reached a village somewhere south of Coventry. Dublin was feeling particularly tired and her body ached with some undefined ill that sometimes came to punish her. For once she could not think beyond pitching her tent and having a thick blanket around her.

The convoy came to a halt in a clearing just north of the village. The women stood in a huddle, their heads all turned in the same direction, drawn by the smokey pall that crowned the jumbled houses ahead. Down there would be warmth and hot food. Before anybody could make a move however, a message was shouted back from the vanguard: 'The Royalists are here!'

Dublin went cold. Her already shivery limbs threatened to give way beneath her. A fight was imminent and she could not bear the thought of the outcome.

'Nothing to fear, Missy.' Obidiah came up to stand beside her, drawn as if by magic to calm her terrors. ''Tis just a few old soldiers settling themselves in. They don't know we're here yet. We'll soon root 'em out.'

His down-to-earth assurance soothed away the fear.

As Dublin watched, her hand clutching the stuff of her bodice, the Parliament's troops marched systematically into the cottages and began to drag the Royalists out. Obidiah was right. They were a small party, surprised and outnumbered.

Waiting in the drizzle, dazed by cold and damp, Dublin felt like a watcher at a stage performance. On this of all occasions she should indeed be afraid, but now she wasn't. At that moment she had infinite faith in their invincible army. Obidiah had once told her how as a child, he and his brothers often poached rabbits from a landlord's warren. Under cover of night they would send in dogs to scatter the quarry, driving them into nets where they squealed and struggled to free themselves. Now their men stole into the houses, human terriers, sending the King's men running out into the arms of the cavalry. Soon the Royalists were routed, racing back into the countryside. The Roundhead party took their places in the cottages and huts.

Seeing that Robert was surrounded by soldiers, Dublin suppressed the wild hope that she might take the same lodgings, and instead found shelter in a roomy, draught-proof cottage, along with two wives of regular soldiers. Stoical, weather-beaten, the two women had much experience of days like today. Their acceptance calmed her. The remains of a fire still smouldered in the centre of the room and they soon found sticks and teased it into life. Crowding round for warmth, their clothes steamed in the tepid glow.

It was some time before the owner of the cottage made an

appearance. She came shuffling into the kitchen without looking at them and began to add more wood to the fire. She was neither young nor old but her face was pinched and she had the air of one who is indifferent to her fate. All this while she had been hiding, waiting to see the outcome of the scuffle. Her manner was sullen and it dawned on Dublin that no matter which army stayed, it would cost her dear. In an attempt to make conversation, she asked: 'Is your husband with the militia?'

'My man was killed.'

'God rest his soul.' She resisted the urge to cross herself, adding: 'I pray it was not the Parliament men who took his life.'

The woman sniffed and wiped her nose on her sleeve. 'Parliament, King, it makes no difference.'

Dublin felt confusion. She wanted to believe that Robert's cause was just, but even she could see that sometimes it served innocent people ill. What meaning had the war for this poor woman? Tonight they took the very bed she had shared with her man, and what would they leave her in return? The army carried no money, and a promissory note to pay for food and lodging was hardly worth the ink used to write it. She wondered if this was how it was destined to be.

A raiding party returned after dark with four sound horses and some two dozen sheep. The villagers were then conscripted to the ovens to bake sufficient loaves. Late that night the convoy ate well of bread and mutton. Dublin made sure that the widow had a share.

Early next morning they were on the road again. Dublin was glad to get away from the two army wives. Their inquisitive eyes bored into her like wasp stings. Spiteful tongues had gossiped. Silences had spoken volumes. She knew that they had branded her a doxy, a woman with no man of her own, but available to any who would take her. Thinking of Robert and the purity of her love, she dimissed them with contempt.

As they continued south, the uncertainty of the future preoccupied her to the exclusion of most things. Round and about other women travelled, some with children, following their menfolk wherever the war took them. It seemed strange to her that they should put their infants to such hardship but in answer to her question, one of them said: 'My man was in the cells. We had no place to go. Compared to that, this life is a paradise. I've got clothes and good vittals.'

144

She held out the skirts of her thick worsted gown and wrapped her shawl closer about her. Dublin wondered if she had taken them from some place where they had been quartered. Killing, stealing – one by one, all the Commandments were being broken in the name of a just war.

In her arms the woman carried a babe of no more than a few months, and two other tots, perhaps of three or four years, clung to her skirts. She looked old to be the mother of such children, her face yellow and lined where privation had taken its toll. Her name was Polly Cranford.

Walking with her, Dublin became aware of the increased number of people converging just ahead of them. Their party, perhaps two hundred souls when they left Hull, was nearer now to a thousand. They had nearly reached Reading.

Scouts were sent ahead to see how things stood and soon the news was passed along the lines. Some ten days before, on 15 April, Lord Essex with several thousand men had laid siege to the town. His men now camped in great numbers on each side of the river, waiting for the Governor to see sense and surrender.

There was no sign of Robert or Obidiah. The women started to set up camp on the outskirts and Dublin attached herself to Polly Cranford. The woman having no shelter of her own, Dublin invited her into her tent.

'You're kind,' Polly said. 'How are you called?'

She hesitated. Long ago on the other side of the Irish Sea, there had been Sorcha O'Neill. That name belonged to another girl, another time before Robert Hammond came to the rescue at Carrickmain. An English name would have been safer, but it was what Robert called her that mattered.

'Dublin.'

'You're a Papist?'

That question again. That was what Caleb had said to her that very first day, warning her to take care. She remembered that he had shown no hatred for her on account of her religion. Caleb Gosden. She shook the thought of him off. In any case, she was no longer a Catholic. Her allegiance was to whatever cause, or faith Robert espoused. Aloud she said: 'My master, Captain Hammond of Lord Essex's own bodyguard, has instilled in me true Christian values.'

'You have a man in the regiment?'

145

'I am here as servant to my master.'

Polly nodded philosophically. 'Praise God this war will soon be over and then perhaps my man will get a pension, or regular work.'

Now that the subject had changed, Dublin felt on safer ground. She asked: 'Where are you from?'

'London.'

Her voice was nearly drowned as a volley of shot rang out in the distance. Musket-fire was a familiar sound but there was something about the volume and rapidity of this cacophony that made them both stop.

'What's happening?' Dublin scrambled up and outside. About half a mile away, a pall of smoke and the report of muskets underlined the deeper boom of cannon.

As they strained their ears to listen, the shouts of men reached them, their cries heightened by fear or excitement. When the smoke parted it revealed distant figures hurrying in all directions. The centre of their activity was the bridge.

Polly grabbed her children and held them close. Her face was stiff with alarm and she frowned into the distance as if by so doing she might make out the very faces of the men. 'God help us.'

Moments later a troop of soldiers marched by.

'Where do you go?' Dublin called out, caught up in the excitement.

'Caversham Bridge. The King has come to relieve Reading.'

Helplessly the two women stayed where they were, spectators at another peepshow.

'My man,' Polly whispered.

Dublin said nothing. She had her own nightmares.

The battle raged at Caversham Bridge and Dublin stayed rooted to the turf outside her tent. Polly Cranford had her little ones to nurse. Dublin had only her fear.

They could see nothing through the dense smoke, but their ears gave them clues as to what passed at the river. The cries of men and horses painted pictures more terrible than any witnessed with the eye.

Late that afternoon, news reached them that the King's forces were repulsed. Dublin felt as if a garrotte had been whisked away from her throat and she was near floating with emotion, but the initial euphoria soon turned to dread. Men began to drift back to the camp and it was clear that there had been many casualties. There was no sign of Robert. The garrotte was back in place.

'I must go.'

Polly looked at her. 'Where to?'

'To see that my master is safe – his servant, too.'

Polly glanced round quickly then called the children to her. 'I'll come with you, to find Amos.' Dublin's own fear was reflected in the other woman's eyes.

Struggling against the tide of soldiers the sight that greeted them turned their hearts to ice. Men lay in extreme distress, some along the route where they had been placed to await help, others where they had fallen, nearer to the bridge.

At a glance it was not possible to know whose men they were. Already some of the Roundhead soldiers were going amongst them and if they could not give an account of themselves, they began to strip them, taking anything of value. Dublin watched in disbelief as they took one protesting prisoner and threw him, wounded and bloody, into the river. His screams were like to freeze the waters before they gurgled to a chilling end.

'No!' She started forward to help him although she could not swim, but the troops had the look of crazy men and to defy them would have brought disaster. For a while she stood helplessly, watching the spot where his head had last broken the surface of the water. There was nothing. Shaking with disgust, she moved on.

Soon it was impossible to go any further. The bridge was securely guarded by the Earl of Essex's men and the sheer press of numbers made it impossible to advance. Behind Dublin, Polly called out, anxious for the safety of her little ones.

Reluctantly Dublin turned back and at that moment Polly let out a scream that would freeze hell.

'God have mercy! No!!' She began to wail and twist as if in a trap.

'What is it?'

Her little ones stood frozen beside her and the babe joined in her lament.

'No!!' she cried again. 'Please, God, no!'

Dublin followed her glance and her stomach retched with disgust at the sight of a man twisted awkwardly at the foot of a tree. His face was the most hideous spectacle, having been blown away

147

by a musketball. By some cruel blow of Fate his eyes, pale blue and staring as if startled literally out of his head, hung forward upon the angry flesh that had once been his cheeks. His jaw hung by a thread, swinging with a grotesque grin.

'No-oo!' Polly rocked herself like a lunatic.

'Is he . . .?' Dublin glanced again at the creature but could not bear to look on him.

'Amos.' Polly fell to her knees and began to pray, abasing herself to entreat her god to change what she had just seen. All the while the creature was making a terrible noise through the hole that had once been his mouth.

Dublin did not know what to do. It took all her courage not to run away. Instead she put her arms about the woman and her children, gathering them all close. 'You are sure it is him?'

'They're his clothes, the colour of his hair.' His wife turned her head a fraction but could look no further. 'He has a finger missing, on his right hand.'

Drawing in her breath, Dublin went closer, almost tiptoeing so that the injured wretch should not feel her presence and call out for help. He continued to grunt to himself, thankfully unaware of her approach. She took another deep breath, bent down and looked at the wretch's hand. His fingers were clenched around a pole as if in the rigor of death but all the while he was mumbling and exuding pink dribble from the gash in his face.

Dublin's hand shook so much that she could scarce touch him but she forced myself to turn the hand enough to reveal the stunted finger. Its soft human warmth only added to her outrage. 'I'll get help,' she said uselessly.

Turning back she stood with no idea what to do. Polly now moved towards him. Smoothing down her hair, bodice and skirts as if she were making herself beautiful for her lover, she pushed the little ones behind her and walked across to the tree.

'Amos, my heart, there's nothing to fear. It's me, Polly. I'll have you well in days.'

The poor creature continued to burble and dribble, and watching, tears flowed down Dublin's shocked and helpless cheeks.

A moment later someone touched her arm. 'Praise God you're safe.'

She could only look into his healing brown eyes. 'Ro . . .' She nearly called him by name.

148

If he had fought in armour, he had removed it and now wore the familiar buff coat against which she had once, so long ago, rested her cheek.

'You aren't hurt?' He stepped back to look her over and she shook her head, pointing with her eyes to the horror beneath the tree.

'That's her man.'

His face tightened but he walked calmly over and bent down beside the woman and her husband.

Gently he patted her on the shoulder and Dublin could feel that pressure on her own flesh. He said: 'I'll get a surgeon,' then to Dublin: 'Stay with her. I'll be back.'

Dublin's mind had now grown numb to everything outside herself. She waited near to Polly, not looking at her, not looking at him. With selfish guilt she felt only relief that Robert was alive, not desecrated like Polly's man. There was no sense to it.

At last Robert returned with a companion. The man carried a leather bag which he placed on the ground beside Amos Cranford but it was clear from his expression that he did not know what to do. Finally he took a flask of wine and poured some into the hole in what had once been a face. The poor wretch gagged and struggled but finally allowed the liquid to funnel down his throat. Much of it ran over the parody of his features, cleaning the ravaged flesh.

The surgeon then proceeded to bandage him, lifting the jaw back into roughly the place it had once been, easing the eyes back into the sockets and leaving space for air and liquid to reach him. When the face was decently covered he looked round at Robert and shrugged.

Robert turned reverently towards Polly. 'Do you wish to have him with you?' he asked.

She was too stunned to know.

'I'll help her look after him.' Dublin wondered at the voice which had escaped from her lips. How she would bring herself to do so, she did not know.

'You are sure?' He gazed long and hard at her and she drew strength from him.

'Will he live?'

Robert looked at the surgeon for confirmation. The man shrugged again. 'Not if he's lucky.'

149

Polly was now kneeling beside her man, holding his hand, crooning to him in a gentle monotone. Beside her, the little ones scraped up handfuls of pebbles and built a castle. The baby slept.

Dublin looked at Robert to find him watching her. 'You are a brave girl. I'll send food and blankets and wine for you all. If the task becomes too much, then I'll have him moved to the town. We'll pay someone there to care for him.'

'You aren't hurt?'

'No.' He smiled. 'This town will fall any day now. Then I'll be moving on, perhaps to London.' He met her eyes. 'This life isn't good for you. It's time you were settled somewhere.'

The panic at the thought of losing him was lessened by a frail hope as she remembered what Polly had told her. 'That family come from London. I could travel with them, see them back home.'

He nodded. 'So be it. When they get back I will make sure that they have sufficient means to survive.' He met her eyes again. 'Then we must think on your own safety.'

Safety had no meaning for her except at his side, but she remained silent.

With a nod he stretched wearily and took a step back. 'I must go. There is much to be done.'

She asked: 'Have you seen Obidiah?'

He shook his head. 'Pray God he is safe.'

Pray God, indeed.

Against all nature, Amos Cranford remained alive. Lying in the dark at night, Dublin had terrifying dreams about his injuries, how the flesh beneath the bandages putrefied and fell from his bones. Her stomach churned at the imagined stench of rancid meat. Whenever possible she stayed outside, driven from the tent by her own imagination.

Meanwhile, Polly sat with him day and night, answering the dreadful distorted noises he made as if she understood their meaning. Dublin busied herself with other tasks, collecting firewood, going for the rations – a penny loaf, a piece of meat and some barley each. With this she made broth and watched in macabre fascination as the other woman spooned it into the maw beneath the mask.

'That's the way, Amos, we'll soon have you better.'

Then: 'Do you think he'll live?' she would ask the surgeon for perhaps the hundredth time.

'It is in God's hands.'

Polly tended him as if he were beautiful and precious; at the thought of Robert hurt and helplessly dependent upon her, Dublin's heart grew tight. She would gladly give her life to care for him. It was then that she understood how Polly felt.

In the meantime, Robert's prediction proved right and Reading surrendered. The Reading garrison was offered safe passage back to Oxford but things soon went disastrously wrong. Having no pay and little prospect of any, the Parliamentary forces decided to celebrate victory in their own way. Unchecked, they stormed into the town and began to plunder.

As the garrison went to move out, the victors fell upon them and stripped them of everything they owned, sometimes even the decency of cover. A torrent of heady abuse fell upon the vanquished. The Earl of Essex and his officers seemed powerless to stop it.

Stores of wine were uncovered and the troops became increasingly wild. They set about systematically ransacking the houses, driving the occupants out into the streets and killing on a whim – that man's nose is too big, cut it off . . .

When Robert returned to the camp, Dublin told him how Amos Cranford still hung onto life. He praised her for her dedication and she felt like a cheat, not daring to tell him how she really felt. Instead she diverted her thoughts to safer ground. 'The troops are still rioting?'

He sighed ponderously. 'They are. We did not act fast enough to prevent it. It must not be allowed to happen again, but you can understand their actions.'

She raised her eyebrows in surprise, not believing that he could approve. Sensing her shock, he continued: 'Once I would have thought like you, but war teaches us many things. Not long ago these men were face to face with death. Now they have before them food and clothing and treasures for the taking. They might never again lay hands on such things. Who can blame them if they choose to live for today?'

Dublin knew there was some injustice here. 'The people in the town did not choose to take sides,' she said. 'Yet it is they who suffer.'

151

He nodded. 'You are right, it is so. That is the harsh truth of war, the innocent always suffer. A few of our men have been strung up for disobeying orders, but it has had little effect on the others.'

He suddenly looked so drained that she risked touching his hand, for a terrible moment remembering the warm feel of Amos Cranford's clenched fist. To shut it out, she asked: 'Where do we go next?'

Robert seemed to shake off his gloom. 'I have been charged to take a report to Colonel Hampden. I shall tell him how it went here and also that we most urgently need money. At the moment we can barely afford bread or fodder. All the coats and boots need replacing and many of the horses are without shoes.' She listened intently, trying not to think of John Hampden's daughter, defying herself to confuse Robert's duty with his desire. He continued: 'Colonel Hampden can relay the request to Mr Pym and then on to the Parliament.'

'Shall we travel together?' She willed it to be so. Her question was an attempt to predict the future. If it were otherwise then surely Robert was abandoning her in favour of her rival.

'We shall. There is no sign of Obidiah.'

Her immediate elation was deflated and she felt a pang of fear at the thought of the old man alone. 'Do you think he's safe?'

'Pray God that he is.' He made ready to leave.

Not wanting to be parted from him, Dublin asked: 'When do we go?'

'On the morrow. The Cranfords will travel with us and you can help them. The main army are moving on towards Oxford and I shall join them as soon as I can.'

At this point her courage failed her and she did not ask what would then become of her. It was better to live in hope, than to ask and be vanquished.

Chapter 21

London was visible long before they reached it, a distant jumble of orange-pink haze. Roofs, chimneys, awesome spires . . . all fought for supremacy. From a distance it was hard to imagine that there were roads and squares and dwellings within such a contorted mass. The whole was topped by static palls of smoke so that one could smell it long before setting foot within its boundaries.

They came in via Holburn Street, and crossed the Fleet over a congested bridge. Reaching New Gate, they were admitted through the City walls. Robert had all the necessary documentation and there was the merest delay before they set off again. Somewhere along Candlewick Street, they turned sharply towards the river and down a warren of lanes in search of the Cranfords' home.

The spring sunshine that had bathed them since leaving Reading was blocked out now by overhanging buildings, all jammed together in chaotic disorder. Underfoot, filth and excrement sent up a bad but familiar stench. Only a few, defiant nosegays reminded them that it was May Day.

With a start, Dublin realised that it was a year to this very day that she had made her escape from Wolverton, only to end up at the bothy with Caleb. Without thinking, she reached down and touched her ankle, rubbing the tiny scars which Caleb had so gently treated. She thought of his 'good' face, compassionate, tender and her mind was filled with unnamed regrets.

Coming back to the present, she watched anew the thronging mass of city-dwellers going about their business. This overcrowded, smelly place could equally have been her eponymous city – one poverty was much like another.

153

Finally crossing the Ropery, they reached a jumble of dilapidated huts. This was the aptly named Chepeside.

'That's where we live.' Polly looked anxiously along the row of dwellings and gave an audible sigh of relief. 'There is no need to worry, Amos. Praise God, it looks as if our place has not been taken.'

Amos Cranford continued to mumble unintelligibly. The journey had been like purgatory, for each time the ox-cart hit a rut, and that was every few yards, he had groaned out his pain. Dublin imagined that the tender flesh must burn with torment at the lightest touch even from the protective bandages. It would be such a relief to be freed from the burden of his suffering.

'We'll manage,' Polly said as Robert and the carter placed him on the earth floor of the foetid lean-to. He lay whimpering on some old sacks and to Dublin's relief, they made ready to leave. Neither man said anything but she guessed that like her, they were anxious to be released.

Polly's face was taut with worry but she turned and took Dublin's hands. 'I'll miss you, Dublin. God go with you. You have been kindness itself.'

The guilt of her true feelings weighed Dublin down and she felt a sense of betrayal at leaving them in this evil-smelling place.

'We'll meet again,' she said, knowing that they probably wouldn't. As recompense for her weakness she took off her shawl and wrapped it around Polly's shoulders.

'Oh, I couldn't.'

'Then use it for the children.' Dublin hugged her, feeling the fragile skeleton beneath the skinny flesh, then with the merest hesitation, she patted Amos on the hand.

'God go with you.'

Robert stood behind her. Part of her seemed to have a will of its own and wanted only to lean back against him. Fearing his rejection, she forced herself to move away.

'This is to tide you over.' He handed Polly some coins. From their sound, they were gold. 'And this is where a message can be left. If you need help then let me know.'

His kindness to the Cranfords added to Dublin's yearning. Here he was, a man of noble birth, yet he concerned himself with the welfare of this poor, peasant family. Then she remembered how he had cared for her and a strange mixture of tenderness and regret

154

mingled in her heart. She did not want to be reminded that like Polly Cranford, she was only a humble peasant.

They drove back the way they had come, with Dublin perched in the back of the wagon, while Robert rode on ahead on his mare. As they squeezed their way past piles of filth and between scattering pigs and geese, she wished that she could sit behind him on the mare and clasp her hands around his waist as she had on that first, momentous journey to the Isle of Wight. Such daydreams made the jolting of the cart more tolerable.

Suddenly the chaos of Chepeside was left behind them. With the river glimpsed only along narrow alleyways, they began to pass by mansions which dwarfed even the house at Wolverton. Dublin wondered who could live in such splendour and when Robert reined in briefly to wait for them, she asked him, wanting to keep him near.

'That,' he said, 'is where my godfather, the Earl of Essex, has his London dwelling.' She could think of nothing to say. The opulence left her overwhelmed.

'Where do we go now, master?' the carter called out.

'West Minster. We'll be staying at the house of the Hampdens.'

This news hit Dublin like musketshot. He was going to see his betrothed! Her face suffused with jealous blood and she crushed her hands together to calm her turmoil, wondering how he could humiliate her by taking her to the very house.

For a brass farthing she would have leaped from the cart and run off down an alleyway, anywhere to get away from the knowledge that he was going to his future wife, but she sat there, leadenly. No matter how desperate matters seemed, there was nothing to do but stay, for how else would she find a way to set him free? Perhaps she could slay the other woman – challenge her to a duel as jealous suitors might do. Then in spite of herself, she could not stop the awful doubts – supposing he did not *wish* to be released?

The Hampden house was square and stonebuilt. As with those houses they had passed along the Stronde, there was space and quiet and fresh air. At the entrance, Robert reined in and waited for them to catch up.

'You, Tom, take the cart and the mare and get them stabled,' he said, and turning to Dublin: 'And you'd better come with me.'

She scowled at him, doubly ashamed of her stained skirts and the grey bands of her collar. Her hair was all afuzz and she felt dirty, ugly, common. How could he humiliate her by parading her thus before her rival?

Grabbing her bundle, Dublin jumped sullenly from the cart and shrunk back behind him. He was looking up at the windows of the house and she knew that he only had eyes for the wealthy woman inside.

The door was opened by a servant and they were shown into an entrance way from which a solid stairway led off to a gallery above. Candles burned in braziers attached to the walls. They sent out a liquid glow. Dublin wondered if they were gold. The heavy dark table in the entrance way had intricately carved legs, oak leaves and acorns climbing up its sturdy limbs, solid, opulent, and on the floor was a rug, woven in rich blues and burgundies. This place was as grand as a cathedral.

In the waning tide of light, Dublin kept close behind her master, hoping that no one would cart her off to the kitchens. She could not have borne the shame.

'Robin!' It was a man who came to meet them, slender of stature, brown of hair and eye, with a long thin face, impressive in his bearing.

'Mr Hampden, sir.' Robin bowed his head in respect and the older man took his arm.

'Come along in. No need for formality. We are not soldiers here but kinsmen. Come, I pray you, take some sack and tell me all the news.'

Like a shadow, Dublin followed behind, willing herself to be invisible. It did not work.

'Who is this?' Mr Hampden cast shrewd eyes over her and to her shame, she blushed.

'One of my servants. I came across her in Ireland and somehow Fate seems to have decreed that she should travel with my party.'

Dublin's legs were almost betraying her and she huddled her bundle close to her chest and prepared to resist any attempt to take her away, ready to shout out loud and tell them that he was hers. Any rich, spoilt lady who thought she could have him by right of her position had another think coming.

Mr Hampden looked uneasily at her. 'Is an Irish servant wise? There are spies galore. A Popish girl sounds a dangerous travelling companion.'

Robert shook his head. 'She cares for me. She would do me no

156

harm.' He spoke with such confidence that some of Dublin's bitterness evaporated.

Leaving her to stand where she was, the men seated themselves on each side of the fireplace and began to talk. Dublin was so preoccupied with her feelings that she heard little of what their host had to say.

In his turn, Robert told of the siege at Reading, and of the looting, and Lord Essex's desperate need for money and equipment.

'It is the same from all sides,' Mr Hampden observed. 'There's hardly a horse to be had, for every animal has been taken for the cavalry, and fuel is like gold.'

Dublin stared fixedly at the ground and wondered what God would accept in exchange for letting her wash and change into a clean gown and dress her hair.

A knock at the door caused all three of them to start.

'Enter.' The latch was lifted and the door pushed inwards. The recent damp had swollen the wood and it dragged harshly across the floorboards.

'Mary! See, here is Robert come to visit us.' Mr Hampden turned in his chair and beckoned his daughter over.

Dublin felt black with spite, having difficulty in controlling her jealous breath. She kept her eyes lowered so that her enemy would not have the advantage of ignoring her. A slight figure moved past her and made a modest curtsy. Now that her back was towards Dublin, the Irish girl looked up, boring her hatred into the other girl's spine.

'Mary, praise God that we all meet again in good health.' Robert rose to his feet and bowed formally over her hand.

Now Dublin stood upright and stared unabashed at the creature before her. Small, compact, very straight-backed, her hair beneath her cap the same colour as her father's . . . Dublin looked in disbelief at Mary Hampden. Her feared and hated rival was all of twelve years old!

Dublin's initial euphoria at finding that Robert's betrothed was only a child, ebbed away as she realised in what high esteem her father was held.

After some little time the three of them were joined by a fourth person. He knocked briefly on the door panel and walked in without waiting. Both Robert and Colonel Hampden stood up.

'Robin, this is my kinsman, Oliver Cromwell. Like you he is here to impress upon the Parliament the need for equipment and money.'

Robert took the man's hand. Other than being dark of hair, Mr Hampden and his cousin did not favour each other. Mr Cromwell was a big man, swarthy of complexion, jowly, and not of the cleanest disposition, but his manner and the confidence with which he discussed affairs of the country, marked him out as being of importance.

'Hammond, I have heard very good reports of you. I hear you conduct yourself bravely in times of danger.'

Robert's face flushed with pleasure and Dublin warmed towards this visitor. Robert said: 'My only wish is to see a noble end to this conflict, sir. To see the King back where he belongs.'

Mr Cromwell inclined his head and his expression was hard to read. Then he said: 'I fear that unless we have a military victory, the King will not be persuaded to yield,' with the briefest hesitation adding: 'If it be God's will then victory will be ours, King or no King.'

'Surely you wish for a peaceful settlement?' Robert's face was guarded.

'My cousin is of the view that a bad king is worse than no king,' Mr Hampden said.

Mr Cromwell bowed his head. 'Indeed I wish for a speedy settlement, but I have to say that if I came upon His Majesty in the heat of battle and it should prove necessary, I would not hesitate to shoot him as I might any other private person.'

'You would kill the King? That is not why I am fighting this war!'

Dublin felt Robert's shock and her own pulse increased in sympathy. The English King had little meaning for her, but in the context of right and wrong, clearly Robert knew best.

'You fight to rescue him.' Mr Cromwell answered Robert's question with a statement. There was something about his expression that implied he thought her master to be an innocent. With a wry smile he went on, 'I honour your noble sentiments, but whatever Our Lord wills, I shall obey. Only God's laws are clear. Be true to those and you cannot then be wrong.'

Robert still looked uneasy and Mr Cromwell continued, 'At the moment East Anglia is ours. We need to move west now, fast,

158

consolidate our gains and close on Oxford. Only when our sovereign has no other option, will he accept our terms.'

Discussion of the war and affairs of Parliament continued. Dublin noticed that covertly, Robert continued to scrutinise Mr Cromwell. She could not interpret his expression.

In the meantime she had more important things to consider. Mary stood very still between Robert and her cousin, Mr Cromwell. From her demeanour she seemed to know all about the conduct of this war. It was little wonder that Robert welcomed a union with such a family.

But Dublin's earlier despair had ebbed away. She knew now that it was not possible for him to love this child. Dublin was three years her senior at the very least. The feelings she nurtured for him were those of a woman, and somehow soon she had to ensure that he began to think of her as such.

Her reverie was interrupted by someone calling her name.

'Dublin, go along now. You will be given shelter and clean clothes and perhaps you can help with the duties.'

Her face grew red again. Robert was waiting for her to move and she felt ashamed to be ordered around in front of this girl, who was now looking at her with curious brown eyes. Dublin hated her mild expression. But worse was to come. As she bowed her head so that her resentment should not be seen, Robert added: 'I think it would be wise for all concerned if, when I leave here, my servant could remain behind.'

'No!'

All eyes turned upon her. There was rebuke on the face of the two older men and Mary merely looked fascinated. Robert gave a deprecating laugh.

'Please excuse her. She lost her family at Carrickmain. Since then she has been part of my train.' To Dublin he said, 'I am not asking you, I am *telling* you that you shall remain here.'

With a glance at Mary, he added, 'Perhaps you could look after Dublin, my dear – teach her how to conduct herself.'

The young girl smiled, sure of herself, anxious to please him and Dublin was assailed by defeated tears.

'Don't cry,' Mary Hampden said. 'God will protect you. You will be safe here. I have five sisters and three brothers. The house is always full of people.'

Dublin fought back her weakness and refused to look at

anyone, least of all her rival. Feeling the weight of defeat on her shoulders, she turned and followed Mary Hampden to the door. The whiff of herbs from the stuff of her dress contrasted with Dublin's own travel-stained self and only added to her sense of failure.

As they went to leave the room, Robert stepped forward and caught Dublin's arm. 'Don't grieve, child. Believe me, I do not wish to leave you behind. In all conscience though, I cannot risk your life by trailing you round the countryside.'

'But I want to come . . .'

'No! You stay.'

She pulled her arm free and straightened her back so as not to give them the pleasure of seeing her anguish. She was aware that Robert looked embarrassed by her conduct, but as she turned to follow her enemy from the room, he quietly added: 'Remember that your behaviour is a reflection upon me – so serve me well.'

She was already halfway across the hall when he added something else. Although she hesitated, it was too late and she could not be sure what it was, but it sounded like: 'And never forget that I shall miss you.' She hoped with all her heart that her ears had not played her false.

Chapter 22

The Hampden household was not as Dublin imagined. Although the house itself was large and there were clearly masters and servants, the children of the family had their duties as did the lowliest of scullions. Dublin too, was expected to play her part.

The domestic arrangements were in the charge of Mary's stepmother, Mistress Letitia. She was Mr Hampden's second wife. Although she had borne him no children, by his first wife he had produced nine, of which Mary was the sixth. Her sisters, Ruth and Anne and a young son, William, were at the London house, while two older children were away from home altogether and the remainder stayed in the family house at Great Hampden.

Dublin discovered all of this in the first few minutes of being alone with her rival. Seemingly unaware of any hostility, Mary talked incessantly as she led the way into the hall and then up the stairs to the gallery above. Dublin followed her around three of the four sides, past portraits of relatives and ancestors, and then stopped outside one of the many identical, panelled doors.

Dublin was prepared to be difficult and to find fault with everything, but to her surprise she found herself taken directly to Mary's bedchamber.

'You will share with me.' She opened the door and stepped back to let Dublin see inside. The room was beautiful, fully-panelled, with a large, deep window and velvet drapes. The warmth of the wooden floor was further enhanced by a rug in blues and creams, and the chamber itself was dominated by an ornately carved, pillared bed, with drapes that matched the window covers. Hangings on the walls portrayed rural scenes and Dublin almost felt herself to be in the countryside.

'My bed is large,' Mary said. 'It is part of my dowry. It will go with me when I marry.' She walked across to the window and seated herself in the deep recess. Silhouetted there she looked calm and confident and suddenly older than her twelve years. She continued: 'There is plenty of room for two here and we can talk together. Is it true that you come from Ireland?'

Dublin had no wish to talk with her at all, and certainly not about her origins. The thought of this as Robert's marriage bed made her rage inside. Aloud, she said: 'I remember nothing of Ireland. My life began when Master Robert brought me to live with him.'

Mary's expression did not change so she continued, 'My only wish is to serve him.' Anguish bubbled up and she blurted out: 'It's not fair that I should have to stay here!'

Mary continued to stare, offering no response.

'He doesn't want to leave me here, not with you. He's simply afraid for my safety.'

Without speaking, the younger girl crossed the room and opened the door of the armoire which stood along the inside wall. It was high as the ceiling and contained neatly folded piles of blankets and clothing. That same smell of herbs wafted out as she sought among the piles and extracted a grey dress and shift and crisply starched bands. 'Your bag of clothing has been sent to the wash-house. If you would like to refresh yourself . . .' She nodded towards a ewer of water and a basin.

Shamefaced, Dublin accepted the clothes. Mary made no attempt to leave so Dublin untied the laces of her skirts and slipped out of them. Now wearing only a tattered bodice and stained stockings, she threw them off and turned her back.

She was half-ashamed of her nakedness, but a perverse streak told her that she already had a beautiful body. Her breasts were firm and her waist slender, widening to hips that were rounded but not too big. She had started her courses back in Ireland, a lifetime ago, and knew herself to be truly a woman.

'You are very beautiful. Brave too, I think.'

There was no malice in the younger girl's voice, no sarcasm or envy. She spoke with a candour that was confusing. Dublin found it difficult to hate someone who spoke well of her.

'Are you afraid for him?' Dublin blurted out, rubbing the cloth provided under her arms. The cold water felt fresh and soothing.

162

'For my Papa?'

'For Robert.' How could she be so stupid?

'But of course.'

'You must love him.' Dublin ached with envy.

Mary was a long time answering, picking absently at the bed-cover with delicate fingers. 'I hardly know him. Papa arranged our settlement some two years ago. It was Robert's godfather, the Earl of Essex, who acted for him. Papa and the Earl are friends. Robert's father died when he was but ten.'

Dublin wanted to tell her that she knew his family well, his uncles Henry and Thomas of whom he had spoken, and his brother John who was godson of the dead Prince Henry, but she said nothing.

Mary said, 'With six daughters, Papa has been hard-pressed to see us all well provided for. I am sure that Robert will be a good husband.'

Dublin turned round to look at her, wanting to appeal to her to let him go, but the honest, child's face confused her. Instead she said, 'Can you read?'

'Of course, can you?'

Dublin's embarrassment must have shown for her hostess quickly said, 'Then I can teach you. Papa likes us to read from the Bible and I have several other books.' She sank back upon the bed. 'Your hair is the most beautiful I have ever seen,' she confided.

Dublin's spirits lifted and she tugged the comb through her hair until each strand was loose and smooth. 'When will you wed?' she asked, tormenting herself for no good reason.

'On my fourteenth birthday – at least, that was the plan. Now that we are at war it may change. Papa is so much away. He has recruited his own regiment.' She gave a brief smile. 'Papa is so popular where we live, there was little difficulty in getting men to join him. My stepmother grieves because he spends most of his time away, either with the Parliament or with his troops. Tomorrow he goes to see Mr Pym and then the day after, he and his men are leaving to join the Earl of Essex. They will be heading for Oxford.'

'Will Robert go with them?' Dublin's chest tightened at the thought of his imminent departure.

Mary stood up and came across to her. She began to pin the

clean white bands about her guest's throat. Her hands were small and short-fingered and their pressure against Dublin's neck was not unpleasant. Her jealous mind thought that Robert would like the touch of these hands. As Mary fastened the last pin, she stood back and nodded in satisfaction, then said: 'Oh no, Robert is not going with Papa.'

Dublin's relief lasted for the time it took her hostess to add, 'He'll be leaving to join the Earl's bodyguard at first light on the morrow.'

Mary must have seen her alarm, for she said kindly, 'I think you are truly fond of your master. Tonight we will both pray for his safety, his and Papa's. If we ask God to protect them then they will surely be safe.'

In the face of her simple faith Dublin nodded her agreement. In her secret heart the terrors remained.

She did not see Robert depart. In truth she could not have borne to witness his leave-taking from his future bride, or face the risk that he might overlook her. In any event he left early the following day and Tom More, the carter, went with him.

A day later Mr Hampden also left as planned. In the hallway, his wife, daughters and youngest son stood together to receive his blessing. Tenderly he kissed Mistress Hampden, holding tight to her hands and talking quietly so that no other should hear. He finally released her and moved on to Ruth, Anne and Mary, who all curtsied and received his kiss upon the forehead. Each girl cried silent tears. Only young William put on a brave face.

'Farewell, Papa. God go with you!'

'Hurry back, John!'

Dublin could not help but share their pain and this confused her. How was it possible to fight for Robert if she sympathised with her enemies?

She was assailed by a sense of displacement. This house was alien. Of the city of London she had no knowledge other than that brief visit to Chepeside, and England in general was still a dangerous place for an Irish girl to be. She felt betrayed, abandoned and with no energy to fight back. At the same time, some innate sense of survival made her stay quietly at the Hampden house, salting meat, drying and bottling fruit and generally laying up stores for an expected siege. Once again, life was in limbo.

True to her word, the day after Mr Hampden's departure, Mary began to teach Dublin her letters. She was quick to learn and Mary gave her the horn book that had been her own. Dublin feigned indifference, but secretly she longed to master the mysteries of reading and writing. Whenever possible, she went into the garden and painstakingly scratched the letters into the dusty soil. Before long she could write her name.

In her mind, the period spent with the Hampdens seemed to last for a very long time, months, perhaps even years, but later she knew that it could not have been more than six weeks, for two events occurred in June that would stay with her for ever.

Chapter 23

Although Colonel Hampden was away with his regiment, there were so many visitors to the London house that Dublin was never short of news. Hardly a day passed when some story did not reach her of murder, rapine, arson, and infamous acts of betrayal carried out by the King's men.

This knowledge served only to confuse. As far as her understanding went, the King had the loyal support of his Catholic subjects and it was difficult to believe that followers of the true religion, into which she had been born, would act so wickedly. As the rumours persisted however, she grew increasingly to fear and then hate them. Clearly Robert and his Protestant cause must have right on their side. Nothing was what it seemed.

At night she lay awake in the big bed next to Mary and remembered Carrickmain. There, her mother had died at the hands of the invading troops – Robert's troops. Dervla must have suffered, as the English peasants suffered even now. Not knowing of her going was a torture. Dublin's imaginings could not have been worse if she had witnessed what had befallen her mother. She tried to draw comfort from the old beliefs, her mother's acceptance that death was merely a respite, a chance to heal before rebirth in a fresh young body, but her own doubts were too potent. When sleep did come, such terrible rememberings haunted her that she awoke crying and drenched in sweat. There, by her side was Mary.

'Dublin, what is it?'

'It's naught but a bad dream.'

'You were calling on Robert to help you.' Mary waited for an answer but there was none to give. Always, at the memory of what had passed, Dublin's tongue became tied.

She wanted to tell the younger girl that her father had fallen in battle, or been slain afterwards in the bloodlust; that her mother had been violated and murdered. What would she think then, this upright English girl? And what would Mary say if she knew that Dublin had slept in Robert's bed, albeit a makeshift one beneath the hedges, or shared his room at an inn, or bathed his naked body? But it was impossible to tell her these things; they were too private. She also feared that no matter what Mary learned, it would make no difference. A marriage settlement was just that, practical, convenient, for social and economic advancement. A servant's passion would have no place in such considerations.

If Dublin's thoughts were morose, in the city itself things were exceedingly gloomy. There was an outbreak of pestilence which many blamed on the ungodly acts of the army, in this case meaning their own Parliamentary men. As far as the war went, the King seemed to fare the better, although it was hard to believe that God was on his side.

Visitors to the house complained about the latest demand for money to finance the war. It was impossible for anyone to refuse. In the face of monthly and sometimes weekly assessments, they felt that the past injustices of the King's demands now seemed insignificant. There were still those in the city who were loyal to Charles and fears grew that they were increasing in number.

For the moment at least, London seemed safe from attack, but if King Charles ever hoped to regain his kingdom, then his capital would have to be taken, perhaps by storm. For Dublin, nightly the bad dreams returned.

'Beware the enemy within,' Mistress Hampden warned. 'Do not tell anything that you know to strangers.' This seemed an empty warning as Dublin knew nothing and had little contact with the outside world.

She hardly ever went out, except to church on Sundays, where the vicar preached long, impassioned sermons; or with one of the servants to the fish-market on Wednesdays and Fridays. In the city, she was half-fearful, half-intrigued by everything about her. Here, there were more beggars than ever she had seen in Dublin, but when she remarked upon this, Mary said that they were victims of the war, seeking refuge.

Dublin thought about Polly Cranford. She was certainly a victim of the war. She wondered if Amos still lived and how Polly was managing to support him. In spite of her earlier revulsion, she vowed one day soon to visit her friend.

Although there was much complaint everywhere, the Hampdens did not go hungry. Coal was the biggest problem, for the routes from Newcastle were barricaded by the Parliament's own troops. They succeeded in strangling the trade, but in the process their own side suffered too. Meanwhile, wood became so scarce that it cost treble its rightful price and everything that could be burned, was.

At church on Sundays, the ministers entreated the congregation to pray for the Puritan soldiers and to give every penny they could to help the refugees fleeing from Ireland. At first Dublin thought that they meant Irish people and her heart lifted with compassion, only to realise that they referred to those English who had been driven out. She wanted to stand up and shout: 'What about the Irish you have slaughtered?' but she did not. They were bound to have an answer. There was no understanding it all.

Thus, the month of May and most of June passed. When Dublin could forget Mary's place in Robert's life, she liked her. At other times she wondered how to dispose of her, then seeing her pleasant, innocent face, guilt weighed her down.

It was in the third week of June that the messenger came. Dublin answered his knock and it was immediately plain that he had something serious to impart.

'Mistress Hampden?'

'She is resting.'

'Then arouse her. She must hear what I have to say.'

Shutting the door in his face Dublin scurried along to Mary's chamber, where she was writing in a diary that she completed each day.

'There is a man to see your Mama.'

She laid her quill aside. 'What sort of man?'

'From the military.'

They both hurried along the gallery and Dublin waited outside, while Mary went in to arouse Mistress Letitia. Moments later they both came out and hastened down the stairs with Dublin in their wake.

Anne and Ruth must have heard the commotion, for they too appeared in the hallway. Mary opened the door and asked the man inside.

For the first time Dublin looked at him properly. He was an older man, travelworn, and the Hampdens recognised him as someone from their estate.

'Richard Lowell. What is it?'

'Madam, I come with grave news. I fear that your husband has been wounded.'

'Badly?' Mistress Hampden's face was a mask.

'I fear so. He is at Thame. His forces ran into the King's troops at a place called Chalgrove Field. They were led into an ambush. Colonel Hampden was struck in the shoulder.'

Mistress Hampden grasped Mary's hand, squeezing the fingers until they went white.

'I shall make ready to leave, immediately. You can guide me there?'

'I can, ma'am, but . . .'

She looked around at her stepdaughters and said; 'I want you to take William and travel back to Great Hampden. As soon as it is possible, I shall have Mr Hampden brought there.'

'But Mama, you cannot go alone.' Dublin looked at Mary's stricken face and remembered their nightly prayers. Clearly God had paid scant regard to Mary's entreaties for the safety of her father. As for their other prayers – her heart froze.

Their stepmother said, 'Richard Lowell will guide me and I will take a groom and a guard and . . .' She turned. 'You, Dublin O'Neill, you have been on the roads. You shall accompany me too.'

Her daughters started to protest. Dublin felt rigid with fear, but already foremost in her mind was the thought that once free of this place, she would be able to seek out Robert. She wondered if, unlike Mary Hampden, her prayers had been answered . . .

They had been on the road but one day when their party was intercepted. At first they thought the approaching cavalcade were enemy troops. Dublin's instinct was to flee, for Mr Hampden was one of the most loved yet most hated men in the kingdom. If the enemy learned who they were, then they would surely be undone.

'You stay hidden, ma'am, I'll see to this.' Richard Lowell wiped his hand across his mouth and moved to meet the approaching troop. His face was grim with anxiety. Mistress Letitia ignored him and descended, ready for the confrontation.

'Praise God, they're Parliament men!' As they drew near Dublin saw that the soldiers wore orange sashes, but the relief was shortlived. The Captain dismounted, removed his hat and bent his head in reverence. When he looked up, his eyes were black with pain.

'Mistress Hampden? I have been commissioned to find you and accompany you home.' He hesitated. 'I fear that the Great Patriot is dead.'

Mistress Letitia did not move. It was almost as if she had been turned to stone. 'Ma'am,' Dublin reached out to touch her hand but she seemed unaware of it.

The Captain continued: 'Much of the country is in mourning, ma'am. Your husband was one of our great heroes. Colonel Hampden is being escorted home for burial. You will wish to be with him.'

The Captain was a young man, dark-haired, much the same age and colouring as Robert. His slight build and gentle manner brought home to Dublin the frailty of these soldiers when faced with the wrath of their fellows.

Taking courage, she asked: 'Have you any news of Lord Essex and his bodyguard?'

'I fear not.'

The agony of ignorance remained.

In silence they changed course and travelled the miles to Great Hampden. Sitting opposite Mary's step-mother, Dublin marvelled at her composure. There was something about these English, their self-control in the face of tragedy. If it was Robert who had been mortally wounded . . .

The Hampden house was one of the grandest that Dublin had ever seen. Imposing, big as a fortress, with a central square tower and castellated walls, the many windows looked out across a sweep of lawn. Open fields and fine mature trees made a fitting backdrop. Again, the wealth and power of Robert's friends intimidated her, yet it struck Dublin with sad irony that even the protection of so many worldly goods could not save a man from the mortal thrust of a sword.

At the house she was left to her own devices. No one had the will to see to her, for the death of their master had paralysed them all. At the same time people were coming from near and far to pay their respects.

170

The weather did not match the sadness of the occasion and for want of anything better to do, Dublin left the house and wandered the grounds. She felt sobered by the great man's death, and yet distanced from the family grief.

The gardens were beautiful, well-maintained and there was a sense of peace as she walked along the narrow, grassy pathways between the low box hedges. The scent of lavender and hyssop hung sweet in the air. In the distance, ducks were calling. She was suddenly in awe of so much beauty. There must be a purpose in living – and dying.

She walked full circle and was about to cross the courtyard back to the house when there came the sound of horses. There was no need to look. Some things are known without the power of the five senses.

Running around towards the stables, she was in time to see Robert dismount and make for the house. Dublin did not know quite what she felt – enormous relief that he was safe, a grinding sense of sadness that he had come to comfort Mary. She longed to run and cling to him but could only shelter behind a pillar and watch.

The door to the house opened and Mistress Letitia herself came out. She wore mourning and even from that distance, she looked drained of hope and colour. Robert took her hand. His expression was one of deep regret. Moments later the rest of the family appeared and Mary was in his arms.

Her head nestled into his shoulder and he rocked her, his lips resting on the crown of her head, creasing the cap that covered her hair. She was such a little thing, so vulnerable. Dublin could feel his tenderness and the knowledge dragged her to despair. Turning away, she wandered towards the cow byres and nursed her loneliness.

The great man was laid to rest the following day. His coffin was borne to the village church and Dublin was immersed in the universal sense of loss. Somehow, along with his friend Mr Pym, John Hampden epitomised the Parliamentary cause. Now that he was gone, she wondered if any hope of victory remained. It was not for herself but for Robert that she feared defeat – 'If the King takes Hull, I might lose my head' – that is what he had said. If Charles took the whole kingdom, would the same not apply?

The sober party left the church and made its way through the beeches towards the burial place. The mourners walked in convoy. Mistress Letitia was helped along by her eldest step-son, the living image of his father. Watching them, Dublin drew comfort from the eternity of the life-force.

Mary stood next to Robert. A muffled drum measured their foot treads. Robert looked so tall and protective, his expression grave, sensitive to the agony of the occasion. Silently Dublin slipped away and found a dusty spot near the stream where the busy ripple of water restored some of her calm.

'Dublin?'

The sound of his voice had her on her feet. She stared guiltily at him, ashamed that at that very moment he had filled her thoughts.

He in turn sat down wearily on the bank at the spot where she had been resting. He raised his tired face to welcome the sun.

'A terrible business. I cannot believe that God would call such a man to Him if He wishes us success.'

This echoed her own thoughts but she remained silent.

'There is worse.' He picked up a stone and threw it idly into the water. 'Prince Rupert is after Bristol. If Charles succeeds in taking it, he will hold the second biggest port in the country. Throughout the west, towns are falling to him.'

'What will happen?'

'What will happen is that the King will go for London. Meanwhile poor Essex has no troops, no money and very little discipline. He is weary and demoralised but they won't take his resignation.'

'Does that mean you are going back to London?'

He shrugged. 'It seems most likely. Here . . .' He patted the earth beside him. Her throat was dry as she sank down.

'You are well? You are getting along with Mary? She seems pleased with your company.'

Her eyes flashed her jealousy and he raised his eyebrows. 'You don't like her?'

'I like her, yes.'

'Then?'

'I don't want to stay there.'

'Then where do you wish to be?'

She dared not say.

'I want you safe,' he said, anticipating her answer.

'Could I not be safe with you?'

172

After a while he looked away and then threw another stone into the water. 'There are different kinds of safety.'

'If I came with you no one could hurt me.'

He scrambled to his feet. His boot was inches from her face and she longed to nestle her head against his leg.

Just as the silence became unbearable, he said, 'There are many ways of being hurt too, you know. If I keep you apart from me, it is because I have good reason.'

He was looking down at her and for a second she saw behind the soldier's mask, remembering that evening in Hull. 'Trust me,' he finished.

She wanted to cry, to have him hold her like he had Mary, tender and loving. Instead she asked: 'When will you leave?'

'This same evening.'

There was nothing to be said. He kicked the dusty turf with his boot and then straightened up. 'God be with you, Dublin. I must go back to the house.'

'Your betrothed will miss you.' Her voice was bitter but he did not respond.

Instead he said, 'I don't know when I shall see you again, any of you. That is in God's hands. Pray for me.'

She turned away and looked out across the countryside, waves of sadness churning like a plough at the furrow. She had to fold her arms across her chest to hold back the swaying emotion. When she finally dared to look round, he had gone.

Dublin remained by the stream, gazing out across the vast grounds of Hampden House and trying to pretend that everything was well – only she knew that it wasn't. Robert was slipping away and there was no means of stemming the tide of loss.

For what seemed like hours she stayed in a state of suspension, not really thinking or feeling anything, for thoughts and feelings were too painful. Then, as the sun began to lose its warmth and the grass grew damp, she started reluctantly back towards the house. She didn't belong here. Her life only had meaning away from them all, the Hampdens and the Hammonds – high-born, powerful people from another world. She belonged with that other Robert, just herself and him, travelling the roads together – but such a time would surely never come again.

Halfway across the courtyard, she was distracted by the sound of hooves. A single horse came in at a canter and the rider's urgency brought her back from her troubles. He dismounted and hurried to the door.

Dublin hesitated, wondering whether to go on around to the back entrance, but her curiosity got the better of her.

'Captain Hammond?'

Robert appeared at the door. He wore only his shirt and breeches and the informality of his wear showed clearly how much he felt at home here. Dublin drew back into the shadow of an oak tree, straining her ears to hear.

'Captain Hammond, sir, your commanding officer requests that you go home immediately. There has been a tragedy.'

'Tragedy?' Robert's eyes narrowed and Dublin moved closer, no longer caring if she was seen.

'Some trouble with a foraging party. It seems they came to take cattle and your brother tried to stop them. I'm afraid he's dead, sir.'

'Oh, Robert!' Mistress Letitia stepped out from the dark hallway and went to him and Mary too, ran to put her arms about him. Dublin stood alone, feeling his pain, unable to offer the comfort he needed.

Robert released himself gently from Mary's grasp. To the soldier he said, 'I thank you. I will leave without delay.'

For a moment he put his arm around Mary's shoulders again, and squeezed her. The act was as much that of a brother as a lower, but Dublin envied the girl the easy contact. In the face of this latest tragedy, she was drowning in a sea of uncertainty.

Robert leaned close to Mistress Letitia and spoke to her. She nodded and they both looked round.

Robert's eyes came to rest on Dublin and she lowered her gaze, ashamed to be caught openly spying. He said, 'I am going back to Abbey House tonight. I have changed my mind about leaving you here. Get your things together.'

For a moment she thought that her ears had deceived her. This was what she wanted to hear. Surely, in reality, he would not take her to the mother he had once refused to burden with her presence? But he was looking at her, waiting for her to move.

'Come along, girl! We must leave without delay.'

In her haste to be ready, Dublin almost ran for the house, wondering why it took the death of Robert's brother to make her dreams come true. Surely this life held no sense!

Chapter 24

As the house at Chertsey Beomond came into view, there was an immediate and terrible sense of desolation, as if the place had been despoiled and then abandoned. The only thing to move as they crossed the yard was the swaying body of a man, hanging from one of the elm trees. Robert reined in his horse. Dublin glanced at him, feeling his fear at not knowing who he might find. After a moment he rode ahead then called back, 'He is a stranger.'

Moments later, the door opened and a lady of older years came out into the cooling dusk. Dublin was immediately struck by the dreadful similarity to the image she held of Mistress Hampden, newly-widowed and bereft, as she had waved them farewell the day before. Here was another woman of like age, mourning the violent death of someone she loved.

'Oh, Robert! I cannot believe such a thing!' Mistress Hammond clung to her second son, letting out her pain in the safety of his arms. Next to her stood a younger, tight-lipped woman. In her arms she held a very small baby.

Robert rocked the older woman to him. 'Hush, Mother. Hush, now. I am here.'

Gradually Elizabeth Hammond's grief subsided and wiping her tears, she released herself from her son's embrace, glancing round at her daughter-in-law. At this, Robert too, turned to the young mother.

'Margaret, there are no words to say what I feel.'

The widow looked at her baby as if to draw strength from its existence. For a moment her voice threatened to fail her. 'See what a fine nephew you have, Robin. John was so proud. He had the child baptised in your honour.'

'Then I am proud.' He touched the shrouded face of the baby, then the tender expression hardened again. 'Can you recount what happened?'

Margaret glanced at her mother-in-law and Elizabeth Hammond began to tell the story, twisting a sodden kerchief in overwrought hands.

'It was near supper-time, three days ago. John had ridden over to check on the stock. A mare was due to foal and he wanted to make sure that she was well. I was carving beef. Suddenly I thought I could hear shouting and when I went to the casement, it was to see a troop of soldiers down in the meadow. John was in their midst. He was dismounted and they seemed to be harrying him, riding into him with their horses. He was waving his arms about and he seemed very angry.'

Mistress Elizabeth glanced quickly at her son. He nodded encouragement.

'Well, quick as silver I went outside to see what was happening. When John saw me, he shouted that I should go indoors. I turned back to the house but the cavalry came cantering over.' She shook her head. 'I was afeared by their manner, so arrogant, provocative. They demanded food and shelter. John came running after them and called out that I should refuse them entry but they ignored him. Their Captain, a wild-looking young fellow, rode past me and straight into the house!'

She shook her head again at the memory. 'There must have been about ten of them. They went into the kitchen and began to take everything that they could find. The beef on the table was consumed there and then, with gallons of ale and the bread which was still hot from the oven. The crocks were overturned and smashed against the floor.'

She turned to Robert as tears welled up. 'They even smashed the benches and threw them onto the fire.'

Robert held his mother close. 'And John?' he asked gently.

'John first tried to reason with them, telling them that he was neither for nor against them, but they ignored him. Two or three went up to the chambers and began to empty out our chests, flaunting themselves in our clothing, making mock. Then they began to pack our finest ware into their saddlebags to take away.' Tears poured down her face. 'They discovered Margaret, still abed, and made foul insinuations. One threatened the babe if she would not . . .'

176

Margaret cut in. 'I'll tell it, Mother. You don't have to say it. I stabbed him.' Her voice was obscenely calm in the face of what she was saying. 'He had a knife in his belt. He was so busy trying to unbreech himself that I simply took the dagger and plunged it into his chest. He died in seconds.'

Dublin held her breath, visualising the scene.

Robert asked, 'What happened then?'

'The soldiers were holding John captive, wanting him to witness my violation. Then he broke free and set about them, hitting out in his anger. One of them, a common soldier, carried an axe. He . . .' She clung to her brother-in-law. 'He's in there.' She indicated the hall.

Robert opened the door and went ahead. Silently the others followed, Dublin trailing uncertainly behind. She felt doubly uncomfortable witnessing this tragedy, seeing for the first time the family where her master belonged, where she so much wanted to belong.

John Hammond was laid out on the table, a wall-hanging draped over him, a Bible on his chest. His face was unscarred. He looked so calm, so handsome in the stillness of death.

'I'll find them,' Robert vowed. 'I'll kill the man who did this.'

'You are too late, my son. The Captain had him slain. It is he who hangs outside.'

Dublin felt Robert's disappointment. He was denied even the release of revenge.

His mother added bitterly, 'I don't think it was the taking of John's life that angered the Captain, but the fact that the soldier was lowborn and John was someone of rank. In God's eyes we are all the same.'

Dublin was taken aback to hear Caleb's words echoed by this aristocratic woman. But in her next breath, Elizabeth Hammond denied the very statement that she had just made. Looking at Dublin as if she had just noticed her presence, her face became closed, suspicious.

'Who is this?' Mistress Hammond asked.

'A – servant. I rescued her in Ireland.' Robert's hesitation threw Dublin into confusion.

His mother frowned with disapproval. 'She is travelling the countryside with you?'

177

'She has been in Mary's care, with the Hampdens.' Dublin saw him blush and this added to her own discomfort.

Mistress Hammond said, 'Have a care, Robert. An Irish peasant – how will people view this?'

He did not reply immediately and Dublin was about to offer an explanation of her own, but at that moment, to distract his mother, he said: 'You will have heard the news that the Patriot is dead? I am come directly from his funeral.'

'God have mercy.' At last, Mistress Hammond looked away from Dublin, dismissing her as if she was of little account. Dublin knew that she had failed some test, but she did not know what it was. She felt angry with herself for not speaking out. Who was this grand lady to look on her as if she were a clod of clay?

She stood by as they made their way back into the parlour and when nothing was said, followed behind, smarting at the injustice of her treatment. A voice in her head said: *'I'm as good as you, prince or pauper.'*

Somehow they struggled through the rest of that day. Other snippets of news were eked out and the family took refuge in discussing the practicalities of their present situation. Robert, as the eldest son, now held the estate in trust until his small nephew should come of age. For twenty years, eleven months and two weeks he would be master of Abbey House and all the lands.

'I shall find a bailiff, a good manager,' he said. 'Then I must return to my regiment.'

'Have you anyone in mind?'

He shook his head. His mother said, 'I can run the estate well enough but I need a reliable man to help me. Old Obidiah Strange is back. He is a trustworthy man, and he won't be leaving here again.'

For the first time in many days, here was some good news! Obidiah's disappearance at Reading had seemed to signal only one thing but now, against the odds, he had turned up safe and sound.

'What happened to him?' Robert asked.

'He was taken prisoner. The Royalists released him on oath that he took no further part in the fighting. He has given his word.'

Dublin secretly thought what a relief it must be to have to fulfil such a promise.

Robert nodded his acquiescence. 'I will go and see Obidiah. With him to help you, I shall rest easier.'

His departure meant that the womenfolk were left alone. Of servants there was no sign. Clearly, the coming of the King's men had driven them away. Listlessly, Mistress Hammond poked the embers in the great fireplace, then she turned to Dublin.

'Here, girl. Make yourself useful.'

A hen lay half-plucked on the table, so without a word Dublin set to work to finish the job. Both women watched her and she hoped for some small measure of approval.

Just as she was beginning to feel safer, Mistress Hammond said, 'Young woman, are you a servant to my son – or what?' Her tone was sharp, accusing. Dublin did not know how to reply.

'Your son saved my life, ma'am. I serve him in any way that I can.'

The older woman's mouth tightened and she rapped out: 'You will not share his bed. There will be no unseemliness here. Our servants ran away when the raiders came. While you are here, you will carry out whatever duties are needed. And you will sleep in the attic.'

Dublin went to protest at the insinuation, but after an initial feeling of affront, it dawned on her that Robert's mother assumed that she was his mistress. The realisation brought a glow of excitement. If his mother suspected it, then surely it was possible. One day . . .

'Are you listening to me, girl?'

'Yes, ma'am.'

'I think it would be wise if, when my son leaves here, you were to remain behind. Following a field army is no life for a chit of a girl. You are near full-grown. My son would not wish you to roam the countryside like a slattern. It will do his reputation no good.'

Dublin looked away. For a wild moment she thought: She's afraid. She thinks that he might feel something for me. Meeting the woman's gaze she responded demurely, 'Thank you, ma'am, you are very kind. I will try to repay you.' Crossing her fingers behind her back she silently added: 'For as long as I stay.'

Mistress Hammond expelled her breath as if some problem had been resolved. She said; 'Good. We need all the servants we can get.'

The sting of her remark made Dublin smart but she hid her feelings. A moment later, the older woman left the room, taking

Margaret with her, and Dublin concentrated on the safe familiarity of cooking a meal.

Once everything was simmering, she wandered outside. At the back of the house it felt peaceful, not the sort of place where murder and pillage had so recently taken place.

She made her way into the buttery, looking for beer or wine for the evening meal. Inside it was cool and restful. She leaned against the cob of the wall and rested her hand on one of the huge casks of wine that lined the walls, opening her heart to the possibilities of an unknown future. Her own plans were for something very different from the one Mistress Hammond wished for her.

She began to feel weary and started back to the house, carrying two ewers of ale. Passing through the garden with its indecently cheerful burst of colour, she realised that on the morrow, Robert would be attending his second burial of the week.

It was Henry Hammond who conducted his nephew's funeral service. As chief mourners, Robert, Elizabeth and Margaret walked behind the coffin along neatly bordered paths which led from the house to the church. Another aunt, Mary, and her son William Temple, a young man who matched Robert in age, were also present. The only family members to be absent were Uncle Thomas who was away with his regiment and Aunt Jane Dingley who was indisposed.

The thought of Aunt Jane set Dublin's heart beating. What would she say, if she found Dublin here at Chertsey? For a while she thought about the Island, about Robert's desertion and Caleb's rescue. Her thoughts threw her into chaos. In one way life was so simple – she loved Robert and would devote her life to being with him, try to stop her how they might. In another way it was more complicated than she would ever understand.

A solitary drummer beat the way from the house to the church. The family bore themselves with dignity, passing between lines of villagers who came to pay their last respects. The babe was carried in front of the mourners, heir to the father he would never know.

The natural grief of any bereaved family was overlaid with

180

other tensions. It did not escape Dublin's notice that Henry Hammond seemed as much in shock as in sorrow. As a servant of the King, whose men had killed his nephew, she wondered if he felt responsible for John Hammond's untimely death. Yet no one could cast blame. This war was like a plague, beyond human control.

The service was simple and such that no one could take exception to its form. The church bore no trimmings that could give offence. This was the way of these Puritans – no statues or paintings, no decorated cloths or fine carvings. For a moment she thought of Glendruid and its simplicity, a stark stone altar, a simple grove of oaks – natural things were best.

At the back of the building, the remaining servants wept openly. Tears threatened to overwhelm Dublin too, not only for poor, dead, handsome John whom she had not known, not only in sympathy for the pain suffered by the widow and the bereaved mother, but also for Robert's loss of his brother. Her own heart was heavy with emptiness. When Robert left here would she be left behind again, alone and deserted as any widow?

At the graveside, Robert's cheeks were wet and she had to fight the urge to go to him, for that privilege belonged to the rest of the Hammonds. It would always be so.

After the burial, a serving girl called Martha Osborne, who had that morning returned to the house to resume her duties, followed Dublin back along the lane. Her eyes were red and swollen with sobbing. Some instinct told Dublin that she too, cried not only for John but for some absent sweetheart.

''Tis a wicked thing, this war,' Martha choked out. 'Master John was the finest man that drew breath.'

Dublin said nothing. After they had gone a few yards, Martha added: 'You can't know what it's like to love someone, to live in fear for his life.'

'I can imagine.'

'No. Imagining ain't the same. Every time I think of my Tom, I find it hard to breathe. They all keep telling me he'll come back, but – I'd go and look for him if only I knew where.'

Dublin looked into her poor desperate eyes. 'There are thousands of men away from home. Your Tom will come back safe.'

181

As they entered the gates of Abbey House, Martha told her: 'If ever he comes back, I'll never let him out of my sight again.'

Thinking of her master, Dublin silently echoed the vow.

Robert left Chertsey the following morning and Dublin had no difficulty in slipping away. The foraging party that killed John had taken all the horses so he left his mare behind and set out on foot. It was therefore easier to follow him.

The countryside teemed with wanderers – soldiers, vagrants, bandits. Being alone and on foot, Dublin felt the fear of capture grow by the minute. Panic threatened to overwhelm her but she hung on until they were a mile or two away from Chertsey before making her presence known.

'You again!'

He stared angrily at her and with sinking heart she realised that it had been a mistake to reveal herself so soon. Her throat grew dry.

'We agreed that you should stay at Abbey House. Can I not trust you to keep a single promise?'

'I misunderstood,' she lied miserably.

He snorted. 'This nonsense of following me has to stop.'

Her world began to crumble, sagging under the weight of his criticism.

Not meeting her eyes, he said: 'You must go back – now. You found your way this far so there should be no difficulty in returning.'

'I—'

'Now.'

'I hate you!' Summoning a semblance of dignity she turned away, holding herself erect in defiance of his dismissal but quaking inside with fear and hurt.

'Dublin!'

For a heady moment she turned, her eyes large with appeal. He said, 'It is for your good.'

She turned away again and kept walking. Now indeed there was nothing. Everything was bearable but his rejection.

There was no question of going back to Abbey House. The thought of Mistress Elizabeth's disapproval, the return to being a servant, was abhorrent, to be rejected out of hand. But what else was there? Her small, remaining knot of pride would not allow her to continue following him like some abandoned cur, in the hope that he would relent.

Suddenly she thought of Polly Cranford. It was not a happy prospect, but Polly did live in London whence Robert was bound. The memory of Amos, the grinding poverty of Polly's hut, the intrusion of her brats, all appalled Dublin, but Polly was the only person in the whole world who might make her welcome. Summoning what little resolve remained, she set off again, along the route to London.

Chapter 25

It took Dublin a long time to find Polly Cranford's house. So many lanes looked the same and she had to keep going back to the river to try yet another smelly alleyway before finally coming upon it.

One of Polly's little ones was playing outside. The sight of the child carried Dublin back to Reading, the horror of the battle, the hopes she had then nursed for her own future. She felt an almost physical pain at the thought of her own abandonment.

The small girl looked up in answer to Dublin's call and quickly retreated through the sacking that acted as a door. Hesitantly, Dublin followed.

It took a few moments for her eyes to accustom themselves to the gloom, and longer for her nose to adjust to the stench. The place was much as she recalled it in her worst dreams – tiny, dark, foetid, the earth floor cluttered with rubbish . . . and along one crumbling wall on some sort of pallet covered with sacking, lay the stinking frame of Amos Cranford.

Dublin wondered whether to speak to him, but there was something amiss. Taking a step closer the expression 'still as the grave' came to her. She knew that he was dead.

'Where is your mother?' The child shrugged and went back outside. Quickly Dublin ducked out after her, breathing with difficulty, for the air without was not much sweeter than that within. She did not know what to do. Surely Polly could not have abandoned the girl? Did she know that her husband was dead?

It had been a mistake to come here. Quickly she glanced back along the shambles but already it was too late for Polly was approaching from the direction of a well, carrying a wooden bucket from which water seeped in lazy runnels along the seams.

'Dublin!' She started to run, the water slopping over her feet. Dublin put on a brave face and turned to her.

Polly looked older than ever, her features strained, her hair a nondescript grey-brown that blended with her general pallor.

'Oh, Dublin!' She seemed overcome with emotion, and the younger girl hugged her, aware of her scrawny frame, the sickly smell of illness. Polly's chest rasped harshly as she breathed, exhausted with the effort of fetching water.

'How are you?'

Polly shook her head. 'Amos is dead. This morning. He could not swallow. He's been a long time dying.'

'I'm truly sorry.'

'Don't be. He's suffered too much.' She rubbed a weary hand across her forehead. 'My second child, Thomas, was taken with the coughing sickness a month past. And the baby died soon after we got here. I had no milk.'

Dublin looked away, oppressed by so much suffering but Polly shrugged it off. 'What of you? Where have you been? How is that master you are so fond of?'

She blinked back the pain. 'I have left his employ.'

'You have?'

It tumbled out then, all of it. It was a relief for Dublin to tell what she felt and an escape for Polly to listen.

'It strikes me that you disturb him,' the young mother said, as the tale drew to a close.

'How?'

'You are a woman, my dear. Men cannot help themselves.'

'You think he likes me?' Her spirits soared.

'Oh, I'm sure he likes you well enough.'

Polly sagged back against the outer wall of the hut and Dublin chided herself for her thoughtlessness but there was nowhere to go except inside the hut, and she never wanted to enter there again.

As if reading her thoughts, Polly said: 'I will not ask you in.'

'You must come away with me, you and the girl.' The little one was swaying against her mother's leg, holding fast to the tattered material of her dress. For a moment, Dublin saw herself, a tot back in Ireland, clinging to the safety of Dervla. She forced herself to pick the girl up.

'What is her name?'

185

'Sarah.'

She was light as chaff. For a moment Dublin hesitated, wondering about the body of Amos. Again Polly seemed to read her thoughts.

'He's gone. The real Amos went months ago. That bag of bones in there isn't the father of my – child.' She hesitated over the word as if the memory of her other babes came to confront her. 'They'll put him in a pit. There's nothing to stay for.'

'Then come with me.'

'Where to?'

She had not thought that far. After the merest hesitation, she said, 'Mr John Hampden's house.' The thought of the airy rooms and the full larder drew her like a moth. Whatever the Hampdens might think, the servants would certainly give them charity. And surely, sooner or later, that was where Robert would come . . .

Polly pulled a face. 'You don't mean *the* Mr Hampden? There's no place there for the likes of me.'

'You think they're better than you?' Dublin felt angered by her friend's humility, that touched too nearly on her own sense of inferiority. Again, she felt the image of Caleb urging her on.

In the face of the challenge, Polly acquiesced.

Polly turned back to the hut and Dublin waited outside so that her friend could say goodbye to her man. It was a long while before she came out and her face was impassive. She was empty-handed.

'Are you bringing nothing with you?'

'I sold everything we had long ago, when the money your master gave me ran out. He sent more, by the way.'

The news opened the void of longing.

'Now I have nothing but the child.' She reached out to take Sarah and the two women's eyes met. Polly said, 'Only God knows which of us will go first, her or me but if it should be me, will you look after her?'

Dublin glanced at the spindly scrap of humanity and then back at the pale woman who held her. 'I could die too.'

'No.' There was certainty in her voice. 'You have a long way to go.'

'How do you know?'

'I just do.'

Hesitating, Dublin said, 'If you can see the future, then will I . . .'

'He cannot wed you but that does not stop him from feeling.'

She blushed at the transparency of her thoughts. 'What *does* he feel?'

Polly gave her the ghost of a smile. 'Why, he loves you.'

They set off together, taking it in turns to carry Sarah. It was a hot day, oppressively so. Dublin feared that the bad city air would make her breathe in the pestilence or some other foul pox, though if Polly was right, there was no need for alarm.

Everywhere there were soldiers. Many of them were young men, apprentices. The gaols had long since been emptied and now master, man and boy abandoned their crafts to rally to the call. There was hardly a man left who had not enlisted.

The city was alive with expectation. Most of this army would be moving out any day to go to the aid of poor besieged Gloucester. Everywhere girls walked brazenly on the arms of their sweethearts. These uncertain times made them bold.

As they drew near to the river, another kind of activity caught their attention. Suddenly the roads were blocked with women in their dozens, nay hundreds. They walked in formation, many of them carrying children – mothers, grandmothers, daughters, all bent upon some mission.

Bystanders stopped to watch the procession. Dublin was struck by the contrast between the quiet dignity of the women and the jeers and catcalls that greeted their parade.

'Where do you go?' she asked one matron as they drew near.

'To the Parliament to implore them to settle this war. There is hardly a woman who has not lost a loved one through the fighting. It is time it came to an end.'

In those few words she voiced all that Dublin felt to be true. She looked round at Polly. 'Shall you come?'

'You think the men will listen to us?'

'Perhaps if we shout loud enough.'

She gave a cynical smile. 'It is too late for me. My man is gone.'

'But not too late for others. Would you want a country where no men remain? What will Sarah do for a sweetheart if every man dies in battle?'

187

'A world without men would be a more peaceful place.'

'It would soon be a world without people.'

They fell into step and followed the gathering crowds.

'Get you back home to your fires!'

Dublin was hit on the arm by a ball of dung and resisted the urge to turn her fists upon the wretch who had thrown it. Hitting back was how it had all started – and hitting back meant that it would never end. To hide their fear, these men were taking refuge in laughter.

The woman next to Dublin said: 'They can't abide the thought that we have a voice. They are afraid that when the war is over we won't be content to stay home and tend their fires.'

Dublin lifted her head high and marched on. If men had no more sense, then perhaps women should not stay meekly at home. The war had got to stop. What would be the point of a victory to either side if no man came back to reap the rewards?

The crush was getting stronger. A little way ahead a scuffle broke out as the leading women tried to force a way past a barrier of soldiers blocking their path.

'Let them through!' Dublin called.

The women's voices grew higher, more raucous. The men, at first good-humoured, began to react more violently, faced with the marchers' determination. Now people began screaming. Somewhere ahead, musket-shot rang out. Those in front tried to turn back but the crush behind was as great. Dublin looked around anxiously for Polly but could not see her. There was no choice but to go with the crowd, first forwards and then back, buffeted like leaves in the wind.

'This way!' Someone grabbed her arm, extricating her from the throng. They dashed down the narrow alley and away from the fighting, coming out into a square where there was space and respite. She turned to thank her rescuer but already he had disappeared. In the distance, musketshot still reported, punctuating the screams.

Part of her wanted to go back to find Polly. It was Dublin who had encouraged her to join the demonstration; now she might be in trouble. At the same time there seemed little likelihood of finding her, and any hope of presenting a peaceful petition was lost. In defeat, Dublin looked around to get her bearings, once more with no clear idea of what to do or where to go. It would be pointless to return to Polly's hut. She would not go there again.

A group of men were watching her. An unspoken sense warned her of their lust, the base carnal drive of the mob. The best defence was to have a sense of purpose. Dublin thought again of the only other place in London that she knew. Once she was away from the heat of the young bulls, she stopped the nearest bystander, and asked, 'Do you know the way to the home of Mr John Hampden?'

It still took her the best part of two hours to find the Hampden house. By then, her thirst and exhaustion were such that she had no thought beyond finding comfort. It did not matter if Mary was there, for it would be easy to make up some tale to explain her arrival, and Mary would understand about the women's march.

Dredging up the last of her courage, Dublin knocked hard at the door panel and waited.

'Lord have mercy! It's Dublin!' Tilly White, elderly, constant, in the Hampden family service since childhood, held out her arms in greeting. She felt like an old friend.

'Am I allowed inside?'

'Course you are.'

Dublin was about to offer some explanation, invent some tale, but Tilly said, 'Where have you been? They'll be that pleased to know you're safe.'

'They?'

The old servant busied herself picking up some pieces of straw that had blown in or been dropped from someone's boots. 'Word came from Great Hampden that you was lost. They searched everywhere for you, Chertsey, even here. Where have you been?'

Dublin remained silent. The fact that everyone knew of her disappearance filled her with panic. She asked, 'Is Mistress Mary here?'

'No they're still at Great Hampden. We don't expect 'em back yet. There's no one here now except Hezikiah and me – except today, that is.'

'Today?'

'Master Hammond's just come over. His regiment moves out tomorrow and he's using the master's study.' At the mention of John Hampden, old Tilly crossed herself, an automatic gesture that signified Rest in Peace. Seeing Dublin's face grow pale, she said, 'You afraid he might beat you?'

Dublin shook her head.

'Then it looks like you need a drink and a rest, you've gone that pale.'

'Don't tell him I'm here!'

Tilly frowned. 'He's the one that's been searching for you.'

As they started down the passageway the door to Mr Hampden's study opened. Dublin fought down the urge to run and hide, instead increased her pace, hoping to reach the safety of the kitchen before she was spotted, but ahead of her, Tilly stopped.

'Look here, master. Look who's turned up.'

She could not face him. When she finally raised her eyes, he was watching her with an expression so strange that it made no sense.

To deflect his fury, she said hurriedly: 'I've been with Polly Cranford.'

'Come with me.'

He led the way into the study where Dublin had first set eyes on Mary, that day so long ago, back in the spring.

The silence seemed oceans deep before he broke it. 'Why did you do it? How could you run off?'

'You sent me away!' She forgot her position in the face of his accusations.

'I sent you *back*. Did you not think for one moment what might happen?'

'Happen to whom?'

'To you, you foolish girl. Don't you know how much I . . .'

'Care?' The word blurted out, betraying her feelings.

'. . . feel responsible for you?'

Dublin snorted in disbelief, trying to hide her shame at showing her true hopes. 'Well, I'm grown now. You don't need to feel anything for me.'

Obliquely he said, 'Need and fact are not the same thing.'

This remark made no sense and the ensuing silence was taut as binder thread.

When the silence grew unbearable, Dublin repeated: 'I'm a child no longer.'

'That is true.' He rested back against the bureau and sighed. 'And that is the problem.'

'I don't see—'

'Just go and have something to eat now, and change that filthy gown. We'll talk later.'

190

She blushed at the criticism of her appearance, feeling crushed again. In defence, she scowled at him. 'Don't think I want to go with you, because I don't!'

He did not reply and she tottered down the passageway to the kitchen. Suddenly she had no appetite.

After picking at some cold mutton, she slept in one of the empty rooms normally used by the younger Hampden children, deliberately avoiding Mary's chamber. The presence of Mary's marriage bed, the certainty of her union with Robert was too much to bear.

Sleep came quickly and was dreamless. It was several hours before Tilly roused her with a mug of ale.

'It's past supper. You've been dead to the world, my lass.'

For a terrible moment Dublin feared that Robert had gone. Although not expecting to find him here, the prospect of letting him slip away again was intolerable. 'Where is everyone?' she asked.

'Hezzie's out in the stables.'

'Has Master Hammond left?' Her traitorous cheeks coloured.

'No. He left instructions that he wishes to see you when you awake. He said not to disturb you till you was ready.'

Dublin was thrown into confusion. He was waiting on her convenience like a lady of quality, not summoning her like a common servant.

Tilly produced a plain grey dimity gown, and the all-too-familiar smell of herbs conjured up an instant vision of Mary. Would Robert recognise it as one that she had worn? Dublin slipped it over her head and it was tight across her breasts, a little too short in the skirt but at least it was clean. The very closeness of its fit emphasised the maturity of her body, reminding her how much more of a woman she was than her rival. He could not fail to notice. Laboriously she combed her hair and pinned it demurely at the nape of her neck.

Tilly gave her a jug of ale to carry down to the study. With trembling hand, she knocked and walked in as soon as he answered. The jug shook on the tray and drops of the liquid splashed onto her skirts.

Robert was slumped in Mr Hampden's chair near to the window, his back half to the door. Only the top of his dark head was visible, that and his legs stretched out in a long vee.

'I bring you some refreshment.'

'Good.'

He rose to his feet and indicated that she should put the ale on the table. It juddered against the wood as she tried to put it down without shaking. For a moment she was back in Hull, in the room where he had worked and slept, the hallowed sanctuary where, just occasionally, she had shared some precious intimacy with him.

Taking a horn cup, he poured some of the ale and held it out to her in silence, then poured a second measure for himself.

Like hers, his hair was tied back at the nape of his neck for coolness, and he wore no boots. The sight of him was so beautiful that it overwhelmed her.

It was the same feeling that had been there since she first set eyes on him at Carrickmain, a sense of reaching for the moon and knowing that it could never be touched, of wanting the impossible and finding that there was nothing less.

'Where have you been?'

At the tone of his voice she felt a moment of rebellion, a remnant of the pride that the marching women had shown so briefly that afternoon in town. She fought it down. At this moment, she could not bear to quarrel with him.

'I went to see Polly Cranford. Her man is dead. We became separated when some women tried to petition the Parliament for peace.' She hesitated. 'I was one of them.'

Robert's expression did not change. After a moment he said heavily, 'Then you were too late. The Peace petition was defeated in Parliament yesterday.'

'Then it was a bad day for us all.'

He took time to consider her words. 'Your thoughts do you credit,' he said eventually, 'but to settle this war from weakness will only bring greater suffering.' He put his drink down, sank back into the chair and stretched out his legs again. His stockings needed darning. 'The Peace Party want to hand over control of the armed forces to the King, but control of the army is the very backbone for which we have been fighting.'

She felt disturbed at his line of thought. 'But your own brother died. My family are all killed. Amos Cranford had his face blown away. How can this be right?'

Robert regarded her seriously. 'If we were to give in now, all those people would have died in vain. We must have a just settlement if there is to be any lasting peace.'

192

He must have seen her doubt, for he added: 'This business is God's. We've kept our faith with Him and now the tables are turning. You have to be prepared to give your life for what you believe to be right.'

She went to protest but he stayed her with his hand. Its pressure against her wrist was like magic. 'I would not fire one more musket-shot than was necessary. I respect your desire for peace but I hope you do not misjudge my motives when I say we must continue with this war.'

She met his eyes, the dark honest warmth in them . . . and there was something more. Her throat felt dry and she could not look away. Quietly, he said, 'You should have stayed at Chertsey, or at Great Hampden.'

'Why?'

'You know why.'

She shook her head, waiting for him to transport her from her empty, hopeless world, into heaven. She wanted to yield her body, her very soul to him.

With a sigh he dropped his hand and looked away. 'It's late. Get back to bed.' His tone was sharp and she drew back as if he had slapped her. She wanted to run and hide for shame. With as much dignity as she could dredge up, she left the room.

In the bedchamber, she rent the sheets with pain and frustration, stuffing them into her mouth to drown the hurt. How could he do this, play hot and cold with her feelings, hint at affection then dash it with never a thought to her pain? Leaving here, going anywhere away from him was the only answer.

She slept badly, tormented by dreams and forlorn hopes. Her first hope on waking was that he would be gone, but Tilly told her otherwise. The only answer was to keep out of his way. After that she had no idea what she might do.

Suddenly she remembered Polly. Supposing after she left, Polly were to come looking for help, for shelter and a position? At the very least, someone with authority in the house should be alerted. There was only one person who could give those instructions. With misgivings she sought him out.

He was in the hallway pulling on his boots. Moments later and he would have gone. The thought of losing him swept her along in a torrent of emptiness. But for the moment she took her courage in her hands. 'You promised to help Polly Cranford. Two of her children are dead. I invited her to stay here but we got lost yesterday in the crowd.'

He looked up questioningly. 'You sound like the mistress of this house.'

The reprimand did not go unnoticed but she continued, 'She has nothing, no money, no food, no man.' He remained silent so she asked, 'Could you not help her, perhaps find her a place in Chertsey – that is, if she comes here?'

'I'll leave word that she is to be attended to.'

'I thank you.' In the tumbling void that followed, she said: 'You are leaving now?'

'Shortly.'

Her tongue refused further utterance and she watched him fasten himself into his buff coat, capturing the images for her empty future. Just as the silence became an agony he said: 'The army moves out today. We have new regiments, perhaps a thousand more horse, coats and boots for everyone. A few weeks ago my godfather, the Earl of Essex, was the scapegoat for all the wrongs. Now he is once more a hero. We march to Gloucester. If the town holds out, we'll drive the King away.' He turned to look at her. 'This may be the turning point in our fortunes.'

'Aren't you afraid to die?' She blurted it out.

He pondered the question seriously. 'Of course I'm afraid. I am young, not yet four and twenty. I have no heir. I have no wife . . .'

She waited. Turning and looking out of the casement, he said: 'I give you the choice. You may either stay here, or I will find an escort to take you back to Chertsey, or –' and he raised his voice because he guessed that she was about to interrupt him '– or you may travel with the baggage train to Gloucester.'

Above her own disbelief, she could feel his embarrassment, then a surge of joy enveloped her. What did it matter? If this was the only way that he could ask her, then it was just as wonderful. He did not look round, and fighting down the wave of triumph, she replied, 'I shall go and pack directly.'

Chapter 26

King Charles's cup of joy was brimming over. On the very site where, last October, the Battle of Edgehill had ended so indecisively, he was at last reunited with his own dear Henrietta-Maria.

Her coming was a glorious sight. She travelled from York at the head of a magnificent army, consisting of three thousand infantry, and thirty companies of horse. Prince Rupert had gone ahead to escort her.

'My lord,' she swept forward and made an obeisance at Charles's feet. 'At last I am here, your very own She Majesty Generalissima.'

Charles was too moved by emotion to do more than hold her dear hands, gaze into her bright button eyes, and know that at long last he could look forward again to her good advice – and to the joys of the bedchamber. As the Queen took his arm and marched empress-like before the assembled gathering, the royal loins stirred.

In all the time that they had been parted, Charles had remained faithful. It was not only a question of Christian devotion. Try to ignore it as he might, wenching and whoring were an everyday pastime at his court, although conducted with discretion in the face of his own abstinence. It was not that Charles was unmoved by a pretty face, or unaroused by a beautiful body. There were times when he had been tempted, but something in his make-up, an inherent shyness, made it impossible for him to launch into an affair. Secretly, he feared that his potency might fail him, then he would be a laughing stock. He also worried that a troublesome mistress might not be so easily got rid of, and besides, Henrietta-Maria would be in a fury. With his wife he felt safe. There was

195

something about the Queen's small bony body that gave him courage, and her cheerful enthusiasm for his love-making provided him with everything that he could ask for. He offered up a silent prayer for her safe return.

On 14 July they rode triumphant into Oxford to be greeted by celebrations that reminded him of the olden days. Poets waxed lyrical about the sterling bravery of Lord Hopton's Cornishmen, who had won a famous victory at Landsdowne and now, as he accepted the adulation of his loyal supporters, further news came of a noble battle at Roundway Down, where the enemy had been defeated by a force of half their numbers and were now in disarray. Victory could only be a short while away.

This happy state of affairs continued, and the crowning news for which he had hardly dared hope, arrived towards the end of July. Prince Rupert, supported by his brother Prince Maurice, with a heartwarming display of fraternal genius, had taken Bristol. Now Charles had the port that he needed. His Irish troops could be shipped in and victory was staring him in the face.

He personally would leave at once and go to reward his noble nephews, his glorious troops. Together they would move on to Gloucester and when that was in their hands, they would sweep towards the east and London would feel the weight of their presence! He raised his eyes heavenwards. God be praised!

Chapter 27

With the added responsibility of a loving wife, Caleb abandoned thoughts of leaving the village. In spite of his wild imaginings, he knew that he could neither take Sara with him, nor leave her behind.

Another year unfolded and deny it as he might, each month marked an anniversary of the time that he had shared with Dublin O'Neill. Caleb tried to remind himself that this year was different in a far more important way, for he was now a married man. Hardly a day passed when Sara did not struggle up to the downs to bring him some token of her affection, – a fresh pasty; a new jerkin, painstakingly sewn; a shirt, the folds of which were lovingly stitched to disguise his misshapen shoulder. He cherished yet resented her concern.

'Stay with me.' Caleb would mouth the words, wanting her to drive the spirit of Dublin out, and Sara, adoring and acquiescent, would bare herself to him, hold him close, comfort him, love him. He experienced only emptiness.

The time for the shearing brought its own ghosts. Caleb devoted himself single-mindedly to the work, beating his own record in fleecing eighty-seven lambs. Sara worked at his side. It was a good partnership, well-tried and trusted, but as he clipped away, he could not shut out the thought that this time last year he had planned a very different future for himself.

He remembered the last night of the shearing, his craziness, the angry humping with Annie Colenutt. He must have been possessed. Her brat had been born some nine months later . . .

'Here, pass me that salve.' He nudged Sara and pointed to the pot, refusing to think any further.

197

At the shearing feast, Lizzie Gosden added to her son's unease. 'That little lass of Elijah Wavell's is bonny. Such a pretty, blue-eyed babe. She doesn't favour her parents.'

He wanted to tell his mother to desist, yet he could not. 'It's not deformed?' he asked.

Lizzie looked puzzled. 'She's a pretty baby, perfectly healthy – look, she's over there. Why do you ask that?'

He shrugged, hot around the collar, refusing to look across the green to where Annie Wavell and her meek husband were gorging themselves on venison pie. Tightly, he said: 'I was the first man she saw after the wedding. She thought it was bad luck.'

Lizzie sniffed derisively. 'Such superstition. Anyways, that young 'un was conceived afore the wedding.'

Sara was watching him, her eyes large and troubled. With an effort he slipped his arm about her shoulders and squeezed her to him. Annie Wavell's baby was in its mother's arms. It had large blue eyes and waving dark hair.

'Aren't you going to play?' asked Lizzie, nodding towards his abandoned fiddle.

'Not tonight.' Turning to Sara he mouthed: 'Tomorrow I'm going into Newport, to take some fleeces.'

'I could take them . . .' she offered in sign language.

'No.' He wanted to get away, but not back to the emptiness of his hut. Trying to make up for his secret thoughts, he winked at Sara, letting her know that everything was well, only it wasn't. A pall of gloom had settled on him and with a dreadful certainty, he knew that unless some miracle occurred, things never would be well again.

Caleb awoke at first light and shifted his position in the bed, pushing down the spiky straw that stuck through the ticking of the mattress. Sara lay against him, her face snuggled into his shoulder. Her hair was loose and a long strand lay across his chest, damp and silky. He brushed it away, thinking that it was beautiful, although not as beautiful as . . .

Quickly he sat up and the movement jerked Sara into wakefulness. With a start she too, went to get out of the bed but almost immediately she fell back, her hand over her mouth, swallowing.

'Are you sick?' He touched her shoulder and even as she turned her face towards him, he knew.

He could not look at her. The knowledge felt like a thong,

pulled ever tighter around his chest until he could scarcely breathe. Patting her on the shoulder he pushed her back onto the bed and got up. 'Stay there.'

Hurriedly he dressed and made ready to leave. His chest was still constricted and he longed to run out into the clear morning and draw in great gulps of air, to liberate himself from this cloying, female world.

As he walked the six miles to Newport, the sheepskins grew heavy upon his back. He almost welcomed his aching shoulders, anything to distract him from his thoughts. At home were Sara and Lizzie, good women, adoring him, wanting to contain him. Out there was – what? A battle raging for good and evil, unexplored villages, cities, foreigners, strangers, *Dublin O'Neill.*

To reach the market he was forced to pass the pillory. The sight of it stirred such a turmoil in him that he hardly knew which way to turn. If there was anyone held there, he knew that he would have to release him, although to do so would bring inevitable retribution upon himself. As he approached, he could see a crowd gathered across the Square. His heart quickened but the pillory was empty. The focus of attention was the woolman, holding court.

'Think on it, brothers and sisters. No more punishments for sins that aren't sins. No more tithes for ministers you don't need. Make your voices heard, tell the Parliament what we, the true citizens want.'

Caleb stopped to listen, enthralled by the man's manner.

He continued: 'The war is going badly. What we need are goods and money – and men. The King's forces have taken Bristol. Now they have the port, they'll be importing foreigners, Irish Papists, to crush us into the ground. If you are a true-born Englishman, then stand up now and be counted. If you have no goods, if you have no money, then give yourselves! Come and fight for the cause!'

Nearby a military man waited, a large pouch about his waist. The orator said: 'Sergeant Howard here will swear you in, give you a whole shilling to seal the bargain. Food, stout clothing, the knowledge that you are fighting against evil, will all be yours. What are you waiting for?' Already a group of youths were lining up.

Flinging his fleeces at the woolman, Caleb said: 'Take these.'

'Good man.' He looked Caleb over, considering, before saying:

'Why not take your silver? Before long, the tide will be right. We'll be sailing for Southampton before dusk.'

Looking around the Square, Caleb noticed Michael Tribe from the village. He swallowed hard, his mouth dry with apprehension, then he called out: 'Good day, Michael. I would ask you to perform me a service.'

The village wheelwright came over, nodding his greeting. 'Of course, Caleb. Of course.'

The shepherd hesitated a moment then drew in his breath. 'When you return to the village, I pray ye, go to my cottage to see my mother and my wife. Tell them not to worry about me. Ask them to pray for me. Tell them that Caleb Gosden has rallied to the cause.' He lowered his head a moment then looked up again, defying the other man to comment. At his feet, the dog Tyke was seated patiently, glancing up now and then to check on the welfare of his master. Caleb said: 'Give my dog into the safekeeping of my wife. I am going to the wars, to serve my country.'

The army was gathering at Hounslow Heath. A multitude of men and horses, cannon, wagons, tents, women and children thronged together on the grassy outskirts. In the village itself, there was hardly a cottage that did not throw open its doors to bring out ale for the men. It felt more like a fair than a prelude to war.

Robert had not yet joined his men and Dublin stood at his side. She felt joyous, powerful. At this moment he was hers for all the world to see. Maybe her role was only that of servant and cook, but just this once she felt that she truly belonged, like any other wife or sweetheart who had chosen to travel with her man rather than stay behind.

'How far do we go?' she asked him.

'At least one week's march. It won't be easy. We have to cross hilly country. Once the King gets wind of the fact that we are coming, he'll send troops to try and turn us back.' The sobering news clouded this otherwise happy day.

Leading the parade, at the centre of attention, was Robert's godfather. Dublin studied the Earl of Essex with interest. He was an old man, probably in his late forties, austere-looking, but the excitement of the day seemed to have infected him and he rode amongst the ranks of men, raising his hat and bowing to all and sundry. Everywhere he moved, a cheer went up.

The bands started to play and one by one, pennants were raised as brigades prepared to move off, horses to the fore and rear, the artillery, pikes and women in the middle. With regret, Dublin drew back, now assigned to a wagon drawn by a stringy-looking mare. It was going to be heavy work and the nag did not look up to the journey. Dublin felt a pang of sympathy for this lowly creature. From now on the horse would be her responsibility.

It was time for Robert to move on. His eyes shone with emotion. The handsome black gelding that carried him had cost ten pounds and it was sleek and restless and on its toes. He sat proud in the saddle. Dublin thought he looked like a god.

Robert turned to her as she stood by her mare's head, stroking the horse behind the ears to soothe her. For a terrible moment, Dublin wondered if this might be the last time they would ever speak. Robert met her eyes and she guessed that he felt something similar.

'God be with you. So that you need have no fear, I have made provision for you in my will. If anything befalls me, give me your word that you will go back to Chertsey.'

'Robert . . .' Terror forced out every other thought. For the first time she used his name and he shook his head to stop her.

'There is nothing to fear.' He gave her a tight smile that said everything, and nothing. Spurring the horse forward he turned his head to take one last look back. 'You are a very special woman,' he said. 'God go with you.'

Such was the press of numbers, that it was about an hour after the first cavalry troop moved off, before the infantry began their march. Caleb was already fatigued by the prolonged drilling that had started at the moment of his enlistment. Now he hoisted the long ashpole of his pike, blinking as the sun flashed across its metal tip. His hands were raw from the drilling. He lifted his pack across his shoulder and fell into step, keeping pace with his companions, his stride in rhythm with the beat of the drum. In his pack were enough supplies for a week. By that time they should have reached their destination and once there, the relief of Gloucester would be their objective.

Caleb did not know where Gloucester was. In fact, he did not know where he was at that very moment. Once away from the Island shores, he had no clear vision of the geography of his country. The knowledge made him feel uneasy, dependent on those around him. He was not used to relying on anyone.

As they marched, preachers were exhorting them to do God's work. Their message was passionate, but it did not tell Caleb what he wanted to know. Fornication, theft, praising God were foremost in the recitals. Caleb's thoughts rested always on the aftermath of this struggle – what then? What would be the future for this land? King or Parliament, he was not sure that either would improve the lot of the landless and the lowly. Too late, he asked himself what he was doing here.

A little to his right, a wagon trundled along, pulled by a sickly-looking ox. On board, a young woman unhitched her bodice and gave suck to her babe. He thought that back at Caulbourne, Sara's already ample breasts would soon be swelling to hold the milk that would nourish his child. He visualised his wife clearly, her round, grey-green eyes, long, straight, light-brown hair, plump cheeks and short neck . . . a plain woman made fair by her love for him. He could almost feel her desolation when she learned of his desertion. Leaving her was the cruellest thing that he could have done, but he comforted himself with the thought that his mother would take care of her.

When he finally returned home, he would be a hero and a father, but between now and then was the unknown. Would he kill, *could* he kill . . . or would he himself be killed? Would he wound, or be maimed? Would success or failure be theirs?

The countryside looked familiar yet different. Around him the land showed signs of devastation where hungry armies had stolen anything that grew. It was the peasants who suffered, their very livelihoods snatched away from beneath their noses.

Already his feet ached and his face glistened in the late summer warmth. Thinking of Sara had been a mistake. The memory of her quiet, constant presence, the certainty of her, the comfort of her soft, yielding body opened up a void of loneliness. Suddenly he missed her very much.

Chapter 28

The euphoria that carried Lord Essex and his troops out of London with such high hopes, soon seeped away. Before long, the infantry became tired and footsore. All their drilling and parading had not prepared them for the long, gruelling march, day in day out, and their laments soon became a common chorus as they negotiated the endless, cratered lanes. Each man carried a week's supply of bread and cheese and when this ran out, they were still less than half way to Gloucester. Some fell sick and horses went lame.

Gradually the troops became spread out and the several thousand souls who had marched so jauntily together from Hounslow, were no longer one army. While the main party forged ahead, small groups became separated. Stragglers fell further behind, slipping away in the night, running back to their homes. Fear of recapture was less urgent than the current privations.

Robert's party was nearing Bicester when trouble struck. It was near dusk and Dublin had just erected her tent for the night's camp. The evening was chilly, made sharper by the empty velvet of the sky. The jolting of the wagon had made her stiff all over, and the dank night air ate into her bones.

The army had not stopped to eat since daybreak and she no longer felt hungry, but the acrid scent of venison, already roasting over the fire, began to torment her nostrils.

Suddenly, musket-fire stopped her in her tracks. From all sides, horsemen appeared as if from nowhere, wielding swords, shouting blasphemies, a deafening, unstoppable force.

Instinctively Dublin dived for the tent and fumbled for the knife she used for cutting meat. Her fingers scrabbled about in vain. In the dark she froze. The earth shook with the stampeding of horses and at any moment her tent threatened to be trampled underfoot. She was back again at Carrickmain.

Dublin covered her ears against the battle cries, the strange distorted howls of fear and bloodlust only feet away, expecting that at any moment the tent-flap would be torn open and she would be dragged to a bloody death. In the back of her mind, distanced by her own immediate danger, was the terrible thought of what might happen to Robert. Silently she began to pray, offering anything, everything if only he should be safe.

The skirmish did not last long. Ere dark, the sound of hooves grew more distant. Outside, occasional voices pierced the shocked silence, then the volume of sound expanded and changed to cries of jubilation.

As the remnants of the raiding party limped away, Dublin crawled outside. Nearby a group of soldiers danced and whistled, unable to contain their exultation. They had repulsed some four hundred Royalist horse.

'You did it!' The men were patting their leader on the back, shaking his hand. 'Well done, Robin! Bravely fought, sir!' She realised with a mixture of disbelief and horror that it was Robert who had led the counter-attack. Pride in his courage was immediately outweighed by shock at the danger he had risked. At the thought of what might have been, she began to tremble, sinking down onto the wet grass near the dying fire. She started to sob.

All around, relief rippled through the camp, rising to a wave of joy which in turn gave way to sober grief as the dead were counted. There were some twenty casualties.

Desperately Dublin wanted to speak with Robert, to tell him what she felt. But for the grace of God they might have already lived through the last moments of their lives. Before she died she had to tell him, but he was now nowhere to be seen. His responsibility for his men, his loyalty to the regiment, outweighed any other thoughts he might have.

As she watched, a large grave was hastily dug by firelight. She stood helplessly by. Then she saw him, standing at the edge of the pit, praying over the bodies of those who had given their lives. He was bare-headed, his hair lifting in the sharp wind. His voice was strong and carried far but was tinged with emotion. Once he hesitated and she knew that he was near to tears. Each man present bowed his head in silent acknowledgement. After the last body was lowered into the pit and earth dropped by the handful onto their dead brothers, the assembled company began to drift away.

One by one the army returned to their tasks, trying to put some normality back into the night. All the time Dublin wondered if the enemy still watched and whether they would return like wolves to a flock. Robert had retired with the other officers. She spent the night alone in the dark, kneeling on the damp grass, praying to Robert's God, to her mother's God, to anyone who might bring them safe from this hell.

By dawn, she knew that her prayers were answered. The enemy did not reappear. As soon as it was light, the army moved on.

The next day, 1 September, the soldiers met up with the London Regiments at Brackley. From there they still had sixty miles to go across the Cotswolds. Strain showed in each man's face, for every ridge, every hill might hide Prince Rupert's demon cavalry, hell-bent on turning them back.

To make matters worse, a rumour spread that Gloucester had already fallen. Colonel Massey, the Governor, was a young man of Robert's age. He had not long taken his commission with the Parliament, having been disaffected with the Royalist cause. There was little to suggest that he could be relied upon once the going grew hard. On firm authority, they had it that he had asked for a settlement even before the siege began. Their mission seemed hopeless.

As they continued westwards, the weather became increasingly cold. Day and night, rain fell in unrelenting sheets and it was hard to recall what it was like to be warm. Everything, everyone was weighed down by the icy chill. Wagons were stuck to their axles in mud, and even under cover it was no better, for clothes clung heavy and freezing to exhausted limbs.

Just once, Dublin wondered whether it would not be better to have the warmth and comfort of Abbey House or Great Hampden, but the thought soon passed. She lit a fire but it was immediately doused by the torrent. Her toes tormented her with chilblains.

She tried to lift her spirits by reliving over and again the moment when Robert had called her 'special'. She saw him only to deliver food to his quarters and he was ever in the company of others. Yet he always acknowledged her, with a nod of thanks or a brief, tired smile. She wondered if the time would ever come when they should be alone.

The raids became more insistent. Prince Rupert descended upon their troops with the savagery of a heathen, but the pike held their positions and forced him to retreat. Yet the Parliament men were losing heart. Only the knowledge that it was now further to go back to London than to continue, stopped them from deserting in droves. Inexorably they moved on.

At night it was so cold that no one slept. Even when the rain ceased they dared not light fires for fear of giving their position away. All the time they did not know whether Gloucester had already fallen to the King.

Finally, on the dark, miserable evening of 5 September, they reached the brow of Prestbury Hill. Cannon-shot fired out to alert the citizens of Gloucester that relief was on its way.

Dublin's wagon struggled up the incline. She felt too cold, wet and tired to go on. There had been no sign of Robert for two days. Suddenly the scene ahead caused her to catch her breath. The valley of the River Severn spread out below like a strange fairytale land, the wide curving sweep of the river shimmering in the rain. Towering over the landscape like a true pillar of strength, was the mighty Gloucester Cathedral. For a moment it reminded her of the stone at Glendruid, a symbol of life and power.

Between the besieging army and the city walls, pockets of fire burned – for the King's force was still outside the city walls! The Roundhead cheers must have been heard in Gloucester itself. They raised their flagging energies and were all for hurrying on to make the descent and rescue the besieged city, but conditions were so bad that the wagons became stuck fast and some even overturned on the sharp descent. Lord Essex ordered the troops to wait until morn.

Dublin's mare – which she had graced with the name of Fortune – struggled gamely on, although there had been little enough fodder on the way. She was now no more than a bag of bones. By some miracle the wagon was still intact, although one wheel was beginning to wobble dangerously.

There was no point in erecting tents. Dublin unhitched the

wagon and prepared to sleep beneath it on the wet grass. She had reached a point where she was immune to rain.

Before crawling beneath it, she pulled her dripping shawl around her shoulders and gazed at the flickering lights in the valley. Nearby, Fortune tried to graze on the stunted, trampled grass.

Someone approached them. She did not need to look round. Something about his presence transcended sight or sound. Robert joined her in silence and together they observed the scene below.

'Tomorrow will see the showdown,' he said.

'Do you think we will succeed?' She wanted to talk of other things, but tonight no one could think beyond the taking of Gloucester.

'If God wills. We have sent scouts ahead and it seems that the garrison are in good spirits.'

The question she most dreaded asked itself: 'Think you there will be much bloodshed?'

He did not answer straight away. His profile in the gloom was shadowed. His hair, normally soft and lightly waving, was plastered against his skin. He looked weary and she felt a mother's need to comfort him. She said nothing, not wishing to hurry his visit to an end. He seemed content just to stand there, watching. She screwed her toes up inside her shoes and squeezed the water out through the soles.

'If I should not survive this siege,' he said evenly, 'I would like you to know how much I think of you. You are loyal and brave – and very beautiful.'

She listened in a dream.

Robert continued to address his remarks into the dark. 'If I do survive, then I must do what is best for you. When we get back to Chertsey, I will settle a sum upon you and you must seek a husband – not a labouring man, someone with his letters or perhaps a yeoman with some land.'

'No! I'll never wed!' A slap across the face could not have been more painful.

He was silent a long while. 'It would be best if you did.'

'Best for whom?' The hurt made her sharp and accusing.

Again he was a long time answering, then straightening up he said, 'For you. Otherwise I might do something that I would regret.'

'What sort of something?'

207

He turned towards her. His eyes were large and serious and there was longing in them. 'Don't you know? Don't you know how much I think of you?'

She was too stunned to reply and he took her silence for shock or perhaps disapproval.

'I am sorry. I have no wish to offend you. Just get yourself safely wed.'

'Never!'

'Then that makes it harder.'

'I want to be with you.' Desperation made her bold and he suddenly looked angry.

'You want to end up like the leaguer ladies? Believe me, it would be best for you to be a wife rather than a punk for the taking of any enlisted man, which is where you'll end up if . . .'

'I'd rather be your – punk.' She stumbled over the word, knowing little of its meaning, knowning only that he must forget about Mary Hampden.

She waited, hoping that he would kiss her, ask her to lie with him.

Instead he told her: 'I should never have said anything. You must forget it. As soon as this siege is over I will have you escorted back to Chertsey.'

'I won't go!'

'You will.'

'I'm not your hired maid.'

'No, you're not.' His eyes were black with pain. 'I don't know what you are, but whatever it is, you torment me. Enough. Tomorrow we have serious work to do.'

He turned on his heel and walked back the way he had come, leaving her in turmoil, immune to the mud that now ran into her shoes. Thinking over what he had said, it seemed both the best and the worst thing imaginable.

She did not sleep. In any event, by first light the whole regiment was on the alert, ready for the attack. In the grey gloom of a damp dawn they looked out again across the valley. Below them, enemy camp-fires spiralled.

They expected that soon the besieged garrison would make a sally, and prepared themselves to go to their aid, but as the light grew stronger, the scene before them was clearly revealed. In the valley there were no Royalist soldiers, no tents, no horses between Lord Essex's troops and the city of Gloucester, just a series of sorry fires smokily consuming the damp dross of the abandoned camp. The King's army had gone.

There was such celebration in Gloucester! They were greeted like heroes although they had not in truth fired a shot in the city's defence, but for the moment everybody was a friend. Strangers hugged and danced in the streets and everyone had a tale of hardship or bravery to tell.

Dublin's cartwheel had become so rickety that she abandoned it and led her mare instead, with her belongings tied about the horse. Around her, wives and sweethearts broke rank and mingled with their men, so Dublin took the plunge and sought Robert out. His half-declaration of the night before gave her courage.

He was mounted on his black gelding, waving to the citizens who lined the streets to welcome the cavalcade. He looked relaxed, exhilarated by the success.

'This is a happy day,' Dublin called, swallowing her fear and riding up beside him.

She thought his face grew red but he reined in to wait for her. 'It is indeed. Tonight we dine with Governor Massey.'

For a wild moment she hoped that by 'we' he meant himself and her, so she asked: 'Where do you stay?'

'At the Governor's house.' He paused. 'One of my Lieutenants will find you quarters.'

There was the familiar pain of rejection, but she knew that it was not possible to stay with him. It did not lessen the longing, however. She made an effort to be cheerful. 'Will you tell me about it on the morrow?'

'I will. You must be safely quartered.' His face coloured as he added: 'When time allows, I will call on you.'

There was a sudden awkwardness. Neither of them could acknowledge what they were thinking. The cheering made it difficult to hear. Secretly she wondered if he would really come and seek her out. She tried not to think ahead because the pain of disappointment would be too great.

He called to one of his Lieutenants and gave instructions to have her found lodgings, then with a brief nod of his head and a brief wave, he rode off into the town.

Dublin held Fortune by the bridle and rested her face against the mare's neck. The warmth and light went with him.

She was billeted upon a family of carters who lived in the centre of Gloucester. They were kind enough, willing to share what little they had with the relieving army. They were hungry for news and it was easy to satisfy them with an account of life in London and of the trek across England. Even her accent passed without comment, for there were no enemies here. By the time Dublin took to her bed, she was filled with food and ale and content to slip into a peaceful sleep.

The following morning she awoke with a muzzy head. She was still abed when the wife of the house came to rouse her.

'A gentleman to see you.'

She scrambled into her clothes and stepped out into the street to find Robert waiting. He was on foot but he carried a saddle. 'Here, I bought this. If you are going to ride that mare, you'll need it.' He wore clean linen and his hair was dressed. The celebrations of the night before did not show on his face.

'I thank you.' She took the saddle and hastened to put it safely inside the house. As she came back out, he indicated that they should walk.

'You are comfortable here?'

She nodded. As if acknowledging their mood the sun broke through and a warm breeze touched the air.

'Was it a good evening?' she asked, struggling with her envy. There must have been women present, either young girls of quality or even camp followers. The thought of any woman capturing his attention, stealing his smile, sent spirals of despair tumbling in her breast.

'It was a good evening, yes.' As they walked, he continued to talk. 'Saving Gloucester is the best thing to happen to Parliament in many months. Governor Massey is an able man. He inspires confidence. When the enemy dammed the water supply he diverted the river so that the mills kept grinding. In the whole duration of the siege, not one of his officers deserted. A lesser man would not have held the town.'

Secretly, she thought that the description could equally have applied to Robert.

'What will happen next?' she asked. 'Have we now won the war?'

210

His face clouded and at the same moment the sun was eclipsed. In his carefully measured way he said: 'This is just the beginning. When we left London we had no thought but to prevent the fall of Gloucester. Well, we have succeeded but I have to ask myself at what cost.' He nodded across at the distant hills. 'Somewhere out there, between us and London, is the King's army. It is our duty to get back to the capital as quickly as possible – and it is their duty to stop us. Come what may, there will be much blood spilt before this conflict sees a happy ending.'

Chapter 29

With great reluctance, the Parliamentary army set out for London. On the outward trek, assaulted by foul weather and held back by lumbering wagons, progress had been slow. On the return journey they travelled at speed, not following a direct route but feinting to throw a hidden enemy off their tracks. All the time they lived in expectation that day or night, a marauding troop of Royalists would descend upon them.

Since leaving Gloucester the army had had little rest. Before long their pace slowed. It was made worse by the leisurely gait of the cattle they captured en route and with which they resolutely refused to part. These men had known hunger and would go to any lengths to avoid it again. From now on their food travelled with them.

At first, Essex's troops avoided the King's army. Reaching Reading, the Earl ordered the remaining garrison to abandon the town and come with them. In all, they were some fifteen thousand souls. Now their sole aim was to reach London first and save the capital from attack. The race was on.

After Reading, they set their sights on Newbury, a town of good size which promised to offer free quarter. There was not one of them who did not long for a dry billet. As they drew near, scouts were sent ahead to arrange accommodation.

Along with everyone else Dublin rejoiced at the prospect of some respite. She was relieved of the responsibility of a wagon but the riding was hard and her poor Fortune could barely keep pace with the main army.

Just as they were preparing their minds for the comforts ahead, the news filtered back – the King's men were ahead of them! Just

212

two hours earlier, the Royalists had installed themselves in Newbury and now barred the way to London. If the Roundheads wanted to pass, they had no choice but to fight.

Dublin thought to herself: If I am going to die, then it will be at his side. There would be consolation in sharing his last moments. Together they would step from this world to be made whole in the next. Mary Hampden would have no part in this. Then came the awful thought: What if he alone should die . . . She offered up the prayer: '*Please God, don't let him perish without me.*'

It was easy for Dublin to pick out an Ensign from Robert's troop and in return for five shillings, she bought from him a change of clothing. It was all the money that she possessed, given to her in case she should become separated from the main column, but the price was worth it.

The Ensign was a small man, jokingly called King Charles by his friends because of a supposed resemblance to His majesty. Even so, his breeches were large and she had to tie them up with cord. The rough cloth shirt was loose, fortunately, and hid her breasts, but the spare boots that had been taken from a dead musketeer were alas, also too big. Dublin had to stuff the toes with her stockings to make them fit. With her hair pinned up, she would pass well enough for a man. In the heat of battle, who would be looking? With trembling hands she tied the orange sash around her hat, and waited.

The countryside around Newbury was undulating. Stands of trees outlined the enclosed fields. Away to their left, the land was more open but the Parliamentary forces had the advantage of higher ground. Raising their heads and voices, the Parliamentary ministers asked for God's blessing upon their cause.

At first light, unnoticed, Dublin rode Fortune into the ranks of the cavalry and chose her spot. For once the men had to go into battle sober, and as their Captain, Robert had to encourage them, by making jokes. Dublin positioned herself just behind him. She looked with dismay at his taut face and dark-rimmed eyes. Her heart threatened to give her away by its beating.

Suddenly in the distance a charge was sounded, and out of nowhere Prince Rupert's cavalry came up across the fields. Within moments Dublin found herself in the centre of a yelling, frenzied mêlée. She closed her eyes, waiting for the blow that would take her to her Maker.

213

But the cavalry were powerless to run them down, for the hedges and narrow lanes constrained them. Pistol-shot, muskets and cannon boomed their death-knells. The sky was black with choking smoke.

From the first, Dublin lost sight of Robert. In panic, Fortune wheeled and carried her mistress away from the fighting. Try as she might, it was impossible to turn the mare. The horse did not stop until she had put half a league's distance between herself and the centre of the battle.

Panting and with aching arms, Dublin turned to look back at the sight. Pockets of dense smoke obscured the action but the screams of men and animals painted a picture more macabre than any canvas.

She watched, paralysed, as between the gusts of smoke the hedgehogs of pike repelled all attempts to dislodge them. Behind them the artillery discharged round after round of shot. An explosion near to hand shook her from her trance. An entire column of men were split asunder by a single cannon-shot. Whose cause they championed Dublin could not tell. Arms, heads, bowels, brains, splattered the ground. These were some mothers' sons, some women's sweethearts. Beneath her, Fortune trembled, rigid with fear. She soothed the mare to turn her own mind from the unbearable. Somewhere down there was the man she loved.

The fighting lasted until dusk. She had no idea if they were victorious or in defeat. The cries of the wounded chilled her blood. Already, systematically, survivors went among the bodies, stripping them, taking anything of value. She watched in horror as a soldier hacked the finger from a wounded man to gain his ring. There was a time when she would have run to prevent such barbarity, intervened to protect the innocent, but now she remained paralysed. War drives out such noble instincts. Could this be what they were fighting for?

Fear for Robert's safety outweighed everything else. Fortune still refused to turn back so Dublin dismounted and began to run, searching for news of her man, hardly daring to look on the dead for fear of seeing his face. Many of the corpses were naked. Some were so disfigured that it was impossible to identify them. She fought back the bile and covered her nose to escape the sickly-sweet smell of blood.

'Dublin!' It was Robert who found her. Her hat had fallen off and her hair was now loose. She had not even noticed.

'In God's name, child, what are you doing?'

He leaned forward and pulled her up onto the saddle in front of him. She felt an insane mixture of affront and relief at being designated a child. His physical presence overwhelmed her. To her shame, tears showed in her eyes.

'I am not a child and I was looking for you.'

'And putting yourself at risk in the process.' He rode away from the carnage, back towards the town. They passed the spot where she had abandoned her horse and in the company of the gelding, the mare now kept pace.

'How stands the battle?' she asked, fearing the response.

'We have routed them. Come, we are free now to take accommodation.' She knew that the flippant remark hid the true nature of his feelings. Robert reined in and set her down in the street and as he did so, he gave a little grunt of discomfort. Looking up, she saw for the first time that his shirt dripped red with blood.

'You're wounded!'

He looked down at his arm and seemed as surprised as she was. Cautiously he felt the blood as if not believing that it was his own, then she saw his expression change as the pain began to claim him.

'I didn't realise. In the heat of battle . . .'

'We must find you a surgeon.'

'I have something to do first.'

'No! What?'

'The Royalists are asking if we have taken Lord Falkland as prisoner. I must find him.'

'But why?'

'He was – *is* – a friend. There is no more noble spirit than his.'

She looked helplessly at him. 'Please, don't go back.'

'I must.' Seeing her expression, he said: 'You go ahead and find accommodation. Later I'll seek you out. Tell them you act on my behalf.'

Before she could protest further, he wheeled the gelding and rode back out of town.

There was nothing else that she could do. Selecting a house of good size she walked to the door and simply asked for quarter for: 'My Captain and myself.' To her amazement, Fortune was taken

215

from her and she was immediately shown to an upper chamber by a girl of about her own age.

'We are pleased to welcome you,' she said, unlatching the casement to let the late evening warmth into the room. The window faced away from the battleground, across the stables. The sweet smell and comforting sound of horses assailed Dublin's nostrils and in that balmy September air it was hard to believe the destruction that lay within walking distance.

The girl said: 'Our sympathies are with your cause. Last night the King's soldiers took much of our meat and wine but there is more hidden.' She turned with a smile. 'My father is a mercer. His trade is sore injured by this war.'

Dublin nodded her sympathy. 'My Captain is a good man. He will pay for what he takes.'

The girl smiled again, suddenly coquettish. 'Does he pay you?'

'For what?'

'For what he takes.'

'I serve him willingly.' Then getting her meaning, Dublin blushed.

This pleased her hostess and the girl patted the mattress on the great four-poster. 'Not a word to my Mama. She would whip me if she heard me, but I believe in making most advantage of what God has given me. A Captain is coming back for me soon.'

She preened herself and Dublin could think of no answer.

When Robert arrived she knew immediately that he had found his friend. His face was drained of colour and he held himself stiffly because of the wound but over and above that, the pain of loss showed in his face.

For the moment however, more pressing things concerned her. With difficulty Dublin helped him off with his buff coat and then tore away the blood-soaked shirt. A wound perhaps an inch long and half an inch wide gaped in his upper arm. Within the ragged, bloody hole the dull metallic lead of shot showed. Her stomach contracted and she swallowed down her nausea.

Taking clean water and cloth she attempted to clean his arm. 'You need a surgeon.'

'Can you not take it out?'

'No.'

'Why not?'

'It will hurt you.'

216

He straightened up. 'Surgeons are in short supply. There are worse hurt than me. If the shot stays in it will cause harm.'

He handed her the dagger that hung in the scabbard at his waist. She willed him to change his mind but he held her with his eyes, the handle of the knife resting against her unwilling hand.

'Please.'

Some untaught knowledge made her take his match and cord and making a flame, she baptised the blade with it. Fire purifies.

He nodded his head to her to continue and fighting down her fear, she tried to prise the lead from the hole. It did not wish to budge. Twice he could not swallow back the agony that her probing inflicted. 'Robert . . .'

'Don't stop!'

There was no going back. His scarlet life's blood ran over her fingers. Averting her face so that she should not see his pain she tried again and this time the lead came away. She held it in her palm like some malevolent eye.

Now the shot was out she took clean linen and lined it with cobwebs to make a bandage. When the arm was covered she let out her breath and sank back onto a settle feeling weak and faint.

'Brave girl.' His face was grey.

'Not as brave as you.'

He gave her a wry look. 'I would not choose to go through that every day.'

'Are you in pain?'

'Enough. Go and see if they have any sack.'

She washed her hands in the basin then went to do as he bid. Downstairs they gave her a flask of wine. Robert drank deeply then he held it out. She started to shake her head but he nodded encouragingly. 'It is good for shock. You need something to calm yourself after your ordeal.'

The taste was harsh but within moments it seemed that new blood coursed in her veins.

'Did you find your Lord?' she asked.

His face hardened. 'I did. He was only recognisable by the mole on his neck.' He gazed away from her, cut off by grief. 'The passing of someone such as he makes me question this war.'

'I cannot believe that any man's death justifies it.' The memory of the women's peace march was clear in her mind. She said: 'He must be a loss to the Parliament.'

217

Robert shook his head. 'Lucius was fighting for the King. He was the most honest man I ever had the joy of meeting.'

'Was he not then your enemy?'

'Never. We simply saw the road to honour in different ways. They say that he deliberately rode to his death because he could not bear the conflict.'

These tangled loyalties left Dublin confused and she remained silent.

'His widow will be distraught,' Robert said. 'Theirs was a true love-match. He married against his father's wishes, to a woman of modest means.'

Dublin felt a mixture of envy then pity for that woman who had been so loved. Aloud she said: 'Another widow.'

He did not comment. His eyes were heavy and sinking back on the bed he closed them, but after a moment looked up again.

'Have you eaten?'

'I couldn't.' The thought of what she had witnessed that afternoon crowded in on her.

'Then where are you sleeping?'

The question caught her out. She had not thought past finding this safe place for her master. Seeing her hesitation, he caught his breath as if about to speak but then was silent. Finally he said: 'I would prefer not to sleep alone this night. I give you my word that I will do you no dishonour but – lie here with me.'

Not quite believing what he was asking, she began to remove the Ensign's cumbersome boots and rough breeches then clad only in his shirt, she climbed uncertainly onto the bed. For a while she sat looking down at him as he lay dozing, the line of his jaw, the curl of his hair, the flickering of his eyelids, then carefully she lowered herself beside him. This was a scene she had enacted a thousand times but now she trembled with emotion.

After a moment he reached out with his good arm and pulled her close.

'Thank you,' he said.

'For what?'

'For staying with me.'

'I would not wish it otherwise.'

With a little grunt of exhaustion, he leaned his head against her shoulder and fell into sleep.

Sometime in the night Dublin surfaced into the warm dark cocoon of Robert's bed. She could feel the heat of his flesh and a magic more potent than any spell drew her closer to him. She knew that he was awake.

Pushing the cover back, he raised the shirt above her waist and gently began to caress her naked flesh. She was suspended in another world. There was no fear. His patient hands soothed her until she would have fain melted into his probing fingers. He kissed her hair and eased her over.

Just for a moment she hesitated. A lifelong taboo instilled into her long before coming to England, held her back for a fleeting second but the magic of this journey could not be denied. His prick was hard and moist, seeking her out. She only wished to grant him the release he sought, to please him. Even the pain of his penetration was overlaid with joy that she, Dublin, should take him into herself. She cared nothing for the blood that stained her legs. The sacrifice was as it should be.

Afterwards he lay on his side, his injured arm uppermost. She felt as one with him, enveloped in a sense of peace. She wanted to hang onto this moment for ever.

After a while he shifted his position and let out a sigh. Into the darkness he said, 'Forgive me.'

She kissed his shoulder but he did not respond. Tendrils of fear began to touch her. 'I love you,' she said.

'I know that you do. That makes it so much worse. I tried to warn you.'

'About what?'

He sighed again and moved onto his back, separating himself from her. She fought down the need to grab hold of him, keep him close.

'I didn't mean to use you. You deserve better.'

'I don't want anything better. Robert, please . . .'

'You mustn't have any foolish hopes.'

Fear twisted her heart. He was going to send her away. 'I haven't,' she lied.

'It isn't that I don't care for you. You must know that I do, but I gave my promise to John Hampden. Mary has already paid her portion to my uncle. When the war is over and she is of age I shall honour my bargain.'

'You will still wed with her.' She faced the pain of defeat, a long dark journey which she would have to make alone. 'Do you love her?'

She felt his shoulders move in a shrug. 'What do you mean by love?'

She sat up and hugged her knees, trying to instil some warmth into her emptiness. 'I mean caring for someone more than yourself, wanting to be with them. Not wanting to live without them.'

'That isn't love, that's abandon. You should not put that burden onto someone else.'

'I don't ask anything of you.'

'No, you don't, but one look at you and I see a fragile flower that can so easily be crushed.'

Dublin turned away from him, struggling to still the dread. 'I'm not fragile. I don't need anyone.'

He was silent for a long while then he said: 'That might be so, but God help me, I surely need you.'

She turned and put her arms about him, kissing his brow and temples and eyelids. Her heart was bursting with love. 'You have me,' she replied. 'You always will.'

He pulled her close and she clung to him, trying to lose herself in him, never to be separated again. She thought: Thank God, now everything is going to be well.

Chapter 30

Caleb endured the march to Gloucester without complaint. Each time the army was attacked he found himself responding by instinct, standing with his companions, presenting a united, impregnable front of pikes that offered protection to the musketeers and cavalry. As the lines held and each man kept his nerve, he began to feel pride in the courage of his companions. He defended them stoutly.

In spite of the fatigue engendered by too little sleep and the constant fear of night-time assaults, he retained his good spirits. As the days went by and the attacks increased, he recognised that he conducted himself well in battle, but by the time they rode, triumphant into Gloucester, he had not in fact killed a single Royalist.

He joined in the city's celebrations, drinking too much ale, singing in the streets, storing up tales to tell when he returned home. Gradually, this alien way of life was becoming familiar.

On the journey back he began to feel a sense of excitement. Once they reached the capital, a decisive battle would be fought. He, Caleb, would be one of those who charted the future. When years ahead, men looked back, they would see the battle for London as a turning point in England's history. Once the King was defeated, a new future would dawn for this land. Now Caleb had a sense of purpose.

The setback at Newbury therefore, took him by surprise. He had not foreseen more fighting until they reached London itself and then there would be one, life-or-death struggle for right and honour. For this he would have died. Instead, finding the way blocked, there was no choice but to take up positions and wait.

221

Lined up with his company, Caleb felt calm and confident that this fray would be no different from those other skirmishes that had dogged their outward journey. At first light a man of about his own age, mounted on a handsome black gelding, stopped to offer encouragement, empty words that Caleb accepted without believing them.

'Today will see God's will done. Hold your line when the enemy attack, my lads, and have no fear. By tonight, we shall all enjoy the blessing of heaven – either here on earth – or with God's own assembly.'

Caleb grinned wryly. If he had a choice, he would experience heaven here, on earth. For a moment he felt a flicker of resentment. The young Captain appeared to have all of God's gifts – good health, a good countenance and a fine, athletic body. His clothes were weatherproof, of excellent quality and he held himself with an inborn pride, the rich son of a rich son. Caleb wondered what it was like to have all the world's blessings.

Then, within seconds, the distant rumbling of a charging force turned every head. Clouds of dust marked the galloping approach of cavalrymen. Clearly the Royalists had decided to take matters into their own hands. Caleb gripped his weapon and lowered it as the order came to: 'Charge your pike!'

The cavalry continued to bear down, swerving at the very last second as the pikes held fast. The dust, the heat of men and horses, choked Caleb's nostrils. Beneath the helmets he could see eyes ablaze with zeal, hatred, excitement, fear. He felt nothing.

Everything was confusion. The fighting continued throughout the day. Caleb found himself advancing with the pikemen, pushing forward over uneven ground. Behind him his own troops drove the company on. Ahead, enemy horsemen challenged yet again.

The advancing pikemen began to ascend a soft, uneven mound. Caleb stumbled, and glancing down, saw with disbelief that they trampled over the bodies of dead and dying soldiers. All his certainty crumbled.

Suddenly the ranks broke. Caleb found himself standing alone. Directly in front of him a single horse charged forwards, the rider brandishing a sword. Caleb lowered the pike until it was level with the man's chest, knowing that he must kill or be killed. At the last moment the Cavalier hesitated and Caleb could clearly see his

222

face. It was young, wide-eyed and fear showed in the open mouth, the frozen stance.

Now was Caleb's chance to save his own life, but he held back. Before him was a boy. He could not, would not strike the lad down. In the eternity that they faced each other, a sudden, unseen missile hit the rider. He jerked back in the saddle and his breeches showed red. The boy cried out, his eyes flickered and he fell from the horse.

Caleb did not stop to think. Throwing his pike aside he dashed forward to his enemy's prostrate form, warding off the trampling hooves, immune to the iron and shot that criss-crossed the air about him. Bending down, he hoisted the boy up and turning from the hell around him, carried him away.

Using four of his last six pence, Caleb found accommodation at an inn. There, he stripped his captive and tended to the ragged wound. It was within an inch of having blown away his scrotum. Fortunately, the shot had passed clean through the fleshy part of the upper leg.

The clothing that Caleb tore away was of the best, finest lawn, good cambric, all deeply trimmed with lace. The young Cavalier wore good worsted breeches and supple leather boots, which the shepherd could not help but covet. He thought briefly that here was another of God's favoured sons, but the earlier resentments did not trouble him. Wounded, the boy was as vulnerable as the poorest peasant.

In his saddle bag Caleb carried a pot of his sheep salve, and this he applied to the laceration, bandaging it with strips torn from his own shirt. He could do no more.

The boy lay semi-comatose, his body pale and childlike on the pallet. His hair was long and golden, dressed in lovelocks. His body was slim, almost girlish, and apart from a fuzz of ginger in his groin, hairless. His naked vulnerability roused in Caleb a sense of pathos, a feeling, half-paternal, half-maternal, wanting to protect this man-child from further harm. The feelings were alien, dangerous. Simple hatred for the enemy would have been easier.

He fetched a flagon of ale and sat in the window recess, slowly drinking, watching over his charge. One penny remained in his satchel. He had no idea what to do next.

After an eternity the boy's eyes flickered open. A series of

223

emotions passed over his features – confusion, pain, fear, a child-like anxiety. He looked to Caleb for reassurance.

'You're safe. The wound isn't serious.'

'You were fighting with the enemy,' said the boy.

'No. *You* were fighting with the enemy.' Caleb raised the lad's head and trickled some of the ale into his dry mouth. 'Drink up, now.'

'Where is my horse?'

Caleb shrugged. 'I had enough trouble rescuing you.'

'My father paid fifty guineas for her. He'll not be pleased if I've lost her.'

'Your father is lucky to still have a son. How old are you?'

'I'm past sixteen.'

The shepherd felt the weight of his twenty-two years.

'Where do you hail from?' he asked.

'I am Tristram Fortunatus. My father is Lord Tring.'

The name meant nothing and Caleb waited. His charge looked displeased with the blank response and added: 'You acted dishonourably in leaving the field.'

'I saved your life!'

Tristram shifted himself painfully up on the mattress, easing the weight of the cover away from his lap. He said: 'Technically you are a deserter.'

Caleb blinked in disbelief. 'You would rather I had left you to die?'

'Naturally not.' The young man paused. 'Who are you and what is your station?'

Caleb told him his name and the name of his village, adding: 'I am a shepherd – and of an independent mind.'

'Am I your prisoner?'

The thought had never occurred to him. He raised his eyebrows and shrugged.

'Then I should take you prisoner. That way you can redeem yourself. I'll release you on condition that you come and fight for the King.'

'Never!'

'Then consider yourself in my employ.'

'That neither. I have no wish to be servant to any master.'

Tristram frowned. 'You speak like a Leveller. Then what shall you do?'

224

Caleb considered, fetching the pisspot for his patient. He was pleased to see that the liquid flowed clear and golden, no internal injuries. 'What shall *you* do?' he countered.

'Return home, to my father's estate. When I'm healed I'll take up arms again.' Tristram looked around, and seeing his satchel on the settle, indicated to Caleb that he should fetch it. After a moment's resistance to the imperious command, he complied, noticing the heavy silver clasps. The young man fished inside and produced a leather pouch.

'Here. Take this for your trouble. And go and find my horse.'

'I don't want your money. And I repeat, I am *not* your servant.'

Tristram looked crestfallen. 'Then can you find a Royalist officer? Anyone. Tell him to send word to Lord Tring that his son is at this inn. Please?'

Caleb grinned, the boy's wheedling charm winning him over. 'I'll do that.'

'And – take this money. You may have to pay a messenger, and I owe you for this accommodation.'

Reluctantly Caleb accepted the pouch and put it inside his shirt. It had been his intention to go to London, to get there before the city was attacked. Clearly, this was what he should do, try to find his regiment and join the campaign. The memory of the battlefield at Newbury, the noise, the stench of death, the soft, yielding flesh beneath his feet, stopped him short. He had no idea if his army had been victorious.

'I'll find help for you, then I shall leave here,' he said aloud. He picked up his own satchel. 'Farewell then, Cavalier. I wish you health – and a pox on your cause!'

The young man bowed his head good-naturedly. 'God protect me from a masterless man!'

Outside, Caleb stood indecisively on the pavement. Before seeking out a messenger, he wondered about his own journey. It was a long and dangerous walk to London. He thought of the youth lying upstairs in the inn and was suddenly struck with the futility of war. Had they blown each other apart that afternoon, what would have been achieved?

Now he was free. Did he really believe in the struggle enough, to go to London and die? Unbidden, an image of Sara's face came to him. Her pregnancy would now be some five moons advanced. Would that there was a way to send word to her.

With a sigh he pressed his hand against his side, feeling the bulky presence of the pouch. Curiously he took it out and weighed it in his hand. It was surprisingly heavy. Opening the thongs he tipped the contents into his palm. There, gleaming dully, were ten gold angels. Never had he seen so much money. He half-turned back, intending to return it to the lad, but remembering the fine clothing, the fifty-guinea horse, he resigned himself to Fate. Suddenly, another, far more powerful realisation came to him. With ten angels, he was a man of substance. Why go to London to die? He would go home, and unlike Tristram Fortunatus, he would never take up arms again.

Caleb set off on foot towards the south. He estimated that if he was lucky, it would take him about a week to get there. Before leaving Newbury, he took the precaution of hiding some of the gold angels about his person, cutting open the lining of his shirt and concealing a few inside, tucking others into his neckband and more behind a buckle on his boot. That way, if he were to be accosted by a footpad, or a deserting soldier like himself, he would not lose all of his fortune. Only three of the angels remained in the pouch tucked into his shirt.

The knowledge that he had deserted from the army weighed upon him. He felt no actual sense of betrayal, more the burden of an inbuilt belief that you should always finish what you had started. He was not a coward and the thought of his own death had not dismayed him, but he could no longer accept that butchering boys was a solution to the Roundheads' cause. When he arrived home he would find his own way of building a better future.

On reaching Portsmouth he wandered along the waterfront looking for a craft bound for the Island. Until this moment it had not occurred to him that boats might not be free to come and go as they pleased, but everywhere there was a strong military presence.

He was immediately drawn towards a barque loaded with sheep, guessing that they were being shipped across to the Island, ready to overwinter. Biding his time, he waited until there was nobody about then accosted the skipper.

'Hey! Where are you headed?' The boatman looked suspiciously at him.

'Who's asking?'

'Caleb Gosden. I'm – I'm a shepherd, on my way home.'

The man looked ill at ease. Caleb suddenly became aware that he was not alone. Two men carrying pistols had come up behind him and now stood one on each side.

'What the . . .' Before he could protest, they grabbed him by the arms.

'Some sort of spy, are you?'

'No! I'm going home.'

'Where have you been then?'

Caleb hesitated, loath to recount his brief sojourn in the army. His delay seemed to confirm the men in their suspicions. Swiftly they began to search him and immediately came upon the pouch.

'What's this then?'

'Payment for a job.'

'What sort of a job would that be – a stealing job?'

'No!' He tried to pull himself free but his resistance was taken as further evidence of his guilt.

'Right, young feller-me-lad. You come along o' us. I don't know if you're a common thief, or a spy, or a deserter, but whichever it is, you're up to no good.'

Try as he might to explain, the men would not listen. Within an hour, Caleb found himself once more incarcerated in a common gaol.

The next morning, he was charged with theft, the presence of the three gold angels making this the easiest felony to prove. Having nothing to lose, Caleb told of the rescue of Tristram Fortunatus, omitting to mention that he had left a field of battle before the issue was decided. The name of Fortunatus, or that of his father, Lord Tring, meant nothing to those on the Bench. Remembering Sir William Meux, Caleb tried his best to keep patient. The Justices conferred together and for a terrible eternity he suspected that the sentence would be one of hanging. He was not prepared to die like this.

The spokesman cleared his throat. 'Prisoner, we are not convinced that you acquired the money about your person in the way that you say. In fact, we are confident that such an amount could only have come into your hands by malicious means. However, while being sure that you have lied to this court, since your story cannot be disproved with absolute certainty, we have decided not to introduce the full weight of the sentence upon you. Instead of

227

being taken from this place and hanged, as I am no doubt sure that you deserve, you will be incarcerated instead in a place of safety, there to serve out three years of your life in hard labour.'

'Never!' Caleb began to struggle, but in vain.

'It's no good, lad. Thank your God that a noose isn't facing you.' One of his two escorts, built bigger than a bull, held him with ease, his gentle voice belying the force of his massive body. 'Do you have any means to support yourself?'

'Some small amount'. Caleb was unwilling to admit to having any money besides the three angels which had been confiscateed.

'Well, as long as you are able to pay, consider yourself lucky. It's my belief that every event in this life has a purpose. I don't know where you've been, but there's a war out there with no sign that it is going to end. You might just live to be glad that you spent three years in gaol and away from the conflict.'

Remembering Newbury and the trampled corpses, Caleb wondered if the prediction could just be true.

Chapter 31

Dublin awoke in the night to the warmth of Robert's body, but this time it was not the glow of love but the feverish heat of sickness that roused her.

'Robert?'

He grunted.

'You are in pain?'

'I'm burning.'

She hurried out of the bed, fumbling to light a candle, then fetched cold water and a cloth. Hastily she stripped the covers to sponge him down. His breathing came shallow and fast. Sweat glistened on his upper lip and his head felt like an oven.

Exposing his wound, she looked with dismay at the yellowing ring of pus on the cloth and the angry red rim to the ragged tear in his arm. As she gently squeezed around it, thick globs of filth oozed from the centre, making her shudder. His arm was hard and inflamed. All the time she thought: *He's going to die*!

'Try to rest. I'll be back.'

Struggling into her clothes, she hastened down the narrow stairway and knocked loud on the door of the landlord with no thought to the fact that it was the middle of the night. After an eternity he came to answer her call, owl-eyed, his hair awry.

'My lord is sick. We need salves for a wound and something for fever. Where can I find a surgeon?'

He looked at her curiously, his face crumpled from sleep, blinking his eyes the better to focus. She realised then that when last he had seen her it had been in the guise of an ensign. Her face grew hot with shame at the unintended deception.

Mercifully he allowed her inside and after a hasty consultation with his wife, who was hidden from view in the alcove that served as their bedchamber, he returned to rummage in the long sideboard that filled the length of their parlour, finally producing a phial of liquid. In silence he held it out.

'Poppy juice. It will soothe him, ease any pain. Keep him cool and if he's no better by the morrow then send out for someone. You need help?'

She shook her head. 'God bless you.'

Upstairs, Robert tossed restlessly upon the bed. He had thrown the covers aside and now began to shiver with the rigors of fever.

Dublin always carried comfrey with her. Working fast, she spread a paste upon a piece of petticoat to make a poultice, then bound the arm again. Silently she prayed that the medicinal powers of the herb would work.

Somehow she forced a spoonful of the laudanum between Robert's teeth. He was rigid with trembling and seemed hardly to be aware of her presence. A terrible fear claimed her. Climbing back into the bed, she pulled the covers up and tried to warm him with her body. There was nothing to do except pray. All the time the nightmare thought tormented her; that in such cases, half the victims die.

After an age the trembling ceased and Robert grew silent. The initial feeling of relief was quickly overlaid with another, worse fear. Holding her breath, Dublin rested her cheek against him, waiting for the rise and fall of his chest. Mercifully there was a gentle but regular movement.

Exhausted by both lack of sleep and fear, she dozed fitfully against his back. By the time she opened her eyes the candle was gutted and the early sun filtered through the casement. Beside her, Robert was cool and still. Again terror threatened, causing her to jump up. In response he gave a grunt of protest. Thank God!

It was three days before he was fit enough to travel or, more precisely, he considered himself fit – Dublin would have kept him abed for another week. But the fever had subsided and the wound was now cool. A healthy crust began to form as it started to heal. Soon they were packed and mounted and heading for London.

It was a terrible journey. Robert still looked grey with suffering and barely spoke. Dublin worried herself into a frenzy. They travelled alone and at every turn she feared that the King's men might come upon them, or a band of deserters take all that they had, including the horses. Either way, she did not expect to reach London alive, but God smiled upon them and after two days of almost solid riding, they finally saw the distant haze of the city.

Her first thought was to find good lodgings. 'Where shall we stay?' she asked as they reined in for a few moments' rest.

'You must find somewhere clean and safe.' His voice was flat with exhaustion.

'Just me? I should not find shelter for the both of us?'

'I must go to Hampden House.'

Raw jealousy scalded her tongue. 'Will *she* be there?'

'If you mean Mary, I know not. I will come to you this night, or tomorrow.'

'Why bother?' Now that Robert had made her his own creature, she felt more, rather than less jealous of her rival.

'You are being foolish. This is not the time.'

She opened her mouth to protest, but on seeing the black circles beneath his eyes, the extreme pallor of his face, she bit her tongue, instead asking: 'Who will look after you?'

'Tilly will be there. Don't fret for me. Just make sure that you are safe.'

His concern mollified her a little and at his bidding, she found lodgings at an inn in Clerk's Well. They parted in silence, her heart still heavy with affront, he insisting upon riding on alone.

Somebody took Fortune to be stabled but Dublin barely noticed. All the time she visualised Robert with Mary. The girl might dress his wounds, sit close to him on his couch, hold his good hand, and he would find pleasure in her company. The rage burned ever deeper into her heart.

The inn boasted a good table. At any other time Dublin would have appreciated it. Here indeed was comfort, her own chamber, a fireplace, a good solid bed and chest. There were even rugs upon the floor but such trimmings could not distract her from the thought that he had chosen to return to his other life. The jealousy was like an illness, burning her up, turning her cold, taking her appetite and reducing her to misery.

In spite of such rebellious thoughts, all evening she sat at the window and looked out for him. The fire died unnoticed in the grate. Minutes dragged, hours lasted a lifetime. By ten of the clock, a lamp-lighter doused the burning flame across the street and she was plunged into darkness. Without even bothering to undress, she climbed into the lonely bed and nursed her pain.

Awakening heavy and unrefreshed, she forced her thoughts for the first time to other matters. It was her duty to seek out Polly Cranford. Before leaving London she had given her promise to Polly to take care of her bairn. Instead, Dublin did not even know if they had survived the demonstration unscathed. Polly might have followed her suggestion and gone to Hampden House, be installed there even now, but it would do no harm to look elsewhere. The only place to search was in Chepeside. Whether or not she found her, the mission distracted her from a miserable and perhaps fruitless vigil at the hostelry.

It was difficult to recognise Polly's hut, or more precisely, where it had been, for in place of the row of tumbledown tenements, the alley was now exposed and bare. Fire, that most cleansing of agents, had raged along the narrow lane and wiped the fragile houses away. A few charred posts and heaps of ash were all that remained.

'Do you know where the Cranfords went?'

The man in the nearest surviving hovel shrugged without interest. A similar question was dismissed by a woman fetching water from the well. Clearly there was nothing to be gained by staying, so with some relief Dublin set off back to Clerk's Well.

As the inn came into view, somebody rode up and dismounted at the entrance to the yard. The black gelding was instantly recognisable. Her spirits lifted and she ran to catch up with Robert before he went inside. He turned in answer to her call and it was a relief to see that his face looked more rested.

'Where have you been?' he asked.

'To seek out Polly but she was not there.'

He shook his head. 'There is no word of her at the house either.'

For the moment there was nothing more to say. In silence they entered the hostelry and mounted the stairs to the upper floor. Opening the door, Dublin stepped back for him to enter but he in turn ushered her in ahead.

Unspoken feelings tugged at the air.

'You are comfortable here?'

'You didn't come last evening.' It was an accusation blurted out in pain.

'Forgive me. I had no strength to ride out again.'

Her face felt tight with the imagined slight. 'Did Tilly look after you so well?'

'She dosed me with some concoction to make me sleep.' Guessing Dublin's true concern he said: 'Mary and her family are still at Great Hampden.'

Mention of her rival's name drove home the nagging hurt.

'Robert . . .'

'Dublin . . .' They broke the silence together. After a moment he said, 'We have to be clear about our future.'

The word 'our' gave her a glimmer of hope, but not the certainty she craved. At the same time, her jealousy was spoiling the very thing that mattered. Swallowing down her envy, she said, 'Forgive me for being so foolish . . .'

'You are not foolish but I cannot give you what you seek.'

'I only want . . .'

He took her hands and sank wearily onto the bed. 'I beg you to think again. I can only hurt you. There is no shortage of good men who would take you to wife.'

'No.'

Standing before him, her hands still held in his, she willed him to love her. Leaning forward, she rested her cheek against his and in response he nuzzled his face into her neck. Some force beyond her will pulled her ever closer, pressing her breasts against him.

In a sudden frenzy of need he began to kiss her eyes, her temples, her neck, seeking out her mouth, hastily tugging at the strings that held her gown. His urgency lit the touch paper of her own and she hurried out of her clothing, pressing herself to him, willing him to merge their two selves.

Within seconds she was beneath him, her limbs parted, welcoming him into her very soul. This time there was no pain, only sheer concentrated delight. She joyed in the rhythm of his passion. When he was spent, a calm she had never before known settled upon her. Cosseted in his embrace, she drifted naturally into sleep.

It was an hour, perhaps two before she awoke gradually into the afternoon light. Outside, cartwheels rumbled along the cobbles. A dog barked disconsolately. Stretching and filling her lungs with wakening breath, she looked around the room. Robert was dressed and standing near the casement. At the sound of her rousing he turned.

For a long while he looked down on her, his smile compassion-

233

ate, his expression gentle, then a cloud of unease crossed his face. 'On the morrow I must leave London again. I have been ordered back to Gloucester.'

She grasped the irony of his mission – making this journey only to go straight back. It deflected her from the fear of what he would say next. Reaching out, he took her hands and sank down. He seemed to seek some solution from deep inside himself, finally saying: 'It would be best if you go back to Abbey House.'

'I cannot!'

'Why?'

'What would your mother think? How would your sister-in-law treat me if she knew I was your – doxy!'

'A doxy sells herself for gain. You have given yourself. There is no comparison.'

'Are you saying your mother would approve?'

He shook his head at her intransigence. 'You know she would not. If the times were different, I would find us a place of our own. You could stay there, be independent. You would have servants and I would be with you. As it is, I have to leave. Where else can you go? Any other course of action is too dangerous.'

'You don't want me. Why do you not have the courage to say so?' She tried to free her hands but he held them fast.

'Because it isn't true.'

The denial gave little comfort. 'If I did have a place of my own, what would become of me when you wed?'

His patience was running thin and he released her hands. 'Have you forgot there is a war? At any time I may be called to my Maker. Can you not value what we have now? Where is the sense of worrying on a future that might never happen?'

The mention of his mortality shocked her into silence. Shamefaced, she closed her eyes against the bolster, trying to find courage within herself. With a sigh he patted her on the shoulder and a thought came to her. Pressing home her case, she said, 'If we might all die soon, then can I not travel with you as I have before? This may be the only time God grants us.'

'It was different then. You are no longer part of a baggage train. You are no longer my servant.'

'Then what am I?'

He was a long time answering. Her hands lay unresisting again in his and without awareness he gently kneaded her fingers. When he replied, his voice had the tense edge of extreme emotion. 'You are someone who brings joy into my life. You are a source of comfort to me. You are the woman that I love.'

Robert and Dublin set out for Gloucester in the company of a troop of soldiers. Mounted upon her own Fortune, Dublin rode triumphant at her lover's side. To her joy, he made no attempt to disown her. Wherever they took quarters she slept openly in his chamber, glorying in her role. When they dined she sat at his table, waited upon along with those officers invited into his company. He made no secret of his commitment to her and in turn the officers were attentive, admiring – and perhaps a little envious, which added to her sense of wellbeing.

Their lodgings were always good and comfortable and servants attended to their needs. At first Dublin found it difficult to accustom herself to this new status, for in the past it had been she who waited upon others. Now she spent much time before a glass, dressing her hair, brightening her lips, scenting her gowns with lavender and rose petals, immersed in her role as mistress of the man. Since meeting him this had been her sole purpose in life.

Her efforts did not go unnoticed.

'Dublin, you are beautiful! You smell like a herb garden.' Nothing could quell the ecstasy of every waking moment, the anticipation of each night, the sheer satisfying joy of sating her body with his.

'You are wearing me out.' In a hostelry at Cirencester he pulled away from their third love-making and slumped, spent, onto the mattress. 'Never have I known a woman with such an appetite.'

'You have known many women?' A familiar tightening of the chest accompanied the question.

'You would wish me a virgin?'

'I'm jealous of every woman who has so much as looked on you.'

'And I am jealous of every man who casts an approving glance in your direction.'

At his remark her fears evaporated. 'That is different.'

'How so?' He snuggled her against his chest. The wiry hair scraped pleasingly against her cheek.

'I cannot help it if men look at me – I don't look back.'

He raised his eyebrows questioningly. 'Never?'

'Never! I shall never look at another man.'

He gave a half-laugh and pushed her onto her back again. 'Now, you bawd, you have awoken my beast once more.' He kissed her long and hard and she pressed herself to him so that he had no choice but to push inside the soft folds of her flesh.

'You temptress!' When he was done he stretched out on his back and she bent her head to kiss his damp, salty cock. He murmured: 'Don't waken him again, he's past recall.'

With a sigh of pleasure, she slid up his torso until her chin rested comfortably in the hollow of his shoulder. His hand tightened on her arm. 'Let's sleep.'

But her mind was at work. 'We'll be in Gloucester on the morrow?'

'We will.'

'Where shall we stay?'

There was silence and she guessed that he was thinking of all the implications. Eventually he said: 'Governor Massey will house me. I shall make it clear that there must be provision for you.'

'In your house?'

'In my house. I am not the only soldier travelling with his – sweetheart.'

He hesitated when searching for the right word and she felt the tension gnaw at her again. Love her he might. Travel openly with her on the road he did, but when it came to moving back into his own world, back with his own kind, she knew that her presence was discomfiting.

'What is Governor Massey like?' she asked, to dispel the fears.

'Able, competent. He is a God-fearing man.'

'Then he will disapprove of me?'

'Perhaps.'

She sat up. 'Would you wish to hide me away?'

'No.'

'What if Mary were to visit?'

'She will not.'

'What if she did?'

He sighed. 'If she came I should not share an accommodation with her.'

'Not until you are wed.'

'Desist. You will have to learn to accept that I love you. You

236

bring me greater joy than I have ever known. If I do my duty by my wife it will be because that is how it has to be.'

'Suppose I were to have a child.'

'Suppose you were.'

'It would be a bastard.'

'It would be a child. My flesh. Please, now let a man get some rest.'

She snuggled into his shoulder but try as she might, the cold shadow of doubt remained.

Governor Massey arranged their accommodation in Westgate Street, not far from his own. Whatever Dublin had said to Robert about other men, she could not help but notice that Edward Massey was of fair countenance, though at the same time there was something of the Puritan about him. During the siege he had, by dint of his own personality and courage, swung the majority of Royalists to support the Parliamentary cause. Looking at him, she could understand why.

To Dublin he was polite but distant. She sensed that he was both disturbed by yet disapproving of her presence. It did not make for easy conversation.

Meanwhile, the newly-arrived Captain Hammond was immediately called upon to confer with the Governor on the best way to restore the ailing city walls. Prince Rupert's efforts at mining had done their work and the unending bombardment left scars throughout the town. In addition, a strategy for defending the west had to be worked out. It seemed unlikely that the King's army would return to Gloucester itself, but nothing was certain.

In the meantime, other towns fell like cards before the Royalist advance. The news came that Exeter had fallen to Rupert's brother, Prince Maurice. This was another reminder of the precarious future.

Dublin felt almost wicked that in such circumstances she could be happy, but in truth she was. Briefly, Robert and Massey were drawn away to fight at Tewkesbury. Left alone in the splended isolation of their lodgings, she was beset once more by all the old fears, but both men returned unhurt and victorious. Now she had her lover, his adoration, the pleasure of his body, the safety of his patronage. Her life was truly blessed.

237

Chapter 32

King Charles sat alone in his chamber, intent upon his devotions. He was in sombre mood. The change in his fortunes was such that he could not but wonder at God's purpose. Even the news that his nephew, Prince Maurice, had taken Exeter did little to ease his gloom.

Since the Queen's triumphant return to Oxford, so many petty squabbles had broken out among his courtiers, that Charles was at his wits' end. The Queen and Prince Rupert were always at loggerheads. Backbiting and scandal-mongering upset him and he was at a loss to know how to make peace between the jealous factions.

'Can you not, please, open your heart to my nephew?' he begged of Henrietta. 'The lad is reckless, yes, but he is a brave soldier, and so loyal to me.'

'He is arrogant beyond bearing. I will not endure his presence.'

His appeals to Rupert met with no greater success. 'Nephew, I command that you show respect to Her Majesty.'

'Uncle. I respect her. Now, when are you going to purge your court of all the Catholics and ne'er-do-wells?'

The Lord had seen fit to bless Charles's reunion with dear Henrietta, and a ninth child grew large in her womb, but since conceiving, the Queen had been beset by illness, which past experience told her were unrelated to her pregnancy. A harsh cough tormented her and violent aches and pains drove her to distraction.

'If I remain in Oxford, then surely I shall die,' she moaned.

At the thought of her death, Charles, already low in spirits, hit unplumbable depths and though his heart ached to think on it, he could not deny her wish to seek a more conducive climate for the forthcoming birth. Henrietta chose Exeter and on 17 April Charles, along with his two eldest sons, accompanied her to Abingdon, and there, amid tears and heartache, he said goodbye.

'Give me your blessing, dear Husband. I know that through this birth, God will see fit to call me to Him. My great regret is that I shall never see your dear face again.'

'Henrietta, please! Trust in God. All will be well.' He tried to convince them both, but the spectre of their parting shattered his courage. Only the presence of his dear children gave him the strength to go on.

Holding his beloved close, he touched her mouth, loving the way her upper lip protruded over her too forward teeth. He gazed long and hard at her, determined to capture for ever the minutest details of her sweet visage.

He was consoled by news of her safe arrival at Exeter, then by the glad tidings that on 16 June she had been safely delivered of a baby girl. But the Queen's health was poor and in her wisdom she decided that only the climate of her native France could cure her. As soon as she could slip out of Exeter, she made her way to Falmouth and set sail for home.

Charles had other worries. Oxford was surrounded by the enemy. Three armies threatened his capital and in a fit of daring, he decided to take matters into his own hands. Withdrawing all troops from the neighbouring towns, he strengthened the garrison at Oxford then made a dash for it, moving west between two of the besieging armies and hoping to draw them away. To his chagrin, the Roundheads immediately occupied all the towns that he had abandoned. Oxford was still under threat.

Charles now felt himself to be out of his depth. Secretly he thought that he should have followed Prince Rupert's advice and sat tight at Oxford until more recruits arrived from Wales. He could not quite bring himself to order Rupert back from York, but he wrote with some broad hints.

To his delight, Charles then had his first, truly personal, military success at the site of Cropredy Bridge. Flush with the joy of victory, he began to think that perhaps things were not so desperate after all.

Then came the news that following the relief of York, Prince Rupert had engaged the enemy in what was clearly an ill-advised battle at Marston Moor. In its wake, York surrendered.

Reports hinted that the Prince had made mistakes. Not least, he was at supper when the battle began, convinced that the Parliamentary forces would not attack until morning.

The King rose from his knees and stood gazing from the casement. He did not entirely blame his nephew. Even he himself occasionally made an error of judgement.

There again, things were really not so bad. Calming his palpitating heart, he thought: Surely God will provide for this, His most humble and specially chosen servant . . .

Chapter 33

As the summer of 1644 blossomed, Dublin found to her great and secret joy, that her courses ceased. She said nothing. Robert was too preoccupied with the war to notice. By dint of laying abed after he rose in the morning, she was able to disguise the sickness that came upon her as soon as her feet touched the floor. On the first morning of August however, he stopped his grooming and turned towards the bed, a frown upon his brow.

'Your face lacks bloom, are you unwell?'

At the surprise remark, her cheeks betrayed her. He raised his eyebrows and then the dawning knowledge caused his mouth to open although no sound emerged.

'I am well.'

He continued to scrutinise her and it was impossible to keep the secret. 'I am with child.'

Robert sank back onto the bed as though an invisible hand had pushed him. 'This is . . . This is . . .' He did not finish the sentence.

'You are not angered?'

'Angered? How should I be angered? A child is God's blessing.' He shook his head to himself as if the knowledge was hard to comprehend.

'You will not send me away?' Her greatest fear was voiced.

'As long as we remain here and Gloucester is safe, then there is no need for such a plan.'

Suddenly he kissed her, tender, gentle, the kiss of a father rather than a lover and she put her arms about his neck and held him close. 'I want your child.'

'Then God has heard your prayers.'

She was aware of a sudden change in him, a holding in of his

241

breath, a tensing of his body. Drawing back, she saw concern on his face. 'Something is wrong?'

He shook his head but his expression remained guarded.

'You are worried what others will say?'

'Others?'

'Your mother, your aunts and uncles, Mary.'

He shrugged. 'The news will cause pain in some quarters.'

She sank back onto the bolster and looked away into the distance. 'Then you do not wish for this.'

He sighed. 'Why do you always put words into my mouth? I welcome the thought of a child but I also know that it will cause distress to others.'

As she turned away from him, he added, 'Now do not start to imagine things. If it were the other way around and Mary was with child, then my thoughts would also be for you.'

It was impossible to speak. The thought of Mary bearing him a child, the idea that she should be his wife was too cruel. She thought bitterly that in some quarters there would be celebration indeed, when Mary came to his marriage bed. Far away, Dublin's own voice asked, 'You still intend to wed with her then?' Such foolish hopes had filled the past weeks.

'You know that I must.'

'Then go to her!'

'Dublin, why do you torment yourself? I give you my love and every waking moment of my time, either by being with you or keeping you in my thoughts. Yours is the first name to appear in my will. Whether alive or dead, you are foremost in my consideration. Do not spoil it by unfounded jealousy.'

She could not look at him and after a while he got up and finished his toilet. He left the chamber in silence.

All morning the weight of Robert's cool parting stayed with her, turning a golden day grey. She was short with Leah who cooked for them, sending her twice to change pears that were yellowed and soft. Stewed in rosewater they would have fared well enough, but her pain had to find relief and poor Leah bore the brunt of it.

At midday she walked to the linen shop and purchased a length of cambric to make a child's gown. Since the lifting of the siege, trade had filtered its way back into the city. The act of sewing the garment would be such a comfort and she distracted herself with

242

imagining which silks would best decorate the bodice. It would be a joy to do something practical for the child, Robert's child. Happier thoughts began to occupy her mind.

What should his son be called? It did not even occur to her that it would be a daughter. Men like Robert always fathered sons. Whose name should he bear, this perfect boy? His father's, or perhaps his grandfather's – but then they bore the same name. Then there was poor dead John – or her own father . . . With shock, she realised that she no longer remembered her father's name. Her picture of him was blurred as if some mist now stood between herself and the past. Her history was fading.

So deep was she in reverie that the voice which finally intruded seemed to come from a very long distance. 'Mistress O'Neill!'

Turning, she saw Sergeant Digwood hurrying along behind her. He was a short man, stockily built, one of Robert's subordinates. The effort of catching her up had turned his face quite red. His eyes however, were wide, anxious and Dublin's heart missed a beat.

'What has passed?'

'Mistress, there has been some trouble.' Without grant, Digwood grabbed her elbow and urged her back the way he had come.

'What trouble?' She stumbled in her efforts to keep pace. His story came out in short bursts.

'Some disagreement. At the Council of War. Major Grey. He insulted Captain Hammond. Called him names.'

'I don't understand.'

She stopped to catch her breath and Digwood gasped out, 'Captain Hammond tried to calm him but he won't have it. He seems to think himself insulted and is set upon revenge.'

They hurried on and all the time she waited for the worst. As they rounded a corner, Digwood said, 'They have gone even now into the streets. Major Grey insists upon satisfaction. He smote Captain Hammond across the face with his fist. Please hurry, ma'am. They have taken their swords and are about to fight a duel.'

Dublin saw them immediately, two half-circles of military men standing upon a dusty expanse near to the river and in their midst, like prize-fighters in the arena, her own true love and his enemy.

'Robert!' She screamed his name with no thought of decorum, unheedful of anything but the need to stop this madness. 'Robert, please!'

Her shouts went unnoticed. Their swords were drawn and they faced each other, seemingly calm, bent upon a serious job.

'Robert, please stop!'

She was now within yards of their circle and Robert glanced at her for the merest second. His expression did not change. Sergeant Digwood placed a restraining hand upon her arm and she looked on helplessly. Robert appeared calm, assured. The other man, Major Grey, looked older, florid of countenance. Indignation seemed to emanate from his dark cheeks. All the time he was mouthing words, but so low that she could not hear.

'Let us settle this amicably.' Robert spoke clearly, his sword drawn but held low, the point towards the dusty earth.

'Whoremonger. You're a hypocrite, man. A Pope-lover. I'll have none of it. Stand and fight!'

'Then shall we begin?'

She could not bear to look and yet she could not look away. Her eyes were held by the ghastly spectacle of the two men circling, waiting, watching for the merest weakness or slowness of movement. All the time she prayed out loud, words tumbling to prevent the unthinkable from happening.

Suddenly, Major Grey lunged. The sword whooshed through the still air but Robert evaded its lethal blow with a quick shift of his weight. He did not move from the spot.

Again Major Grey thrust hard at him and this time he leaped aside, but at the same time his own sword drove forward with such speed that she hardly saw its advance. Whether Grey saw it or whether he was just too slow, she could not tell. The cruel blade went unerringly to his throat and its momentum carried it deep into his neck. For a moment, it seemed as if Robert tried to hold back, but too late. Major Grey staggered several paces and a scarlet fountain arced from beneath his collar.

Immediately Robert threw his sword aside and caught his adversary even before he hit the ground. 'Quick, a cloth to bind this before he bleeds to death!'

Dublin thrust the new-bought cambric at him and watched appalled yet hypnotised as he bound it firm around Grey's throat.

With each breath, a sickening, gurgling sound emanated from the wound. At the same time a growing pattern of poppy red spread across her child's intended gown.

The surgeon intervened but after little more than a glance, he shook his head. Robert cradled the big man, reciting the Lord's Prayer, holding his fading eyes, willing him to live. After an eternity, Grey grew still and his life's torrent became a flow, then a trickle, then stopped.

Very carefully, Robert lowered him to the ground and stood up. He swayed unsteadily and Dublin reached out to support him. With barely a movement he shook his head and she drew back, excluded from this most awful event.

When the silence became intolerable, she asked, 'Why did you fight?'

It was several moments before he looked up. 'His prejudice.'

'It was because of me.' Shame and guilt weighed her down.

Robert shrugged, neither admitting nor denying it. 'There were many things. He never liked me.'

'What will happen now?' she asked.

'There will be a court martial.'

'But you were only defending yourself!' Such injustice roused her flagging courage.

'That is what I have to prove. I have just killed a man.' He looked into her eyes and she saw his shock and pain.

'Oh, Robert.' In silence they drew together and gently rocked. Searching for some inner strength, she said: 'All will be well.'

He nodded his head and at that same moment two of his fellow officers arrived to escort him away.

'Robert!' She clung to his arm but gently he released her grip, willing her to have courage.

'Stay where you are, Dublin. Governor Massey will see that you are taken care of.'

'Please come back! The baby . . .'

With a bow of his head he walked away between the two guards, composed, dignified and as she took a step back, she was aware of a nagging ache in her belly. 'Robert!' His name was little more than a whisper.

She wanted to sit down but there was nowhere to hand. Shakily she turned and began the long haul back towards their accommodation. No one escorted her. Her hands shook so that she had to clasp them one in the other to stay the movement. She felt cold. Her head started to pound.

It took all her strength to push open the door of the inn. Wearily, she dragged herself up the mountainous stairs, wanting only to lie in their bed, rest her body where his had lain that very morning. She did not bother to remove other than her shoes. Inside, she felt heavy as lead. As her head touched the bolster and her eyes closed, there was one more, terrible blow – a warm and unmistakable flow between her legs.

On that day, 1 August 1644, two men gave up their lives, one in full manhood on the streets of Gloucester, the other barely formed in his mother's womb; and in that same afternoon, Dublin lost both lover and son to this most foul war.

Laid low by her miscarriage, Dublin remained many weeks at the inn. The loss of her child was followed by heavy bleeding and she had not the energy to rise from her bed. Copious doses of motherwort finally stemmed the tide of loss, but nowhere could her thoughts rest safe. Leah nursed her diligently for she was greatly indisposed.

Colonel Massey sent word that Robert had been escorted to London where his court martial would take place although when, he could not say. In the meantime, financial provision was made so that she should rest and recover undisturbed. The words were solicitous but no one from Robert's regiment paid her court and she felt snubbed, abandoned. Without his protection, she was as nothing. The days became weeks and there was no news from Robert himself. The anguish grew worse.

Already autumn was upon them and lying helpless in bed, Dublin realised that ere long it would not be possible to leave the city at all. The roads would become impassable and she would find herself as much a prisoner in Gloucester, as Robert was in London. In the meantime, his trial might take place. If he were to be found guilty . . . The thought was the spur that finally forced her from her bed.

'You shouldn't be abroad, Mistress.' Leah frowned at her intransigence.

'I cannot lay abed for ever.'

The maid sniffed disapprovingly but Dublin ignored her. Fighting down the weakness, she set out to find where Fortune was stabled. Her legs were so shaky that she could barely walk the half-mile to the livery.

It was both a surprise and a relief to discover that the horse was still there and looking better than ever before. There had been some grass during the year and with Robert's influence, Dublin had been able to resist the pressure to hand the mare over to the militia. Throughout the summer she had grazed and rested.

As Dublin pushed open the door of the barn, Fortune turned her head, ears forward with curiosity, then came across to nuzzle her visitor. The sight of the mare brought back memories of the trek to Gloucester and back. Dublin ran her hand down the animal's neck and rested her cheek against the velvet muzzle, trying to draw some comfort from the living warmth. For a few moments the peace and strength that comes from communing with a large, docile beast bathed her battered spirits, then making sure that no one was abroad, she picked up each of the horse's feet in turn. She had been recently shod.

'You are well-named.'

Fortune crunched the apple brought for her, shaking her head up and down as she sampled its sweetness. For their mutual pleasure, Dublin scratched the hollow behind the mare's left ear then made ready to depart. 'Right, lady, it is time we said goodbye to Gloucester.'

Without word to Leah, she packed as much as possible into two saddle bags and left the inn at night. It would have been sheer madness to attempt the journey alone, so before dawn she presented herself at the door of the Blue Boar, joining a party of travellers leaving that morning for London.

She began to wonder what she should do when she reached the capital. In spite of past visits, she still knew only Polly and those who resided at Hampden House. Polly might be anywhere and there was no question of going to Mary's home.

Another doubt plagued her. Athough Mary Hampden had treated her well, it was a sad fact that the family servants were more her friends than those with whom she wished to be an equal. Fortune flattened her ears at the feel of Dublin's resentful heels, driving against her flanks.

As they trudged along the endless miles, Dublin resigned herself to her fate, which brought in turn a cautious optimism. In her

247

luggage were five sovereigns. She was well-dressed and well provided for. There would be no need to go in person to Hampden House at all. She would set herself up at an inn and a messenger could be despatched to find out all that she needed to know. Once Robert's whereabouts were established, then all would be well.

Chapter 34

Dublin reached London on a Friday. It was immediately clear that the city had grown accustomed to war. Every gate was fortified and wherever her eye rested, there was evidence of soldiers. On her person she carried a pass ensuring acceptance with Parliamentary sympathisers everywhere. She duly handed it over and was granted admittance. In London at least, she was safe.

At Cripplegate she parted company with her fellow travellers and set out alone towards Clerk's Well. A bonfire of Popish books burned in a clearing, sending out a fierce blast of heat, and a group of young zealots called anti-Catholic slogans across the Square. Their ardour no longer troubled her. Her religion, unformed though it was, was that of her lover.

Nearby, a miserable column of prisoners were digging a drainage trench. A few citizens gathered to watch for there was little enough by way of entertainment these days, the theatres and even the bear-baiting having long since been banned.

At last she found the inn where she had stayed before and requested the same chamber. Immediately she was alone, the memory of that other time engulfed her. Here, they had slept together in total commitment to love.

Loneliness submerged her, as bad as anything that she had known. For a while she gave into it, letting her tears flow, berating the war that had taken her love and cost her her baby, then as the deluge cried itself out, she felt a curious kind of calm. Wiping her eyes, she sent for a messenger to be despatched immediately to Hampden House.

Dublin chose her words carefully so that no matter who was in residence, the message would not give rise to suspicion. Little as she cared what the Hampdens thought, she had no wish to lose Robert's favour. With bitter humour she told the man: 'Say that you are sent by a gentlewoman from Gloucester.' He left clutching a silver penny with the promise of another when he returned. There was nothing to do but wait.

Time passed snail-like and she reckoned twice over that he should have completed his mission and returned, yet still there was no sign of him. Fretting with impatience, she descended to question the innkeeper and it was then that the emissary returned.

''Tis no good sending a person there. They took me for a spy and boxed my ears!' He sniffed indignantly, and held out his hand for the remainder of his money. There was nothing to do but pay him. Still there was no news of the man that she loved.

Only one course of action remained. Dublin dressed carefully in a gown of brown wool, warm but modest, not wishing to appear as anything other than her former self. Nervously she set out towards Whitehall.

Her palms tingled as she approached the house. Her stomach was so knotted, that she wavered in her intent to march to the door and ask outright where Robert was. But as she hesitated, the door opened and somebody came out, stopping on the top step. With sinking heart Dublin saw that it was Mary. The sight of her rival threw her into confusion. She could not face the humiliation of having to ask. Mary's right to such knowledge struck cruel as a sword.

At first Mary did not see her. She stood looking across the square as if searching for someone, but apart from Dublin the place was deserted. Painfully, Dublin recognised that she had grown. The child of long ago was now replaced by a maid on the very verge of womanhood. There was something at once dignified yet fiery about her which sapped the small amount of confidence that Dublin retained.

For a moment she was tempted to turn and creep away but the need to know was too great. She took a step nearer. Mary glanced across, then away, then turned her eyes again in Dublin's direction, staring now, wide-eyed.

'You!' She was clearly shocked, but there was something more.

Dublin blurted out: 'Is there news of the court martial?' Any carefully-worded beginnings were blown to the wind.

'What are you doing in London?' Mary's voice was sharp.

'What of the trial?'

250

After too long, Mary said: 'The Council of War meet this very day to decide upon his fate. I wait even now for news.'

Mary's calm acceptance filled Dublin with frustration. Impatiently, she said: 'Then can we not go now, to find out?'

'*We*?' Mary drew herself up and her tone was imperious. Too late, Dublin realised that something important had changed. After an impossible silence, Mary said: 'How did you come to know of it?'

'I was in Gloucester.'

'With Robert?'

Dublin did not deny it.

Mary said; 'I should have known.'

There was no answer to the unvoiced accusation. Instead, Dublin said, 'All that matters is that he is safe.'

Mary regarded her as if she was something familiar that was not quite what it seemed – as if a dog had spoken, perhaps. She said, 'I know that he is innocent.'

'He did kill a man, but he acted in self-defence.'

'You were there?'

'I witnessed it.'

The younger girl digested this like some strange meat, slipped unsighted into her mouth, to be savoured and experienced. Finally, her voice heavily laden with sarcasm, she said: 'A gentle-woman from Gloucester.'

Dublin blushed.

It was clear that they were both equally out of their depth. Mary went to speak then swallowed down her first thought, saying instead: 'We can only pray.'

'As we did that time before, for the safety of your Papa?'

'You do not believe that God hears our prayers?'

'If He does then He would not seem to care about what we want.'

'You think then that we know better than the Almighty, what is right for us?'

Dublin hesitated. 'I think we must strive for what makes us happy.'

'What are you saying?' There was a harsh edge to Mary's voice and Dublin did not enlighten her. The atmosphere between them was prickly as holly. Suddenly the younger girl's reserve began to crumble. Her eyes brimmed with tears and her lower lip trembled. 'I don't want him to die!'

As she voiced Dublin's greatest fear, the Irish girl moved towards her, compassionate but unable at the last moment to offer comfort. Instead she said, 'I too pray for his deliverance.'

Mary's eyes were suddenly hard. 'You are more than a servant to him.'

There was challenge in the statement and a hundred answers tumbled through Dublin's mind but before she could utter one, her attention was distracted. Following Mary's gaze, she saw with relief, disbelief, joy, that he was there, striding towards them. In unison they gasped.

'Robert!' Mary picked up her skirts and ran, any semblance of dignity thrown aside. Unable to move, Dublin watched as her rival flung herself at him and he swept her into his arms and swung her round. There was something familiar, comfortable about their closeness. This was the girl he would marry.

His head rested against the crown of Mary's hair but as he turned, he held Dublin with his eyes. She could not interpret his expression – pleasure, confusion, it was all there.

Without looking away, he set Mary down and came across. For a moment Dublin was reminded of a father returning home, embracing a favourite daughter, now moving towards the wife. Every part of her wanted to run to him as Mary had done, be held, feel his strength. With a supreme effort of will, she stood her ground.

'Dublin!'

'You are safe?'

'Praise God they have acquitted me.'

His arm was still around Mary's shoulders and she was looking from one to the other. Her expression became guarded. She said, 'Your servant arrived here this very morning.'

Dublin flashed her an angry look and Robert glanced down at his betrothed then released his hold. 'Go, ask the servants to set me out food. I'm hungry as a hunter.'

Dublin saw the girl tense, affronted at the order. She turned towards Dublin. 'You heard what your master said.'

'He was speaking to you.'

They both looked to him for support. He said to Dublin: 'Where do you stay?'

'The inn at Clerk's Well.'

'Then go there now.'

She hesitated, then walked past them, not meeting their eyes.

Was he dismissing her like a common servant? She felt weighed down by emotion, then the thought came to her that neither of them had won the battle for his support. Mary was her superior in birth and to her belonged his loyalty by right of their betrothal, but he had not upheld her order. Implicit in his remark was a promise that he would come to her. Grasping this gleam of comfort Dublin went back to the inn to wait.

The hours dragged painfully. Dublin tormented herself over and again, knowing that Mary would win. By the very nature of her position, she would persuade him not to come. In one breath she believed that he would not be blackmailed, then with the next she was certain that he would submit to his bride's wishes.

As the sky turned to midnight velvet, she heard his stride along the passage outside her chamber.

'Dublin, forgive me, I could not come before.'

Her relief was total.

He removed his coat, flinging it across the oak blanket box. She noted with jealousy that he now wore rust-coloured breeches and a fine linen shirt that she did not recognise. He had been shaved and his clothing bore the musky smell of Mary's house. She remained seated, pretending to gaze out across the stableyard, not acknowledging his greeting.

He drew in his breath to speak then changed his mind. As she continued to stare through the window, he said, 'It seems that you are incapable of doing as I ask. Even in such extreme times you disobeyed my orders and left Gloucester.'

This stung her into replying. 'I am sorry that my presence here offends you. You did not even bother to write! For all I knew, you might have been hanged.'

'I sent messages. Edward Massey knew of the progress of my trial. I asked him to take care of you.'

'He sent money,' she grudgingly admitted, then the injustice of her situation bubbled up. 'None of your friends considered me worthy of a visit.'

Robert sat down on the bed and sighed. 'These are distracted times. I sent messages, many of them. Massey himself informed me that you were taken care of. What more could I do?'

'I lost the child.' The words blurted out, cold, as if such an event

253

was of little import. The knowledge engulfed her again with hurt.

From his face she could see that he was shocked. 'Oh my dear, I am truly sorry.'

'That leaves you free to go back to Mary.'

'Dublin!' He sank on his haunches and gazed into her face. 'We have been through this before. Remember that for the past months I have been on trial for my life. Today I am reprieved and I find Mary in high dudgeon and you accusing me of neglect.'

His mouth was tightly drawn and a nerve twitched along his jawline. The normally warm brown eyes became remote. He said, 'I am truly sorry about the child. But there will be other times.'

'Perhaps God is punishing me. Perhaps He does not approve of our love.'

He repeated. 'There will be other times.' She could feel his discomfort. Then: 'Just tell me one thing,' he said. 'Do you wish to continue?'

She looked away and he added: 'My marriage to Mary will still go ahead.'

'Now that I am not with child . . .'

'You have already said that.'

Louder, she repeated: 'Now that I am not with child it is you who are free to choose.'

In response, he pulled her up from the chair and held her close. She felt stiff, unable to give vent to her need. After a while he released his hold. It was his turn to gaze from the window.

'Why do you torment yourself? You know how much I care for you. While I was waiting for trial I made plans.' He turned round. 'You will not like them. They were intended for you and – the babe, but it makes sense that you follow them anyway.' Taking her arm, he steered her to the bed.

'This has been a terrible year. In two days it will be December, then 1644 will be over. This war has raged more than two years and we are still no nearer victory. I have spoken with Colonel Cromwell and we are all agreed that if Parliament is to win this cause, then we have to re-form the army. What we need is a truly Parliamentary force with officers answerable to us.'

He paused. 'I have been asked to be part of this re-modelling. Once we have formed, there will be an all-out campaign to end the conflict.'

The cold fear of death was back. In all the time that she had known him, his life had been in danger. Today he was released only to face another threat.

'I need to know that you are safe.' His tone had hardened subtly. 'Child or no child, there is no question that you should continue to travel with me. From now on, I must be free to move wherever I am needed.'

He pulled her round to face him. 'If the situation was reversed, would you willingly put me in danger?'

There was only one answer but she did not utter it.

'Then accept that I cannot have your safety threatened.' His voice softened and he lifted her chin. 'When this is over I need you to come back to.'

'You intend to send me away?'

'Yes.'

'Not to Abbey House?'

'No.'

'Not with Mary!'

'No.' He gave the semblance of a smile. 'I want you to return to my Aunt, at Wolverton.'

She tried to interrupt, to tell him that it was impossible, but he brushed her objections aside.

'There is nothing to fear. Aunt Jane is aware of my feelings for you.' He smiled at some secret thought. 'I am her favourite nephew, she will do this for me.'

Dublin felt only numbness.

Robert said: 'I implore you not to do one of your running-away tricks. The Island is the safest place you can be. Once the war is over I shall send for you.'

'And then?'

'We will be together.'

She could not let it rest. 'What of Mary?'

'Wherever I end up, you will be with me. My wife will have her own residence. That will have nothing to do with you and me.'

It was useless to express her feelings. Instead, she said, 'Mary hates me.'

'I fear she is aware of my feelings for you. I cannot hide them.'

'It is because she loves you too. Supposing she makes conditions that we part?'

'I would not accept it – any more than I can break my vow of marriage to her.'

Dublin was silent. At the moment any future looked bleak but one without him, one where he was no longer part of her life, was no future at all. She was tired of running away. Suddenly overwhelmed by it all, she moved into the shelter of his arms.

'There, my love.' He kissed her hair, hugging her close, rocking her against his chest. Into her hair he said, 'Sometimes I thought I should never see you again, never hold you like this. It was only the hope of such a time that kept me sane in the dark days before my trial.' He kissed her on the mouth, tender, long and gentle. It was like coming home.

'Robert.' She guided his hands to her breasts, longing for the comfort of his touch, parting her legs to have him ever closer. 'Make love to me.'

'My dearest.' Within moments she was in the only place she ever wished to be, upon the bed, beneath him, united in this heaven-sent act of love.

Afterwards they dozed, kissed as if they would never get their fill, then made love again. Like a coin tossed high, she now came down on the side of hope and happiness. At that moment she could face anything.

'How soon before I have to leave?'

'Soon. Perhaps a few days, a week, no longer. I give you my promise that I shall write.'

She put the thought of departure from her mind. He said: 'I miss the Island. As a boy, with my cousin Robert Dingley, and my brother John, I had such a wild time. The Captain of the Island himself took us once to Parkhurst Forest to shoot deer.'

'The Captain?'

'These days they call him the Governor, the most important of men. He is appointed to govern the Island by the monarch, or in these times by the Parliament. The post is now held by the Earl of Pembroke.'

The thought of important men entertaining him was not to Dublin's liking, so she changed the subject. 'Tell me about when the war is over.'

He did not reply immediately. When he began to talk it was as if he was the cunning man, making a forecast, seeing into the future. She soaked up his bedtime tale.

'We shall raise a new army. The King will be defeated and return like a chastised son to his rightful place, remorseful, obedient. The rest of us will go home, make love to our sweet-hearts, try to heal the wounds.'

She asked: 'What if the King will not repent?'

'He must, for we shall be the victors.' He squeezed her closer to him. 'As far as the King goes, it may be necessary to pull a few of his teeth, make it harder for him to bite.' As an afterthought, his voice light with humour, he added, 'There will be no need to take off the whole head.'

She was hardly listening. The soothing effects of love, the glow from the fire, his sheltering arms, all lulled her into a state of bliss then, in the way of things, the sudden terror of parting destroyed the paradise.

'Robert!'

'What is it?'

She held him so fast that he could scarce breathe. 'I don't want you to go, ever. If you are going to die, let me be with you!'

'I am not going to die. Not now. I give you my word that I shall struggle back to you no matter what! Please, just accept what I ask. I shall lead a victorious army and you will be safe in the care of my aunt. What is more, my love, I will ensure that your mare is shipped over, then you will be able to explore the countryside. Now, stop frightening yourself.'

She lay down beside him, pretending to settle to sleep. He said, 'I have news from Chertsey. My uncle Henry is in Oxford with the King. His Majesty thinks well of him. Strange to consider how our paths have diverged.'

She nodded in the dark and kissed his shoulder. Within moments he was gently snoring.

Inside the room it had grown dark. Outside, the rise and fall of a westerly whooshed around the inn, enveloping it, cutting it off from the world. She wanted to stay there for ever. Questions jostled for answers in her mind.

A month, a year – how long before Robert's predictions came true and he returned for her? Another, tormenting imp asked, Will the future be as he sees it? With a sinking feeling, Dublin wondered if he would survive this terrible war? Then the merest glimmer of hope raised her from despair.

Please, God, let me again be with child . . .

Chapter 35

Dublin awoke to the familiar cold of her chamber at Wolverton. The end of her nose felt like a snowflake and the moment she moved, her toes began to itch with chilblains. Each morning she dipped her feet in the piss pot, which everyone swore would cure the affliction, but it did not seem to work.

For several minutes she huddled under the covers, preparing herself for the ordeal of getting out of bed. The coverlet felt damp and icy beneath her fingers. Another day stretched ahead and she was weighed down by boredom. Aunt Jane's son, Robert Dingley, was coming to escort her around the Parish. Cousin Robert's calling was to the Church. Dublin thought rue-fully that his mission in life seemed to be to ensure that she made recompense for her wicked, Catholic beginnings. Dutifully he trailed her around the village, preaching the gospel as they rode and as she carried out an endless stream of good works. At the thought of this devout, humourless companion, she groaned.

Her return to the Island had brought home to her how much she had changed since that first agonising journey, riding behind Captain Hammond. Then she had been a child, a lost orphan, bat-tered by ill-fortune. Yet now, in spite of her maturity and the knowledge that Robert Hammond loved her, she still felt herself to be a misfit in this company. In fact, she was a misfit everywhere – neither fish nor fowl.

She turned restlessly in the bed and a chill column of air shafted between her and the covers. She sighed and lay still, suspending that train of thought. Her ever-present longing to have Robert back was deepened by the need to find out where she belonged.

He had promised that she should have a house of her own and she suspected that only then would she truly know who she was.

Taking a deep breath she flung the bedcovers back and leaped up, stamping her feet on the rough, cold floorboards, dragging her gown over her head and suffering the clammy dampness of the cloth as it slid over her person. She brushed her hair with vigour to bring some warmth to her hands then pushed her feet into chilly slippers and skipped down the stairs.

Mistress Dingley was in the kitchen discussing the day's duties with Jennet who now had the dual distinction of being head of the kitchen, and a married woman. They both nodded towards her as she came in and this underlined the confusion of her position, for she was companion to both of them.

When first she had returned to Wolverton, Jennet welcomed her with pleasure, unashamedly avid for news.

'Dublin, you're back! Have you returned to marry your shepherd?' Jennet had giggled, pleased with her joke, but gradually, as she had taken in Dublin's fine clothing, the hesitancy of her manner, the kitchen girl had withdrawn. Now, Dublin often caught Jennet watching her, her expression wary, as if she was trying to assess a stranger.

As for Aunt Jane, she had greeted her with courtesy, ever mindful of her comfort. Dublin guessed that a wish to serve Robert rather than concern for his protégée, was foremost in Aunt Jane's mind. When they were alone in the house, Dublin took her meals with Robert's aunt, but on those occasions when her husband returned from London, or one of her sons came to stay, or any visitors called at the house, Dublin was consigned back to the kitchen to pass an uneasy time with her former companions. Neither fish nor fowl.

Aunt Jane said: 'I was about to send and waken you. My son will be here shortly.'

Dublin suspected a reprimand but she did not respond. Resisting the temptation to pour some ale, she waited while the two women continued with their deliberations. When cousin Robert arrived he would breakfast with them, after loud and prolonged prayers. At the prospect, she wilted.

Later that morning, cheered by a cool clear sun, Dublin and cousin Robert Dingley set off on their mission to the neighbouring villages. They took with them gifts of salt and loaves and cheese

259

which Aunt Jane regularly distributed to some poorer families.

Riding through the forest, Dublin had a rare sense of wellbeing. For once the ground was neither boggy nor frosty, and having cantered up a long incline, she felt exhilarated. Now that Fortune had cleared the cobwebs from her lungs, she walked quietly and her mistress relaxed.

'I am sorry it is a long way to make this final call,' cousin Robert called over his shoulder. 'Old Micah Dore used to live in Shorrel, but then he moved to be with his sister. Since she died, my mother has continued in her responsibility to him.' After a moment's silence, he added: 'We should thank God for this opportunity to serve Him.'

Dublin nodded. She did not really want to talk, trying instead to imagine what it would be like to ride in this forest with her own Robert. Cousin Robert was plump and staid beyond his years. His calling to the ministry was always in the forefront of his mind and conversations were sprinkled with rejoinders to keep God ever-present, even in the most mundane moments.

When out riding, caution was always his first consideration so that canters such as the one they had recently enjoyed were rare, as he constantly expected his horse to stumble, or gallop off with him. Guiltily Dublin wished for a more adventurous companion.

'If it will not inconvenience you, while we are at Caulbourne I shall call briefly upon the minister,' cousin Robert said. 'You might like to use the time to enter the church and pray.'

'It is Caulbourne we visit?' Immediately Dublin's heart jolted. Caulbourne was Caleb Gosden's village.

Since returning from the mainland, she had often imagined calling on the shepherd. Always a nagging doubt troubled her at the memory of leaving him to face the consequences of sheltering her. As usual, her mind tried to shy away from the memory of that summer. She had been such a poor, lost creature, so in need of protection.

She had a sudden clear image of Caleb's face, the intensity of his expression, the way he would suddenly withdraw from her, leaving her feeling to blame for she knew not what. Without thinking, she reached down and touched the tiny scars on her ankle. Then he had been no more than a hair's breadth away from her and she remembered the disturbing feelings aroused by his presence. There was something about the particular shape of his body, his deformity excepted, that had a lithe, male quality which transcended thought. His compassion, his gentle ministrations stirred another feeling in her heart. She refused to dwell on it.

She felt distanced from him now, a grown woman, sophisticated. Her place in Robert's life gave her a sense of safety, but . . .

To her cousin she said: 'While you visit the minister, I will look around the village.'

'I hardly think . . .'

'I shall be quite safe.' Her tone defied argument.

The parcel to Micah Dore delivered, Robert Dingley and Dublin parted company outside the church. Dublin rode with the illusion of purpose, back across the Green towards the stream. Some distant memory of Caleb's description of his home pointed her in that direction. Down near the water a man was chopping firewood. Dublin reined in and asked him: 'Where would I find Caleb Gosden?'

The man pushed his hat back and scratched his flattened hair. 'That's a good question,' he said ambiguously, then after a moment added, 'That's his cottage, over yonder.'

Dublin followed his gaze. Unaccountably, her heart began to race and she wanted to get away. This now seemed a bad idea, but the woodcutter was watching her and she had no choice but to follow his directions. Swallowing down her unease she rode on across towards the cottage, dismounted, left Fortune to graze on the swathe of stunted grass, and knocked shakily on the door.

An older woman answered her knock. Dublin knew immediately that it was Caleb's mother. Her colouring was quite different – coppery hair, green eyes – but the shape of her face, the fine features, were Caleb's.

'I – er – I was looking for Caleb Gosden.' She knew that her face was flushing and any veneer of self-possession deserted her.

The woman looked at her guardedly. 'Who's asking?'

'He – he did me a kindness, some time ago. I wanted to thank him.'

'Caleb isn't here. He's gone to fight for the Parliament.' She paused. 'His wife's here.'

'Wife?'

'Sara.' Lizzie Gosden looked suspicious in the face of Dublin's ignorance.

261

'I see. Er – it does not matter. I was passing . . .'

At that moment, the cottage door was pushed wider and Sara Gosden went to step out onto the path. It was clear that she had no idea her mother-in-law had a visitor, and seeing Dublin, her eyes widened in surprise. They grew even larger as she recognised the caller.

Completely out of her depth, Dublin nodded to the girl, staring at her huge belly.

'Sara's due any day,' Lizzie announced.

There was nothing to say. Dublin wanted to turn and run away. Her feelings were swirling in great bursts of undiluted force – embarrassment, shame, jealousy, humiliation. Backing away, she grabbed Fortune's rein and struggled into the saddle, gabbling: 'There's no message.'

Across the green she heard the sound of cousin Robert's voice. Quickly she rode onto a narrow path between some bushes, not wanting to be seen. She felt terrible, out of control. All the time the question asked itself: *What is wrong with me*? In the whole of that summer, Caleb had kept her as distant as the beacon she could just espy on the brow of the down, always angry with her, resentful, treating her as if she was some alien creature. As soon as she had left, he had taken Sara into his arms, into his bed, and now she bore the fruit, almost ripe in her womb.

Robert had kept himself away from her too, until his sickness, and simple male lust, had weakened his resolve. Then the child that had promised to flower inside her had sickened and died. Now she was barren, empty. The clear morning turned grey.

Dimly she became aware again of cousin Robert's voice. He was enquiring of the woodcutter if he had seen a young lady on a black horse. Quickly fighting down her turmoil, she rubbed her eyes with the backs of her hands and rode out to face him.

Mercifully, he was preoccupied with some aspect of dogma which the minister of All Saints had seen fit to discuss with him. As they made the return journey to Wolverton, cousin Robert rode ahead, keeping up a monologue. Dublin was able to pursue her own thoughts.

'How long do you think it will be before the war is over?' She asked, suddenly cutting across his pronouncements.

He looked round at her in surprise. She realised that her question had no relevance to his own train of thought. 'I hardly see . . .'

Taking up her theme however, he gave her his view of the progress of the conflict. With unusual insight, he observed, 'I imagine you are wondering when you may expect my cousin back and move into your own establishment.'

She felt herself grow hot beneath the winter chill. When she did not answer, he said: 'I would advise, dear young lady, that you prepare yourself to stay under my mother's patronage for a good few months yet. I shall, of course, keep an eye out for a suitable property, as this is what my cousin wishes,' here he hesitated just long enough to make it clear that in his own view, cousin Hammond's plans were at the least, misguided. He then added: 'But really, I do not advise any hasty decision. You have a lot to learn. My mother is kindness itself. For the present you should pray for guidance and take pleasure in doing God's will.'

Behind him, Dublin felt herself to be in an aura of increasing gloom.

It was past midday when they arrived back at Wolverton. As they handed their capes to a servant and made for the warmth of the hall fire, Aunt Jane came to seek them out.

To Dublin she said, 'The coneyman called, not ten minutes since. He is going to Freshwater to collect rabbits and will call back on his way to the port – he has brought a letter for you.'

Dublin's heart skipped and she followed Aunt Jane's gaze across to the oak table that dominated the room. There, bound with ribbon, lay a folded parchment. Curbing her desire to run with it to the privacy of her chamber, Dublin walked casually over to the table and retrieved it.

For a moment she felt panic, wondering if she would remember anything of what Mary had taught her. She glanced at her own name, scrawled on the outside of the parchment, with relief recognising the letters and their meaning. She looked up to find Aunt Jane watching her. The older woman said: 'Would you wish me to read it for you?'

'Thank you, ma'am, but I know my letters.'

She saw a flicker of surprise cross Aunt Jane's face. 'Then why not take it and read it in peace? But be sure to tell us the news.'

'Of course.' Dublin smiled uncomfortably and withdrew.

Once alone, she untied the strings, fumbling in her haste to open this lifeline. She folded back the sheets and stumbled through the words:

263

My Heart,

Since we parted, my life has been grey, empty of joy. I pen these lines in the hope that the coneyman will bring them to you.

As I spoke with you on our last occasion, our main task has been to re-model the army. Ere long, we shall be leaving here, although I do not yet know our destination. I hope you will be proud to learn that your Robert has been granted command of a regiment of Foot, being now, my dearest, Colonel Hammond!

It is thought that Lord Fairfax will command our forces. In spite of our best efforts, this new army is still not up to strength. We even closed the shops to encourage recruitment but more men will have to be pressed. It is a measure I detest but, God willing, morale is high. It is quite a sight to see our infantry in their new red tunics.

You will not have heard, but Oliver Cromwell has completed his tour of duty and will soon return to Ely and retirement. I would give much to follow his example and come to you but this war has to be won. He will continue the fight for the Cause in Parliament, while I shall do so on the field of battle.

It near slipped my mind to tell you that the Hothams, first son then father, met their end by hanging on Tower Hill. God's mills grind slow but correspondence taken at Marston Moor proved beyond doubt their treason at Hull. May God have mercy upon their souls.

Dublin, not a night passes but my body aches for you. Your smile, your laughter – they are my life's blood. If it be possible, please, I pray you, send a letter by return for I do not know how much longer I will remain here.

Has my cousin had success in finding you a property of your own? It is my earnest wish that you should have security and independence, no matter what my fate. Does Aunt Jane treat you well? I know that your role in the house must be a difficult one, but have faith. Once you have your own place, this embarrassment will be eased. In the meantime, take comfort in prayer and service to my aunt.

Pray for your Robert that he may come safely back to you.

In true love, RH.

Dublin read the letter again and again. He felt at once so close, yet distant as the moon. Her hand came to rest on her belly, its flatness a cruel reminder of what she so desired. She rocked herself in longing for the man, for his child. Caleb Gosden and his pregnant wife no longer mattered.

Pushing her sadness aside she sat down to reply, a short letter, not saying what she felt because she did not have the words, but her very heart was spilled onto the page.

My Dere Lov,

I thank thee most kindly for thy leter. We do well here, with no batel to cawse us payne. I mis you so sorely. Do you think to be home afore Eester? I praye for you, dayly. We all feel prowd of you.

Cosin Robert has fownd me no howse as yet, but afore you cum, I hop to have a harth to welcom you.

Your loving Dublin.

The letter went some way to easing her longing. Once it was collected, she tried to look forward to better times. Robert Dingley would soon find her a house of her own. Then she would have servants to oversee and much to occupy her to keep it in readiness for the day when at last, her beloved returned.

Chapter 36

Daily, Caleb and a gang of fellow prisoners were herded from the gaol to Portsmouth dockside, there to build boats for the Navy. From first dawn to twilight, it was Caleb's job to saw and soak, steam and strip the mighty oak trunks until they were malleable planks. Compared to shepherding, this life was immeasurably hard, made baser by the mean rations and impure water that was the only source of succour.

In the end, nine of the ten angels given to him by Tristram Fortunatus had been confiscated upon his imprisonment. The change left from the tenth, which he had used to pay for food and accommodation on the journey from Newbury, was eked out to supplement his rations. After two months in prison, it was gone.

Caleb knew that he would die. Without the help of some outside agent, no one could survive both prison and hard labour. Now that he had no money, disease or starvation would claim him. Part of him looked forward to the release, for it would be easy to succumb to the grinding labour and deprivation, but two things forced him on – a seething sense of injustice at his imprisonment, and a longing to see his child.

By his reckoning, the babe would be due, perhaps already born. The thought of it filled him with unaccustomed feelings of tenderness, and a fierce need to protect it from the evils that had so longed dogged his own existence.

Waking in the night, cold beyond endurance and crushed between two stinking prisoners, he had a terrible sense of the peril facing his family. Sitting in the acrid, piss-soaked straw, he knew that whatever the risk, on the morrow, he would find a way to escape.

Next morning, as he travelled to the quayside in the misty drizzle that seeped unmercifully through his coarse hessian shirt and breeches, Caleb took note of every ship tied up along the wall. Soon he picked out a barque loaded with hides, which he guessed was bound for the Newport tanneries. It was a calculated risk. The ship might equally be headed somewhere along the south coast and he would find himself even further from home, a wanted man and penniless. But there was nothing for it. He could not enquire as to the destination. Throughout the day he looked for an opportunity to slip away unnoticed, all the time noting the tide and praying that he could escape before the barque sailed.

His chance came when the gaolers stopped for their own refreshment. Such a luxury was not permitted to the convicts. They were expected to continue with the backbreaking work with the minimum of overseeing while the guards stuffed themselves with bread and cheese.

On the pretence of needing to piss, Caleb moved to the water's edge and once there, slipped silently over the wall and into the water. It was so cold that for a moment, he thought his heart would stop. With fingers deprived of feeling, he made his painful way, hand over hand, along the wall in the direction of the barque. He was unable to swim and the fear of drowning was only overcome by the desperate need to reach home.

When he came to the barque, somehow he hauled himself up on the seaward side, thanking destiny for the heavy ropes that looped over the prow. Unseen, he slid behind a pile of hides and studied his bleeding, frozen hands. He prepared to wait.

It was about an hour before they set sail. The wind was frisky and before long, the ship was out on the open water. Peering cautiously over the side, Caleb saw with inestimable relief that the ship was headed due south and that in the distance, the thickly wooded, undulating spread of the Island beckoned them on.

The crossing took about an hour and as the barque neared the shore, Caleb lowered himself over the side, jumping clear at the last moment and landing, to his relief, in a few feet of water. Hastily he waded ashore, putting as much distance between himself and the craft as possible. Weighed down by waterlogged clothing, he struggled up the beach and set out due north. It was already fast growing dark and he thought that it would be safer to travel by night. Praise God, before first light he should be back in the arms of his wife.

He pressed on relentlessly, his feet now raw and bleeding, stumbling and forcing his way across fields, through copses until at last, as a small, watery sun braved the clouds to cast a pale light across the Island hills, Caleb dragged himself into Caulbourne Village.

A dog barked as he descended the final slope, glancing with full heart at the church on the bank to his left, then allowing his eyes to feast on the familiar stream which formed part of the sheepwash. At last, he was back where he belonged. He vowed never to leave again.

Walking faster now, he passed several wooden houses, then approached the halfdozen stone cottages, in one of which he had been born. His heart thumping with emotion, he banged on the door, at the same time lifting the latch and pushing his way inside.

The first thing he saw was his mother, but not as he remembered her. Here was a woman older by at least ten years. Her back was to him and she was bending over a wooden box, drawn close to the fire. The dog, Tyke, near to the embers, leaped to his feet and flung himself at his master.

'Hello, boy.'

Stiffly Lizzie pulled herself up as he fussed the hound.

'Mother.'

'Caleb – is it really you? Oh, my boy.' She stumbled towards him and near fell into his arms, rocking against him with extreme emotion.

'There now, 'tis all well. I promised I'd come back safe.' He looked around the room for signs of Sara, wondering if she might be up in the little cubbyhole of a bedroom.

Before he could ask, Lizzie said, 'Oh Caleb, how could you go?'

'I had to. It was my duty.' The half-truth discomfited him. Still he looked around. 'Where's Sara?'

At this, Lizzie shook her head and her eyes were blinded with tears. 'Sara's dead. She died in childbed.'

The news poleaxed him. All feeling drained from him and he gazed disbelieving at her. 'When?'

'A week since.' She glanced now towards the box near the fire. 'You have a son.' She shook her head and a second hurt tore at his guts.

'Is he . . .?'

'He's very weak. Mistress Holbrooke puts him to her breast twice a day, but 'tis not enough. There's no one with milk to spare.'

Caleb crossed to the box and knelt down. The sight of his tiny, ill-nourished son unleashed the dam of pain that bore him down. *'No-oo!'* he roared. 'He shall not die! He shall not!' Picking up the infant and holding it to his chest, he rocked the babe as if to force life into him.

'Caleb, if it be God's will . . .' Lizzie grasped his sleeve, exhausted, imploring, but he shook her aside.

'No! A curse upon your God. He can take my life if He pleases, but He shall not have my child!' Even as he spoke, he could feel that the child's heart was little more than a flutter, a mere butterfly's breath, growing lighter and lighter until it stilled almost imperceptibly into a sigh on the March morning air.

Caleb buried his son in the newly-dug grave that, a few days earlier, had received his wife back into the earth from whence she had come.

He was drunk. Since the child had died, he had not allowed himself a moment to be sober. As soon as the baby lay with its mother, he set out for the hills, having nowhere in particular to go, but not being able to stay.

'Caleb!' He ignored his mother's anguished cry and increased his speed. At his heels, the dog, Tyke criss-crossed his way along the path, his eyes never leaving his master. Caleb ignored him. He saw nothing but the blackness of his pain.

During his absence a new shepherd had been appointed in the village, so even the refuge of the bothy was denied him. He walked and walked until his legs refused to carry him, then sat on the grass and gazed into emptiness. His heart was cold as marble. There was no tomorrow. There was no yesterday.

As dusk fell, his brother John found him but he refused to return to the village.

'You must come, brother. Think of Mam. She has suffered a loss too. You only add to her distress.'

Caleb had run out of beer. He had no money. Sobriety faced him, the worst of all futures.

'Lend me sixpence.'

'Not to drink away. Come home, please.'

Caleb dragged himself up and turned in the opposite direction. 'Leave me!'

John gazed after him, defeated, then returned home alone.

Once he was by himself again, Caleb stopped. In the valley below was West Over House. He had no desire to see another human soul but need drove him on. At the back door, he knocked and waited. A girl answered his call.

'Alms,' he said.

She stared at him, wide-eyed, suspicious.

'I'm a soldier, returned wounded from the war. I need sustenance.'

She hesitated, glancing back into the room behind her, looking for support.

Quickly Caleb said, 'God will reward you if you take pity on me. I only ask a quart of ale, a jug of wine. I need it to ease the pain.' He hinted at his back as if it was some affliction suffered in battle.

Making up her mind the girl nodded briefly, closed the door and after an eternity returned with a jug of cider. 'Here, drink this,' she said. 'And may God bless you.'

With a nod, Caleb drained the ewer and handed it back. Turning away he moved his lips in a brief, bitter grimace. Now there was the merest glimmer of hope. If he played his cards right, he could find the escape he needed. As the cider began to claim him, he stumbled his way back up the hill and into oblivion.

Chapter 37

For the first time in thirty-six hours, Robert permitted his boots to be pulled off by his friend and servant, Obidiah Strange.

As he sank onto a settle in the unfamiliar room where they had taken quarter, he felt his hands to be tingling still, with excitement. To Obidiah he said: 'Well, old man, is not today the greatest of all?'

'Aye.' Obidiah struggled painfully up and placed his master's boots beside the hearth in the billet.

Outside, the symphony of victory echoed around the village, performed by men drunk on success and survival.

'I've found some good brandy in the cellar.' Obidiah poured the Colonel a generous measure which he took and drained in one swallow.

'Take some for yourself,' Robert commanded. 'And find me pen and quill, quick as you can. I have letters to write.'

Obidiah grunted, muttering under his breath in his accustomed manner. Robert grinned to himself, knowing that the old man disapproved of what he saw as over-devotion to duty. He didn't hold with letter-writing. In his view, this preoccupation with 'scribblin', 'as he called it, was unnatural. He snorted as he put the writing materials on the desk.

Grinning broadly now, Robert said, 'When I write to my mother, I'll send word to your wife. Go now.'

Left alone, he pulled the desk across to the light of the window, plonked himself down and stretched out his long legs, wriggling his toes, glorying in the sudden sense of freedom. Today was a day to remember.

Picking up the quill, he dipped it in the inkpot and began to

271

complete the various despatches. When they were done, he poured himself another brandy and spread a sheet of parchment before him. He wrote:

Naseby Village,
14 June, 1645

Dublin, my Dear Love,

Forgive your Robert for his silence. We have journeyed to north, south, east and west before coming to this place.

Tonight is a great night indeed. Moving against the King and Prince Rupert we have today had a fine victory. Praise God, loss of life was small but we have taken some thousands of prisoners and arms to match.

I wish I could share with you our sense of joy. As the time for battle approached, Lord Fairfax gave us the word for the day: 'God is our strength,' – and truly our faith was rewarded.

Before battle commenced, the enemy, although outnumbered, had about them an air of such certainty. What a display of banners, silks, taffetas, damasks, and velvets met our eyes! The King put himself at their front and fair blinded us with the light from his golden armour. The sight alone might have subdued a lesser force but our men took courage in the knowledge that those with so much could only be reduced, whereas we, in our humility could only prosper.

During the battle there was much disorder but our men fought bravely, never weakening. In the end it was the enemy who fled, leaving many prizes behind.

Our greatest find was the King's correspondence. It came to light that he has been communicating with the Irish, encouraging them to invade, welcoming the Papists – forgive me for reporting what might be painful to you, but I think of you as an Englishwoman, and you can imagine how such news strengthens our cause.

Lieutenant-General Cromwell, leading the Horse, was second to none. His planned retirement was delayed at Lord Fairfax's request. He now has a voice in both the Parliament and the army. This makes him of the greatest importance.

Dearest, this is a brave day. I doubt the King can recover from this set-back. Shortly we leave here in pursuit of him.

I pray that you are well. This separation must be hard for you. I trust that my Aunt Jane treats you well and that soon you will have a home of your own.

I long to hear from you which greatly pains my poor, lonely heart. My greatest fear is that you may regret your association with this, your most devoted servant.

Praise God this war will soon be at an end so that I can return to the only place where I belong, at your side.

Your loving Hammond.

Carefully he folded the letter and bound it round with ribbon, then sat staring through the window. He was assailed by a bitter-sweet conflict of feelings, the glory of the victory at odds with the longing for his mistress.

The passage of time had not lessened the amazement he felt at the situation in which he found himself. Dublin's simple, unrelenting love was something that he had never expected. Other women had blossomed in his life, companions with whom to pass a few hours, or even weeks. This child had flowered before his very eyes, constant, passionate in her feelings and finally he had been unable to resist it. Once drawn in, he knew that he was trapped by his own sentiments, yet the affair could only cause grief. He was ashamed because he did not have her courage, her ability to give everything and not worry about the consequences.

At Gloucester, heady on adventure, living for the day, it had been easier, even under the quizzical gaze of Edward Massey. Now victory was within their sights and everything would change. Whenever his thoughts drifted to the future, clouds of anxiety gathered. Without Aunt Jane's compliance, he would even now be in a fix.

Other men had mistresses of long standing, maintained in separate households. They seemed able to juggle the needs of family and position with the pleasures of extramarital love, skilfully, without complication. At the thought of his own standing, the expectation of the Hampdens and the Hammonds, Robert felt weighed down. He was not a rebel at heart. How much easier to succumb to social pressures, to enter his marriage without complications. These disloyal thoughts made him feel undeserving of Dublin's love. They also left him feeling unworthy of that other, stalwart girl who would pass on the blood of the Hampdens to his own descendents. At the thought of possessing her young woman's body, his cock stirred.

Perhaps they would both find him out, leave him. He quickly

273

turned away from the thought. At heart he was a coward and yet he could not conceive of life without either of them.

Before he could allow himself the luxury of his couch, two other letters remained to be penned. He deliberated whether to write first to his mother, but for the moment he did not know what to say.

Pouring himself a third, generous measure of brandy, he re-sharpened the quill, dipped the new point into what remained of the ink and began to write again:

Naseby Village,
14 June, 1645

Mary, my Dear Love,

Forgive your Robert for his silence. We have journeyed to north, south, east and west before coming to this place . . .

Chapter 38

As the months passed, Caleb's reputation as a vagrant and a sot became widespread. Sometimes he found it difficult to get alcoholic liquor. When this happened, he began to feel desperate, the need for the drink now overshadowing the original reason why he had wanted it.

He stayed nowhere long enough to catch the attention of the Justices, gauging by instinct when it was time to move on. Travelling across country, he moved from Parish to Parish, taking nightly refuge in barns or under hedges, the faithful Tyke at his side.

From whispers, he knew that people suspected him of witchcraft, and his misshapen form to be that of the Devil. His Familiar, in canine form, was always at his heels. It pleased him to encourage the myth, knowing that fear was a potent weapon in getting the draughts of fermented spirit which were now his life's blood. Similarly, uncertainty about the nature of the dog ensured that it was well-fed.

Caleb tried to live in the present, his need for liquor becoming the driving force in his mind. He knew where he was with drink, what it could and could not do for him. There was nothing else that he could trust.

Resolutely he erased his past history. Never had he been a husband, a father. Then his traitorous thoughts conjured up an image of the baby, helpless, reaching out to him for salvation, a lost lamb. Angrily he kicked a pebble which skittered down the lonely hillside path, taking others in its wake.

It was at night that the thoughts were worst. Memories of Sara came to torment him, her essential goodness, the generosity of her love. He tortured himself with cruel thoughts of what might have been.

In an effort to evade these memories, his mind, ever punishing, escaped into that other purgatory – the contemplation of Dublin. There he tortured himself ruthlessly, pouring blame on his own head for the feelings he could not help, attributing Sara's death to his own weakness in not loving her enough. It was all Dublin's fault, and yet it was all his own, his baseness in putting a pretty face before the spiritual beauty of his wife. But he knew that Dublin was more than a pretty face. In her there had been the help-lessness of a trapped bird, the wildness of a faun. How he hurt inside.

As summer drew to an end, he became increasingly unsuccess-ful in his attempts to beg for drink. He was overcome by rage. Stopping at a cottage on the outskirts of Motestone Village, he banged angrily on the door. An old woman peered out at him, owl-like, distrusting.

'What d'yew want?' She looked him over with distaste and he was aware of his own smell, the dirt, the hopelessness.

'I need a drink.'

'There's water in the stream.'

'Damn you!' He grabbed hold of her, gripping her arm until she squawked with pain and fear. 'Haven't you got any wine, beer, cider, anything?'

She was shaking her head furiously, a gob of spittle running down her chin. 'Here, I've got a penny,' she gibbered. 'It's all I have. Take it, but don't hurt me!'

Caleb looked down at the coin she had fished out of her bodice. It lay warm in his hand. He still held the woman's arm and he could feel how frail she was, how bony. Suddenly, unbidden, tears began to run down his cheeks. He was in the middle of a night-mare and he was the monster.

Flinging the coin down, he let go of the woman and stumbled back down the path, sobbing as he went, blind, hurting. The ubiquitous Tyke shadowed his every move. Caleb did not notice which way he was headed but when he ran out of breath – which did not take long for he was very weak – he realised that he was travelling in the direction of home.

Defeated, utterly lonely, he increased his pace again, praying that his reputation, so actively encouraged, would not now backfire on him, and that his family would not disown him. 'Dear God,' he mumbled to himself, please let me be welcome.' Only there could he find the haven of comfort he so desperately needed.

At the cottage he did not have the courage to walk in, so he knocked and waited. Lizzie opened the door and stood silently gazing at him.

Fearfully he raised his eyes, meeting hers, seeing the pain and worry.

'Oh, Caleb.' She reached out and took his arm, leading him inside.

'I'm sorry,' he groaned.

'Hush, now. Come you in. What a mess you're in. First food, then a wash, then sleep.'

He gave himself up to her, a child again, obeying her gentle commands. He started to ask for a drink, but bit back the request, accepting instead the ale that did little to assuage his longing. Finally, stripped, washed and fed, he fell onto the bed and slept for fourteen hours.

When he awoke he felt strangely detached from everything around him. Lizzie immediately brought him bread and ham and more ale, but although he drank, he had little appetite.

'Come along now, you must eat. You're like a skeleton.'

He forced a few scraps of meat down his throat. He was still tired, heavy, and he had a frightening sense of drifting, not knowing quite who or where he was.

Lizzie had laid out clothes for him, ancient breeches which he recognised as having been his father's. He thought of his mother's loss, the attachment that had bound her and his father so close. He was suddenly ashamed of his own weakness.

Lizzie talked of village matters, weddings and births, good and ill fortune that had come to their neighbours. He did not need to listen. The accounts were familiar, part of his early life, a continuous saga of highs and lows. As he heaved his legs over the edge of the bed and permitted his mother to push his feet into the legs of the breeches, she said: 'I expect you knew that Elijah Wavell died, some time back. You won't have heard, though, that that young flibbertigibbet he married, Annie Colenutt, she's run off with a soldier.'

Now Caleb began to pay attention. 'When? What about her daughter?'

Lizzie's eyebrows raised a fraction, questioning, but she simply added: 'Her mother left a week since. Poor little mite, she's on the Parish.' She eyed her son shrewdly. 'Thank God she's past weaning. I expect they'll farm her out. If she's lucky, someone kind'll take her in, put her into service when she's big enough.'

Caleb was standing now, pushing his mother aside as he struggled to fasten the breeches about his waist. He was so thin that they threatened to fall down.

'Where do you think you're going?'

He shook his head and Lizzie pushed him back. He fell defeated onto the bed, his legs refusing to hold him. His hand shook uncontrollably.

She sat back on her haunches and looked into his face. 'That maid, she's yourn, isn't she?'

He lowered his head and sighed. 'I think so.'

'I can see it.' She was silent for a while then forcing him to look at her, she said. 'We don't have much. There's nothing coming in, but if, when you're strong enough, you were to seek employment, perhaps we could afford to keep her.'

He met his mother's eyes and the tears were there again, shameful, weak, but cleansing him of his pain.

He vowed, 'Come the Hiring, I'll get a place.'

Chapter 39

At last, cousin Robert heard of a property which he thought would suit Dublin's needs. The house, once belonging to a Royalist family, had been confiscated, and for a reasonable sum he was confident that they could acquire it. Hence, on a clear Friday morning in late October, having first attended church, Dublin rode with him to Limerston, where, facing across the southern channel towards France, stood Foxton Manor.

The moment she saw it, she knew that she wanted it. She felt a frisson of excitement, a sudden sense of joy because her secret daydreams of sharing a home with Robert were at last being translated into reality.

The house was of Tudor vintage, having been constructed about fifty years earlier, and was showing serious signs of neglect. It had stood empty for about two years and the gardens and courtyard were overgrown, the thatch in urgent need of replacement. Built from locally quarried stone in pleasing hues of yellow, red and black, it struck Dublin as original and beautiful. She felt that rare sense of destiny, as if Fate had steered her along the path she must take. She turned to cousin Robert.

'Oh, I like it!'

Ignoring her excitement, he began to wander around the outside, tilting his head to examine walls and gables, poking at window-frames. His expression was not encouraging.

Impatient to dip under its deeply shelving roof and explore, Dublin left him. With difficulty she forced open the swollen door, undeterred by the spongy wood, the paint that flaked away around the latch.

Inside she absorbed the spirit of the low-ceilinged, abandoned

279

rooms, where items of furniture and hangings still adorned the place. She knew with certainty that this house had been waiting for her.

Cousin Robert continued to view it with more serious intent, poking into corners for further signs of decay or subsidence. Dublin already knew that even if it was falling down, she still wanted it.

Outside, the courtyard was the deciding factor. Surrounded by six-foot walls, shrouded in vines and creepers, she stood on the uneven pavings and breathed in the heady smell of apples. Choked with weeds as it was, here was a piece of heaven, a perfect retreat. There were various byres and outbuildings, a buttery, dairy, a wash-house, and pastures where ancient oaks had seeded long before the house had been thought of. Plum trees, cherries, medlars – the orchard was even now a profusion of unpicked fruit. Dreamily she plucked a sweet damson and joyed in the taste of juice trickling down her throat.

With good stabling and grazing, the place offered everything she could conceive of in the way of perfection. 'Oh, yes! Please, Cousin, please go ahead.'

Cousin Robert, predictably, pointed out various shortcomings, but Dublin stood firm. 'I know that Robert would approve.'

Reluctantly her companion ran out of obstacles. 'It will need considerable work. Some time needs pass before you can move in.'

'That does not matter.' To herself, Dublin thought that she would be delighted to move in that very afternoon, but she kept her thoughts private. As long as cousin Robert agreed, then she would be patient. Her excitement threatened to erupt into cries of delight, into her skipping for joy.

'You will need servants,' he said. 'Most important, we must find a good bailiff, someone we can trust with running the place.'

Dutifully Dublin nodded, anxious to reach home and write the good news to Robert, except that it was now many weeks since she had heard from him and she had no idea where he might be. A suffocating cloud of fear threatened her happiness. In these times of conflict and suffering, such a display of joy might invite disaster.

Her instinct was to make the sign of the cross, but at the thought of cousin Robert's horror, she could not help but smile. She felt the fear recede. Instead, she silently promised the God who ordered all their lives that she would be patient, so long as Robert came safely back to her.

Robert Dingley brushed invisible pieces of fluff from his doublet. Dublin realised that he had been speaking. 'I beg your pardon?' she asked, shamefaced.

His chin shook with disapproval and Dublin felt duly chastened. As if addressing his congregation, he repeated: 'I said, my dear, that come the Hiring, we will find the very bailiff we need.'

As always, the Hiring took place at Martinmas, on the low flat ground below Carisbrooke fortress.

By first light, Dublin was already dressed. She wore her thickest cloak with a lined hood, and stout shoes against the damp November day.

'I really believe that you should stay at home,' Aunt Jane admonished. 'You should leave the hiring to my son and our bailiff. They know what they are about.'

At the words, Dublin felt a stab of disappointment. Ever since setting eyes on Foxton, she had been counting the days until workmen should be found for her prospective home. Feeling that perhaps she was breaking some code of etiquette, she was about to acquiesce, when a rebellious inner voice reminded her that she was shortly to become an independent woman of property. Robert would understand. Aloud, she said, 'Thank you, ma'am, but I should like to be present.'

Aunt Jane's eyebrows shot up in disapproval, but she merely nodded her head. 'In that case, you will stay close to my son and Isham Carter.'

'Of course.'

As they approached the Hiring Ground, Dublin's sense of excitement rose. Not since the market at Chester had she seen so many traders.

'Isn't like what it used to be,' said Isham, the Dingleys' bailiff. 'Before the war you'd have had ten times as many people – jugglers, Moorish men, folks from the mainland come to tell fortunes, gippos selling love-potions. Then there was the dice-games and the bear-baiting.' He shook his head in regret at the passing of a lost era.

Dublin reined in Fortune and looked across the field. Apart from those traders hawking pasties and baskets, coney-skins and trussed fowls, the only other people not for hiring were the preachers, standing at every corner, exhorting the gathering to turn to God. Following Isham Carter's train of thought, she noted that there was no liquor, no music, no dancing.

Those who came to do business were divided into two groups, men and women who came to sell their services, and employers who came to buy them.

Isham went immediately to look for servants for Wolverton, while cousin Robert dismounted and made a business of easing his tired legs and shoulders. Ignoring him, Dublin pushed Fortune on, riding around the perimeter of the site, watching the dairy-maids with their milk-pails, the cooks and skivvies jostling to be noticed.

The craftsmen had selected their own corner of the field and Dublin set out in that direction, fretting that neither of her escorts seemed in a hurry to engage of the best.

As she rode along, she passed a group of outworkers, men and girls, cowmen, shepherdesses, holding up crooks and stools, and sporting pieces of wool in their hats to denote their trades. Her eyes skimmed over them without interest, until they came to rest on the black-haired, silent man, holding himself apart from the mêlée. At his feet was a black dog.

For a moment her breathing stopped and her eyes were trans-fixed by the solitary figure. She could not look away. He turned his head and his eyes met hers. Quickly she looked down, lost, not knowing what to do. She had rehearsed this meeting often enough, but always at her behest, in some quiet place where she could explain what she felt.

Glancing up she saw that he was still looking at her. His face was impassive and she had no idea what he might be thinking.

'Caleb Gosden.' Her voice wavered with embarrassment.

'Mistress.' There was the merest hint of mockery in his tone.

She was shocked by his appearance. He was thin to the point of emaciation and his face was shadowed, haggard.

'You don't look well.'

He shrugged. 'You look very well.'

Again she blushed, discomfited by the quality of her clothes, her role as employer. It did not fit easily. She said nothing.

At that moment Robert and Isham came to join her, seemingly unaware of the tension between their charge and the hireling.

'Come along, my dear, you are in the wrong place.' Cousin Robert indicated with his head where they might find suitable employees.

'I – I thought this – man might be suitable.' She chose her words painstakingly, trying to control her sense of confusion.

'You aren't needing a shepherd.' Cousin Robert spoke as to a child, while Isham looked with disapproval at Caleb, his reputation clearly having preceded him.

Robert went to move on, but Dublin stuck her ground. 'I know this man,' she said, now meeting Caleb's eyes. 'He is a good worker. Reliable. Experienced. He would make an excellent bailiff.' Her cheeks blazed under Caleb's regard, his slow, cynical gaze.

Cousin Robert was shaking his head. 'I cannot allow . . .'

Ignoring him, Dublin said to Caleb: 'Are you still for hire?' When he did not reply, she added, 'It's a bailiff we're seeking, someone to oversee a manor farm – are you interested?'

He pulled a quizzical face that she could not interpret. All the time she felt increasingly angry with him because he was putting her in a more and more foolish position. He should be trying to sell his services to them, not permitting her to persuade him.

'Dublin, please . . .' Cousin Robert, in hasty consultation with Isham, was determined to put an end to the interview.

'There's a condition.' As the shepherd spoke, they all regarded him with varying degrees of surprise.

'What sort of condition?' Dublin answered quickly before the others could intervene.

'That I bring my child.'

The hurt started, that old, empty wound, because she was not a mother – and because he was a father? The thought took her by surprise. It could be of no interest to her that he had fathered a child, and yet she felt . . . jealous? It could only be because he had achieved something that was denied her. She looked at his shaggy, unkempt head, his skinny, hunch-backed body. Inside it made her feel hungry to be touched.

Turning to Isham Carter, she said imperiously: 'Will you see to

283

the arrangements? You'll know what the wages are set at.' Isham looked to Robert Dingley for confirmation but he did not overrule her order.

Dublin addressed Caleb. 'There is a cottage you can use. It is permissible to bring the child and . . .' She shrugged, wondering about Sara, why he had not mentioned her, but that was another avenue she did not wish to explore. Turning pointedly away, she said to cousin Robert: 'Now, shall we seek out a carpenter and mason?'

With marked disapproval, he followed.

Dublin could not wait for the rest of the day's business to be conducted. In the increasing cold of the November afternoon, she fretted while Robert Dingley and Isham completed the hiring of all the staff that were needed for both Wolverton and Foxton. Having been hired, Caleb had disappeared from the field. Dublin wondered what sort of a fool he must think her, and her anger with herself only increased the anger she felt towards him. She had thought herself free of his influence but already, within minutes of meeting with him, she was behaving like a child.

At last they arrived back to the calm of Wolverton. As they shook the frost from their cloaks and let the servants pull their muddy boots from their feet, they were welcomed by Aunt Jane. Dublin eyed her cautiously, wondering if her behaviour of the morning still upset her guardian, but Aunt Jane seemed otherwise occupied.

To cousin Robert she said, 'My dear, your father has arrived from London.'

Dublin breathed a sigh of relief, knowing that she could now escape back to the kitchens. It struck her as ludicrous that she had just been instrumental in hiring the very servants with whom she would now share much of her days.

Before she could leave the hall however, Aunt Jane said: 'My husband has something for you; a letter from my nephew, from London.'

With beating heart, Dublin accepted the longed-for epistle.

Retreating to the window to take advantage of the fading light, she started to read.

Dearest,

Against all odds I find myself in London. The last weeks have been packed with such experience that I know not where to begin.

In September our massed troops stormed Bristol. In the mêlée I received a scratch but it is nothing – although I miss your tender ministrations. To defend the port was a hopeless task, and the Royalists wisely surrendered to prevent unnecessary loss of life. The city is now ours, praise God!

From there we marched direct to Winchester which surrendered after enduring much hardship. Lieutenant-General Cromwell sent me to negotiate the terms of surrender and in one night we succeeded in reaching agreement. Can you imagine how hope of victory spurs us on?

We moved then to Bazing House. A year now this stronghold has defied our attempts to subdue it. It is one of the biggest Royalist strongholds in the south, and the need to destroy it has been our goal for many months.

Bazing is the property of my kinsman the Marquis of Winchester and without doubt the biggest habitation within these shores. One would think to have arrived at a city, instead of a single dwelling.

The lie of the land, the vast perimeter of the walls, their thickness, all added to our difficulties. The Marquis and his supporters are Papists to a man. Some five hundred traitors sheltered within.

I came there in the second week of October, the purpose being to end the siege. On my second day, after church parade I went with Major King to inspect the cavalry on the northern side.

Fog settled upon us in extremis. Whether it was the foggy air, or my being fatigued I know not, but I was not as alert as I should have been. We came upon a guard who challenged us. Immediately I replied: 'For the Parliament,' too late realising that here were Winchester's men. Major King shot the guard but he and I were taken prisoner.

Everything we had was taken from us, down to the very boots that we wore but we were not ill-used.

On hearing of our capture, Lieutenant-General Cromwell sent message that if we should be harmed then even their most noble should suffer in return. Offer of an exchange however, was refused as they considered Major King and me to be of value in negotiating a settlement.

My dear, it is hard to describe what happened next. Our men set upon storming the house. Nothing was spared. Such a battering I have never experienced. The Papists fought gallantly, expecting no quarter, filling the very breaches with their bodies. It was both noble and terrible.

When it became clear that victory was ours, my kinsman, Winchester,

285

threw himself upon my mercy. His neighbour, Sir Robert Peake, gave me the very key to his chamber, offering me all his jewels in return for the sparing of his life – although the treasure had already been looted.

After much torment the new house succumbed but still the old house held defiant. There was little mercy to be had. Before long the whole was afire. Many perished in the flames or were suffocated in the vaults below, – a terrible mixture of arsenic and sulphur was used to poison the rebels. Our men were out of control, venting their rage against them. I spared those whom I could, but many succumbed. Such was the sad condition at Bazing. For me, it was Carrickmain over again.

Dearest, I was sent to report upon this to the Commons and in compensation for my losses they have granted me £200. The money seems tainted with blood.

Before long I shall be moving on. Now everything must be concentrated in the west. Word of you would be like manna but I am nowhere long enough to receive your missive.

Having met with Sir John Dingley, it pleases me to hand this poor record of my life to him. He tells me that a house is now yours. I spend many an hour trying to imagine what it is like, and what it would be like to share it with you, my dearest love.

Meantime, I am sending a surprise for you. Sir John will make you acquainted with what I mean. I am confident that it will meet with your approval.

Pray for me, Dublin. Wait for me.

Yours in exhaustion, Robert.

Dublin hugged the letter to her, bathing in the love and longing it conveyed. Caleb and the Hiring were forgotten. Again she prayed to the ubiquitous spirit that shaped her destiny, begging that her man should be safely returned.

After a while she thought about the last part of the letter: '*I am sending a surprise for you.*' Her spirits lifted and putting the letter aside, she descended the stairs, wondering what Sir John had brought with him.

Sir John and Lady Jane were still in the hall. They did not look up as she came in and Dublin suddenly felt awkward, an intruder. Sir John finally turned and said: 'Get you to the kitchen, girl.'

The command stung her with embarrassment, knowing that he was putting her in her place, reminding her that she was no more than a servant, living there on sufferance.

In heavy mood she made her way along the corridor. As she pushed open the kitchen door, she heard voices, Jennet's immediately familiar, and a second female voice. Slowing her pace and peering cautiously into the room, it was to see the almost-forgotten figure of Polly Cranford.

'Polly!' Dublin was overjoyed. After a moment of disbelief, she held her arms wide and hugged her friend to her. 'I cannot believe that you are really here.'

Her last memory of Polly was of a sickly, half-starved widow, hanging onto life by the merest thread. The woman who came to meet her had colour in her cheeks, and her body filled out the warm but modest gown. In her wake was a slender child, also touched with the bloom of good health.

'Oh, Dublin. It is so wonderful to see you!'

After they had marvelled at each other and embraced again, Dublin asked, 'How came you to be here?'

Polly accepted the invitation to sit on the long bench, the child, Sarah, standing silently at her side. She said, 'I have been staying at Hampden House. After I lost you at the peace march, I was at my wit's end. Sarah and I wandered around the city with no idea what we should do. I did not have the courage to follow your advice and present myself at the Hampden residence.' She glanced up at her friend apologetically.

'Anyway, just when all seemed lost, we came upon a group of pressed men digging new fortifications. In return for food, I started to work beside them.' There was a silence before she continued. 'We slept in the trench we had dug out by day. It was backbreaking work and I hardly had the strength, but somehow we survived.' Polly sighed at the memory, her eyes shadowed with pain, then made a visible effort to throw off the ghost of the past.

'When the task was finally finished, I took courage and threw myself on the mercy of the Hampdens.' She paused. 'They are truly good people.'

Dublin felt her jealousy rise. 'Was Robert there?'

Polly nodded. 'He came there not two weeks since. It was at his suggestion that I travelled here, with Sir John.' Her voice was deferential. 'Your master wishes you to know that he is well.'

'Did he stay – with Mary?'

Polly looked up questioningly. 'He stayed at the house, yes, but

287

not, I think, as more than a guest.' She asked: 'Do I hear jealousy talking?'

'There is no mention of his marriage?'

'I am not aware of it.' Polly tilted her head to one side. 'It sounds as if you are uneasy, not sure of where you stand.'

Dublin shook her head, unable to voice her fears, but there was no need. Quietly, Polly said, 'Do not reach for the moon. In having him, you already have the highest mountain. It is madness to wish for more.'

Dublin's eyes prickled with tears. 'I love him,' she answered. 'I cannot bear to think of any other woman sharing his life.'

Polly raised her shoulders in a gesture of resignation. 'None of us get all that we would wish in life. I think, my dear, you either have to accept it – or look elsewhere.'

Chapter 40

At Foxton, Caleb found that he had much to occupy him. The house was grievously in need of repair and the land, overgrown and neglected, had to be brought back into use. As a first step, he acquired some sheep to reduce the grass. He knew where he was with sheep.

Little Annie, his infant daughter, was taking a long time to recover from the ordeal of being abandoned by her mother then foisted upon the Parish. The child, at first unresponsive, became increasingly clingy, not letting him out of her sight. The sensible thing would have been to leave her with Lizzie, or to hire a girl to care for her, but Caleb felt the need to raise her himself. Flying in the face of convention, he proceeded to do so, his working day constantly shadowed by his small and persistent burden.

When the child slept, he scrutinised her for signs as to her true paternity. Her hair was dark and curling like his own and her eyes were large and blue, which Lizzie insisted was proof of her kinship, but still Caleb did not know for sure. Many men had dark hair and blue eyes. There was Mortimer Cheke or Nat Jolliffe. Annie Colenutt had been a slut, prepared to lie with anyone who offered her a few coppers. He cursed his own stupidity.

All the time he remembered that last occasion when he had spoken with her, on the night of the shearing – 'if it comes out bent and twisted, they'll know it's yourn.' This child was straight and healthy, strong enough to have survived the deprivation that had been hers so early in life. He thought of the son that Sara had borne him. He too had been straight, but also weak and quickly snatched away. There at least he had been sure. At the thought of Sara, he longed for a drink.

289

At that moment little Annie gave a small, snuffling grunt and opened her eyes. Immediately she smiled.

'Da da da.'

'Go back to sleep.' Caleb's hands began to tremble and once more he was beset by the other problem that tormented him. Since Annie had come into his care, he had eschewed all liquor, excepting the weak ale that formed his staple drink, but he was constantly driven by the relentless urge for something stronger. For the most part, his shaking was beginning to steady, and the anxieties that knotted his belly gradually eased. In the main they were only resurrected by one thought – the mistress for whom he worked.

To his relief, Dublin had not ventured near the house. When he could, he asked about her but he found out very little for certain. Ned Norris, the mason, thought that she was some sort of distant relative to the Dingleys, but remembering the frightened waif he had found in the trap, Caleb found it difficult to believe that she had any blood connection with such an aristocratic family.

It was Ephraim Cawse, the carpenter, who told him a more disturbing version of events, but one that he felt more likely to be true.

'She come 'ere, two year since, brung by milady's nephew. Some say as 'ow she's 'is fancy woman, frowned on by the family. 'E brung 'er back from Ireland and 'e's set 'er up 'ere till the war be over.'

'She's done well for herself then.' Caleb covered the seering jealousy with a snort of contempt. He vowed then that come the next Hiring, he'd look for work elsewhere.

When Dublin had first set eyes on Foxton Manor, she could not wait to move in, but once Caleb was installed as bailiff, she found herself making excuses not to visit. She could not have defined what it was that held her back, but she knew without doubt that she did not wish to see her former rescuer. This did not stop her from gleaning intermittent progress reports from Isham Carter, whom cousin Robert despatched regularly to oversee the new and ill-received bailiff.

'The work is going apace,' cousin Robert informed her, as they rode out to Hulverston to take penny loaves to the poor of the Parish.

Dublin tried to disentangle the myriad questions that plagued her, none of which she dared ask, instead saying: 'How long before it will be ready?'

Cousin Robert reined his cob in, waiting for Fortune to draw level. 'There is a lot to be done, both to house and estate.' He puffed his cheeks out in the pompous way that he had, adding: 'In my view, it is best to delay any thoughts of living there for the time being. I feel that you should remain with my mother at Wolverton, until you have definite news of my cousin's return.'

His plump face turned quite pink and Dublin felt embarrassed, suspecting that at heart, he disapproved of her. Preoccupied with this possibility, she found herself saying, 'How fares the new bailiff?'

Cousin Robert shrugged. 'He works well enough. He's a surly devil though. He shows no respect.'

Already her chest had grown tighter. She asked, 'Has he moved into the cottage – with his wife?'

'I hear he is widowed.'

'Then he lives there alone?'

'With the child.'

She wondered why the news made it so difficult to breathe. Finding cousin Robert watching her, she said the first thing that came into her head. 'If he serves us well, might it not be best to let him remain?' Seeing his surprise, she quickly added: 'No point in thinking of changing bailiffs at the next Hiring; not for the sake of it.'

'That's a long way ahead.'

She could tell that he was curious and already she regretted what she had said. Far better to have endured the time until next Martinmas and then sent Caleb away. She had a sudden vision of his face, his mouth turned down in almost permanent derision, the way he stood as if nursing his disfigured shoulder like some ever-present burden, then those probing, all-seeing eyes. She knew that he would stay and the knowledge gave her a drowning sense of helplessness.

Next morning, one of her prayers was answered. A pedlar, making his annual visit to the Island, called at Wolverton to display his laces and ribbons. He also carried with him a letter from Robert.

Silently thanking her Maker, Dublin took it outside to read.

291

Sneaking behind one of the barns, she perched herself on a staddlestone and unfastened the seal. Her eyes hungrily scanned the paper.

Exeter,
May, 1646

My Life,

So much has passed since this year dawned. I regret that I am not an attentive correspondent but what I lack in writing I more than make up for in thinking of you.

It will surprise you to learn that I am now Governor of this place. It is an honour not without difficulties, but more of that anon. Before settling here I was much involved in subduing those strongholds which kept Exeter safe. My travels read like a gazeteer – Dartmouth, Torrington, Powderham, St Michael's Mount – if nothing more, I know this land better than I would ever have thought possible.

Each place has its story to tell, some brave, some tragic, some miraculous, as at Dartmouth, where a bountiful harvest of fish fair leaped from the sea and restored our failing and ravenous army; or at Torrington where the church exploded, showering us with lead and timber. It was a miracle that we survived, not least among us Lord Fairfax who led the assault and won the city over by giving to each defeated soldier half a crown – or three shillings if he would join with us. Our numbers swelled amazingly!

At Powderham we found ourselves in trouble. Attacking the castle, we learned too late that reinforcements had been newly smuggled inside. There was nothing to do but wait for more men of our own. We took refuge in the church where in the evening and pitch black, we were of a sudden attacked by the garrison. A barrage of granadoes were launched at us while we found ourselves trapped inside. Only by diverting the Royalists did we succeed in escaping across the waterlogged fields to the river and so live to fight another day – which in the case of Powderham turned out to be three weeks later. This time the garrison was quick to surrender in return for the sparing of their lives.

Here at Exeter the people are lukewarm about our Cause. Necessity has made us strip the very roof from the Cathedral for lead to make ammunition, and this goes badly with the citizens. The church is now divided into two to provide a place of worship for both Presbyterians and Independents alike. In other places, lack of accommodation has forced us to stable our horses in disused places of worship, which again brings shock to the pious. Part of my army, with great zeal, preaches at every corner of the city, a practice which is viewed locally as a great heresy.

I know not how long I shall be here. The King is all but defeated.

Since Bristol, Prince Rupert has been in disgrace which, fortunately for us, means that the King deprives himself of one of his most able men. There are now those in our army who hint at a very different future to settlement with King Charles. It is not a philosophy that I can support.

Dearest, Praise God I will be with you ere long. This war is all but ended. I ask only to complete my duty and return to your arms.

In love and longing, Robert H.

Robert's words, so lovingly penned, gave her the strength she needed. In her own love and longing, Dublin vowed that she would set out straight away for Foxton and prepare it for his homecoming.

When she arrived unannounced at the Manor, the first person she saw was Caleb, helping Ephraim Cawse the carpenter to bind some stout poles to make scaffolding. She reined in far enough away to watch them without being seen, so that she could compose herself. Ephraim was an older man, stockily built, stained chestnut-brown by the sun. Bareheaded, Caleb stood beside him, his shirt billowing in the breeze, his body straining to hold the poles fast while Ephraim tied them with twine. It was the bailiff who held her attention.

At Caleb's feet, hanging onto the rough cloth of his breeches, a small child chattered away to herself. Dublin felt the familiar emptiness but already she was mystified. Sara's baby could surely not be so big? The little girl was the first to hear her and turning her large blue eyes in Dublin's direction, she began to tug at Caleb's breeches and point.

It was too late to escape. Dublin swallowed down her unease and stuck out her chin, determined to take control of the situation.

As Fortune crossed the grassy path towards the two men, Ephraim stepped back and raised his hat. Caleb glanced round and went to continue with his labours, but then she saw him visibly stiffen. Flinging his hammer aside, he straightened up and turned to face her. His expression was impossible to read, eyebrows slightly raised, no hint of deference.

It was Ephraim who took the horse's head and, already flustered, Dublin slid awkwardly to the ground. The situation was running away from her.

'I have come to inspect the work.' Her imperious tone served only to embarrass her more. Caleb's eyebrows shot up a fraction higher.

'Mistress.' He half-bowed, indicating that she should go ahead.

Holding herself rigid, she walked unsteadily towards the house.

Much had changed. Woodwork had been repaired, the thatch replaced and crumbling walls restored. Inside, the furnishings had been cleared into one room and now the place seemed cavernous, big enough for a large family.

Unbidden, Caleb began to explain what had so far been done and she listened with her head slightly bent, nodding to show that she understood.

'You wish to see outside?'

She assented and followed him across the courtyard, into the beautiful walled garden. It was nearly June and the sun beat warm and enveloping onto the borders where peas and vetch, asparagus and beans grew among the gillyflowers and honeysuckle. The air was thick with bees and perfume.

'All looks well.'

'I'm glad it meets with your approval.'

She felt like an intruder, an uninvited guest, offending some protocol she did not understand. She wished that he would go away. The child was still trailing along with him, observing Dublin with huge, unblinking eyes.

'She favours you,' she said, for want of something to break the tension.

He shrugged. 'So they say.'

'I expected her to be much younger.'

'My boy – Sara's boy, died.'

'Oh, I'm sorry.' The sadness of the news made her forget the awkwardness.

Again he shrugged.

They both stood in silence, and all those explanations from so long ago slipped away from her. To relieve the tension she said: 'I did not realise you had an older child.'

He grimaced. 'Fate has decreed that she should come to me. Her mother abandoned her.'

She was confused now. 'I – I thought . . .'

His expression was sardonic. 'You forget, I'm Devil-touched. You see here the fruit of my fornication.'

He held her eyes and her face grew hot.

As if pressing home his advantage, he asked: 'You're not wed then?'

She shook her head, realising that he was taking control. 'I'm waiting for – for Master Hammond to come back from the wars.'

'Ah yes, I remember. Your master. Is this to be your conjugal home?'

Dublin blushed. 'It's none of your concern.'

'Of course not. Forgive me for speaking out of turn.'

She knew that he was mocking her. Caleb stepped back, indicating that it was time to go and she brushed past him, trying to keep some semblance of dignity.

'May I ask when you plan to move in?' he asked as they arrived back by the scaffolding.

'I can't say. When . . .'

'When your master comes?' He gave the so-familiar derisive smile, catching Fortune's rein and offering his cupped hands to assist her to mount.

With a brief nod of her head she acknowledged his help and sprang into the saddle. The pressure of his hands beneath her shoe felt like lightning, tingling, dangerous. Now that she was higher than him, she made a last attempt to gain control of the situation.

'My lord enjoys the hunt. Before he comes I want the stables in excellent order, and I shall be looking out for some good dogs.'

'Mistress.' He inclined his head, raising his cynical blue eyes to meet hers.

She could not stop herself from saying: 'I tried to intervene for you, at the Petty Court.'

'That was good of you.'

She shook her head. 'You think I left you to face the consequences of helping me.'

'I don't think of it at all.'

'Well . . .' She did not know what else to say. Reining in Fortune and turning her towards home, she pushed the mare forward. 'I commend you on the good work you have done.'

As she moved off, she was aware again of the mocking acknowledgement, the smirk that touched the corners of Caleb's lips, the crinkling lines about his eyes. She felt a crazy desire to burst into tears.

*   *   *

After her visit to Foxton, Dublin resolved never to go there alone again. On the next occasion, for good measure, she invited Polly to accompany cousin Robert and herself.

'Dublin, you are so fortunate!' Polly gazed with disbelief on the house, turning to look at her friend to gauge if truly, this was Dublin's own property. 'Are you really going to live here? You'll be as great a lady as Mistress Hampden.'

'I shan't be any different from what I am now.' Dublin's voice was sharp. She disliked the comparison with Mary's step-mother. Then her mood lightened. The pleasure of her new house, the satisfaction in gazing across the acreage of meadow and orchard was such that she would not allow herself to be disturbed.

'When you move in, shall I be able to work for you?' Polly was undaunted by her friend's mood.

This was another uncomfortable question. Dublin was assailed by a guilty sense of deserting her old life and setting herself up in a station where she did not belong. The ever-acute Polly added: 'You will fulfill the role of mistress with credit.'

Cousin Robert went to inspect the building works so the two women made their tour alone. As they wandered into the walled garden, it was to find Caleb and his child intent upon tying back the great swathes of mallow that threatened to spread across the path. At the sight of him, Dublin stopped short and drew in her breath. Polly, following her example, slowed to a halt. She looked at the mistress of Foxton for some explanation but none was forthcoming.

Little Annie immediately saw them and tugged at Caleb's shirt-sleeve to alert him to their arrival. Slowly he straightened up and waited for them to approach.

Dublin hoped that he would say something, do something, but he didn't. After an uncomfortable silence she said, 'I bring my companion to see the house.'

He nodded to Polly. He seemed very much a man in command of himself and at home in his surroundings, beholden to no one – prince or pauper. Dublin shut out the memory of the downs above Caulbourne. She noticed that he looked in better health. His face and arms were brown and he no longer had that gaunt, haunted air that had so shocked her at the Hiring.

'How go things?' she asked, determined not to let her discomfort show.

'The roof is finished, the inside work completed.' He paused. 'The stables are repaired and I have found two good horses – fit for a lord.' His mouth twisted slightly.

'Are they ridden regularly?' She fired the question at him, angry with him for baiting her but powerless to challenge something she could not even acknowledge.

'I ride them myself.'

She was surprised, not thinking of him as a horseman.

He did not let the moment pass. 'I maybe a peasant, but I can handle a horse.'

'I didn't mean . . .'

He bowed his head as if accepting her apology, then met her eyes. 'If you would care to try them? They are fit for a lady, too.'

'Thank you, but no. I will stay with my own horse.'

Once again there was silence. Little Annie had come across and Polly bent to speak with her, holding the child's hands, looking into her face.

'What a pretty maid.' To Caleb she said, 'She favours you.'

He nodded at Polly, acknowledging her remark, his expression suddenly open, friendly. Again Dublin felt the pain of exclusion. She announced: 'We must be going.'

As they walked back towards the courtyard where Fortune and one of Aunt Jane's palfreys awaited them, Polly said, 'That is an interesting man.'

'You think so? He is very disrespectful. You are welcome to him.'

Polly looked across at Dublin. 'I cannot believe that you are too great a lady to appreciate him for what he is.'

'What is he, then?'

'His own man – proud.'

'If he is so much to your liking perhaps you should tell him so.' Dublin knew that her voice was betraying her. Even to herself she sounded like a small girl deprived of – of what she did not know. The feeling made her angry. As cousin Robert came into view, she hurriedly mounted her mare. 'If you want him you had better make haste,' she said sharply to Polly. 'Come the next Hiring, he'll be gone.'

When the Hiring came, Caleb did not leave Foxton. Acting upon Dublin's earlier and foolishly expressed wishes, Robert Dingley

297

did not even attempt to replace the bailiff, so she found herself faced with him for another year. In the event however, it made little difference. In spite of the King's surrender, there was no early sign of Robert returning to Wolverton. The house remained empty, and an empty future stretched ahead.

On those occasions when cousin Robert sent Isham Carter to Foxton, Polly would often accompany him.

'You won't come? You don't wish to visit your house?' Polly asked, clearly not believing that Dublin would forgo such a pleasure.

'No.'

'You don't object if I go? 'Tis such a beautiful place, I can't help but wish to see it.'

'And the bailiff?'

Polly did not appear to hear, and Dublin felt annoyed with her friend, or should she say servant? She could not decide. Since the coming of Polly, her own position in the house had been even more confusing, neither mistress nor maid. Polly knew her place all right. She worked in the kitchens, cleaned and cooked, and she slept with Sarah and the other servants in the attic. Dublin had her own chamber and although she too contributed to the daily labours, it was at her own behest. Aunt Jane never directly instructed her in her daily work. In every way she felt an outsider, a misfit.

Thinking of Polly conversing with Caleb, making him smile, sharing laughter, Dublin felt so indignant that she wondered whether to beg Aunt Jane to send the woman back to London, but then guilt and shame weighed her down. What was the matter with her? Meanwhile another year was coming to an end. Soon it would be 1647, and perhaps God, in His mercy, would bring her beloved back to her.

298

Chapter 41

1647 was turning into a terrible year. Cold, rain, failing crops . . .
all added to the hardship suffered by rich and poor alike, but by
the poor in particular. The pestilence made a savage, ill-timed
eruption. The spotted flux swept through some villages. The
Godly pointed accusing fingers at the Godless, and berated them
for bringing a plague on the land. The Godless in turn blamed the
war, the King and the Parliament.

For Dublin, this particular ill wind blew some comfort in her
direction, for with so much help needed by the vagrants and desti-
tute, she threw herself into good works, labouring alongside Aunt
Jane, Jennet and Polly to make the lot of the humble a little less
grinding.

'I do dread these wicked days,' said Jennet. ''Tis a bad time to
be bringing a young 'un into the world.'

Dublin glanced at the housemaid's belly, large and round. The
girl seemed to be in full bloom, rosy-cheeked, sleek, contented as
a brood mare. Raw envy made it difficult to speak.

Nearby, Polly and Sarah sat sewing. As the child grew, she came
to resemble her mother more and more. Their needles moved in
unison, giving them a complete look. Even without a husband, Polly
looked fulfilled. That, Dublin thought spitefully, was probably
because of Caleb. There was hardly a time when Polly did not find
a reason to ride with Isham Carter, the carpenter, to Foxton. Not
that Polly said anything to her. Indeed, she was deliberately reti-
cent, sensing Dublin's disapproval. If she shared her secrets, it was
with Jennet – two servants together, knowing who they were, where
they were going. Only Dublin was cut off, an outcast, drifting. The
sense of hopelessness increased with each passing week.

The house at Foxton was rarely talked of. As far as Dublin knew, everything was in perpetual readiness for the day that she chose to move in, but she did not ask. Let Polly visit there with Isham Carter. Dublin had no wish to accompany them, to see her beautiful, empty house, to witness the growing friendship between Polly and Him, Caleb Gosden. The thought of his rare smile, the occasional flashes of humour, the hint of tenderness . . . Once Robert came . . .

Robert's letter arrived at the beginning of September, brought over by a trader, hoping to find again those markets that had once been so lucrative before the war. It was months since Dublin had heard from her man and the arrival of his letter knotted her belly. As she took it upstairs, she prayed, 'Please God, let it be good news.' She hardly dared read the words for what they might reveal.

Saffron Walden,
August, 1647

My Dear Girl,

It is with heavy heart that I pen these lines. I had hoped long since to be at your side but necessities of state have decided otherwise.

I know not how much news reaches you on those distant, peaceful shores but I will endeavour briefly to tell you how things stand and my part therein.

It is now more than a year since the King surrendered to the Scots. In my innocence I thought this to be the end of the war, but with his capacity for confusion, His Majesty entered into negotiations with all and sundry, causing great division in the process. When at last the Scots handed him over to the Parliament, I again thought that a settlement would be forthcoming, but not so.

For myself I was offered command of a regiment to go to Ireland, the belief being that until Dublin is secured, the King might still look there to be rescued. Accordingly, in March we made the journey to Chester ready for embarkation, only to return again as agreement over our rights and duties became impossible to reach.

My Dear, the army has become a force to be reckoned with. Many months without pay, the threat of summary disbandment, lack of help for widowed and wounded – and most of all the birth of new radical ideas – have turned it from an instrument of the Parliament into a power in its own right.

At first my sympathies were very much with my men. It was I who gave voice to their grievances at the bar of the Commons.

Then however, a faction of the army took matters into their own hands and stole the King away first to Newmarket, now to Hampton Court. My fear is that they intend to do away with the monarchy altogether, replacing it with I know not what. The struggle between Parliament and army increases and I no longer have the stomach for it.

Some two weeks since, I met with my uncle, Henry Hammond. I last set eyes upon him at John's funeral and his war has indeed been very different from mine. He has passed most of the war in Oxford, serving as a public orator, then as Chaplain to His Majesty.

After the King's capture, Charles was refused access to his chaplains but now Henry is reunited with him and upon my uncle's most urgent request I agreed to accompany him to meet with the King.

My Dear, I did so with such a mixture of feelings. I had not set eyes upon King Charles for many years and found him aged and worn but there is something about him, an air of grace and courtesy that reduced me to my knees in sad remembrance of how low our country has been brought. In spite of myself, tears came to my eyes and I kissed his hand.

Dublin, I am much troubled. I can see no way forward with the army other than more disorder and bloodshed. I am their servant yet my loyalty and friendship is also to those within the Parliament. The division causes me much torment.

I have decided upon a course of action and I know not where it will lead. I am today requesting that I be released from my command. I know not how they will respond. Hence, I will have to wait and see what God has in store for me – the words 'death or glory' come to mind.

Whatever my future, remember that I truly love you. In the event that I am deprived of my liberty, think only of your own future. My Aunt knows that your welfare is of the utmost importance to me.

My most ardent prayer is that some day, somewhere, I shall again be reunited with you, my dearest love – and yet even this dream is fraught with fears, for how can I be sure that after three such barren years you would wish to be united with a tired, disillusioned man of little importance?

Whatever, remember me in your prayers.

Yours in God, R. Hammond.

Once more the shadow of death threatened the future. Hugging the letter to her, Dublin tried to draw comfort from this small but tangible link with the man she loved. His words echoed in her mind – 'death or glory'. Glory had little meaning for her, but death – death was the ultimate terror.

Chapter 42

On the afternoon of Monday, 13 September, Sir John and Lady Dingley, Sir Robert Dillington, Sir William Meux, Sir John Oglander and his son John, Captain Brett, Mr Bowerman, Sir Thomas Cheke and Dublin, waited upon the quayside by Cowes Castle. They stood in a row, an assembly specially invited for the occasion. A striped awning had been erected to give shelter from the elements, whether rain or shine.

The autumn sun was behind them, and ahead a sparse stretch of woodland reached down to the gently lapping water of the Solent. It was a calm day and the sea snaked incessantly in gentle undulations, grey and silver by turn.

A guard from the garrison of Cowes Castle stood in formation to their right and as they waited, Captain Baskett inspected them one final time. To their left Mr Moses Read, the Mayor of Newport, along with various other aldermen, Justices and gentlemen of the Island, formed their own guard. Further away along the narrow strip of stony beach, local people without rank waited to see the spectacle.

Dublin tried to think of anything other than the reason for which they were there. Her heart hammered incessantly and there seemed no way to still it. It was difficult to resist the urge to wander off just to release the tension but any unseemly behaviour would bring embarrassment to the Dingleys. Breathing deep for the umpteenth time she clenched her fists against the folds of her skirt and stood her ground.

The pinnace crossing the Solent was already within yards of the quay. A pennant flew from the mast and she studied it intently to keep her mind occupied, but in the frivolous fluctuations of the wind it was not possible to make out what it portrayed.

Next to her, Lady Jane Dingley glanced round and smiled. Dublin tried to smile back but her face felt like wax, hard and glistening. A sailor from the boat was already ashore and the vessel was soon secured to the solid wooden bollards on the quay. As a landing-board was flung across, several passengers came to the rail and prepared to walk ashore. Mr Bulkeley and Mr Lisle, the Parliament's men, sent expressly from the Commons to act as hosts, were the first to disembark. As they reached dry land they turned to attend upon their charge.

Dublin could hardly bear to look. Her eyes of their own volition turned away but were again drawn back to the sight of the next figure who skipped nimbly down the gangplank.

If she had glimpsed him in a crowd, she might not have recognised him. He was familiar yet different, thinner, his shoulders held stiffly as if under strain. His hair had grown long and his chin was bearded, the hair redder than that upon his dark head. In spite of the dignity of his bearing on this most solemn occasion, she could not help but notice how lean his face had become and how haunted. For a moment, it reminded her of Caleb Gosden.

Mr Bulkeley presented their guest in turn to those waiting. Dublin lowered her eyes, but she was aware of his progress along the line of dignitaries. People bowed, shook his hand, saluted and he drew ever closer. Next to her, he took Aunt Jane Dingley's hands and squeezed them in his.

She said: 'Welcome, my dear. It is so good to see you.'

He kissed her upon the cheek and then he was standing in front of Dublin. Somehow she dragged her eyes up to meet his. He gazed intently at her face with tired eyes that had seen much pain, a hint of embarrassment perhaps, a questioning look.

'Mistress O'Neill. It has been a long time.'

'Sir.' She curtsied and looked away.

Keeping his voice low, he said, 'This is a difficult time. As soon as I am free of the formalities expected of me, if you will permit I shall ride over to see your new home at Foxton.'

'Sir.' She lowered her eyes.

He moved on down the line, stopping for a few words with all and sundry. She felt like a limp cloth, wishing only to be away. Again Aunt Jane glanced at her and she made a feeble effort to smile.

'Well,' said Mistress Dingley. 'This is a proud day for us all.'

Dublin looked round to see where Fortune was. Soon they would be riding in convoy from Cowes, stopping en route for speeches and formal welcomes in Newport.

After that Sir John and Lady Jane would go on home to Wolverton Manor. Dublin, accompanied by Polly and escorted by Isham Carter, would ride to Foxton Manor. At the same time Colonel Robert Hammond, the newly-arrived and newly-appointed Captain and Governor of the Isle of Wight and all its ports, forts, towers and places of strength, would take up his official residence in Carisbrooke Castle.

For Dublin, the next days passed in a kind of agony. In spite of her most cherished hopes, Robert did not during that time come to Foxton. Foolishly she had expected him to visit on the very evening of his arrival, to explain to all and sundry at the Castle that he had an appointment of such importance that everything else must take second place. Although she knew it was unrealistic, the disappointment tormented with an almost unbearable ferocity.

Pride mixed with despair. He was come to the Island as Governor, the most important figure, courted, cosseted, flattered by the gentry, his appointment expressly approved by Lord Fairfax, overtly encouraged by the Parliament. Lord Pembroke himself had willingly stood down so that Robert could have the reward he so richly deserved for his loyal military service. Mr Cromwell wrote of him in glowing terms.

Dublin paced the walled garden, now ripe with offerings. She fancied that the very soil was affronted because the new master had not come at once to see its beautiful harvest.

Thankfully Caleb was hardly to be seen, and when she did glimpse him he was always engrossed with some member of the household, labouring to keep the place in near-perfect condition – which it was. Occasionally Dublin espied him talking to Polly and a wave of indignation swept over her. Here at Foxton she wanted Polly as a companion, not one of the servants. Her friend's easy way with the bailiff was another assault on Dublin's failing confidence.

She sank onto one of the stone benches, especially crafted for the garden. Discarded leaves drifted from the trees and made a gold mosaic along the path. Water trickled from the fountain, soothing, almost luring lovers to come and be bathed in its gentle music. Dublin felt as stony as the bench.

Locally, matrons and unmarried girls alike were speculating on the new Governor's qualities, with a predatory, almost carnal anticipation. Dublin knew that they would not be disappointed, but she feared that for her, he had become a stranger. Secretly she was afraid that there was no going back to the heady days of Gloucester. All the dreams and hopes in the world might not be enough to permit them to pick up the loving threads which the war had so brutally severed.

To avoid this painful possibility, she tried to turn her thoughts to other things. In the barren, silent months of his absence, she had somehow tamed the wildcat of her emotions, locked away the raw hunger for him, consigned him to a secret, gentle, remembered place in her heart which occasionally threatened to break free, but was for the most part securely under control. Now he was back – not the same Robert she had loved and worshipped but a stranger, exalted in rank, wiser in experience, older in years. The fear of the unknown haunted her. If he could not make her dreams come true, then to her despair, she resented his coming.

Her thoughts seem to portray the very opposite of what she felt. It was the hope of Robert's return that had made life bearable all this long time, but on the quayside at Cowes she had glimpsed in Robert's eyes the pain of all that he had endured since their parting. Alone in the shadowy stillness of her wonderful garden, she shivered. Perhaps by coming here he would desolate the very way of life she had come to love. Perhaps by coming here he would also destroy himself . . .

Dublin was in the parlour helping Polly to plan a menu when the sound of horses reached them. They both stopped what they were doing and raced to the window. Two riders were approaching across the courtyard. Their horses moved with a jogging gait, giving the illusion that they were not making progress, but the cavalcade quickly drew near. Dublin's heart lurched as she recognised the leader, riding slightly ahead.

Immediately her insides felt gripped by a vice. Flinging her receipt book aside she turned to the door. 'Let's go and meet him!'

She was tense as a lute-string, not knowing whether to give into one desire – to run and fling herself into his arms, or to obey the opposite urge – to fly away and hide. Uncertainly she hovered in the porchway while the hounds bounded out into the yard, barking their welcome.

Robert slipped easily from the saddle and handed the reins to one of his companions. His hand ran like a blessing over the heads of the dogs. After a brief discussion, the two men rode round to the southern aspect of the house taking his horse with them. As Dublin watched, Robert came slowly towards her and hesitantly she stepped out to meet him.

'I can scarce believe that I am here,' he said.

She stood aside to let him pass and uncomfortably they walked into the house. Robert gave his cloak to a servant and looked about him. 'This place is exactly as I imagined.' His face relaxed and she felt a glow of pleasure at his remark.

'We are exceeding proud to have you here. 'Tis good that your service has been recognised.'

Immediately he appeared to grow tense again. Avoiding her eyes, he said, 'It is no easy thing to think of the past. There is much that any man would want to forget.' He was silent as if disregarding his own advice, then visibly pulling himself back to the present, he went on, 'We all need to look forward now, to the time when the country can truly be at peace.'

Dublin took advantage of this safer, impersonal ground. 'What is happening in the country?'

At that moment Polly came into the room with a ewer of home-grown cider and poured a large measure which she handed to the guest. He drank deeply and Dublin saw that his hands shook. She was glad when her friend withdrew.

Robert sighed. 'The King is elusive as an eel. He juggles all and sundry. For my part I cannot tell you how glad I am to be out of it. Now that I am here I intend to lead the life of a gentleman, not a politician or a soldier.'

As he talked, little bubbles of anguish stirred in Dublin, sparked off by that strange alchemy that binds a woman to one man. Try to protect herself as she might, she knew that she was still held prisoner by her feelings for him. It was as if the years were dissolving by the second and she was once more the girl who had ridden with him across England, who had shared his tent, his chamber, his love-making. She was instantly, hopelessly in need of him. The knowledge scared her.

'Would you like to make a tour of the grounds? It is too fair a day to remain indoors.'

Draining the last of the cider he nodded and with nervous pleasure she preceded him outside.

As they walked she kept talking, about meadows and pastures, acreage and yields and tilth. She wanted to impress him with her knowledge of the land, their land.

'And this is the kitchen-garden.' She led him into her sanctuary and was startled to see the bailiff and his child carrying out a tour of inspection of their own. Caleb did not look up as they approached.

Knowing that her face had coloured, Dublin said, 'That is the bailiff.'

Robert nodded in his direction and Caleb then looked round at his master with an expression that Dublin knew well. His mouth was slightly drawn down and she had the impression that he was the one carrying out the inspection and was not unduly impressed by what he saw.

She wanted to nudge him, remind him of his manners. Aloud she said, 'Caleb's been working very hard to restore the house and the land.' Even as she spoke she wondered why she needed to explain, perhaps to justify her choice of overseer?

Robert's eyebrows rose a fraction. 'Caleb?'

'Gosden, my – our bailiff.' Her face began to burn.

'Ah, I see.' Robert regarded him with interest, assessing him in turn, his expression hinting that the man was not what he might have expected.

'Where do you come from, Gosden?'

Caleb told him. Dublin noticed with unease that he offered Robert no title, not Sir or Master. He simply answered everything asked of him as if conversing with an equal.

'Shall you go to the stable?' she suggested to ease her own tension. 'Gosden has found you some good horses.'

Her guest acquiesced and the three of them set out in that direction, Caleb leading the way. Uncomfortably Dublin studied his hunched form as he walked ahead. His black head was bowed and she could almost feel his dismissive mood, sense his indifference to the nobleman who paid his wages. Her own feelings were too tangled to consider so she simply shut them out. Beside her, Annie skipped along, talking away to herself.

Dublin noticed how clean the child was, how her hair shone. Her father cared for her well.

Once at the stables, Caleb brought out the two horses he had purchased for his unseen master. Immediately the two men were drawn together, discussing, examining, conversing in a low, companionable tone. Dublin felt shut out and the realisation stirred again the anger that she felt towards her bailiff. He had the ability to exclude her from everything. The only thing she did not understand was why it was so important to be part of whatever he did.

Not far away a welcoming woodland offered some privacy. Louder than she intended, she said, 'Shall we walk?' She had the impression that Robert was reluctant to leave, but he agreed.

Beneath the trees it was cool and boggy. A stream whispered its way between the willows, and mistletoe hung in clumps from the emaciated oaks. Resentment and unease still tugged at her, but gradually it began to subside. She had not noticed before how magical this place felt.

'I still cannot quite believe that I am here,' Robert said, his mood suddenly lifting. 'It is as if I have been plucked from hell and placed in some strange limbo – I dare not believe that I am in heaven.'

'I think of this place as heaven.'

In silence they walked further into the copse. The path was muddy and Dublin had to pick her way carefully to protect the flimsy shoes which she had neglected to change.

'You look well,' he started. 'It comforts me to see that you are so much at home here.'

She could not stop herself from saying, 'The local people believe that I am Sir John's baseborn child.' She gave a small, embarrassed laugh. 'I do not know who my mother is supposed to be, but your Aunt Jane treats me well considering I am rumoured to be the fruit of a rival's womb.'

Robert's reply was so quiet that she could barely hear. 'If what they believe were to be true than that would make us cousins. I could even wed with you.'

'You are already spoken for.' She hardly dared to think what he might mean and he did not enlighten her. Sadness seemed to weigh him down again.

'Are you prepared to stay here?' he asked.

'That depends in what capacity.' Again she did not know why she spoke as she did.

He did not reply and she immediately regretted her challenge. Finally he said, 'I would ask of you to be patient. At the moment I am finding myself again.'

To break the tension she said, 'The local maids are all agog at the thought of a bachelor for Governor.' Her remark betrayed her jealousy and it did not go unnoticed.

After a very long time, he said, 'Much has happened to me during our separation. You will find that I am not the man you remember.'

'I must be a different person too.' In the face of his desolation panic began to claim her. Just then she would have accepted any conditions he chose to lay down if only he would promise that everything was going to be well, but he did not. She managed to say, 'It will always be my wish to serve you.'

'I thank you.' He turned to her and she was shocked by the pain in his expression. Not meeting her eyes he said, 'Sometimes I have black moods, bad dreams. If you have any concern for me at all, I beg of you to be patient.'

She nodded her head and he leaned forward and kissed her chastely upon the brow. In response she moved closer but the tension of his body, his trembling hands, restrained her from more than resting her cheek briefly against his shoulder. None of his letters had conveyed this change in him, prepared her for the effects of what he had so clearly suffered. She merely whispered, 'I have missed you.'

'I have missed you too.'

Painfully she thought of her imagined reunion, the running into each other's arms, being swept along in a tide of passion, carried up to the chamber, loved until every moment of loneliness had been compensated for.

She felt a great chasm of sadness inside, a certain knowledge that something very precious had been irreparably damaged. Walking behind him she cried silent tears, wiping them hastily upon her cuff so that he should not see.

They had neither of them seen anything of the countryside.

Robert stayed for dinner. At first he seemed reluctant but finally succumbed to the urgency of Dublin's pleading. She felt an unreasoning terror that once he left he might never return.

'Polly has gone to such lengths to make you welcome,' she urged. She had the impression that he was too weary to resist.

Wrestling with her own turmoil, Dublin wished that they could dine alone, but Robert's escort joined them. He was a short man, restless, with the sort of ill-repressed energy that threatened to erupt at any moment. He wore his hair very short in the Puritan fashion and his mouth had a determined set, ruthless almost. Something about him reminded her of a terrier. His name was Edmund Rolph.

Later, she could imagine him discussing her with the rest of the garrison, perhaps making lewd jokes about her relationship to the Governor. Her response was cool.

A goose had been laid up ready for Robert's coming and the best linen and wine, donated from Wolverton, were brought out, along with nuts and fruit from the estate. Perch and eels, larks and quail were accompanying dishes. For the briefest moment, Dublin remembered that it was Caleb who had reared the birds, organised the fishing.

Whether Robert's gloom lifted or whether he was expert at hiding his true feelings she did not know, but during the meal he set about entertaining them with anecdotes from his travels, sometimes making mock of his own misfortunes, recounting the foibles of the great and mighty. Dublin noted that he made no reference to the many battles and skirmishes that he had experienced.

All the time she watched and listened, glancing often to the window as the sun made an early descent towards the west. Too soon its departure would mark the time when Robert would also go away and like the sun his going would leave her world the darker. Inside she longed to howl and rage at the unfairness but she merely sat there, smiling, listening politely to his companion, eating her meal. Each mouthful was like gall.

As they prepared for their return journey, Robert said, 'You must forgive me if I am unable to call upon you very often. For the present at least, such a programme of visits and duties have been devised for me that I scarce have time to sleep.'

The news felt like an insult, a warning that she must remember her place and not expect to be a part of his official life. She tried to blink back the hurt, not let it show in front of Captain Rolph who was watching her with black, cynical eyes, hungry as a ferret.

With an effort she bowed her head, offering a formal farewell.

Her heart screamed with hurt. As the horses were brought round she watched the two men mount. There was no opportunity to be alone with him. The visit felt like a disaster.

Numbed with disappointment, she stood in the damp gloom, watching their diminishing shapes, until they were no more than an indistinct blur in the greyness.

A movement behind her, felt rather than heard, made her jump. As she turned, it was to find Caleb watching her. Her heartbeat quickened and she wondered what he had seen. For a moment she was not sure if she had voiced her misery aloud. Quickly she pulled herself upright, hoping to take control of the situation.

'Mistress.' Caleb raised his eyebrows questioningly. 'Everything is well with you?'

She suspected that he was taunting her, although his face was serious. Too quickly, she said: 'It's none of your business!'

He shrugged as at the mystery of women. 'I merely wondered if all was well.'

'No. It's not.' To defend herself, she said, 'You spend far too much time gossiping with the servants.'

She could see that he was mystified, but a moment later, his scornful expression was back. He said, 'If I neglect my duties, perhaps you'd like me to leave.'

He had trapped her. He knew only too well how efficiently he carried out his work.

Scowling, she mattered, 'That won't be necessary, but stay away from the maids.'

'Ma'am.' He bowed his head with exaggerated deference.

I hate you, she thought. I hate your certainty, your confidence. I hate the way you take away my composure. She knew that he had seen past the grand lady, witnessed the frightened girl inside. The memory of his tender care forced its way into her thoughts. Involuntarily she looked at his hands.

With an attempt at dignity, she turned away, saying, 'Remember what I say.'

'You want some advice?'

His question drew her up short. 'I do not.'

'You won't like it.'

Dublin felt her face freeze, afraid she might show some weakness, unsure how to stop him from overstepping the invisible barrier that kept her safe from him. He ignored her answer.

'It always amazes me,' he started enigmatically. 'I'm always amazed by the power of a pretty face, a pert arse.'

She felt the glow of shame start in her cheeks. 'What are you talking about?'

He shrugged. 'Take a man like your Governor – so upright, such a gentleman, yet one look at a fair lass, and he forgets himself, gets into such a pickle.'

'I don't know what you're talking about!'

'Perhaps you don't. Perhaps all pretty girls have no idea what power they have – what misery they can inflict.'

'I . . .'

'You think I mean you?' He raised his shoulders neither confirming nor denying the fact, then he continued: 'There's the joke of it. A pretty girl has so much power that when a man comes to defend himself against it, he has to use powerful weapons. Ofttimes those weapons are so cruel that it's the maid who is worst wounded.'

'I don't know what you mean.'

'Don't you?' He folded his right arm about himself, raising his left hand to cover his shoulder, in the habitual way that he stood, rocking slightly, nursing his own pain. 'I'm just trying to warn you.'

Before she could interrupt he added: 'Don't let yourself be the worst wounded.'

She was tongue-tied, shamed by his perception, humiliated because her precarious role as mistress of this house was exposed at fraudulent.

Gently he added: 'Never let anyone use your beauty against you.'

Without replying, Dublin turned back to the house. Tears prickled against her lids. She was so preoccupied by Caleb that it was not until she was back inside, that she remembered Robert and his denial.

Chapter 43

November came in cold and wet. The afternoons were dark by three of the clock although it was several weeks before the shortest day. Even with fires in all the chambers and every lamp and candle burning at Foxton, the house was perpetually gloomy. Marooned in her empty love-nest, Dublin thought that the season mirrored her mood. It was going to be a long winter.

She sat in the window recess watching the muddy sky empty its offerings upon the already waterlogged fields. A walk would have skimmed off the worst of her dissatisfaction, made it possible for her to remain still rather than to jump up at intervals and pace the floor of the hall, looking in vain for some purpose. It was too wet for riding.

Polly was upstairs with Dora, the maid, sorting out linen. It was a relief to be alone. The first lines of a couplet began to form in her head but she could not be bothered to go up to her chamber and scribe them. Sometimes she took pleasure in making odd jottings although of late she had had such gloomy thoughts that they were best forgotten. This was no more cheerful a rhyme but she liked the feel of the words on her silent tongue.

Something then happened that made her forget everything.

The wind had got up and being preoccupied with stoking the fire, she heard nothing until a thumping on the front door reached her. After a few moments Dora knocked timidly on the parlour door and poking her head around, announced: 'His Lordship the Governor to see Mistress O'Neill.'

Her choice of title would at other times have brought a smile of amusement to Dublin's lips but the surprise of Dora's announcement startled her so completely that she was dumbfounded.

Robert came into the room shaking the rain from his hair. Rubbing his hand briefly over his wet head he wiped the raindrops onto his jerkin and held his damp hand out in greeting. Somewhat shamefacedly, he echoed Dora's words: 'The Governor to see Mistress O'Neill.'

They both looked at the maid who came to herself and retreated. As soon as the door was latched, Robert turned into the room. He looked so different that Dublin's gloom was for the moment forgotten. His eyes were flecked with crystals of excitement and his whole demeanour spoke of anticipation.

'I have come here to tell you something – and to ask you something.'

She waited, trying to keep her suspense under control. His breath came fast and his expression softened into a smile.

'I have reached a decision. I cannot marry Mary. It is not because she would be a less than perfect wife. I could be a good husband too, dutiful, a credit to all who know me.' He turned towards Dublin and held his hands out in an open gesture as if inviting her understanding. 'But I cannot do it. I want you for my wife – not as a mistress, not as my acknowledged companion. I want you with me on formal occasions. I want you to preside at my table. I want our sons to inherit everything that I gain in this life. I want to provide good dowries for our daughters.' He gave an embarrassed shrug. 'Will you?'

Dublin shook her head in disbelief. Whatever else he might have come to say, she could never have expected this.

He took her hand. 'In making this decision, such a burden has been lifted from me. We could marry here. My chaplain, Mr Troughton, would conduct the ceremony.'

'And Aunt Jane?' She could not take it all in. The thought of his aunt's reaction was one way of questioning the reality of what he was saying. She needed to hear him confirm it again and again.

He said: 'I shall tell my aunt that this is what I want.'

'And Mary?'

His face clouded and her chest tightened in response. She was right all the time, it couldn't be true. But with the merest hesitation, he said: 'I shall go to London to acquaint her with this, on Monday or Tuesday. I feel like a criminal, but of course she will be compensated and there will be plenty of would-be husbands willing to take on such a respected and beautiful woman. I hope that she will forgive me.'

The niggle of jealousy was quickly crushed as she allowed her disbelieving feelings to try out what he was saying – that she, Dublin O'Neill, would be Mistress Robert Hammond, wife of the Captain of the Isle of Wight, mother of his children. 'I can't believe what you are saying.'

'Dublin.' He pulled her to him and pressed his mouth hard against hers. This long-awaited kiss was like powder igniting her. The explosion of joy reverberated through her very being.

'Robert!'

'You say yes, then?' He pulled his head back far enough to look down into her eyes.

'I still cannot believe it.'

He hugged her close. 'I've been a fool. I have known this was how it must be since long before you left London. Something made me believe that because I wanted it for myself it was wrong, when in fact I've been stupid. You, Mary, everyone has been ill-served by my refusal to face the truth.'

A strange feeling of calm settled upon her. Loyally, she said, 'You were doing what you thought was right.'

'Perhaps. The way to torment is paved with good intentions and I've been there many times these past years.'

She laid her face against his shoulder. She could not stop testing him. 'You said that coming here was a kind of limbo.'

'Limbo is a nothing, a waiting. It is time to move on. Say that you love me.'

'I love you.'

He kissed her again, suddenly alive, wild. 'God, I want you. Why have I been denying myself for so long?'

'Why?' She made no effort to make it easy for him, wondering at the abandoned stranger who held her close.

He took both her hands in his. 'Is there anywhere we could go?' He looked out at the unfriendly weather.

'There is my chamber.'

'The servants would be scandalised.'

'Then there is the barn.'

'Right.' He picked her up and carried her, laughing, into the hall, out into the courtyard and across the muddy cobbles to the cavernous stone building. As they went, the rain tapped against her skin and she did not care. She wondered who might be watching but she did not care about that either.

Inside, the barn was half-full of corn and in one corner a milk cow looked up amiably as Robert carried her across to the stooks of straw stacked at the opposite end. Even as her feet touched the ground he was lifting her skirts and easing himself into her. Moist, hungry, she welcomed him, holding him so tight that he might never leave again. His need was so urgent that their loving was short-lived, but it mattered not in the least, for the years stretched ahead. More nights than she could count would be theirs.

'Do it again.'

He laughed. 'You wicked girl. Learn patience!' He took her hand. 'Come along, we must return. This behaviour is shameful between the Governor and his betrothed.'

'It is delicious!'

Back inside the house he poured them both wine and raised his glass in a toast. 'To my bride.'

She raised her goblet in return but the exhilaration began to dissipate. 'When will you tell your aunt?'

'Very soon.'

Dublin did not look up at him. Suddenly doubts began to beset her on a grand scale. 'They won't permit it. Your mother – she'll be scandalised – and what of the gentry here? How will they view their Governor wedded to a peasant?'

'Dublin! If you refer to yourself in that way one more time, I shall be forced to chastise you – severely.'

She smiled, but the ghosts did not go away. She sought safety from them in his arms. 'Robert, I do love you, truly. No matter what happens. I want you to know.'

He shook his head as at an endearing child. 'Nothing is going to happen. Nothing. Tomorrow I want you to ride over to Carisbrooke. I shall receive you, show you around properly. Before the end of the week I shall organise a dinner in your honour and invite the local gentry and their wives.'

She thought with misgivings of all those grand people. Robert reached out and lifted her chin, forcing her to look at him.

'Stop worrying. Everything will be as you always wanted it. I promise.' He stepped back and looked round for his cape and gloves. 'I really must go. Duty calls.'

When he had donned his outdoor clothes, he took her in his

316

arms one more time. 'My dearest, just allow yourself to be as happy as you deserve.'

She hid her face against the rough stuff of his cape. 'I promise,' she murmured, not believing it.

At the door he kissed her once again. Sensing her doubts, he said, 'Sleep you well and happy dreams. In case you have any fears at all, just remember that you are going to marry the Governor of the Island. My word is the law around here, and there is not a soul on this earth who is going to make me change it. So be it?'

Comforted, she nodded her head. 'So be it.'

Chapter 44

What do you think I should do, Will?' King Charles looked anxiously at his servant and friend, William Legge, hoping for some solution to the latest troubles that beset him.

Will Legge hesitated, considering his words carefully. 'Clearly you must leave Hampton Court, Majesty. These threats are serious.' He looked away in embarrassment, before adding, 'Your enemies in the army are saying that you will soon be a dead dog. If you stay here, I honestly fear that your life is at risk.'

The King felt paralysed by the thought. His incarceration by the army was the stuff of nightmares. Turning to Will, he demanded: 'Then where should I go?'

'Perhaps north to Berwick, Sire. Or Jersey? Or to France?'

Charles did not reply. Inside he felt desperate to escape but a nagging doubt held him back. If he were to leave England he would be a monarch in exile. Perhaps he would never again find a way back into his kingdom. He pushed the thought aside.

'Can you arrange it – horses, or a boat, perhaps?'

'Jack Ashburnham will; and Sir John Berkeley will come with us – no one else, though. The fewer of us there are, the less we will arouse suspicion.'

Charles placed his hand over his racing heart, breathing deeper. 'Leave me then, I will prepare myself. I have letters to write.'

As soon as he was alone he went to the window and looked out across the gardens that surrounded Hampton Court Palace. In the grey November day everything looked bedraggled, made brittle by the early frosts. Charles felt the same.

His greyhound, Gipsy, pushed her nose into his hand and he patted her sadly. 'Not you, lass. You must stay behind. One day

318

your master will be safe then he will send for you. I promise.' The oath to the dog gave him the courage to sit down and write.

As night fell, Charles permitted himself to be dressed in the modest clothes brought to protect him from discovery. In happier times he had dressed up to please Henrietta, displaying himself in fantastic costumes at her celebrated masques. Once he had even worn the clothing of a rustic figure, a shepherd, complete with crook, while Henrietta had been his shepherdess. He sighed with tender regret. Meanwhile, these genuine peasant clothes scratched at his neck, and smelled stale.

Detecting his mood, his servants gathered about him. 'Courage, Sire. We will soon have you safe.'

Charles nodded to Jack Ashburnham, drawing strength from each of his three loyal companions. He arranged his letters of explanation on his desk. In a curious way, this flight reminded him of an elopement.

Outside it was grey and damp and silent, the air dripping with fog. The King and his guides moved like dark ghosts, flitting from tree to hedge to wall. As soon as they were safely outside the grounds, they found the horses that had been made ready, and rode in haste towards Thames Ditton. There a boat awaited them.

'Where do we go?' After settling the King aboard, Sir John Berkeley spoke quietly to his companion.

Jack Ashburnham shrugged. To the King he said: 'First we cross the Thames, Sire, then what?'

'All will be well. We shall ride to Bishop's Sutton and change horses.'

The King offered no further explanation and two men looked at each other but did not ask what was foremost in their minds – where would they go next?

Once across the river, Charles acted as guide to the party. Before long, the fog that had so fortuitously obscured their escape from Hampton Court, led him to take the wrong route. Now the winds grew stronger. The party found themselves wandering aimlessly in Windsor Forest.

'I think we need to aim further south, Sire.'

'We will find it.'

By the time they did find their destination, daylight had already broken through. Charles felt weary, longing for some respite so that he could eat and briefly ease his aching back. Fresh horses were indeed ready and in the charge of a loyal servant, but the longed-for rest was denied.

'Majesty, I fear that the County Committee is meeting in this very place. It would be madness to dally here. Please Sire, take the fresh horses and get away as far as you can.'

Exhausted, anxious, he did not demur. When they had put some distance between themselves and Bishops Sutton, Charles reined in.

'Rest your horses,' he advised. 'I need to think.'

'Should we head across the Channel, Sire?' Jack Ashburnham asked.

Charles shook his head. 'I don't think I can leave England. Really, I don't. Who is there nearby who will offer me shelter?'

The three servants looked at each other with guarded dismay.

Jack spoke for all of them. 'I truly think for your safety you would be better out of the country. Within hours the army will be combing every inch of the countryside for you.'

The King shook his head decisively. John Berkeley said tentatively: 'Perhaps the West Country?'

'What about the Earl of Southampton?' Charles said; he appeared not to have heard Berkeley's suggestion.

'Er – he is loyal . . .'

'I am not thinking of remaining there indefinitely.' The King rubbed his hands together in a businesslike way. 'Right, we'll ride to Tichfield straight away then I have a mission for you both. I think I know what I must do . . .'

Chapter 45

The morning following Robert's proposal, Dublin set out triumphant to ride to Carisbrooke. She rode with Polly for company, full of anticipation, anxious to tour the Castle with a bride's eyes, excited as a child offered a treat. For the moment she did not enlighten her companion as to the reason for her visit, savouring the secret, waiting for the time when Robert himself would shout it from the rooftops.

She was therefore dismayed upon arrival to find that Robert was not there but in his absence, Aunt Jane had come visiting. Leaving Polly to join the Castle servants in the kitchens, Dublin allowed herself to be escorted to Robert's quarters.

As she came in, it was to find the older woman already there, seated near the fire. It was immediately clear that Aunt Jane Dingley already knew of the intended marriage and did not like it. She did not deign to speak as Dublin entered, escorted by Captain Rolph.

Sensing the tension, the Captain hovered uncertainly.

'Leave us.' Aunt Jane's tone brooked no argument.

Left alone, Dublin's cheeks grew hot. She felt as if she had committed some crime, and indeed her former guardian's words confirmed the belief. 'You have betrayed us. All of us. Have you no thought of the damage you do to my nephew?'

Indignation overcame Dublin's nervousness. 'How can I damage him when I offer him love and fidelity?'

Aunt Jane did not condescend to acknowledge her answer, saying instead: 'His position here will be untenable.' She scowled, her mouth a disapproving line, unconsciously tapping her foot on the flagstones. She rapped out: 'Do you not have enough already?

You own a house fit for a lady far greater than you can ever be. You have servants, fine clothes – what more do you want?'

Dublin snapped back angrily: 'I want none of those things! I just want Robert, to be with him.'

There was a slight softening of Aunt Jane's tone. 'Then be with him, but as a companion, no more. You will hurt him grievously if you persist with this madness.'

'It is his wish, not mine.' Dublin was trembling, her own doubts making it difficult to defend her position. She wished that Robert was there to state his own views. With luck, he would soon be back.

At last Aunt Jane stopped tapping her foot and looked around for her outdoor clothing. 'Unfortunately I have to leave.' She studied Dublin as if reassessing her, eventually saying, 'Why do you not come too, child? I cannot believe that you are deliberately so wicked. I assure you that you will have everything that you need to make you comfortable, but please, do not continue with this insanity.'

In the face of this appeal, Dublin felt her courage begin to fail but she could not leave. She said, 'Robert asked me to call. I must await him. If he wishes me to leave then I will do so, but otherwise . . .'

Lady Dingley drew in her breath, her nose pinched with pique. 'So be it. Do not however, look for any mercy from me.' Almost to herself she added, 'Once my sister-in-law hears of this there will be such a scandal.'

The thought of haughty Mistress Hammond sparked off the courage that Dublin needed. She answered, 'Ma'am, Robert is a grown man. I do not think his mother can dictate his actions.'

'Don't you, child? I fear you have a lot to learn then. Perhaps his mother can only advise, but there are other, far stronger forces at work and against them you are like chaff in the wind. Never forget that I have warned you.' Tossing her head dismissively, Aunt Jane withdrew.

Left alone, Dublin tried to calm herself. The joy of the morning was swept away. All the old fears were back. Looking out of the window at the parade ground below, she watched Aunt Jane ride out on a postillion behind Isham Carter. She wondered if he knew what had just passed. With sinking heart she felt sure that she and Robert's aunt had been shouting at each other. Perhaps everyone knew.

322

A noise made her turn; Captain Rolph had reappeared. 'Mistress, what would you wish to do?'

Dublin hesitated. Before she had arrived, her only wish had been to explore the Castle, but now she had little heart for anything. She glanced at the Captain and did not like what she saw. There was something insolent about his look. She did not trust him.

'I should like to wait here,' she said. 'So that I can see my lord when he returns.'

With a bow he withdrew, leaving her in anxious solitude.

Robert left Carisbooke simmering with unease. Aunt Jane's unexpected arrival combined with Dublin's imminent visit, meant that he was forced to announce his betrothal before he was ready. His aunt's response was not unexpected but he felt annoyed with himself for not being firmer.

'Your poor mother.'

'Enough, Aunt!'

'What of poor Mary? The humiliation!'

'That is enough, I say! I must leave now to go to Newport. Dublin is paying a visit this day and I do not wish her to be upset. Will you be leaving soon?'

When Aunt Jane stood her ground he had been forced to leave before her. Doubts nagged at him. Would she wait for Dublin and confront her? He was well aware of all the trouble that his decision to wed would bring, but he did not want his betrothed hurt by it. Wherever possible, he would shield her from the knowledge. Once they were married there would be nothing that anyone could do. Just let anybody dare insult the Governor's wife!

He had not gone far when his escort drew his attention to two galloping horsemen coming up behind. Reining in he waited for them to catch up. Immediately he recognised Sir John Berkeley but he had no idea what his arrival meant.

'Governor Hammond, if it pleases you, we need to speak with you urgently.'

Robert glanced round at his escort then rode a few paces distant so that the visitors could speak in privacy.

'Colonel, this is John Ashburnham. Events have occurred on the mainland which have forced us to take drastic steps.'

Robert waited, his expression carefully noncommittal. He knew that something of importance had happened but he kept all show of emotion from his face.

Berkeley said: 'When you last saw the King, he was at Hampton Court. Developments among the army officers have made it imperative to remove him from hence.'

Robert frowned. 'How, remove him?'

Ashburnham said: 'Sir, can you imagine, even now, where the King might be?'

Robert felt his heart jolt. All his instincts told him that a disaster was about to descend upon him. Aloud he said, 'Gentlemen, I hope that I misunderstand you.'

'Colonel, the King is even now nearby. His life has been threatened and in his extreme need he is seeking out someone of honour to offer him refuge.'

Robert was shaking his head. Looking at both men with dismay he said: 'Pray tell me that you have not brought him here? If not, I would beg of you not to do so.' But even as he spoke, he knew that there was no turning back. The King was on the run. If Robert were to refuse to take him in, then who knew where he might go next? He might even flee the country. If he were to intercept Charles however, no matter what his motives, the combined ambitions of Parliament, army, insurgents and church alike would be aligned against him. Aloud he said: 'Oh gentlemen, I fear you have undone me.'

After what seemed an eternity, Dublin was relieved to see Robert come riding back into the Castle, accompanied by several gentlemen. Her relief quickly changed to alarm as she saw her lover fling himself from his horse and begin the most earnest discussions with two of his companions.

At one point, one of the two remounted and started out across the drawbridge but moments later he was summoned back. The three now had a heated discussion there in the yard. Robert was remonstrating with them, his manner so serious that Dublin feared that something tragic was about to befall them.

Finally all three men came into the building. Dublin stood in the middle of the room, listening to their approaching steps, trying to compose herself for she knew not what.

As they came into the chamber, Robert stopped and regarded

her in surprise. With sinking heart she realised that he had forgotten that she was coming. Her confidence took another knock.

'My dear, forgive me but I have to leave again immediately.'

She looked questioningly at him, her own needs overshadowed by the anxiety in his light-brown eyes. 'Something is wrong?'

'That I cannot say, but I have to leave the Island this minute. Something of the utmost importance has happened.' He stood for a moment, thinking, then looked straight at her. 'I want you to remain here tonight.' He took her hand, looking at her for support. 'While I am away, will you see to it that every chamber in my house is thoroughly cleaned and that beds and food are made available? I think, by tomorrow, we will have visitors.'

Chapter 46

No sooner had Robert and his callers left, than rumours began to circulate about the Castle.

'God's truth, mistress, the King himself is across the water. The Governor has gone to persuade him to return here.'

Dublin did not believe Edmond Rolph. The thought of King Charles coming to the Castle was too unlikely. At first she did not reply, resenting the Captain and his condescending manner. He was too confident by half. She had heard that his father was a common cobbler, and the knowledge that, like herself he was base-born, added to her discomfort. She could easily see through his airs and graces to the peasant beneath. With disturbing candour, she thought that perhaps others saw her in the same light.

When she spoke to him, her voice was sharp. 'Why should the King come here? There must be some mistake.'

Rolph fixed her with his hawkish eyes. 'Well, whatever the reason, you'd best set to work to get the chambers in good order, like the Colonel said. God's truth.'

Reluctantly, she concurred.

Along with Mistress Wheeler the laundress, and Mr Troughton, Robert's chaplain, she made a tour of the Castle, examining every room for its suitability as a bedchamber. As they walked, she was aware of her two companions' covert glances, their unvoiced curiosity about her. She wondered what Polly might have told the servants, and what they, in turn, had relayed to the rest of the household. No doubt they wondered what her role was. In the absence of an easy explanation, she did not enlighten them.

Ancient quilts and eiderdowns, blankets and linen were dragged out and hung near the kitchen fire to air. Brooms and besoms were discovered in long-forgotten cupboards and a huge dust raised. Debris was cleared from fireplaces and sticks laid in readiness for the mystery arrival.

'Why are we doing this?' asked Mary, the laundrymaid.

'Mind your business!' Mistress Wheeler answered her sharply and Dublin eyed the older woman, thinking that, like herself, she did not know the answer and did not wish to appear ignorant. In this at least, they shared the same feelings.

As night fell, having found herself a room – hardly more than a cupboard, really – Dublin tried to find escape from the present uncertainties in sleep, but the covers were damp and the wind whistled through the narrow crevice that acted as the only window. There was a severe shortage of covers in the castle and even after piling her cloak and a tapestry onto the bed, sleep remained elusive. At first light, she dragged herself up, cold and heavy-eyed, wondering what the day would bring.

She was on her way to the kitchens in the hope of finding some warmth, when the sound of horses drew her to the nearest window. She looked out across the courtyard in amazement at the approaching cavalcade. Hastily she put on shoes and a cape and hurried outside to watch the spectacle.

The lateness of their coming to the Island meant that the party had passed the night in Cowes, at the Plume of Feathers Inn. When they reached the Castle, they looked travel-worn and dishevelled. There were six of them; Robert, his two companions from the day before, a third escort whom she did not recognise, Captain Baskett whom Dublin had seen inspecting the guard at Cowes Castle and – still she could not believe that the sixth, slight, travel-stained figure could really be King Charles …

As Dublin watched, he dismounted stiffly from a bay gelding. She recognised the horse as Robert's own, one that Caleb had found for him and in whom he put great trust. The King stumbled slightly on landing and Robert put out his hand to steady him. Dublin smiled to herself, pride mingling with excitement. She could not help noticing that Robert stood a foot higher than his royal guest.

She stared, fascinated, as Charles removed his gauntlets and stretched his stiff fingers. His peppered hair hung lank, plastered in strands to his narrow face and as he followed behind Robert, who kept turning to check on his welfare, he limped noticeably.

327

Dublin felt some disappointment. Here was the man who had featured in so many conversations, been the subject of countless arguments, on whose behalf Royalists had gone to war, and against whom many had given their lives. He was not a regal figure.

As they came near, Robert slowed and when the King drew level with herself and Captain Rolph, he said: 'Your Majesty, may I present to you our gallant Captain, and Mistress O'Neill.'

King Charles turned weary eyes upon them. If he wondered who Dublin might be it did not show. His eyes were almost feverish with fatigue.

He held out his hand, the back uppermost. Ignoring the gesture, Captain Rolph made a curt bow. There was something provocative about his action but Charles did not appear to notice.

Some instinct told Dublin what was expected of her. She bent low and rested her lips against the large ruby on the King's index finger.

'Majesty.'

'M-Mistress O'Neill.'

She was surprised that he should have recorded her name and the hesitation in his voice stirred a feeling of compassion. That dimly-remembered conversation at Hull suddenly came to her: the king had an impediment of speech. Poor King. He did not look like the ogre she had imagined.

Robert said: 'It is Mistress O'Neill who has endeavoured to see that you have sufficient accommodation, Sir, although I fear it will seem very spartan. We have little in the way of furniture within these walls.'

'Your h-hospitality is enough in itself.'

Not knowing what else to do, she waited until the King's companions had passed by and the little group entered the Governor's house. Dublin hoped that the modest chambers she had prepared would not be too insulting to these most elevated guests.

Now she was at a loose end. Entering the house, she hovered uncertainly in the hallway, finally making her way to the chamber that she had last night taken for her own. Tucked high up on the third floor, from the narrow window it was possible to see half the Island away to the west, only now cloud and mist made visibility difficult beyond the gatehouse.

Before long Dublin heard footsteps in the corridor outside and moments later Robert poked his head around the door. He looked exhausted and his eyes had that same over-bright look as the King's. Without a word he took her in his arms as if drawing energy from her. 'This has been a difficult time,' he sighed.

She kissed him gently on the mouth and the gloom that had enveloped her ever since her meeting with Aunt Jane, instantly fell away. Now she could concentrate on the present. 'What is going to happen?'

His lips touched her temple and he rubbed his cheek against hers. The contact soothed her.

He said: 'The King is settling into his chamber. I have arranged to meet with the Island gentlemen in Newport so I must leave straightaway, but first I must draft a letter to the Parliament.' He released her and sank wearily onto her bed. 'I spent the whole of last night at Cowes Castle writing letters. Now I must inform them that we are safe arrived. Could I entrust you with the scribing of it?'

'Of course.' She flushed with pleasure at the honour.

'There will be so many rumours, such a furore as the word spreads. That is why I have asked all the Island gentlemen to meet me. I am going to need their support. By my reckoning, there are already Republicans here. No one can gain entry to the Island now other than at Ryde, Cowes and Yarmouth, and then only with my permission. My duty first and foremost is to keep the King safe.'

'You think he is in danger then?'

'He says there were plans afoot in the army to kill him, which is why he fled from Hampton Court. That being so, they will follow soon enough. Only those whom I trust can be allowed into his presence. I have to find more men.'

Having found ink and parchment, Dublin began painstakingly to scribe the words he dictated. It was a long missive, bringing both Houses up to date with events and asking for their instructions. She passed it to him and he signed his name, sealed it with a taper lit from the tiny smoking brazier and fastened it with silk. That done, he stood up.

'Right, I will now entrust this to the good Rolph.'

'You have faith in him.' It was a simple statement.

'I do – is there some reason why you ask?'

'No.' Dublin hesitated. 'It is simply that I find him – arrogant. It strikes me that there is something of the zealot in him.'

329

'You mistake his enthusiasm for something more sinister. He is a good man.'

She shrugged. 'Do you wish me to remain at the Castle?'

'I do. Do not take offence, but for the present I urgently need a maid of all work. Can you fulfill that role?'

She nodded and he smiled his thanks then prepared to make his departure. 'Until I know what the Parliament intends I can make no plans. I pray God that they will see fit to escort the King elsewhere.' He became increasingly serious. 'It seems to me that in coming here he has made a fatal error of judgement. It may prove far more difficult to leave again.'

Dublin tilted her head on one side the better to study him, then asked: 'Why is it that having fought against the King, you now protect him?'

'Because, my dear, he is still the head of our country. Sooner or later some settlement has to be made with him if there is not to be endless bloodshed.' He held her close again and she wondered whether to mention her meeting with Aunt Jane, but in the light of other events it did not seem to be the right time. In any case, he was still talking.

'Whether I like it or not, it seems that I must now devote my life to the protection of the King's. Pray God it does not turn out to be at the cost of my own.'

When Robert returned from Newport, he brought the news that, at Sir Robert Dillington's request, the Island gentlemen were coming to the Castle to pay their respects to their monarch. The news set the household in turmoil. Personally, Dublin was willing to turn her hand to anything, from grinding salt to carrying wood to the chambers. There was a marked shortage of domestic servants, and for security reasons, only those who were beyond reproach could be entrusted to help.

Shortly after the King had dined, the party arrived. Dublin was charged with the task of providing them with refreshments. It fell to her to see that they were comfortable until the King was ready to grant them an audience. Freshly shaved, their hair combed, wearing clean hose – she thought that the delegation resembled a group of newly-arrived schoolboys, spruce and anxious on their first day. They stood around in uneasy groups, glancing regularly towards the stairway that led to the upper chambers.

Some half an hour must have passed while she poured wine and offered sweetmeats hastily baked in the kitchens. Although the gentlemen had little appetite, they took freely of the wine, and the volume of noise grew accordingly. Suddenly there was a hush in the room and they all turned towards the stairway where King Charles, now newly-clothed in a white damask shirt beneath a finely embroidered waistcoat, descended into the hall. He carried a walking stick which tapped his progress, punctuating the growing silence.

'G-Gentlemen.'

As one the assembled courtiers went down on their knees, and in one or two cases prostrated themselves before him. Dublin too curtsied while keeping her eyes raised sufficiently to see what happened next. Amongst the assembled party were those who had fought on the Royalist side, and for them indeed this reunion was an emotional occasion.

One by one they rose to their feet and went forward to kiss the King's hand. It seemed that the hostilities of the past five years were forgotten. Charles had some small measure of conversation with each and finally, when they had all made their obeisance, they waited expectantly for him to speak. Clearing his throat and starting haltingly, he began to address them.

'Gentlemen, I must inform you that for the preservation of my life I was forced from Hampton Court; for there were a people called Levellers, that had both voted and resolved of my death. I have put myself in this place for I desire not a drop more of Christian blood should be spilt.'

'Amen.'

Dublin glanced at the man next to her. She recognised him as Sir John Oglander, who in the course of the war had been imprisoned in London for his loyalty to the King. She looked at his honest, earnest face as he stood with his son, and hoped that the killing and imprisonment would now be at an end.

King Charles's speech was greeted with reverence and in the ensuing silence Dublin began discreetly to collect up the pewter. Still she could not quite believe that she was in this place, with these people, the unannounced bride of the Governor.

Gradually men started to talk in muted voices while a few favoured or bolder members gathered once more around the monarch. Colonel Legge, the sixth man of the delegation, who had travelled from Hampton Court with his master began to question Sir John Oglander about safety.

'What think you that we can do, sir, if Levellers come to the Island in great numbers – more than the local people can repulse?'

Sir John looked distressed, then said: 'I shall make it my business to have a boat always at hand. If a time should come when His Majesty is in danger, then we must make away with him.'

Dublin wondered what Robert, as Governor, would have to say about that.

Later that night, Robert found his way to Dublin's bed. She was already asleep and was only dimly aware of his arrival. Sleepily she turned towards him and as their flesh touched, a welcome heat drew her closer, pressing ever nearer to draw comfort from his presence.

He kissed her and his cock began to push ever harder against her until, with some careful manoeuvring, she turned onto her back. Feeling him move inside her, she thought; If I were to die now, I should go straight from one heaven to another. In the narrow couch they had to move with care for fear of being toppled onto the floor. The idea made her want to laugh out loud.

As his loving came to fruition he gave a satisfied grunt and within seconds was asleep. Dublin lay still, now fully awake, savouring the moment, trying to capture it for those times when he would not be there.

'Will you stay?' She repeated the question several times, nudging him until he roused.

'No, I should go.' After a few more snatched moments he forced himself from the couch.

In spite of the fact that she herself had awoken him, his refusal to stay was a disappointment. She wanted him to make his intentions public. Sleeping with her openly would signal to the world the way that things were, but such indiscretion was not in his nature.

As soon as he was gone, cold permeated the bed and Dublin longed to have him back. She tried to find comfort in the prospect of their wedding but realised with misgivings that with the coming of the King, it would probably be postponed until he left. Please God, she thought. Let him go soon.

332

The next day, accompanied by Polly, she made a brief visit to Foxton to collect some things.

'Bring back every servant you can trust,' Robert said. 'That bailiff of yours, he's good with horses. Fetch him here.'

Dublin remembered Caleb's philosophy with some misgivings, his belief that prince and pauper were of equal worth in the eyes of God. She wondered if this made him one of the insurgents that Robert feared, but not wishing to appear ignorant, she remained silent.

When she reached Foxton, she called on the house servants and ordered them to prepare to leave for Carisbrooke. 'The Governor is putting his trust in every one of you,' she said. 'Pray do not disappoint him.'

As they stared at her open-mouthed, she went out to find Caleb. Polly followed behind. 'There's no need for you to come,' Dublin said, but her friend appeared not to hear.

They discovered him at his cottage, eating his nammet. Annie sat on the floor, a hunk of bread in one hand and a mug of watery ale at her side.

'Plolly.' The child looked at Dublin's companion with affection, holding out her crust.

Sheepishly, Dublin peered through the open doorway, knocking as she did so. It was the first time that she had seen inside Caleb's home. In spite of the simple furnishings – a few rushes, a single stool and a table, a tallow candle in a roughly-hewn sconce on the wall – it looked clean and welcoming. A fire burned bright and smokeless in the hollow and a ladder led to the sleeping space beneath the thatch.

For once Caleb looked disconcerted. Hastily swallowing his bread, he wiped his hand across his mouth and stood up.

'The master wants you to come to Carisbrooke,' Dublin announced, trying not to look into his eyes. When he did not respond, she explained: 'The King's come. You're to help with the horses.'

'What about the child?'

Dublin had not considered Annie. She looked at the little girl and felt something approaching envy, although for what she was not sure. Staring back at her, Annie tugged at Caleb's shirt and he picked her up. His brown muscular arm contrasted darkly against the smooth skin of the child's leg.

'She can stay with me.' Polly was looking at Caleb.

'No!' Dublin's reply was sharp. 'You will be too busy helping me.'

'Am I to come back to the Castle too?' Polly could not hide her excitement and too late Dublin regretted that both the bailiff and her friend should be in the same place. Without dwelling on the reason why, she would have been happier to keep them apart.

As an afterthought she said, 'What about Jennet at Wolverton? Her baby's newborn. Perhaps Annie could stay with her.'

'No.' Caleb's reply brooked no argument. 'I don't leave her with strangers. She comes with me or I don't go.'

'But you have to come!' His defiance left her struggling.

In response he shrugged, then said, 'Perhaps I could take her to my mother. Otherwise ...'

'Right. Take her there then.' Dublin felt unreasonable relief that the matter was settled. She could not have explained Caleb's refusal to Robert without incurring his anger against the bailiff, and the idea filled her with unreasoning disquiet.

When they arrived at the Castle, Caleb and Polly were despatched to their various duties and Dublin went direct to the Governor's house to report on her visit.

Robert had just received a lengthy reply from the Parliament, fetched by Captain Rolph who, to Dublin's disgust, had been voted £20 for his trouble. She was flattered when Robert handed her the letter and painstakingly she followed the words with her finger. It was the Parliament's belief that for the time being the King was in the securest place he could reasonably be. A list of those who could and could not visit the Island was enclosed along with authorisation for Robert to secure the King's safety in whatever way he saw fit. Anything he reasonably asked for would be granted.

As she handed the letter back she looked at him, waiting for his verdict.

'It seems that I am stuck for the present.' He gazed into space, thinking his own thoughts, then: 'First things first, we must make His Majesty's stay as comfortable as possible. I have already arranged for my Uncle Henry to come and serve as his chaplain. Can you scribe another letter for me?'

'Of course.'

'To my mother.'

She felt her pulse quicken at the thought of Elizabeth Hammond and wondered if he had yet informed her of his intention to marry, or whether he would do so in this letter. Her mouth felt dry as she picked up a newly-sharpened quill and waited on his words. He spoke slowly, carefully, enunciating each syllable to make it easier for her.

Carisbrooke Castle
21 November, 1647

Dear Madam and Mother,

I write with news of great import and must ask you to put all other considerations aside and prepare to journey here to the Isle of Wight.

The King has sought refuge at the Castle and it is beholden upon me to guard and entertain him. I urgently request your presence to act the hostess. Please, I pray you, take whatever measures you need to secure an early arrival.

I cannot leave this place so tell Mary that I will personally offer her a full explanation as soon as I reasonably can, but for the moment I prefer that you inform her in person.

Your faithful and devoted son, Robert.

As he dictated the message, Dublin was filled with growing indignation. She could not look at him as she held the finished document out for him to sign.

Reaching for the letter, he looked questioningly at her. 'Something is wrong?'

'Why are you sending for your mother?'

'What else should I do?'

She could not reply because she felt so angry that her voice would of necessity have betrayed her.

He said, 'It would not be possible for you to take on the role of hostess, not yet.'

'On which account? Because I am a peasant, or—'

'Because you are neither my wife – nor my kin.'

His words stung her. 'I see! You do not think me capable of such a role. You are ashamed of me.'

He sighed. 'Dublin, it has nothing to do with my feelings. This is the King we are dealing with. His court runs with the strictest attention to protocol. It is only the extreme circumstance of his

335

arrival that has made it possible for me to treat him as I have so far. Now that the Parliament know he is here and wish him to stay, everything must be done with proper decorum.'

'You prig!'

'You stupid girl!'

He caught her wrist and twisted her hand behind her so that she could not hammer against him with angry fists. 'Be sensible. Whilst my mother is here I can acquaint her with my future plans.' He lowered his voice as she gave up the struggle.

She asked, 'Have you not written to Mary?'

'My mother will inform her that the marriage cannot take place.'

'But you have not written to her?'

'I told you that I will go to see her. I cannot simply write and say that the betrothal is terminated without some explanation.'

'So you will let her think that this is merely a postponement, for political reasons?'

'Hush, will you! As soon as things calm down here I will go to London – a week, no more.'

She was barely mollified. In her secret heart she had imagined Mary already coming to terms with the fact that she had lost the battle, and Mistress Elizabeth bowing to the inevitable. As it was, neither of them knew.

'If you cannot write to Mary then perhaps I should.'

Now he grew angry. 'In God's name, woman! The King of England has thrown himself upon my mercy. At any day the Island may be invaded by insurgents come to kill him. In the meantime I have to act the host, the bodyguard and the nursemaid, and all *you* can think about is some imagined slight!'

She was silent, feeling suddenly chastened. He looked so strained that she felt herself to be an unworthy helpmate, adding to his troubles instead of supporting him through this time of crisis.

'Forgive me.'

'Just be patient. Please. Now, I must go. His Majesty wishes me to accompany him on a hunting expedition. If you have no further complaints to make I will take my leave.'

She willed him to say that he understood, to leave with some sign that she was excused but he bowed formally and went about his duties. Dublin felt wretched.

The day before, she had been confident in her role, kissing the King's hand, acting the hostess to the Island gentry. Now she felt unworthy, an imposter, perhaps even the object of scorn of those around her. Hot tears of misery splashed down her cheeks and she let them fall unchecked. The spectres of Mary and Elizabeth hung heavy in the air.

Chapter 47

As the days passed, the strain of the King's presence at the Castle began to tell. No sooner had news of his arrival reached the mainland than the curious came in droves, some with, some without passes.

Not least were the newsmongers, anxious to glean every snippet of gossip and hasten it back to London. A positive explosion of newsheets and tracts began to appear, some serious, some scurrilous, maligning the new Governor and the Parliament. It was almost impossible to get in and out of the Castle gate without being accosted by a news-hungry scribe, demanding to know how the King fared, what he ate, whether he was in good spirits.

In addition, there were the stricken souls who came to be touched, seizing upon King Charles whenever he left the safety of his quarters. In the public glare he acceded to their requests, handing out coins to the afflicted, making the most of the publicity. For Robert, this pathetic rabble only added to the difficulties of keeping his charge safe.

Correspondence flew back and forth to London from both Governor and King. Instructions and counter-instructions added to the sense of confusion. In such a furore it was impossible to think past the next meal, or the next letter. Everything was permanently on the change.

If Dublin saw little of Robert she had the comfort of knowing that in her alone he confided his feelings.

Meeting him briefly in the corridor one morning, he told her, 'My Uncle Henry is due to arrive at any day. It will be such a solace to have him here, although I fear . . .' He was picking at his cuff with agitated fingers and Dublin reached out her hand to still

338

his, but he did not seem to notice. She was shocked by his appearance. He did not finish his sentence, saying instead: 'I am heartily sick of this sideshow.'

In response, all that she could think of was that today was 29 November. It should have been his wedding day.

'Shall you come to me tonight?' she asked, hoping that the sanctuary of her room might offer some respite.

'If I can. But you must forgive me if I do not find the energy to . . .'

She silenced him with a finger. 'It is you I want, unconditionally. As long as you are there.'

He gave her a tender smile, saying, 'We are still in urgent need of plate and linen. Tomorrow, we could ride across to Foxton, carry out an inventory and bring back whatever we might need.'

'Oh, yes!' She felt like a child offered a treat. The thought of being alone with him, passing a few, brief hours at the home which was intended to be theirs, was such a joy.

'Right, my dear.' He gave her hand a squeeze. 'Duty calls, but I shall see you on the morrow.'

The fact that he did not mention the coming night was a small disappointment compared to the thought of a beautiful day to come.

The next morning Dublin awoke early, immediately wide awake and immune to the damp that sweated its way down her chamber walls. Getting out of bed she walked to the window, screwing up her toes to keep the chill of the floor at bay. Wiping one of the panes with the cuff of her nightgown, she squinted through at the heavy, November morning. Even the enveloping mist could not crush her sense of pleasure. At least it was not raining.

She dressed with great care, spending far too long in front of the mirror, combing and pinning her hair, arranging her gown so that it fitted snugly. All the time the lure of the day created small, bubbling feelings of undiluted pleasure. Today was her day, a time when they could begin to enjoy the reality of their betrothal. She smiled to herself in the mirror.

Her heavy cape lay across the couch along with a fur-lined cap to keep out the cold. Hearing somebody in the corridor she hastily put them on, ready for the summons to leave.

When she opened the door, Robert was there. He nodded to her and did not respond to her smile. Immediately she knew that he was not coming.

'My dearest, I am so sorry. I have received word that my mother is arriving this very day. There are so many other things that need my attention that I fear I must stay here and work.'

The hurt of disappointment was almost physical. She could not hide her feelings. Robert said, 'Do not be angry. I was looking forward to this outing as well.' When she did not respond, he was brisk. 'Anyway, we will go some other day. I am sure that you, too, can find much to do.' Squeezing her shoulder, he added, 'I would appreciate it if you could make a chamber comfortable for my mother.'

Dublin felt that he was rubbing salt into her wounds. The presence of Mistress Hammond was burden enough, without sacrificing her day to making the other woman welcome.

Seeing her expression, he sighed. 'For the moment, bear with me,' he pleaded. 'There are matters of such gravity to impart to her that my own wishes have to take second place.'

'You aren't going to tell her about the wedding?'

'Not at this very minute.' Seeing the look on Dublin's face, he quickly added: 'But I promise I shall do so.'

Heavy with disappointment, Dublin made her way across to the laundry, thinking dark thoughts about her future mother-in-law. Mrs Wheeler, the laundress, looked at her with a pinched expression.

'I have just seen the Governor,' Dublin announced, realising immediately that it was the wrong thing to say.

Whenever Robert was mentioned, Mrs Wheeler sniffed with disapproval. Why she should dislike him, *how* she could dislike him, Dublin could not imagine, but the woman's distaste was evident. For this reason, Dublin's relationship with the laundress was also strained.

'We'll have even more trouble now that his precious mother's coming here to give her orders,' Mrs Wheeler said grimly.

Dublin remained silent. The thought that Mistress Elizabeth would arrive that day, weighed her down. She did not want to face her, see in her eyes the disapprobation when she learned of the marriage plans. Excusing herself, she collected fresh linen and covers, feeling the hostile eyes of Mistress Wheeler and young Mary focused upon her back. With her head in the air, she went

340

from the wash-house back across the yard to the living accommodation.

The room selected for Mistress Hammond was on the first floor; it was spacious, draughtproof and furnished with a fine carved bed. Although Dublin had chosen her own small cubbyhole, she resented the contrast between this comfort and her cramped conditions. Sullenly she began to make up the bed, beating out her resentment on the feather bolster, pummelling the goosedown of the mattress until it was light and fluffy. She would give the woman no room for complaint. Personally she polished the pewter bowl that held dried rose and honeysuckle petals. The sconce, mounted to the side of the bed, soon shone warmly, ready to receive candles that would bathe the whole in yellow, flickering warmth. In the face of a job well-done, her resentment subsided.

Hardly outside the door, she encountered Robert and his mother coming up the stairs. Immediately her mouth went dry and she had difficulty in swallowing.

Robert stared hard at her with pain-blackened eyes, a guarded look, warning of something, but she did not know what. She could not read his expression. His face was taut, as if some tragic news had reached him but although she raised her eyebrows in question, he said nothing. Glancing at his mother, she saw for a moment the dislike in Elizabeth Hammond's expression, then it was gone.

'Well, Dublin O'Neill. I would never have recognised you. You have become quite the lady.'

'Ma'am.' Dublin bowed her head, hating herself for feeling overawed. 'I trust that you had a good journey.'

Mistress Hammond acknowledged the remark but did not respond, saying instead: 'First I must refresh myself, then my son will take me to meet the King. It is a great surprise and honour to serve him.'

'Ma'am.' With a glance at Robert, Dublin walked on past, hurrying for the stairway. There was something badly wrong here but she could not guess what it was. From her demeanour it seemed that Mistress Hammond did not yet know of the new wedding plans. Dublin guessed that Robert was anxious about telling his mother, and his anxiety only added to her own. Suddenly she dreaded the moment when he would do so.

* * *

341

Waiting that evening in her chamber, hoping that Robert would visit, Dublin tried to keep herself occupied by reading from the prayer book, but the light was so poor that she soon gave up. Likewise sewing was difficult, even with keen eyes, and she had to content herself with sitting and thinking. After a while she heard footsteps and half-rose in expectation, but the steps were unfamiliar and to her surprise somebody knocked on her door. Getting up, she went to answer.

She was confronted by one of the serving girls who bobbed her a curtsy. 'His lordship says you're to join him in his chamber.'

Dublin was taken aback by the message but thanked the girl and prepared to go. As she walked along the passageway, which twisted and turned and sloped, she tried to imagine why he should be sending for her. At any other time he would have come himself. Suddenly she felt afraid.

Reaching his door, she knocked hesitantly and in answer to his call went in. He sat at a table under the window and by the light of a candle was penning yet another letter.

'You sent for me?'

He put down the quill and turned round. In response to his serious face, her chest tightened. 'Something is amiss?'

'Sit you down.' She did so. He himself stood up and began to pace the room. 'I do not know how to tell you this. There is no easy way. You will say that I am to blame and indeed, I can blame no one else.'

'For what? What has happened?' She waited, her heart beating fast, her breath suspended as she tried to prepare herself for some blow. He remained silent until unable to bear the suspense, she repeated: 'Whatever has happened?'

'Dublin.' He shook his head and stood as if he could not quite believe what he was thinking.

She went to get up but he raised his hand to stop her. 'It is best that you remain seated.' Taking a deep breath, he announced, 'In response to the letter you scribed for me to my mother, she acted in what she thought was the fittest way.'

Still Dublin waited, certain now that something terrible had happened. 'Your mother has come here,' she prodded.

'Aye. She has come. You will recall in my letter that I asked her to take care of the marriage arrangements, to inform Mary of what had happened here to prevent my coming. Well, she did. I thought it was clear that I wished her to postpone the wedding.' He clenched his hands together so tightly that the veins stood out ridged and blue.

'In fact, my mother approached my cousin, William Temple. As I was prevented from being present in person at the ceremony, she asked William to act as my proxy.' He turned his tragic face towards Dublin. 'The wedding took place as planned. William stood in my place as the groom and yesterday, the twenty-ninth day of this month, Mary Hampden and I were formally wed. She is now my wife.'

In the face of the unthinkable, Dublin was silent. Fate had dealt such a blow that there was nothing to say. Destiny had been playing with her, watching her foolish hopes, her crazy aspirations, and when the game had gone far enough, it struck with one cruel stroke.

'The wedding can be annulled. I did not give my formal consent . . .' Robert's words had little impact upon her. In a swirling, seething tangle of emotion she turned away and swept out of his chamber, hurrying along to the sanctuary of her room. There, she bolted her door.

She found some small protection by being angry. Robert was right, she did blame him, did hold him totally responsible for what he could not, but should have, foreseen. She felt betrayed in the worst possible way.

'Dublin, let me in.'

'Go away!'

'We have to talk.'

'There is nothing to talk about.'

'Open the door, or I'll break it down!'

'If you try, I shall scream. I will say that you ravished me.'

She could hear his exasperation as he thundered harder against the wood.

'Go away!'

'Listen to reason – this can be sorted out. Will you not open the door or must we discuss our affairs in public?'

The thought that members of the household in the rooms along the corridor would all be listening was the last straw. She hauled the bolt back and flung the door wide open. He stood there tight-lipped and tense.

She said, 'I am going away.'

'I forbid it.'

'Who are you to forbid me anything?'

'Who are you to behave like a spoilt brat?'

She slapped him hard across the face, all her hurt directed into the blow. His eyes blinked but he did not move back. Struggling to be reasonable, he said, 'I know that you are hurt. Your pride is hurt. Do you not think I have the same feelings?'

'Your mother did it deliberately.'

'Why should she do that?'

'She hates me.'

'Nonsense.'

'She does! She knows how I feel for you. She has always been determined to separate us. Well, she has succeeded.'

'Are you going to let me in?'

'No.'

He bowed and accepted defeat. 'Then I will see you on the morrow, when we have both had a chance to calm down.'

By first light, Dublin had packed the necessities and crept down to the stables, ordering Fortune to be brought out. The groom, sleepy-eyed, looked at her curiously but did not question her motives.

At the gatehouse the guards greeted her and she forced a smile, hoping that they would not wonder about her luggage. She announced: 'I am making an early morning visit to Wolverton.'

They accepted the explanation and with a sense of relief she rode out across the bridge, at first going towards Wolverton and away from the coast in case anyone should be watching from the ramparts. As soon as it was safe she wheeled round and set off in the direction of Cowes.

It was still barely light and she dared not go too fast in case Fortune missed her footing. The road was awash with mud, beneath which treacherous potholes threatened their safety. All the time she wondered what to do once she reached the mainland.

As she neared Cowes it dawned on her that getting off the Island might not be so easy. She had no pass. Pondering over the difficulties, she made up her mind to go to the top, ask to see Captain Baskett who was in charge of the Castle. They had not been formally introduced, but by dint of careful wording it should not be impossible to convince him that she had the Governor's express permission to leave these shores.

Having thought out her strategy, she rode down to the quayside where, only weeks before, she had stood in the September sunshine to welcome the new Governor. If only it were possible to re-live time.

Thus preoccupied, she rode towards the Castle, but before it was possible to put her plan into action, she was accosted by none other than Captain Rolph.

The sight of him threw her into confusion.

'Mistress O'Neill.' He looked self-satisfied and Dublin's expression hardened in the hope of resisting any questions from him. It seemed infernal bad luck that he should happen to be there. His next words however, changed everything.

'The Governor sent me expressly, ma'am. You are to return with me to Carisbrooke.'

'No! Is there some charge against me that I should be apprehended like a common criminal?'

'No one can leave the Island without Colonel Hammond's permission. The Governor seemed very upset by your departure.'

He regarded her impassively, immovable as a rock.

Clearly, in the time that she had been making a diversion, her absence had been discovered and the Captain had been sent post haste to bring her back. The fact that Robert had sent this man of all others to apprehend her, was the final insult.

'I would rather go to gaol than be taken back there,' she said.

'Ma'am. The Governor would have come himself but he had other worries.'

'He always has other worries.'

'Come, now. I cannot believe you would wish me to carry you across my horse like a common bawd?'

'How dare you!'

'Then perhaps you would like to ride ahead?'

Dublin knew that she was defeated. This odious man was not going to let her go. Suddenly she felt so tired that she would have sold her soul to curl up anywhere and escape from the nightmare of her position.

'Ma'am?'

Dredging up what little pride remained, she rode ahead.

* * *

On reaching Carisbrooke, Dublin did her best to appear in command, riding up to the gate and awaiting admittance. She felt herself to be in deep trouble. Running away was a serious offence, no matter what the reason. Robert would have to deal severely with her or else put himself in an embarrassing position. She wondered how much the tongues were already wagging.

'Dear lady.' The odious Rolph took Fortune's rein, offering to help Dublin down. She swung away from him and landed awkwardly, almost in the path of Caleb Gosden.

The bailiff took one look at her then turned to Rolph. 'What is going on?'

'Mind your manners, groom. This is none of your concern.'

Caleb looked at Dublin. 'Is something amiss?'

She shook her head, not meeting his eyes, feeling faint with exhaustion. Everything seemed to be slipping away from her.

'Out of my way,' said Rolph, leading both horses forward so that they barged into Caleb.

The bailiff reached out and caught hold of Fortune's bridle. 'That's far enough.' To Dublin he said: 'Has this man upset you?'

'No.'

'Well, something has.'

Without warning Rolph brought his foot up and drove it into Caleb's thigh. 'Out of the way when you're told!'

Caleb staggered, losing his footing, and stumbled back onto the ground.

Without thinking, Dublin darted forward and put her hand out to him. 'Are you hurt?'

He glanced down at her hand, resting against his misshapen shoulder, his eyes wide with unspoken questions.

She followed his gaze, then realising what she did, let her hand drop to her side. The action caused his eyes to narrow and he looked away. Without replying, he got up and brushed the dust from his clothes.

Soldier and servant now faced each other. For a terrible moment Dublin thought that Caleb might strike Rolph back. She looked at the knife at the soldier's waist and guessed that he would not hesitate to use it. Quickly to Caleb she said: 'Thank you for your concern, but there is nothing wrong.'

Thrusting the horses' reins at the groom, Rolph took her arm

346

and pushed on past. As Dublin drew level with Caleb, he whispered: 'I'll be here at midnight.'

She gave no sign that she had heard, but as she prepared to face Robert's anger, it was with the consoling knowledge that there might still be a way out.

Rolph escorted her to Robert's study. He kept such a tight grip on her arm that it was too painful to struggle. As they went in, her first instinct was to protest and demand to be released from the vice-like hold, but at the sight of her lover, she stopped. For the first time she felt afraid of Robert. His expression was icy. He gave no indication that she was anything other than a miscreant.

He nodded his thanks to Rolph and only then did the Captain release her. Gently she massaged her bruised arm, looking all the time at the floorboards. She dared not raise her eyes and confirm the anger on Robert's face. For several moments he shuffled papers. She waited for him to dismiss Rolph, but he did not, saying instead: 'Edmund, be seated.'

Dublin tried to still her trembling lower lip by gripping it with her teeth, but she could feel the chattering all along her jawline, down her neck, spreading through her entire body. She was waiting for the executioner's axe to fall.

'Right.' Robert came from behind the table, very upright, remote as the moon. To Rolph he said: 'This girl is to be confined to the kitchen. Put her in the charge of Mistress Wheeler. At night, she is to sleep with the rest of the domestics. On no account is she to be allowed beyond the gates.' Pausing, he then concluded. 'If there was not such a desperate shortage of servants, she'd be in the dungeon.'

'I—' She could not believe that only hours before, she had been his intended bride. The years of love and loyalty suddenly seemed as nothing. In vain she looked for any sign that he might relent, let slip his true feelings, but his face was like a mask.

She went to protest her innocence, to put the blame for her escape firmly where it belonged, but before she could say anything, he rapped out: 'Dismissed.'

Grasped again by the same painful arm, she was dragged back outside to begin a new life as a drudge.

347

Chapter 48

Mistress Wheeler the laundress took pleasure in finding the dirtiest, hardest work for her new skivvy. All day long, Dublin slaved without respite, but exhausted as she was, she would not allow her tormentor to see that she cared. Indeed, her mind was so numbed by Robert's betrayal, that she cared very little about what was happening to her.

At supper, she was the last to eat, and apart from one petrified crust and a few drips of lamb gravy, nothing remained. Polly surreptitiously scraped a part of her own dinner onto Dublin's trencher. Dublin felt her friend's concern, overlaid with confusion because she had no idea what was happening. Dublin had neither the chance nor the desire to enlighten her. It was all too new, too painful to make sense of.

When they retired to rest, Dublin dared not let her head touch the straw. Had she done so, she would have fallen instantly into sleep as a means to escape from her present misery. She desperately needed to stay awake until midnight. Although she was mortally afraid of running away, and perhaps being caught a second time, it seemed better than enduring this living hell.

Other fears assailed her. She wondered what Caleb had in mind. Would he be there? Would he let her down? Even in these extreme circumstances, she found it hard to give herself up to him, to admit that she was helpless, powerless, and that he was the master of her destiny. He might take pleasure in telling her: 'I told you so.' He might seek revenge for the punishment he had endured in the pillory. He might . . .

She jumped, having nearly succumbed to sleep. The only thing to do was to sit up and count the minutes.

When all was quiet, Dublin stole out of the room. Hugging the shadows, she crept along by the walls, the ground icy and sharp beneath her bare feet. She dare not put on her slippers for fear of making a noise. In spite of the fact that some hundred souls dwelt within these walls, it seemed eerily quiet. As she drew near to the drum tower, she heard low voices. Drawing back into the shadows, she froze, watching.

As her eyes grew accustomed to the darkness, she recognised Caleb talking to the guard. Straining her ears, she heard him say: 'You know how it is, Al. There's no privacy inside these walls. I want to take my girl somewhere – quiet.'

The guard referred to as Al, laughed. 'Good is she, Caleb?'

'The best.'

The words put fear into her heart. Did Caleb mean it? Was he intending to take her outside in order to . . . She felt a sense of hopelessness. Overwhelmingly, she wanted someone to care for her, to care *about* her. If Caleb were to let her down now, to use her then abandon her to the elements, there would be no one in the entire world in whom she could trust.

Her unintended sigh brought both men up short. Caleb stepped closer and upon seeing her, he whispered: 'Cover your hair, disguise yourself.'

There was nothing else to do. Dublin pulled her shawl closer over her head and kept her eyes down, hiding in his shadow. He took her arm.

'Thank's Al, I won't forget this,' he said to the guard.

'Enjoy yourself.' The voice was loaded with innuendo.

Caleb held her arm, his fingers closing over the bruise, but they were a gentle pressure. 'Keep your head down,' he said, his face close to hers. She could feel his breath against her cheek. It was sweet and warm.

When they were out of sight, he slowed down. 'Right. There's nothing for it but to walk.' He looked at her bare legs, and taking the slippers from her hands, bent down and put them onto her feet. She submitted to him, steadying herself by leaning on his shoulders, but he did not seem to notice.

'Where are you taking me?' she whispered.

'The only place I can think of. To my mother.'

Sensing her reluctance, he said: 'Don't be afraid. She'll take care of you.'

She nodded her acceptance into the darkness.

As they walked, he said, 'Do you want to tell me what's been going on? What is it that you're supposed to have done?'

'Nothing.' She couldn't begin to explain, least of all to him. How could she ever admit that Robert had let her down, and that Caleb had been right all along. Instead, she asked in her turn: 'Who is it that I am supposed to be?'

'I told the guard I had a date with Polly.'

She hardened her heart against him.

Stumbling along the woodland paths, plunged into sudden pits of darkness, she was glad to accept his arm. He stopped periodically to help her along, steadying her as she slid down banks, taking both her hands as she jumped over ditches. All the time, he remained silent, not intruding into her private grief. She felt pathetically grateful, a whipped puppy, wanting only to be soothed.

Roused from her bed, Lizzie Gosden regarded her visitors with shock.

Caleb said: 'Will you shelter this girl? She's in trouble.'

'What sort of trouble?' Lizzie looked hard at her and Dublin felt her cheeks flush.

'Not that sort,' said Caleb, then he hesitated, looking to Dublin for confirmation. She shook her head, her face red with shame.

Lizzie asked no more questions and Caleb offered no explanation. Instead he busied himself rekindling the fire. Moments later, there was a comforting glow from the shallow hearth.

Hearing a noise on the ladder, they all looked up to see Annie creeping down the rungs, her eyes heavy with sleep, her face crumpled with the lost, pale look of the newly awakened.

On seeing her, Caleb left what he was doing and went across to the ladder. He took the child in his arms and held her close, his cheek against the crown of her head, nuzzling her. 'And how's my girl?'

Dublin watched the scene with a sense of pathos. His tenderness to his child unleashed her own needs – the need to be a child herself, the need to have a child of her own, the need to be loved in this tender, constant way. Shivering, she moved closer to the fire and accepted the ale that Lizzie handed to her.

Moments later, Caleb was back at the door. 'I must go,' he said. 'I can't let myself be missed or they might guess where you are.'

His mother hugged him. 'God bless you, dear son.'

By the fireside, Dublin looked across at him, not knowing how to express her feelings.

Meeting her eyes, he muttered, 'You'll be safe here. Don't go outside until the hue and cry has died down. If the villagers wonder who you are, you can think of something.'

Seconds later, he was gone.

Chapter 49

Dublin's escape was discovered at first light and quickly relayed to the Governor.

Robert listened in disbelief. He was immediately weighed down with guilt. His plans had gone disastrously wrong. He should not have acted as he did. Of course he had been angry with her, humiliated too, and he had wanted to punish her for hurting him, but things had backfired.

There had been another motive in treating her as he did. The Castle was bursting with spies. Hardly one man breathed but another made capital of it. Apart from Rolph, there was no one in the Castle whom Robert could entirely trust, except of course, Dublin, but as long as she remained in his favour, then no one was likely to talk in front of her. But once she was in disgrace, there was no telling what gossip she might pick up. That had been the plan, only he had not had an opportunity to say anything to her in private. In any case, her grief had to be convincing for it to work. Now he realised that he had totally misjudged her feelings. He wondered if, when they recaptured her, he would be able to put things right.

He did not like to admit it, but he had also had his mother's disapproval to swallow. With shame, he recalled Elizabeth's words.

'You are foolish, my son. I warned you that that Irishwoman would bring trouble. You have allowed her far too much familiarity. Sometimes I think she has bewitched you.'

He had felt like a small boy, chided in front of the household.

His mother had cut into his thoughts, adding: 'Anyway, thank goodness you are wed now. You must send for Mary without delay.'

'Not yet.' He had to buy time.

Seeing his mother's sceptical look, he enlarged: 'This is a dangerous place. I don't want Mary at risk.'

Now, the news of Dublin's second escape put everything from his mind. He sent for the guards.

'Did anybody leave the Castle after dark?'

Those who had shared the night-duty shook their heads. Robert studied them closely. He detected a nervousness about one of them. 'You are absolutely certain?' he said, addressing the man directly.

Again the guard shook his head. Still he looked uncomfortable, but in the face of his denial, there was nothing that Robert could do. Instead, he ordered a search-party to scour the countryside. Every port must be watched in case she tried to leave the Island.

Seeing Caleb Gosden, he said: 'I want a deputation sent to Foxton to make sure that she has not made her way there.' The groom acknowledged his orders in his usual take-it-or-leave-it way. Robert eyed him with suspicion. He had never understood how things stood between Dublin and this ill-favoured man, but he pushed the uncomfortable doubts aside.

Sensing the air of surprise at the lengths to which he was going, he said: 'In these dangerous times, anyone who has had any contact with the King whatsoever must be accounted for. The escaped woman knows the Castle well, the entrances and exits, and in the wrong hands, such information could be dangerous.' With relief, he saw that this appeared to satisfy them.

A few minutes later, he was called away to supervise the arrival of the King's belongings, brought down from Hampton Court. As he watched, crimson, gold, green and silver furnishings, brighter than any flower bed, were piled out into the courtyard. Such an array of beds, and bolsters, damasks and velvets were unknown within the Castle walls. Boxes of gloves, trunks of hose, followed each other up to the King's chamber. Charles at least would be pleased.

The spectacle released some of Robert's tension. He drew comfort from the fact that he and the King were on good terms.

When it was all sorted out, he sent for his mare and rode out towards Wolverton. Perhaps, just perhaps, Dublin would have sought refuge there. Then he remembered Aunt Jane's anger at the announcement of his betrothal.

353

Reluctantly he reined in the mare and sat staring into space. He badly needed someone to talk to, but there was no one. He could not admit to Aunt Jane what had happened. He could not even bring himself to tell her that he was now a married man, married against his will, like some weak-willed minor, having no control over his destiny. As Governor, he could not afford to show any doubts, any weakness. Crushed with pain and misery, he retraced his steps. He must keep his thoughts to himself.

Chapter 50

As the months passed, the King found to his dismay that his faith in the Governor of the Isle of Wight was sadly misplaced.

At first all was well. Hammond seemed the perfect host, accompanying him on hunting expeditions, arranging visits to friends. He even defied the Parliament and refused to arrest Charles's companions. No Governor could do more.

Thus reassured, the King busied himself with securing his future. He left no stone unturned – a settlement *had* to be reached.

But then, things started to go wrong. On Christmas Eve, the Parliamentary Commissioners arrived and presented their conditions.

'Gentlemen, I trust you will give me some time to consider these important matters,' the King said.

'Sire. Will four days suffice?'

Once they had departed, Charles looked with dismay at the document. The demands were short and to the point – and utterly unacceptable.

'See Jack,' he said to Ashburnham. 'What shall I do? I am expected to give them control of the army. And all those who have betrayed me during the troubles, they insist that all charges against them are null and void. I will not accept it!'

'Then how shall you respond?'

Charles spent Christmas Day anguishing over the best way forward. Gazing across the wooded hills, he remembered Christmases past, surrounded by his family, the twelve days of holiday celebrated by the masses. Now it was a working day like any other.

His thoughts were interrupted by the arrival of a delegation of

Scots. When he found the chance, he said: 'Gentlemen, I fear I am in danger. I would earnestly ask you to raise an army and come to the service of this, your most loyal King.'

'Sire.' They left with no firm commitment, but he clung to the hope that ere long he would be out of this place.

Meanwhile, he drafted his reply to the Parliament. After four days, the English delegates returned. They were ushered into the Royal presence.

'Gentlemen, may I know if you have the authority to alter any part of this document?' Charles asked.

'Your Majesty, we do not.'

'Then it pleases me to give you this.' He held out his sealed reply. The Commissioners looked at each other, then back at him.

'Sire, we desire an answer. If we are to depart like this, we had as well sent a messenger.'

The King felt his heart-rate quicken. He said: 'I feel it would only be right that the contents are made public on your return to London.'

'I feel it would only be right to return knowing what message we carry.'

Charles glared at the Earl of Pembroke, but in the face of a dozen pairs of unrelenting eyes, he permitted his letter to be opened.

Taking it from his master, Jack Ashburnham read out the contents. Without a word, the Commissioners withdrew to discuss these developments. Within a few moments they returned.

'You refuse to accept the Parliament's conditions,' said the Earl of Warwick.

'Gentlemen, I am merely proposing some possible alternatives.'

Stony-faced, they made their departure.

As soon as they were outside, Charles turned to Ashburnham. 'Quick Jack, I must leave here now, before the Parliament act.'

'There is a boat in Southampton Water, Sire. I will check the tides and make sure that horses are ready.'

'You are a true friend.'

From his window, Charles watched the Commissioners ride out of the Castle and begin the descent to Newport. He noted with misgivings that Governor Hammond was with them.

Quietly, Jack slipped from the Castle to organise the transport.

About an hour passed before Charles saw the Governor riding back up the hill. He came at a gallop and everything about him pointed to trouble. Charles saw him trot in at the gate, swing from the saddle and converse urgently with the guards. Within moments, the great gate of Carisbrooke Castle slammed shut. With terrible certainty, the Royal guest knew that he was now a prisoner.

Chapter 51

During those first days at Caleb's cottage, Dublin waited in continual fear of discovery, but as the days became weeks, she began to relax into the routine of the family.

At first Lizzie was distant with her, treating her with caution. The older woman asked no questions and Dublin had no words to explain her bizarre relationship with her hostess's son. This gulf was always there, not actually acknowledged, but never totally ignored.

Cringing, Dublin recalled how, on the first occasion that she and Lizzie had met, she had come riding over with cousin Robert, a supposed gentlewoman, calling upon Caleb without explanation. Now she had arrived with him empty-handed and penniless.

She remembered her sense of confusion on that first visit, the discovery that Caleb was wed and that Sara, his wife, was with child. She had been jealous. The thought forced its way into her mind. To hide from the admission, she tried to think of something, anything, rather than what it all meant.

As recompense for being there, Dublin offered her services to Lizzie in both house and garden, turning her hand to anything that she could. Lizzie had very little, but what there was, she shared without comment. Finding that the girl was not afraid of hard work, she gradually thawed towards her and the two women settled into a steady, if cautious companionship.

'My poor bones ache these days. I'm glad of your help,' Lizzie finally admitted.

'And I am very grateful for your shelter.'

In the dark winter evenings, they were thrown much together, and eventually forced into sharing their thoughts.

One evening, Lizzie eyed her thoughtfully. 'When first I saw you, I thought you were a lady,' she said.

Dublin felt her cheeks grow pink. 'I – I had the honour to be given a home in the Dingley household. They treated me as one of themselves.' Hesitating for a moment, she added: 'But I was raised in poverty, in Ireland.'

This was the first step. Little by little, she let some of her history be known, but she could not, would not recount her painful romance with the Governor, nor that distant spring spent on the hills with Lizzie's son.

Sometimes brother John and his wife came to call, bringing their little ones to visit. Annie played with her cousins; she was a bright, inventive little girl, striking in her colouring, reflecting Caleb's independent air.

'I am fortunate in my sons,' said Lizzie one night, cradling her granddaughter in her arms. They sat longer than usual over the embers. 'John is so good, so solid. I know I can rely on him to care for me while Caleb is away.'

Just as Dublin thought she had finished, she murmured, 'But I'm ashamed to confess that it is Caleb I love most. It is a terrible thing for a mother to favour one child more than another, but I cannot help it.' She glanced at Dublin to gauge her response, then said: 'I do love John dearly, but it is because he is good and deserving. There is something about Caleb . . .' She seemed lost for words. Her expression was gentle, tender. She said, 'He has caused me much heart-ache. He was always in trouble as a boy. He is still a rebel. I often fear that . . .' She did not elaborate on her worries.

Dublin knew that she had to say something, offer some clue as to what she thought. Carefully, she said, 'Caleb is very brave. But I – I don't really understand him.'

Lizzie looked at her curiously. 'But you trust him?'

'Oh yes, I trust him.' She realised then that she trusted him with her very life.

As the weeks passed, Annie too began to relax in Dublin's company. At first, Dublin found the child looking at her with large, suspicious eyes, in which were reflected the memory of those confrontations with Caleb at Foxton. There were no words to explain them away. Instead, she showed Annie how to make pastry, and which herbs to collect to keep winter colds at bay.

'I like you,' said Annie, in a moment of confidence.

The knowledge was a prize, one that Dublin hoped some day to wave before the child's father, searching for his approval. This was another admission which she did not allow herself to pursue.

The weeks stretched away and Caleb did not come. Dublin guessed that life at the Castle was still fraught with intrigue. She missed the excitement of being part of the momentous events. Sometimes, feeling vulnerable, she missed Robert, but bitterly recalling his betrayal, she gradually hardened herself until her life with him seemed as unreal as that other, child's life, far away in Ireland.

But always, even in her calmest moments, she felt the shadow of her past clouding the most tranquil day. One day, some day, she would have to leave the cottage, and when she did, that past would come to claim her.

One April morning, as Dublin was returning with water from the well, she saw a dog bounding across the grass towards her. With sparkling eyes and a grin on his muzzle, Tyke came panting up. He licked Dublin's hand. Her heart jolted as she smoothed his head, looking around to see if he was alone. Moments later she saw his master coming across the Green towards her. He was riding Robert's mare and leading a second horse, which she instantly recognised as Fortune.

She did not know what to do. His eyes upon her, Caleb slipped easily from the saddle and nodded towards her. 'You are well?'

She nodded, unable to hide her pink cheeks.

He said: 'I am on a mission to Foxton to collect some things. I thought I'd take the chance to ride over.'

Dublin sought refuge in smoothing her horse, resting her face against the animal's damp neck. The presence of Fortune brought hosts of memories flooding back.

'Are you well?' she asked, not daring to voice the other questions that tumbled in her mind.

'Well enough.' He looked towards the cottage and moments later there was a squeal of delight as Annie spotted him. She raced into his arms and he swung her round and round, joining in her pleasure.

For a moment Dublin remembered that momentous meeting at Mary's house when Robert, newly released from gaol, had greeted

360

Mary so. She shook it off. Then, as now, she had to stand by and watch.

Lizzie had come out in response to the noise and in a moment she too was holding her son close. Dublin thought how good it must be to be loved. For the first time she was looking on a different Caleb, one who knew where he belonged, and who was secure in his own sense of worth. She followed the trio into the house and watched as the two women fussed over him. He accepted their ministrations with a tolerant grin.

For a long while they all talked at the same time, but eventually their news was exhausted. At last, Caleb looked across at Dublin and raised his eyebrows questioningly. 'I thought perhaps you would like a chance to ride your mare.'

She blushed. She could not stop herself. For all the world it felt as if he were courting her, finding an excuse to take her out. She looked across at Lizzie who was watching her with knowing eyes.

She did not know if the older woman approved or otherwise. She heard herself say, 'If you wish.'

Hands trembling, she followed him out and for the first time in months, sat upon the mare.

Caleb took the lead, Tyke weaving from side to side, scrambling up the banks, then halting in mid-step to absorb some interesting smell. Dublin rode behind him, not knowing where they were going, or what to expect. At that moment, anything, everything seemed possible.

'Look.' Caleb's voice intruded into her reverie.

'Where?'

'See, on that bank? A cuckoo.'

Dublin followed the direction of his head. For a moment she could see nothing until the pattern of dark and light was broken by movement. The bird hopped a few paces.

She remembered the time, long ago when she had trailed disconsolately behind Caleb and deaf Sara on the Downs. Then, she had watched him take the girl's arm and point a bird out to her. She recalled her feeling of exclusion, a sense of envy because they shared such an easy companionship, while she was a stranger, an outcast. Trailing behind him now, she did not know who she was. Aloud, she said: 'How do you know it is a cuckoo?'

'Keep still. Watch it.'

For an age they remained where they were. The late April

morning was a rare one of diamond-clear air and mellow sunshine. Grass shone sleek with rain crystals, clinging on by invisible threads to the scimitar curve of the stems. Underfoot it was
muddy, and the hollow, squelching sound of damp earth echoed in
the restless hooves of the horses. Dandelions carpeted the
meadow, rich as honey, taking this rare opportunity to expose
their round, loving faces to receive the sun's blessing.

Suddenly crouching low, the bird bunched itself for take-off,
launching into the air with a rapid flapping of wings, its hawk-
like tail drooping with the effort. It landed a few yards away in
an alder, tucking wings and tail neatly away. For several
moments it took stock of its surroundings then, with a quick
throbbing of its throat, the so-familiar song of spring cascaded
across the air.

Dublin let out her breath with a gasp of wonder. Witnessing this
small secret act of nature had filled her with a surge of pleasure.
Caleb in his turn glanced round at her, a brief smile on his face,
which said: 'I told you so.'

'Where do they go in winter?' she asked, riding closer.

'Who knows? Perhaps they hibernate, like dormice, or hedgehogs.'

'Perhaps they do. It seems wrong of them to lay their eggs in
other birds' nests though.'

Although she could not see Caleb's face, his body posture, the
slight tilt of his head, told her that his normal cynicism was back.

He said: 'The cuckoo's no different from many a man. They
plant their seed wherever they can, for other men to raise.'

She flushed, wondering who he was meaning. She thought of
Annie, who was his child. She did not even know who Annie's
mother might have been, but with a sudden, fierce hunger she
thought: If she was my child, I'd never leave her. As the thought
trailed to an end, she realised uncomfortably that the loyalty
extended equally to the child's father.

Caleb added: 'That's what they mean by being cuckolded.'

It had not occurred to her before.

They rode on in silence. Dublin felt strangely fragile, hungry
for some unnamed kindness, in awe of nature and its many won-
ders. Immersed in the sun's warmth and with a growing sensi-
tivity to everything around her, she forgot about the past and the
future. Just being in the countryside, with the gentle rhythm of

Fortune punctuating her own heartbeat, she felt a rare and curious reverence for life.

Caleb still rode slightly ahead. Throughout the journey, the brown mare had become increasingly skittish. She balked at an invisble ogre where a gate stood open, then she shied at some imagined monster behind a solitary beech tree. Caleb sat calmly. Dublin watched the gentle pressure of his calves against the horse's flanks, pushing her on, insistent, confident, instilling courage in the animal. Dublin's eyes rested briefly on his shoulders. In spite of his malformed back, he sat upright, a natural horseman, in tune with his mount.

'What's the matter with her?' she asked.

Caleb delayed replying because the mare took it into her head to have a bucking fit, head down, hind legs flailing, showing her metal-shod hooves.

His body jerked this way and that but he remained securely in the saddle. 'Enough, you witch!' The sound of his voice seemed to calm her. 'Good girl.' As all four feet came to rest briefly on the ground, he ran a strong brown hand along her neck and the calming effect was almost tangible.

Glancing back at Dublin, he said: 'She's in season. She wants a mate. Nature is a powerful driving force. I keep suggesting to the Governor that he has her covered. A foal would calm her.'

The thought of the mare's need mirrored a sudden, terrible emptiness in herself. Bitterly she thought: Robert failed us both, me and the mare. Tears prickled hot and angry beneath her lids. Only her pride prevented them from spilling down her cheeks. Seeking some respite from her hopeless sense of need, she decided there and then that if ever she had Fortune back, she would put her in foal. The mare at least could be spared the pain of being unfulfilled.

'This is a beautiful morning.' She felt the need to draw Caleb into her world and keep him there. She did not want to be alone.

He grunted his agreement, but continued to ride ahead of her. Dublin said: 'This year goes by fast.'

Caleb did not answer her directly. Finally, he said, 'I miss the sense of the seasons, the feeling of being with the earth. Shut up in that Castle, you get out of touch with nature, with its purpose.'

Curiously, she asked, 'What do you think is its purpose?'

He shook his head. 'Birth, death – a natural pattern of life and re-growth.'

'What about God? What about man?'

'There is more to life than God and man.'

'How can there be?' She rode abreast of him, looking across at his handsome face, noticing the gentle dew of sweat that beaded his brow.

He said: 'Your God is that distant, punishing father Who torments men because they cannot live up to His high standards. Your God treats man as if he is at once special, and yet at the same time deserving only of punishment and sorrow.'

She said, 'I don't think that is my God.' Then, wishing to clarify her thoughts to herself, she added, 'Surely we must all strive to be good, like Christ?'

'Surely we are all part of a great whole – man, horses, trees, cuckoos. We come from the earth and we return to it. Power and glory are in everything around us.'

'You are a pagan.'

He did not respond. After a while he said, 'I go to church like the next man. I say my prayers, but it doesn't stop me from listening to what goes on inside of me.' He patted his heart. 'I enjoy the sermons – they are about good and evil, about man and his struggle to make sense of his life, but the other, the ritual, the fear of death and hell – I don't believe it.'

The mare had jogged ahead again, and he eased her back to wait for Dublin to catch up. He said, 'If you wish, I'll show you something – a secret place. There, if you open your mind, you might truly find God – not the God of churches and bishops, but God the creator, God the spirit that is inside everyone. You have to learn to listen for Him, feel Him inside yourself.'

Dublin nodded. She felt slightly breathless, as if on the brink of learning something about this man, for the very first time. Whatever it was, however misguided or foolish the journey, she wanted to know.

After a while they changed direction, riding further south. Dublin did not know where he was taking her, or even if she should be going with him. At the same time she felt that something very important was about to happen.

A mile or so ahead Caleb turned up into the woodland, riding onto a deep, dusty track hollowed out between the gnarled roots of ancient oaks. The trees they supported joined branches overhead to form a sheltering canopy. Generations of feet must have trod this path, but now it was deserted.

All around it was strangely silent. If Caleb had not been present, Dublin would have fled. She had the distinct and alarming impression that the trees, and all that they encompassed, were lying in wait for them. Even the birds were silent.

The climb grew steeper. Tyke, now exhausted by his frequent sorties into the undergrowth, drifted ahead of them, his pink tongue lolling between his strong white teeth. The mare followed obediently behind the dog. It seemed as if they too were in awe of this place.

Quite suddenly they reached the top of the incline, coming out into a glade ringed with oaks. Beneath the trees the grass was short and chequered. Zigzag lines of sun cast golden splashes amid the rich greens and browns. But Dublin was hardly aware of the trees, or the grass, or the intrusion of the sun, for in the centre of the grove, stark, blackened by age and the elements, stood two giant pillars. 'Oh my God!' Suddenly she was back at Glendruid.

Caleb had already dismounted and turning to Dublin, he held out his hands to help her down. She shook her head, petrified by this place.

He said: 'What is it? There is nothing to fear. If you are frightened, the fear is inside yourself.' Beckoning to her with outstretched arms, he placed his hands around her waist and lifted her from the saddle. So overwhelmed by emotion was she, that she almost fell against him, needing another human presence to protect her from the awfulness of her thoughts.

Caleb did not move. His hands came to rest about her shoulders, holding her very still, his cheek just touching her hair. They stood so for an eternity, then he said: 'What is it? What do you fear?'

She told him then. Everything – Glendruid, Carrickmain, the crossing to England, the first visit to the Island, then Hull and Gloucester. As she poured it out, it was almost as if some dreadful Devil was being exorcised. She felt the pain and hurt, the horror of the past pouring away, into the ground, into Caleb, who moved not an inch, supporting her, taking everything that she could no longer bear.

When she had finished talking, he remained silent. At last she raised her eyes and saw in his face a gentle compassion that made her want to be held in his arms, safe as a treasured child. His strength, his silence, were the lifeline she needed.

Taking her by the hand, he led her across to the pillars. 'There is nothing to be afraid of. These are rocks, part of the earth. Here, put your hand on them, feel their texture.'

Still holding her by the wrist, he stretched out her hand and placed it against the gritty surface of the pillar. In the sun's path, it felt warm and vibrant. Reluctantly letting go of him, she transferred her dependence to the column, clinging to it with both hands, eventually resting her cheek against it. After a while, she stepped back.

'I'm sorry. I am such a fool.'

He shook his head. 'You were hurt in a way that no one deserves.'

Her instinct was to move close to him again. Looking at him she felt the magnetic draw of his maleness, the pride in himself that made her want his approval, the compassion that made her want his tenderness.

He asked: 'Why did you feel so much for a man who was part of the army that killed your parents?'

The age-old need to defend Robert was immediately foremost. Drawing back from him, she said: 'He was kind to me. He – I'd never known anyone like him before. I thought he was a good man – so full of honour. I believe he still is'

Caleb sniffed. He gazed past her into the gloom. He seemed to be trying to make up his mind about something, and when he spoke, she had the impression that he was offering a gift to her but was prepared, at any moment, to snatch it back. Finally he said, 'If you want to, you can forget the past now. You've laid the spirits of the dead in this place. As from today you're free to be whoever you want.'

His words alarmed her. So entrenched was she in her past life that the thought of change brought its own fears. Still stunned by the outpouring of all her feelings, she had nothing left. To Caleb she said, 'What of you? What do you plan for your future?'

He wandered to the second pillar and leaned against it, his shoulders pressed back as if in turn drawing something from the stone. He said: 'I never make plans. I just go with the present.'

She thought of Polly. In spite of herself, she asked, 'Do you intend to remarry?'

'Perhaps.'

The answer blanked him off from her. It seemed as if she had spent a lifetime trying to hide her true self, and now, in this place, she had opened her heart to this man in a way that she had done with no other human being. For a while she had felt that something of great import had happened, but now he was drawing away. She caught Fortune's rein. 'We should be going.'

She saw his jaw tighten, the hardness come back into his eyes. With excessive courtesy, he bowed his head. 'As you say, lady.'

The closeness, the tenderness was running away from her. In an effort to rekindle it, she said: 'I can't tell you how much I appreciate your bringing me here.'

'Can't you?' He grabbed Robert's mare's rein and leaped astride her, his foot barely touching the stirrup. 'Come!' He called to Tyke who left the pleasure of a badger sett to obey his master.

In a last-ditch effort to make him understand, she said, 'I need time to think about what has happened here.'

'You do.' His voice was toneless. Already he was riding ahead down the steep path. The mare, catching his mood, began to snort and take exception to the shadows. 'Gedon!' He pushed her hard but did not resort to violence. With sinking heart, Dublin looked at his hunched, resentful back. The fears of Carrickmain were buried, but the ashes of the morning remained with her.

Chapter 52

As the weeks passed and there was still no sign of Dublin, Robert felt increasingly hopeless. As with so many things, it was only now that he had lost her, that he appreciated her true value.

At the same time, such demands were made upon him that he was forced to put the needs of King and country first.

The King's stay was becoming truly burdensome. Each morning Robert paid a visit to his Royal guest, and each morning, Charles greeted him with a list of complaints.

This morning the King was in high dudgeon because a local man, Captain Burley, had foolishly tried to rouse the citizens of Newport into rescuing him. If it had not ended so tragically, the whole thing would have been laughable. A group of women and youngsters, the dim and the dull-witted, had rallied to Burley's support and poor Burley had been tried, sentenced and executed. Charles was taking it very much to heart.

'You are a traitor, sir!'

Robert felt his patience wearing thin. 'And you, Sire, forget your position. Do not push me too hard.'

Charles appeared to struggle to find the right words, eventually saying: 'Do not forget that the time may come when you in your turn are beholden to me for your very life.'

'And do you not forget that . . .' Robert stopped short. He was tired of this bickering. Looking across the parade ground to the east, he said in the most pleasant voice he could manage: 'I have plans afoot to create a bowling green over yonder. Perhaps Your Majesty would find some pleasure in its use?'

Charles sniffed and taking this as a grudging agreement, Robert sought permission to withdraw. Once in the corridor, he stopped to examine the passageway and its exits. As from today, four of his most trusted men would escort His majesty everywhere, being in his company by day and sleeping outside his chamber by night.

Mentally he ticked off Mr Herbert, Mr Mildmay, Mr Preston and Captain Titus for these delicate duties. On these men at least, he could rely.

Returning to his own quarters, it was to find that a package had been delivered from the Parliamentary Committee.

Untying it, he picked up the document addressed to himself and read: '*It has come to our attention that there are traitors about you. A person or persons are conducting a postal service for the King.*' Robert looked at the enclosures, amongst which was a passionate missive from the Queen and an earnest and touching communication from the young Duke of York who, it would appear, had until now been unaware of his father's predicament.

Robert flung them aside and felt himself sinking beneath the burden of responsibility. Who were these traitors? Whom could he trust? As the King had so recently reminded him, his very life might depend on the actions he took now.

In general, there was little to give Robert comfort. Rumours reached him that Charles was planning to escape by drilling a hole in the ceiling. This he could not accomplish single-handedly. Among the men purported to be Robert's loyal servants, there must be spies and traitors. He went through their names – Osborn, Dowcett, Firebrace, Titus, honest men surely, with impeccable credentials, and yet . . .

That night, unable to sleep, he dressed and made his way to the King's chamber. Although it was two o'clock in the morning, he felt that he had to do something. This uncertainty was driving him insane.

Without acknowledging the startled monarch, he marched straight across to the King's cabinet and began to search it.

'Sir, I object most strongly!' Charles struggled into his clothes, unfamiliar in this role of being his own dresser. Outside, Hammond's guards waited. The King could call no one.

Robert continued to ignore him, opening drawers, pulling them out, feeling along linings. He found nothing. Looking round at Charles he noticed how he stood, his hand resting against his pocket. The King followed his gaze and began to back away.

'I demand to search your coat.'

369

'How dare you!'

Desperately Charles pushed him away, at the same time struggling to take something from his pocket. Robert made a grab for it but missed. Inadvertently he pushed the King who stumbled backwards, hitting his face against the cabinet.

'You misuse me!'

Robert made another grab for the papers but with a swift feint, Charles ducked under his arm and threw whatever he held into the embers. As Robert tried to push him aside, Charles stood with his hands held wide, guarding the fireplace.

Finally the Governor forced his way past and tried desperately to rescue what remained in the fire but already the papers had curled and flamed and were now little more than grey ash. 'You will pay for this!' he said in anger.

'Not I. It is *you* who will repent this moment!'

In the face of the King's successful action, Robert withdrew.

As soon as he was alone, Charles went to the wainscotting and lifted the tapestry. There, hidden from view, was a pin-like hole. Harry Firebrace had drilled it so that without the need to open the door, he and Charles could conduct vital conversations.

Pressing his ear to the panel, Charles whispered: 'Harry, are you there?'

'Sire, I am. It is imperative that you escape.'

'What do you suggest?'

'If we could get you out of your room and over the wall, it would be possible to ride to the coast and board a ship.'

Charles thought for a moment. 'If you can find me a cord, I can slip from my chamber window and lower myself down.'

'The window is very narrow.' Harry sounded doubtful.

At that moment Charles heard the heavy footfalls of the guard and the conversation was ended.

Later that evening, he quietly opened the casement. A metal bar divided the opening into two. It certainly looked narrow but he remembered an old adage about a cat – as long as the head could pass through, the body would follow. Cautiously, Charles clambered onto a table and eased his head between the frame and the central bar. It passed through easily. With a sigh of satisfaction he slid back into the room. The next day he said to Firebrace: 'Have no fear. Get me that rope and set everything up. I will be ready to leave whenever you say.'

On the night in question, Charles paced his room in a frenzy of worry. He had to walk quietly in case he alerted the guard outside his door and this tiptoeing only added to his anxiety.

Just as the waiting threatened to become intolerable, there was a thud as a clod of earth hit the window pane. This was the signal.

His heart pounding, Charles scrambled up onto the table and carefully secured the silk cord to the central bar of the window, lowering the rope down to the courtyard below. He paused to listen but all was silent. Outside, he knew that Harry Firebrace would be waiting for him and beyond the curtain wall, Mr Worsley and Mr Osborn had horses at the ready.

With a whispered prayer, he opened the casement as wide as it would go and taking a deep breath, slid his head through the opening. He gripped hard to the bar, fearing that he might lose his balance and tumble head-first into the courtyard. As his shoulders slid sideways on through the narrow opening, he pushed himself forwards, his feet braced against the table. He could already feel the pressure of the bar against his chest and as he shoved hard to ease himself through, the pressure tightened. A moment later and he found that he could go no further.

In his panic, Charles let out a groan. He was so anxious to be free of the Castle that he began to weave and push with increasing panic, but nothing happened. In near despair he realised that the only thing was to go back. Perhaps if he came out at a different angle, he would be successful.

As he started to pull back, he felt the cloth of his shirt pull tight across his chest. He began to struggle increasingly hard but to his horror, nothing happened. He was stuck fast.

'Help!' He whispered the appeal, suddenly afraid that he would suffocate as the pressure on his chest increased.

Now, tormented as an animal in a trap, he began to flail about, abandoning all attempts at silence. Without warning, his torso suddenly slipped back, the ties at the neck of his shirt near strangling him. He hit his nose on the bar as he staggered thankfully into the room, his blood rushing through tortured veins.

Gasping for breath, he sat on the desk, both devastated and relieved at the turn events had taken.

'Sire?' The voice came from the passage outside his chamber.

'What do you want?' he called to the guard.

'Is anything amiss?'

'Nothing. I just had a little nightmare.'

There was nothing to be done. As a signal to Firebrace that he was safe, Charles lit a candle and placed it in front of the window. His only comfort was that the attempted escape had not been discovered.

Chapter 53

Since Caleb's visit, not a day passed without Dublin willing him to return so that she could make her peace with him.

For a brief while she had been closer to him than she had ever dreamed possible. They had been on the edge of the unknown, and only her fear had made her draw back. What had he wanted from her? She dared not admit what it was that she wanted from him. Thoughts of Polly intruded, good, widowed Polly. Caleb had admitted that he might marry. The whole world seemed hopeless.

'Mistress O'Neill!'

Dublin started out of her reverie. A few yards away, coming across the Green from the church, was cousin Robert Dingley. It was no good trying to hide. She did not know what to do. Her mind raced through the implications of discovery. Cousin Robert would surely tell Aunt Jane, who in turn, would relay the news back to Mistress Hammond, if not to Robert himself. Her only hope was that the two women might decide to keep it from him. Once, their feelings would have enraged her, but now, she realised that she shared them. She had no wish to see her former lover.

'Cousin Robert.' She addressed the cleric as she always had done, trying to think of some explanation for her presence in the village. Her being here would almost certainly cause trouble for Lizzie and Caleb, so she said: 'I was just passing through, on my way towards Yarmouth.'

'Yarmouth?'

'I – I have been living out that way.'

'I see.' Cousin Robert seemed to be having second thoughts of his own. Not meeting her eyes, he said: 'Well, I must be on my way. God's work calls.' Bowing his head, he walked on in the direction of the minister's house. Dublin started walking too, in the direction of Yarmouth.

The soldiers picked her up two days later. When she saw them riding along the road to Yarmouth, she made no attempt to escape, having no place to hide. In the lead, his thin mouth tight with triumph, was Edmund Rolph.

'Mistress O'Neill. The Governor will be so relieved that we have found you.'

She did not reply but allowed herself to be seated in front of one of the troopers. Of all the myriad thoughts that enveloped her, one sustained her – at least she would see Caleb at the Castle. But as they rode, it dawned on her that no one must suspect that he had helped her to escape. For his own sake, she must ignore him. So she would be denied the opportunity to make him understand. The knife of disappointment twisted in her heart.

As the Castle came into view she was awash with memories. So much had happened; so much been promised within these walls.

Once inside, she was escorted straight away to the Governor's study. At the sight of Robert, her heart thundered. His hair had grown longer. He was noticeably thinner. His face was furrowed with perpetual worry-lines.

He did not look at her, but addressing her escort, he said: 'Leave us.' They were alone.

The silence seemed to last for ever. As she studied the familiar floorboards, she knew that he was watching her. Her face was dirty and her hair uncombed for she had spent the last two nights under a hedge.

When he spoke, his voice was soft. 'Where have you been?'

She shrugged.

'Who have you been with?'

'Nobody.'

'You cannot have lived all this time in the open.'

She stole a glance at him but was unable to read his expression. She said: 'A kind soul took me in. She did not know that I was a fugitive.'

To her relief, he did not pursue it.

She heard him draw in his breath. His hands were clasped together while he marshalled his thoughts. All the time she waited for the axe to fall.

When he spoke, it was more in sadness than anger. 'You betrayed me by leaving. I would never have thought that you would do that.'

'*I* betrayed *you*?' She looked at him in disbelief.

'You did not trust me. You did not believe that I would annul my marriage.'

She was silent because now she thought about it, he was right. She thought him too weak, too much under his mother's influence, too hidebound by convention to overstep the mark.

He was still talking. 'I was relying on you to help me in these troubled times. I thought that if I made a show of dismissing you, you could work on my behalf, discover what is going on out there.' He nodded towards the window. 'I thought that you would realise.'

She looked at him with shock. 'That is despicable. You intended to use my hurt for your own advantage!'

He shook his head. 'Not my advantage. It was for the good of the country.'

She refused to look at him, still nursing her pain.

He said: 'I cannot prove it, but I know that the King has already tried to escape. I have sent some of his servants away, but others remain. I no longer know whom to trust. I know that he will try again.' Choosing his words carefully, he added: 'You were – are still – in a position to keep your ears open, find out what is going on. You could have access to the entire Castle. If I were to consign you to the domestic staff . . .'

She snapped back at him. 'Why should I do that?'

'For the country.' When she did not reply, he changed his tactics. 'Surely, after all we have meant to each other, you wouldn't desert me at a time like this?'

'Forgive me if I am wrong, but is it not you who have broken your vow to me and then humiliated me like a common thief?'

'Dublin, please . . .' He moved closer but she backed away. She did not want him to touch her.

After a while he said: 'It will be a great pity if you refuse to help me. Unless I can justify your presence in my household, I shall be forced to send you to the mainland. I cannot have spies within these shores.'

'Spies?' She looked at him with disbelief.

'You being Irish, running away . . . people will draw their own conclusions.'

'You told me I had nothing to fear,' she said with bitter irony. 'You said that as Governor, your word was law.'

'Things have changed.' Again he moved closer to her. She could smell the herbs that kept his linen fresh. In contrast, her own stained garments undermined her confidence.

He spoke so quietly that she could barely hear. 'If I were to plead with you?'

She looked up to meet his eyes, dark with entreaty.

He said: 'For some reason, the King seems to have taken a liking to you. He asks after you even now. Charles is lonely, without friends. The laundress was smuggling out his correspondence, but now she is dismissed. If you were to treat kindly with him, flatter him a little, he might confide in you.'

'I won't do it! I thought you had more honour than to ask it.'

Robert shrugged. 'I had honour once. Now the difference between right and wrong is blurred. I only know that I must obey my orders. Keeping Charles safe is all that I care about, by whatever means.'

Dublin tried to think of the consequences of what he asked, but she did not know what they might be.

'There are those about the King who would wish him harm,' Robert said, to add weight to his case.

She sighed. 'And if I refuse?'

'Then you will be on the next boat to Southampton.'

Dublin looked away from him, across the room, out into the courtyard. Her heart jolted. She saw Caleb come riding in and dismount. He stopped and with misery, she saw that he was talking with Polly.

Her voice flat with despair, she said: 'I'll do it.'

Robert let out a sigh of relief. She felt numb, as if the ground had fallen away beneath her and left her hanging over a bottomless void. Unable to meet his eyes, she said: 'There can be no further contact between us. Ever.' Glancing back across the courtyard, where Caleb now stood alone, she added: 'I will do as you ask, but not for you. I'll do it for the country.'

After Dublin left the room, Robert stood in the near-dark, cursing himself for his clumsiness. At the back of his mind, lurking, malevolent, was the thought that perhaps there was someone else. He would not believe it. After all this time, surely she could not have changed her mind? He could only hope that given time, she would come round.

No matter where his thoughts turned, to affairs of state or affairs of the heart, the future looked unrelievedly black.

Seeing Caleb Gosden going about his business in the Castle courtyard, Robert wished for a moment that he could change places with this humble servant. The bailiff did not talk much and probably did not think much either. Although he apparently had a child, it seemed unlikely that he had ever experienced the pain of love. Such a man knew only the base urges of his nature. Turning from the window, Robert confronted his own lonely, complicated future. He thought: Lucky Gosden, unhampered by love or passion, immune to events outside his own narrow life.

Chapter 54

Caleb sat in the Trooper Inn, a tankard of ale on the bench beside him. He was on his way back from Caulbourne. As he drank, his mind pondered the almost physical ache he felt when he thought about leaving Annie. He probed it like a rotten tooth, teasing it out to see if it hurt as much as he imagined. It did. Missing Annie was one of those mysteries that made life a constant source of interest to him. Without her he was free to move about as he pleased, unencumbered by her constant presence, liberated from her endless chatter, and yet . . .

He tried not to ponder on that other great mystery – his feelings for Dublin O'Neill. The visit to the motestones hung like some heavy cloud over him. It seemed as if a power outside himself had led him to show her the grove. Standing there in the shelter of the trees, holding her, feeling her fear and need, he had believed for a foolish moment that his craziest dreams were really coming true. It had been the sweetest moment of his life. But the moment the spell was broken, he had lost her again – to that stuffed, pompous, silver-dipped son who now governed the Castle.

When at last he had found both the courage and the opportunity to return to Caulbourne, it was to find that she had gone.

'I don't know where she is,' said Lizzie, clearly concerned. 'She went across to the church two days since, and has not returned. I pray to God that she is safe.'

Caleb dared not allow himself to believe that she was in danger. Most likely she had wanted to get away from him. He tormented himself with the thought that she was hiding somewhere, waiting for forgiveness so that she could return to Hammond's bed. What weapons did a poor man have against such wealth and power?

Despising the Governor, and the girl, but most of all himself, he ordered another drink.

'What are your feelings about events at the Castle?'

His train of thought was interrupted by the man who sat next to him. He was a man of middle years, respectably dressed, not someone whom Caleb recognised. He guessed he was a visitor to the Island, come perhaps to glean news, or to advance some cause. Idly, he wondered if he had a pass.

'I have no feelings.' Caleb drained his ale and made ready to leave.

'A man who has no feelings must be either empty-headed or tired of life.'

Caleb regarded him again. He was stockily built with a shock of frizzy hair, cut to his shoulders. His pale eyes were shrewd. 'What are *your* feelings?' Caleb countered, welcoming some distraction.

'Well, now.' The man settled himself and prepared to launch into an explanation. 'Any true man must face a dilemma. The King represents different things to different people. To some he is a victim, and they in turn would lay down their lives for him. To others he is the Devil, and for them, as long as he breathes, a curse will lie on our land.'

'And what is he to you?' Caleb accepted the tankard that was placed before him, nodding his thanks to his new companion.

'The way I see it, everything depends upon this one person – whether he lives or dies, whether he stays here, or is taken to London, whether he escapes up north, or flees to the Continent. No matter what, he will be the rallying point for some faction.'

'What if he dies?'

'Then his son will be the new saviour, although as long as he is out of the country his power will be limited.'

Caleb nodded at the wisdom of this observation. 'You still haven't said how you see the situation.'

The man supped deeply of his ale, licking his lips appreciatively. 'I have an overview, as it were. I see it like a game of chess, a strategy. For every move, there are an infinite number of consequences.'

'What do you think is likely to happen?'

'What I fear is that the King will fall into the wrong hands. While the Scots and the Parliament and the army all harangue over him, some faction will take control of his destiny, use him for their own ends.'

'Which faction?'

'Who can say? For myself, I should like to have power to ensure that whatever decision is made, it is for the good of the country.'

'And how would you propose to do that?' Caleb smiled his cynical smile.

'Ah, well now, therein lies the dilemma. Unless I was the person controlling the King's destiny, I would be as helpless as the rest of them.'

Caleb was now genuinely curious. 'What would you do then, if the King was in your hands?'

'Me? – Endymion Salter, by the way.' The stranger held out his hand and Caleb in turn introduced himself, before his companion continued: 'I would ensure that the needs of the poor and the Godly took first place. First and foremost there would be freedom of religion. Then, the landless would be accommodated. Any settlement made would have to be binding and lasting, but it would be the ordinary citizens who came first.'

'Mmn. There, I'd agree with you.'

Endymion leaned closer. 'We meet here each week – to discuss the way forward, as it were. You seem to be a man who thinks, who has ideas of his own. Why don't you come along?'

Caleb drained his ale and prepared to leave, saying: 'Maybe I will.'

When he got back to the Castle, the first person he saw was Polly.

'Oh Caleb, you'll never believe it! Dublin is back! She was captured by Captain Rolph and brought in not an hour since.'

Caleb felt his pulses race. 'She's not hurt?' he said to Polly.

'No.' She hesitated. 'You've no idea where she's been?'

He shook his head. 'How should I know?'

Polly looked embarrassed. 'Well, they've taken her straight to the Governor. What do you think he'll do with her?'

Caleb didn't know. In one breath he feared that Robert might truly punish her, in which case he would have to act. In the next, he visualised a fond reunion between lovers. His brow grew dark.

'Don't fret,' he said bitterly. 'If I know her, she'll wheedle her way out of trouble.'

As he crossed the courtyard, he saw the door of the old Governor's house open and Dublin come out. He pulled back into the shadows. As he watched, she walked across to the kitchens. He could see that she had been crying and he started to walk out to meet her, but already she had opened the door and gone inside. With a sigh he leaned back against the rough stone of the wall.

Moments later, Dublin re-emerged carrying a pile of laundry. Now she looked distant, enclosed in a world of her own. He detected a sense of purpose, as if she had resolved on some course of action and would not be deflected. She made her way in the direction of the King's room, head held high. She did not look like a woman in disgrace.

Caleb burned with resentment. Clearly Hammond had pardoned her – no doubt for a price. He cursed again the rich, pampered man who had control over their very lives. It was time that things changed.

The Society for a Just and Peaceful Settlement of the Troubles in England, met in a small room at the back of the Trooper. Locally their numbers were few, but those present were assured that there was widespread support for their aims across the country.

It had taken considerable skill on the part of Endymion Salter to persuade Caleb that he above all men, was in a God-given position to ensure that their ideals could be realised. As a groom with access to the Castle and on good terms with the guards, if Caleb played his part, a fair, just society for the whole of England could be forced upon the privileged and wealthy, the bigots and the unjust.

'Let's get this clear,' said Caleb. 'If the King were to fall into our hands, we would hold him until Parliament agreed to our conditions.' He stopped and looked round at the nodding assembly. Many of them he recognised, good, steady men and women with more than sawdust between their ears.

Emphasising the point, he said: 'There would be no question of killing him?' In the few dealings that he had had with the frail, gracious monarch, Caleb had grown grudgingly to like him. Although he might represent all the evils of the kingdom, Caleb personally believed that Charles's life had the same value as even the humblest member of the Society. Human life, even a king's, was sacred.

'There's no question of killing him.' Endymion addressed the gathering. 'If we did that then we would have slain our golden goose. Anyway, violence is not our way. Only when our demands have been met, and implemented, and made known to every true-born Englishman and woman, do we hand the King over. By then, they would not dare to go back on the agreement.'

Caleb was satisfied.

'Where could we hold him?' asked a member.

'That hasn't been decided yet.' Endymion turned his grizzled head towards his neighbour and raised his eyebrows.

In response, Caleb announced: 'I know a place.'

'You do? And the business itself . . .'

Caleb looked away. He knew that everyone present was watching him. By virtue of his position, they had marked him out as the unanimously appointed, indeed some would say, the divinely anointed, choice. He looked from one to the other, the expectant eyes, the suspended breath.

Quietly he said: 'Very well, I'll do it.'

With thundering heart, he realised that he had just agreed to kidnap the King.

Chapter 55

Dublin was now responsible for the King's laundry, and in addition, she saw to his fire and the general cleaning of his chamber. Being in daily contact with the Royal prisoner, often she was alone with him. Sometimes she would catch him watching her, his mild, doe-like eyes moist with unnamed regrets.

'Your Majesty, I fear that you are sad.'

'Truly sad, my dear. I fear that I have not a friend in the world.'

'Surely that is not the case.' Dublin spread the fine lace of his collar flat and draped it near the fire to dry. For a moment she was tempted to say that she was his friend, but the audacity of such a claim held her back. In any case, she could not ignore the burden of her true calling, which was to act the spy. Whatever else, she could not, would not lie to the King, mislead him in order to get information. There was something so vulnerable about him, that she felt the need to protect him from further hurt.

By the dying light, he read aloud, part of a sermon which Robert's uncle had preached in the Castle just prior to his recently enforced departure: '. . . And they shall turn swords into ploughshares.' The sentiment brought tears to Charles's eyes.

'How I wish for such a time,' he said, his voice trembling with emotion. 'I cannot believe that Governor Hammond has sent his own uncle away, perhaps to prison for his loyalty to me.'

His words sent a wave of fear through Dublin. Beneath Robert's upright, honourable façade, did there lurk a ruthless man who would sacrifice even his kin for the cause which he served? She shivered, refusing to think of it.

'Is there no way that you can change things?' she asked the King, forgetting her station and her mission. It all suddenly

383

seemed extremely simple. If Charles wanted peace so badly, then why did he not agree to it?

'Come and sit by me, my dear.' The King beckoned to her and after a moment's hesitation, she sank down onto the stool at his feet. For a long while he gazed into the fire, as if reading the flames, then he turned his sad eyes towards her, searching her face. She wondered what he thought about her. Daily, she listened out for any snippets of conversation, and watched for signs that he was conducting some illicit activity, but she had seen nothing. This was a relief because the idea of betraying this gentle, sensitive man weighed heavily.

The King said: 'If God wills, He will use me as His instrument to bring peace to this, His land.'

Dublin did not really believe his words, but neither did she wish to deprive him of hope and comfort, so she waited.

'Could you not agree to what the Parliament wishes, Sire?' she asked. 'If you did so, they would begin to trust Your Majesty again, then you could go back to your palace. The Queen could come back to join you.'

'Ah, my dear.' His voice was heavy with regret. 'I fear you do not understand the tenets of faith, the burden of monarchy.' He reached out and to her dismay, took her hand. For several seconds he was silent, then he said: 'You are such an honest, straightforward girl. I should hate to think that anyone would use you in order to further their own ends.'

His words put her on her guard. 'Like whom?'

'Like, perhaps, the Governor.' He raised his eyebrows questioningly. Dublin looked away, her face red with guilt.

Still holding her hand, Charles rubbed his thumb along the length of each finger, then traced out the shape of her palm. She resisted the desire to pull free. He said: 'Sometimes I fear that the Queen will never return. I fear that I am doomed to spend the rest of my life, however long or short, entirely alone.' He looked at her and quietly asked: 'Would you do a service for a poor, lonely man?'

'Sire?' She stiffened, wondering how to deal with whatever he might ask.

'Would you embrace me?'

'I—' She did not know how to respond. While a part of her was appalled by the thought of kissing this man, another, until now unrecognised part of herself, felt a heady sense of excitement. If she chose, she could seduce this graceful, aristocratic and still powerful monarch. She was shocked yet exhilarated by the discovery.

Charles shook his head. 'I do not ask for a subject's kiss. Not an unseemly kiss. It would please me if, like a daughter, you were to offer some small token of affection.'

'I—'

Again he met her gaze. 'I am not a fool, my dear. I have eyes in my head. Do you not think I realise how the wind blows between you and the Governor?'

Again, she could think of nothing to say.

Charles continued, 'You are an exceptional girl. Forgive me for saying so, but the Governor is a man so devoted to duty that he might forget where to draw the line. I sense that you have your own doubts – perhaps your heart is drawn in another direction?'

'Sire, I—'

'You are truly beautiful, Dublin O'Neill. The Governor knows that I am not easily seduced. Animal attraction, carnal temptation does not ensnare me. But beauty, innocence, might do.'

'I don't know what you mean, Sire.'

He sighed. 'I don't think you do. Well, it seems to me that you might go against your own nature in order to fulfil your sense of duty. I wonder if you would not even sacrifice your honour?'

'The Governor would never ask me to do that!'

'Of course he wouldn't. He is too astute. But he knows you, Dublin. He knows what lengths you might go to in order to fulfil your loyalty to him.'

'It wouldn't be for him . . .' She stopped as she realised what she was saying. Charles was quick to pick up her thoughts.

'Ah. Then there *is* somebody else? Somebody you are protecting?'

She shook her head and Charles gave a shrug. 'It would greatly please me to be comforted by such a lovely girl, but I, like you, have my own sense of honour. I would not use you to feed false information to Governor Hammond.'

'Sire, you misjudge me. I give you my word that I—'

'Hush.' He leaned forward and kissed her on the lips, a tender, parent's blessing, then he sat back with a sigh. 'We will not speak of this again. You will light my fires and do my laundry. I shall not

385

reveal anything to you which will make your tender conscience prick. Do we have an agreement, you and I?'

There was nothing to say. The pressure of his lips, the tickle of his beard, still left their imprint on her mouth. She thought: I have been kissed by a King, whom some say is God's representative on earth. It was overwhelming.

He said: 'Go now. Tomorrow we will both have forgotten that this conversation took place.'

As the weeks passed, true to his word, the King made no reference to the evening that he had kissed his laundress, and Dublin flitted between the Royal presence and the kitchens, the laundry and the stables, the wood-store and her bedroom.

So preoccupied was she with her own confusion, that it was in fact several days before she realised that there was something amiss in the guardroom. She could not have put her finger on it but a certain atmosphere existed, something not right. Every time she walked into the room, there was a sudden silence. In times past the men would have continued with their conversation, or perhaps have made some joke, conducting a flirtation with her. Now they waited awkwardly for her to leave, and she felt the warning glances behind her back.

By dint of casual visits, Dublin came to realise that it was always when the same three men were on duty – and invariably they were in the company of Edmund Rolph. At Robert's behest, Rolph had been promoted to the rank of Major. Dublin tried not to let her dislike of the man colour her feelings, but she could not help but notice that he was more conceited, more jumped-up than ever.

As she came out of the guardroom one suppertime, she encountered Caleb washing off the Governor's horse in the yard outside. From habit she drew back into the shadows, her heart-rate increasing. Since her return to the Castle, she had not so much as acknowledged his presence. He, in turn, behaved as if she did not exist. She did not know how to overcome the barrier.

Robert's horse was lathered with sweat but the rider had already disappeared into the house. Dublin wondered what business had taken him abroad.

'You'll catch cold if you stay there.'

386

Caleb's comment caught her unawares. Although it was a May evening, it was damp and chilly, as were most days in this miserable year. Dublin stepped from her hiding place, making a show of picking up some mysteriously dropped object. Caleb continued to wipe the animal, cursing it quietly as it jumped and snorted at the water.

'The Governor's just come back from town,' he remarked.

'Oh.' At last here was a chance to talk to him, but she did not know what to say.

After an uncomfortable silence, he added: 'Too many spies, too many loopholes.'

'What do you mean?'

Caleb shrugged. 'I reckon it's what might happen that torments His Lordship most. Not knowing who has a knife at his back.'

'Like who?' She moved closer, not sure that she wanted to hear.

Again Caleb shrugged, working consistently, addressing his remarks to the damp air. 'For myself, I wouldn't trust one of those men around the King. But there, their main concern is for His Majesty's safety. The ones the Governor should really worry about are those who want to kill him. Perhaps he should look closer to home.'

'What are you saying?'

Caleb gave the horse a final wipe across the withers and stood back. Still he did not look round at her. 'I don't reckon your Governor's a very good judge of character.'

Before Dublin could protest, or question Caleb further, the guardroom door opened and Edmund Rolph came out, accompanied by the King's page, Richard Osborn.

It was clear that Rolph had been drinking and he strutted importantly past, ignoring Dublin and Caleb, making some joke with Osborn as he went. They appeared to be on very friendly terms.

As they disappeared into the mist, Caleb said: 'Your Colonel thinks highly of Major Rolph, doesn't he?'

'Why should I know?' She hesitated. 'What are you saying?'

Caleb raised his shoulders in a gesture that signified: Who knows? Aloud he said, 'I'm just saying the Governor thinks highly of Major Rolph. C'mon, lad.' The last remark was addressed to the horse and with a nod of his head, he went to lead the animal away.

387

Dublin moved forward to block his path. 'If you know something, you should say.'

Caleb raised his eyebrows and for a moment his eyes met hers. It was just long enough for her to recognise the too-familiar feeling that he could see into her soul. Then he looked away. His customary sarcasm returned. 'Seeing as how it concerns you so much, Rolph's a dangerous piece of work.'

Dublin waited. After a moment, Caleb raised his eyes to meet hers again. They glistened in the damp night, shrewd and unwavering. He said: 'Rolph spreads rumours, lays false trails. Perhaps you should warn your Governor that his trusted major claims that Parliament are secretly pressing Colonel Hammond to do away with the King.'

Dublin thought: It can't be true. Robert is too good a friend to Rolph. Aloud she said: 'How do you know that?'

'Because I overheard him say it. And more.'

'Such as?' Her impatience with Caleb was growing. All the time she suspected that he was trying to provoke her.

Drawing in his breath, he said: 'Major Rolph wants the King dead, you realise that? On the pretext of helping, he's planning to panic the King into making a bid for freedom. When he does, Rolph will shoot him as he tries to escape.'

'Then you must tell the Governor!'

Caleb shook his head. 'I'm telling you. It's up to you what you do about it.'

She was confused by his logic. 'But I have no proof.' In the face of his stoical silence she started again. 'If the King is killed, there will be trouble for all of us.'

'Especially for your precious Governor.'

Her impatience gave way to anger. 'You don't care about anybody! What about the King's safety? What would happen to the world if he was killed? You MUST tell!'

Still Caleb remained indifferent. 'I wouldn't wish to see the King killed,' he conceded, 'that's why I'm telling you – but if you say that I was the one who warned you, I shall deny it.'

'But why?'

Caleb's face remained inscrutable; then with a brief nod of his head, he brushed past her, leading the horse away. Dublin was left to pick the bones out of his remarks.

Her mind was in chaos. She wondered whether to face Rolph

herself and demand that he tell the truth, but at the thought of his wily personality, his sneering conceit, she quaked. The only thing was to warn Robert.

For a moment she wondered what Caleb was playing at, why he had told her. He claimed not to care what happened at the Castle, and yet he wanted the governor alerted. At the same time, he refused to be drawn into the affair himself. Just for a second she wondered if he had some motive she did not understand. It was like a flicker of light, flashing to reveal something in the dark, leaving the merest outline and then disappearing into the blackness.

The only thing was to catch Robert alone, although how and when she did not know. With a sigh she made her way to the wash-house and trying to behave normally, retrieved some hose hung up to dry in front of the great log fire. Using the pretext of returning it to the Governor's quarters, she slipped up the stairs. As she reached his door, she closed her eyes and drew in her breath, then with a determined toss of her head, she knocked on his door.

There was no answer. Quickly Dublin looked about her then cautiously turned the large, round, iron handle. It twisted with a loud click and the door opened under her weight. Inside, the room was empty, although a recently-stoked fire burned in the grate. It sent shadows weaving their way up the rough-hewn walls, across the cluttered desk, licking out towards the narrow couch.

'What are you doing?'

He must have come along the corridor in stockinged feet for suddenly, silently, Robert had come into the room. From the doorway, he stared at her in astonishment.

Utterly flustered, Dublin looked around, her face reddening in the fireglow. Her eyes came to rest on the abandoned hose. 'I brought you those.'

He acknowledged her reply but still waited. The eyes that met hers were lonely, defeated. Trying to keep her voice steady, she said: 'There is something that you should know.'

'And that is?'

'Major Rolph is planning to kill the King.'

He let out a snort of disbelief. 'Nonsense!'

'He is. He is encouraging the King to escape, and when he does, Rolph will shoot him.'

389

Robert shook his head. 'You're wrong. Edmund is acting under my instructions to win the confidence of the King's conservitors. That way he will find out what is going on. Naturally he has to pretend to be on their side.' As if explaining to a child, he added: 'He might collude in an escape attempt, but not in murder.'

'Then you are a poor judge of character!' Dublin flounced towards the door, embarrassed by his response. 'Don't say that I didn't warn you.'

'I won't. And thank you for your concern, but there is no cause for worry.' He came over towards her. 'I – I truly appreciate your concern.'

She deliberately drew away. 'I must go, I have duties to attend to.'

With a regretful look, Robert bowed his head.

For no good reason, Dublin suddenly thought: I wish that I could go back to Foxton, away from this unnatural life. She longed for the house, but most of all the garden. In her mind's eye she saw the profusion of colour, smelled the heady scent of summer, heard the somnolent trickle of the fountain. Then in spite of herself, like a well-painted miniature edged in light, she saw Caleb, his child at his side, working methodically among the asparagus, at peace with the place and himself. Caleb. He was more a part of Foxton than Robert ever was.

Chapter 56

Although some of the King's servants had been banished, they had not abandoned their service to him. Before leaving Newport, Harry Firebrace arranged for the onward transmission of the Royal correspondence, while Captain Titus, establishing himself in Southampton, set about arranging for horses to spirit his monarch away – once his escape from Carisbrooke could be effected.

Meanwhile, Charles anguished over what form his escape should take. Soon after his failed attempt to get through the window, Governor Hammond had moved him to another chamber. A platform had been especially constructed below his window, and day and night guards were present. If he were to escape, then the guards would have to be bribed.

Now, as before, the main obstacle was still the window bar. In his room Charles was surrounded by files and acid but he was at a loss to know how to use them. He wrote frantic letters to Titus, asking for advice.

In the end, his friend Richard Osborn took matters into his own hands, preparing the bar during the times when Charles was on the bowling green. All that the King would have to do was to finish the job.

It was finally settled that Wednesday, 24 May was the best time. Charles went over events in his mind until he was in a fog. Outside the castle, Mr Worsley and one of his relatives would be waiting with horses. A boat lay in wait at Wootton, some six miles away. Everything was ready. Then, on the afternoon of 23 May, as Charles strolled around the bowling green, Abraham Dowcett joined him.

Falling into step with the King, Dowcett said: 'Your Majesty, I fear there is some little difficulty with our business.'

Charles raised his brows, his chest tightening.

Dowcett glanced to left and right to ensure that no one was near, then continued: 'For some reason, and we know not why, the guard rota has been changed. I fear that our friends will not be at our call on Wednesday.'

Charles let out a sigh of such magnitude that Dowcett involuntarily put his fingers to his lips, urging the monarch to caution. Alarmed at his own action, Charles looked quickly around, but no one appeared to be taking any notice. Turning back to Dowcett, he said out of the side of his mouth: 'What does this mean?'

'Sire, the good news is that our team of men has not been split up. They will next be on guard on Sunday. I suggest that we postpone the matter until that night.'

Charles gave an imperceptible nod of his head then veered away across the green, heading for the summerhouse. All that he could do now was wait, for four more neverending days.

When Sunday night finally arrived, the King found it almost impossible to behave naturally. Claiming to have the beginnings of an ague, he retired early to bed. Once in his room he hastened to add more acid to the window bar, wiggling it with tense hands until at last he felt the hint of movement. Hardly daring to breathe, he applied his weight to it and found to his great relief that it could be pushed aside. Thankfully he tugged it back into place, praying that he would have no visitors.

The seconds barely moved. During each minute Charles could have ridden to Cowes and back, have composed ten sonnets, or preached a sermon. Peeping out of the window for the hundredth time, he saw with anxiety that it was the hour for the guard to change. Breath suspended, he could hardly believe that the loyal guards were now indeed on duty. With a trembling hand he wiped the cold sweat from his brow.

After a while he heard lowered voices outside. Two of the guards seemed to have disappeared from their posts and two others had taken their place. Charles found it difficult to breathe. What did this mean? Here he was, alone, not knowing what was happening. No longer caring if he was seen, he pressed his nose hard against the window pane, watching for what would happen next.

392

It was an eternity before, to his great joy, the two guards returned and took up their positions. 'Thank You, dear Lord.' The King of England raised his eyes in gratitude to the King of Heaven.

Charles tried counting sixty at the correct speed to register the minutes. After about six of these, he began to recite verses that he had learned at his tutor's knee. Hesitantly he translated them into French – anything to keep his mind occupied.

At last, the clock upon his desk showed that it was a quarter before midnight. Now he could complete the task of moving the window bar. He pushed the casement open, desperate not to make a noise. The bar seemed to grate thunderously but finally co-operated. Now, all he had to do was to lower himself down the sheer wall. Below, Dowcett would meet him and guide him to the appointed meeting-place where Worsley waited with the horses.

As he raised his leg over the windowsill, Charles heard the low tones of Dowcett's voice giving the pass. Moments later the platform below his window was filled with guards. The frozen King watched as, protesting, Dowcett was overpowered and dragged away.

Half-hanging over the sill, Charles grasped in panic at the handle of the casement and managed to heave himself back inside. His hands shook so much that he could scarce grab the bar and force it back into position. The guards had betrayed them!

Shutting the window, Charles raced for the safety of his bed, diving childlike under the quilt and pulling the cover over his head. Cowering in his couch, he strained his ears for any sounds.

Minutes later, a brief knock on his chamber door was followed by the entrance of Hammond. Feigning surprise, Charles sat up in bed, the covers still clutched to his chin.

Without speaking, the Governor strode across to the window and examined it. Turning towards the bed he said: 'Majesty, I have come to say farewell to you.'

Charles stared at him blankly, wondering if for some reason, the Governor was being called away. 'You are leaving?' he asked in an unsteady voice.

'On the contrary. I was led to understand that it was you who were planning to leave.' Inclining his head, the Governor pulled the broken bar away and held it up.

In the face of his guilt, the King remained silent.

Chapter 57

The news of the King's attempted escape served to remind Caleb that if he was to fulfil his promise to the Society for the Peaceful Settlement of the Troubles in England, then he must act quickly. The burning question was *how*? Force seemed out of the question. Single-handed, he could hardly overpower the King, bundle him into some box or crate and then carry him freely past the mêlée of soldiers and through the Castle gates. The more he thought about it, the more two things became obvious: first of all he would need the King's co-operation, and secondly, he would need help.

His preoccupation with this vital mission helped to distract him from the pain he felt since Dublin had returned to the Castle. She had made a point of ignoring him. Although they had spoken briefly on that one occasion, it had been clear that she was still concerned about her precious master's safety.

Much as it hurt to admit it, Caleb could only conclude that Dublin was still besotted with the Colonel. He swallowed down his contempt. With his intellect, he despised her. With his heart, he yearned for the same blind loyalty that bound her to his rival.

For the past week, early each evening, Dublin had left the Castle taking small items of comfort for the Widow Colenutt. The old lady, who baked for the garrison, had had a fall and could no longer make the journey up the hill. It was Dublin's task to collect the pasties and brawns that Martha Colenutt still managed to bake. Scornfully Caleb thought that she must be back in favour if she was permitted outside the gate.

Her visits meant that Caleb saw her nightly, as he handed over the mare, Fortune, receiving the animal back when Dublin returned. Sometimes he felt so angry with himself that he could not speak to her. At other times, some cutting remark would escape him, designed to remind her that she was only a camp-follower, a whore who had now got her comeuppance. In reponse to his comments, she would look at him with those bewitching eyes, sometimes angry, but for the most part so vulnerable, so mystified . . .

Yet when Caleb's hand happened to brush against hers, every sensible thought went out of his head. If he allowed himself to look on her features, he saw pain and loneliness. This drowned him in a sea of need to comfort her, but he fought against it. All he wanted was to be away, and back with Annie – except that first there was work to do.

For a few days he thought furiously of every possibility with regard to the King's escape. One thing was clear: he needed a chance to speak to Charles personally but this seemed impossible given that the royal prisoner was always surrounded by guards. Then Caleb had an idea. Even as it occurred to him, he baulked at it, shamed and disgusted by what he must do, but for the cause of justice and the greatest good, he steeled himself to attempt it.

As Charles came into the courtyard one morning, his entourage following behind, Caleb stepped forward and said: 'If it please Your Majesty, pray heal me.' He turned his torso so that his back was visible to the King, saying: 'As you will see, I am ill-formed. Your touch, with God's good grace, will make me straight.'

Caleb endured the humiliation as Charles looked him over, his gaze resting on the malformed shoulder. For good measure, Caleb hunched his shoulder higher.

'If you pray for forgiveness for your sins, then God in His wisdom might see fit to cure you,' the King responded.

Inside, Caleb seethed. Aloud, he said: 'With your noble intervention, I feel confident that God would look benignly upon me.'

With a shrug, the King moved closer and his frail hand came to rest upon Caleb's shoulder. Steeling himself to suffer the shame, Caleb bent closer and whispered: 'Sire, it is my wish to help you. You must trust me. I have access to horses. A woman leaves the Castle every evening before supper. She comes to your room with linen. When the time is right, I would beg you to dress in her guise.'

His head was bowed low as he accepted the King's blessing. Charles showed no visible sign of having heard but the merest pressure from the Royal fingers told Caleb that he had understood.

Already Caleb was thinking of what he must do next. Now that he had set these wheels in motion he had no choice but to call upon Dublin for help. She alone held the key in that she had both access to the King's chamber and a nightly pass to leave the Castle.

In creating this situation, it was almost as if another person had acted on Caleb's behalf. He had no reason to think that Dublin would co-operate; indeed, she might equally betray him to the Governor, but even as the thought came to him, he knew why he had done it.

Now was the time of reckoning. Now he must find out once and for all what she really felt. There was no going back.

Bowing again to the King and expressing his thanks, Caleb withdrew. He thought to himself: Desperate needs call for desperate measures.

'You're mad! How could you even think of it?' Dublin gazed aghast at her former rescuer. They stood by the gatehouse in the drizzle, Fortune between them, both clinging to her bridle. The mare threw her head up to ease the tension of their combined weight against the bit in her mouth.

Caleb said: 'As long as the King stays here, we'll all be trapped, perhaps for ever.' In the face of her disbelief he tried another approach. 'What do you think might happen to ordinary folk if the King is rescued and restored to his throne? Do you think the poor will benefit? Or those who do not hold the King's religious views?'

Dublin shook her head, not knowing the answer. He added: 'And what about your precious Governor? Do you think the King will look kindly upon him after he has held him prisoner?' He paused: 'Don't you want to go back to Foxton and act the lady?'

The last remark was thrown at her with ill-concealed contempt. When Dublin did not reply, he added: 'Don't you want that?'

'If Robert lets the King escape, he'll have to answer for it to the Parliament. I can't . . .' She still shrank from the thought of betraying him.

She asked: 'Why are you doing this?'

He relaxed a little. 'So that a just settlement can be reached. For everyone. My friends want a fair society, freedom of worship, fairer distribution of land.' He moved closer. 'Power to change the future will lie with those who hold the King.' His look willed her to understand.

396

'You're mad,' she repeated.

His expression hardened. 'Not mad enough to be used and then cast aside without having the sense to recognise it.'

'What do you mean?'

In his infuriating way, he did not explain, instead saying: 'Anyway, that is what I plan. You would not be taking any risks. I only ask you to agree that you will permit the King to take your clothing. He is no bigger than you. If you wear a veil he can cover his face and hair. No one will suspect.' She backed away a few paces but Caleb followed. 'You would simply go to the King's chamber. He will take your clothes and lock you inside. If he binds your mouth you will not need to explain why you did not call the guards. You will be innocent of any crime.' As she regarded him unhappily, he added: 'If you want to stop me then you had better tell your Governor now, or warn him so that he can arrest me when the time comes.'

'When do you plan to do it?'

'Is that your way of saying you'll help?'

'I can't. I don't know. Why would I do so?'

'To ensure a just future.'

'I'd have to think about it.' She tilted her head, looking at his intent face, disturbed by his zeal. 'How do you know you can trust these people?'

'If you knew them, you'd understand.' He raised his hands in resignation. 'I don't want to spend the rest of my life shut away in this castle. If we negotiate a fair settlement, every man will get some land of his own . . .'

'But they wouldn't . . .' Another thought occurred to her. 'Suppose they kill the King?'

'We're not his enemies. If you shared our objectives you'd know that killing won't achieve them.'

She tried to think but her mind could not grasp all the implications. It fished about for ways to buy time. 'Where would you take him?'

'That I won't tell you.'

She shook her head again, not saying no, unable to say yes. As she met his eyes, she saw the urgency in his request. His very life seemed to hang by her answer. Lamely she repeated: 'I'll have to think about it.'

Chapter 58

The King was shaken by the unexpected offer of help from the taciturn groom. At any other time he would have had the man removed by his retinue, except that there was no one about him whom he could really trust. With a sudden cold wave of fear, he thought: There IS no one that I can trust.

He began to feel desperate. An almost irresistible urge to race for the Castle gate overcame him. He wanted to keep running, even if they shot him down.

'I have got to get out of here,' he said aloud. For a moment he wondered if he should report the incident to Hammond, thereby incurring the Governor's favour, but then he thought that by so doing, he might be sacrificing his last chance of freedom.

Trying to get a grip on himself, he thought about what the groom had said. The man had implied that Dublin O'Neill would co-operate with them, give Charles her clothing so that he could leave the Castle in her place. His first feeling was one of pleasure, a rippling excitement that the girl should take such a risk on his behalf. The fragile, romantic dreams that he had shyly nursed, suddenly had a heady reality.

But when she next came to his chamber, bearing a pile of clean hose and shirts, there was something distant about her. Deliberately she left the door open so that the guard in the corridor outside was privy to any conversation. He was denied the chance to ask her outright.

When she had gone, Charles sank wearily onto his settle. He felt confused and disappointed. He had been a fool to believe that she would betray the Governor. On the other hand, if the groom was right, and she was prepared to betray Hammond's trust, then how could Charles in turn rely upon her? There was no answer.

Weighing up all the possibilities, he asked himself: What have you got to lose? Think, man! There was a good chance that he might lose his life. How could he trust them? Then, thinking of the army, and the Parliament, and the Scots, a despairing voice asked: How can you *not* trust them?

Wearily pulling off his boots and preparing himself for a lonely evening, he thought: If she asks me, I'll do it.

A pile of linen was neatly folded and stacked on a wooden table in the Castle kitchen. It awaited the time when someone would carry it up to the Royal chamber.

Dublin stood before the laundry, her hands tingling with uncertainty. An hour since, she had crossed the yard and encountered Caleb. She had tried to slip by him unnoticed, but as she passed, he had stretched his back and leaned his weight against his large, wooden shovel.

Without looking round he said: 'Tonight. Tell the King, tonight.'

Now she was face to face with the dilemma which tormented her. It was insoluble. Pass on the message, allow herself to be locked in the King's chamber, and she would betray Robert in the most despicable way. On the other hand, if she were to tell him of the planned escape, then Caleb would face imprisonment, even death. And if she did not act? Dublin knew that Caleb would go ahead anyway.

'Have you nothing to do?' Her anguish was interrupted by Mistress Hammond, on one of her tours of inspection.

'Ma'am.' Dublin experienced the familiar resentment as she looked at Robert's mother. But it no longer mattered. She no longer wanted the prize that Elizabeth Hammond so jealously guarded.

She picked up a pair of the King's gauntlets, newly sponged. The Royal hands were slender, not much bigger than her own. Without being seen, Dublin slipped the gloves into her shawl. Suddenly she knew what she must do.

Although Caleb had succeeded in making contact with Charles, and wringing some sort of promise from Dublin, his escape plans were still incomplete. He mulled over what would happen once the King was safely outside the Castle. Even if Caleb was able to alert Endymion Salter to the appointed time of the escape, Charles would probably refuse to entrust himself to strangers. At the same time, in order to avoid suspicion, the King in Dublin's guise would have to ride alone and in the normal way towards Carisbrooke. There was nothing to stop him from making his own dash for freedom.

At last Caleb thought of a solution. It was not very satisfactory, but it was the best that he could come up with. When Colonel Hammond came out to ride that morning, Caleb said: 'Have you noticed, sir, that your stirrup leathers are wearing? The stitching needs attention. Perhaps I should take them to the saddlers, get them repaired, or replaced.'

'Do that.'

As usual, the Governor was distracted. Loud enough for the surrounding troopers to hear, Caleb said: 'I'll take them then, tonight.'

'Very well.'

As the horses clattered out across the bridge, Caleb continued to sweep up the dung deposited by this latest troupe of horsemen. Now he had permission to leave the garrison. No one would question him if he rode out with Dublin, or as it happened, with the King. A moment of elation touched him. His plan was going to work. Once clear of the Castle, he could ride with Charles to Foxton, and hand him over.

It was not easy to remain calm. Now that the wheels were set in motion, there was no going back. If things went wrong . . .

When the time finally came, Caleb saddled up Fortune, and one of Robert's mares for himself.

'You going out?' his companion, Alfred Fleming, asked.

'Aye, to the saddlers with these stirrups. I – I'll ride down when the skivvy goes to Widow Colenutt's for the pasties.'

His mate grinned. 'How did you wangle that? Don't pretend you're not sweet on her.'

'Bollocks.' Caleb pretended contempt, but the reality of his feelings caused him to flush. For a moment he forgot that it was not Dublin who would be riding with him and when he remembered, he felt a prick of disappointment. Then the gravity of his mission came back to him.

'See, you're shaking with excitement.' Alfred Fleming gave a laugh.

In spite of his tension, Caleb's mind began to clear. When the moment came, he could not risk anyone else being present in case they might notice something amiss. To Alfred he said: 'Do me a service, Al, stay out of the way. I – I don't want her thinking I'm waiting for her deliberately. You know how it is in these matters.'

'All right, old son. But watch how you behave.' He was suddenly sly, adding: 'That young lady's used to better manners from her suitors.'

At the thought of the Governor, Caleb felt the sting of jealousy, but he fought the feeling down, rejoining: 'Time she got used to plainer meat, then.'

The minutes dragged by, creeping up to and then crawling past the appointed time for the Royal descent. Something had gone wrong – it must have done! Caleb fought to calm himself. Catching his mood, the two horses were restless in the misty evening.

'Don't show you're that keen!' Alfred teased, preparing to take his leave with a deliberate show of fuss and bother.

'Get away!'

'I'm going!'

At that moment, the door leading from the officers' wing creaked open and a swathed figure stepped out into the yard. Caleb jumped. With total relief he saw the shrouded King hunch his head against the now driving rain and begin to cross the yard. With a brief smile, he thought that Charles was playing his role well.

In a low voice he said: 'Sire, let me hand you up.'

The King shook his head, stretching for the stirrup and hauling himself into the saddle. Caleb bit back the temptation to remind his Royal companion that he must remember he was a lady. In silence he mounted the mare and took the lead.

'Stay close by,' he whispered. 'The mount's quiet. Don't forget to wave to the guards, they'll expect it.'

Beneath the shawl, he glimpsed the King's gloved hands, noticed that a strand of hair, darkened by rain, was plastered across the royal brow. The Royal hair desperately needed cutting. 'Keep your head low,' he whispered.

They rode out of the Castle in silence, the Governor's mare jogging her way down the cobbles, Fortune picking her path more circumspectly.

401

'Have no fear, she's sound-footed.' Caleb sought to reassure his charge. 'Just follow me. When we're clear of here I have a safe place to take you.'

Once out of view of the Castle, Caleb turned in the saddle. 'We'll make what speed we can. I have friends waiting to receive you.'

He spurred the mare forward and to his relief, the King followed suit. Hardly letting up the pace, Caleb pushed on along the four miles, until the familiar outline of Foxton became visible in the near dark.

'We are nearby, Majesty. Believe me, you will be well taken care of.'

Uneasily he waited for the King to ask questions, perhaps express misgivings. He was not sure how he would answer but there was no need, for Charles continued to follow in silence.

As they rode into the yard, Caleb hoped that Endymion would be there. There was a chance that he would not have received the message in time to meet them. If he did not come, it would be up to Caleb to entertain the Royal guest until such time as the Society had succeeded in making their approach to the Parliament. With shock he realised that there was no going back. He was now committed irrevocably to the role of rebel.

Swinging from the saddle, he turned to help his companion to dismount. The King pulled away and with a burst of anger Caleb thought: He thinks he's too good to be touched by someone like me! Then he remembered how Charles had lain his hand upon his humped shoulder. Perhaps fear, not disgust, governed his actions.

'Come.' He dismissed his confused thoughts and led both horses round to the side of the house, loosing them into the paddock. With sinking heart he guessed that Endymion had not yet arrived.

'Come along inside, Sire. I'll find you some refreshment.' He stood back to let Charles pass. The King scurried by him, still muffled in the shawl.

'You're quite safe now.' Caleb threw his own hat onto a table and let his jerkin drop onto the nearby chair.

The King stood awkwardly in the centre of the room, his shoulders hunched up almost as if he expected a blow. Caleb frowned in confusion. 'You really are safe. Sire?'

As he stepped forward, his charge raised his gloved hands to his

402

head and lifted the shawl. It caught against the thick hair, the thick brown hair, that tumbled down to waist-length. Slowly, the Royal head turned and Caleb gazed in disbelief into the eyes of Dublin.

'What the Devil!' Caleb's expression was one of total bemusement. His brow furrowed, staring as Dublin let the shawl fall to her shoulders, revealing her everyday gown. His gaze took in her clothes and shoes. On her hands she still wore the King's gloves and following Caleb's eyes, she glanced guiltily down, letting her hands drop to her sides.

She could feel her heart thumping, her throat grow dry as she sought for some explanation. In the end all she said was, 'I'm sorry.'

'Sorry? Would the King not come?' His eyes narrowed. 'You did this deliberately?'

Dublin saw his fists clench and for a moment she thought: He's going to hit me. Aloud she said: 'I didn't wish you to risk . . .'

'YOU didn't wish?' The fists tightened into angry balls. 'Who are you to decide what I should risk?'

'I . . .'

He snorted at his own private thoughts, and when he looked at her again, his eyes were like flint. 'Did you not even have the guts to tell the Governor? That at least would have been an honest betrayal. That way I would have been captured with some sort of honour. This way . . .' He stepped closer. 'What sort of pleasure does it give you to humiliate me like this?'

'You're wrong!' She struggled to find words that he would accept. 'If you had taken the King away, they would have hunted you down, killed you.'

He sighed, a long, despairing exhalation of breath. 'That was for me to decide. Don't you realise, you have destroyed a chance to find a just settlement to all this strife? Now God alone knows what will happen.'

Dublin seized upon his words. 'That's just it. You can't play God. If you do, they'll strike you down.' Without meaning to, she added: 'I didn't want you hurt.'

'Don't you mean you didn't want your precious Governor embarrassed?'

His contempt roused her anger. In her own defence, she shouted: 'He's NOT my Governor. I hate you sometimes, you and

403

your sneering.' He gazed at her, unmoved, and she added: 'I don't know why I bothered. You don't deserve anyone to . . .' Her voice trailed off as she looked into those cold blue eyes.

She tried again. 'Just accept that I did what I thought was right.'

'You betrayed me.'

'I did *not*.' Fighting to control her sense of inadequacy, she muttered, 'Anyway, you can go back home now, to the Castle. No one will know.'

'You'll know.'

'Why should that matter? I did it for you.'

Again he scrutinised her, seeming to lose some of his anger. Studying her as if she were some mystery specimen, he asked: 'Why? Really, why?'

'Because I – I care about what happens to you.'

'But why?'

She shook her head in frustration. 'How should I know? I just do. I suppose I'm grateful to you for what you did for me.'

His shoulders drooped and he gave an empty laugh. 'Grateful.'

'Yes.'

The blue eyes met hers again, defying her to look away. 'Is that what you feel for the Governor – gratitude, because he dragged you from the bogs in Ireland? Is that it? Gratitude – or is it his position, his power that excites you?'

'Yes. No!' Under his cross-examination, she felt something approaching panic. Stepping back, she said: 'I must go. I'll be missed if I don't get back, then they'll be asking questions.'

'They?'

In a barely audible voice, she said: 'He. I have to report to the Governor on how Mistress Colenutt progresses.'

Now his voice was almost triumphant. 'I see. You have to report on your mission, is that it? And how will you describe it, as a success or a failure?'

Crumbling under his scorn, she turned towards the door, stumbling in her attempt to escape from his searing contempt. As she pulled on the handle, she swung round and spat at him: 'I hate you!'

He nodded and for a terrible moment she thought: That's what he wants to believe.

In silence he followed her outside and caught Fortune. She watched helplessly as he saddled the mare, then with exaggerated politeness, held out the reins. 'Should I help you to mount?'

'No!'

He bowed his head. In spite of her best intentions she asked: 'Aren't you coming?'

'You think I should?'

'I don't care what you do.'

'Then in that case, I'll come.'

They rode to Carisbrooke in silence. Dublin's feelings were manifold – outrage; a sense of injustice; the unfairness of being misunderstood; and just plain, painful hurt. Behind her, Caleb jogged along on Robert's mare, silent, his presence sending out an almost physical wave that seemed to push her on, yet at the same time keep her away. When they reached the Castle she felt an overwhelming sense of relief.

It was too late to think of going to Widow Colenutt's. For the first time she began to wonder what excuse she could make for her failure to do so. As they clattered over the cobbles towards the gatehouse, her worst, hardly-formed fears were confirmed.

'Where in God's name have you been? The Governor's in a fury.' To Dublin, the guard added: 'You're to go to him immediately.'

She glanced round at Caleb but he refused to meet her eyes. Slipping from the mare, he came round and took Fortune's rein, still not looking at her. Dublin dismounted and walked unsteadily across the courtyard towards the living quarters, wondering what storm awaited her next.

'Where have you been? *Where?*'

She was silent.

Robert snorted to himself with indignation. 'I cannot believe that you, of all people, could behave in this way.' He stood behind his desk, formal, coldly condemning.

'I beg you to listen . . .'

'You were commissioned to carry out certain duties. You have failed me.'

'I have not! I – I cannot tell you everything, but please . . .'

He did not appear to hear her. 'That groom, I'll have him flogged.'

'No!'

His cold eyes came to rest upon her face. 'His welfare seems of great importance to you.'

405

'He has done nothing wrong.'

'He left the Castle under false pretences.'

She thought of the petty court, of Caleb left to face the consequences of helping her. Once again she might avoid punishment, but he would take the blame. She caught Robert's arm. 'Please, I beg you, do not flog him.'

Robert scrutinised her face, his expression tight-lipped. When he spoke, there was venom in his voice. 'Where have you been – under the bushes with him?'

'No!'

'You must be under some sort of spell.'

'Of course I'm not – I'm grateful to him because he once did me a kindness.'

Bitterly, he said: 'I trusted you.'

Suddenly her own sense of outrage welled up. 'It is you who have misused me. I am condemned, humiliated. People snigger behind my back. I endure it so that I might find out what you want to know.'

'Dublin.' Robert threw off his cold shield. Before her eyes she could almost see him wilt. His words confirmed her feelings.

'I am under such pressure, I know not which way to turn. Poor Rolph has been arrested. The Royal servants have made false charges against him, saying he wished to kill the King. I am without my right-hand man.'

She lowered her eyes to avoid saying: I told you so.

'I'll dismiss the groom,' he said.

'Where will he go?'

'Why should that concern you? Come the next Hiring, he can find another post.'

Dublin's thoughts came so fast and furious that she did not follow their connection, but she said to Robert: 'I will never go back to Foxton.'

'I see.' He made a show of tidying documents on his desk. 'I thought you loved it there.'

'I love the house, the gardens, but I shall never be happy there . . .' She could not finish the sentence.

With a sigh he came round the desk and placed his hands on her shoulders, forcing her to look into his eyes. When he spoke, he was reasonable, accommodating.

'I know that this has been hard for you. As soon as the King leaves here, we can pick up the threads of our lives again.'

She started to protest but as she stood before him, he bent his head and pressed his lips against her neck, against the rise of her breast.

'Dublin!' Into her hair he whispered, 'It's been so long. I should never have left you like this.'

'No, Robert. Please.'

'Please, my love. Don't make me beg.'

He began to kiss her, lifting her skirts. She started to struggle, beating him with her fists, but he seemed oblivious.

'Dublin.' He moaned her name, forcing her back against the wall, lifting her off her feet. She wanted to scream, to tear at his face, but something held her back. All the time she thought of Caleb, his fate in Robert's hands. Was he capable of taking the ultimate revenge in order to get what he wanted? As Robert thrust into her she began to sob.

When he had finished, he moved away. Standing with his back to her, he said: 'Don't you think I know? You and that ill-formed peasant.'

Trembling, she said, 'Let me leave here.'

'To go with him?' He gave the parody of a laugh. 'He goes, you stay.'

In the face of her silence, he confirmed her worst fears. 'Don't you know that I could have him killed?'

'If you did, I should kill you myself.'

He tried again, pretending that he had spoken in jest. 'In the fullness of time, you'll forget him. He's uncouth, a peasant.'

'Like me.'

'Not like you.' He shook his head, appealing to her. 'Think of all that we have meant to each other . . .'

She did not argue with him. An overwhelming sense of sadness claimed her. The calmness of her voice masking her turmoil, she said? 'May I withdraw now?'

In the face of her self-possession, he acquiesced.

Banished from the Castle at a moment's notice, Caleb collected his belongings, hoisted his pack onto his back and called to Tyke.

'Caleb!'

He heard her call, but kept walking, not looking back.

'Caleb, please wait!'

Reluctantly he slowed his pace, aware of the soldiers watching from the ramparts. She came running after him, breathless. There was anguish in her face. In the half-light, her eyes looked huge. She had been crying.

'I'm so very sorry. I tried to intervene.'

'You've intervened once too often.'

As he went to move on, she said: 'Where shall you go?'

'It's none of your concern.'

He saw the desperation in her face. With a sigh, he stopped. 'Look, I don't know what you want. I don't know anything. Just go back to your Governor.'

She shook her head, gazing at him with her young girl's innocence. Her voice flat with defeat, she said: 'Let me come with you.'

'Don't be stupid.' He dismissed the words as meaningless. 'Leave me alone, is that clear? You've tormented me enough.'

He hoisted his pack higher and began to move away again, then hesitated. 'Your mare, she's in foal.'

'I –'

'I had her covered with the best stallion in the yard. She'll foal next May.' He saw the tears brim over her lids. He could not bear the sight of her pain. Lengthening his stride, he walked away from her, not giving her the chance to say more. When he was safely down the hill, he gave the merest glance back up to the gatehouse. There, silhouetted in the mist, hunched and forlorn, he saw her solitary figure, gazing after him.

He found himself travelling in the direction of Caulbourne but as he drew near the village, he stopped. It was a sad fact that he had no job, no money, and few prospects. He desperately needed a drink. Dropping his sack and surveying the familiar Green, the winding stream, he thought that even if he went to the next Hiring, once a prospective employer learned that he had not served his time, he was unlikely to find a post.

The village was swathed in mist, giving it a silent, deserted look. Little Annie was down there, and Mam. He had a vision of the child curled up against her grandmother, the two rocking in a gentle, enveloping scene of family love. He had nothing to give to either of them.

A few spots of stinging rain hit his upturned face. There had been no summer to speak of and now autumn was already here. Another season. Another year. Another lonely future. Picking up his load, he turned his back on Caulbourne and set off for the hills.

Chapter 59

Just when King Charles thought that all was lost, the Parliament agreed to treat with him. True, the conditions were exactly the same as those offered when he had been at Hampton Court, but it gave him hope. After ten months of imprisonment, he was permitted to leave the restrictive walls of Carisbrooke Castle and take up lodgings in the town of Newport.

To his joy, once again he was surrounded by men of his choice, Captain Titus, Harry Firebrace, all his old servants, with the exception of an unfortunate few who were in prison. In addition, new courtiers came to offer their support, amongst whom was a pleasing young man with golden love-locks and a plethora of lace. His name was Tristram Fortunatus.

'I remember your father well,' said the King. 'I trust that these sad times have not caused him too great an injury.'

'No, Your Majesty. My father is well and his estates flourish.'

'And yourself?'

Fortunatus lowered his eyes. 'Sire, I was wounded at Newbury, but since then, I have tried my hand at politics, hoping to further your cause with word rather than sword.'

Charles bowed his head. He felt sad that such a beautiful young man should be marred by a pronounced limp, but then all, in some way, had suffered. To Fortunatus he said: 'I pray that your sojourn on this Island will be pleasant.'

'It is a fine place, Sire. Soon my father will settle some land upon me. I might do worse than to set up an estate here.'

Charles thought of the homes of his friends, the Oglanders, the Worsleys, the Dillingtons. If things were otherwise, he too might have found this a happy place to settle. He recalled that

Governor Hammond had bought a place. There had been some speculation about it, a hint that he had set up some lady of pleasure in it.

To Fortunatus he said: 'If you want advice about buying property here, you could do worse than ask the Governor.'

At first, the Treaty negotiations seemed to augure well. The King accepted the initial proposals without demur. On leaving the Treaty Hall that night, there was an air of euphoria throughout the town.

But as the days passed, things became increasingly delicate. Whilst he was willing to agree to some points, there were a few upon which Charles would not, could not budge.

'Why can we not pass over these points?' he demanded of the Assembly. 'If you will allow me to come to London, we can come to some arrangement about the areas of contention.'

'Sire, in agreeing to this Treaty, it was made clear to you that each item must be taken in order. We cannot move onto the next, until the former is settled.'

The truth dawned anew upon Charles. He could prevaricate all he liked, but the only way out of this mess was to make his escape.

For Robert, the stormclouds were gathering. Ever since the King had come into his care, a dispute had been raging between the army and the Parliament. At the same time, there were growing elements who believed that there would be no peace at all as long as Charles lived. Robert, the soldier, struggled with Robert, the servant of the Parliament. His sense of honour told him that in the end, the rule of law must be upheld. He would do nothing without the express permission of the Commons.

His deliberations were interrupted by a knock on the door. In answer to his call, Edmund Rolph stepped into the chamber.

'Ned!' Robert's spirits lifted. If everything else was wrong in this benighted Island, then Rolph's return, exonerated from the charge of treason, was one small flame of comfort.

'Sit you down. Take some wine.' Robert poured the Major a generous measure and looked at him with affection. 'My dear man, I know I have said it before, but I have to say again how your presence warms my heart. In the event of anything happening to me, I have left express instructions that the safety of the King is to be in the hands of yourself and Captain Bowerman. Now that you are back, I can rest easy. On you at least, I know I can rely.'

On Monday 27 November, Robert's former colleague Isaac Ewer arrived from Portsmouth.

'Isaac! What brings you here?' Robert was glad to see him, but feared that his arrival could only mean trouble. Noting his rank, he added: 'Congratulations – I see that you too are now a Colonel.'

'Robin, I have express instructions that you should re-arrest the King and bring him back to Carisbrooke, or anywhere else you believe to be safe.'

Robert nodded. 'So be it. As soon as I have confirmation from the Parliament, I will act.'

Ewer shook his head uncomfortably. 'You should do so now.'

'Not without Parliament's agreement.'

Ewer did not meet his eyes. In a low tone he said: 'Then my instructions are that you should accompany me back to army headquarters.'

'What for? What of my duties here?'

'In your absence, Major Rolph and Captain Bowerman will hold the fort.' Seeing Robert's hesitation, he quickly went on: 'I'm sure this is a temporary withdrawal, for further debate on the future.'

Robert nodded, in some ways grateful at the prospect of some respite. Seeing no alternative but to obey, he sent for Rolph.

'Edmund, while I am away, I command that you maintain things here as they are. Keep a close guard on the King. See that at all costs he does not leave the Island. If we travel fast, I should be back within two days.'

'Colonel.' Rolph acknowledged the order. He seated himself on the edge of Robert's desk, swinging his leg, relaxed, confident. To his commanding officer he said: 'Rest assured, sir, while you are away, we will take care of things for you.'

As Robert went to prepare for his departure, he noted with misgivings that Isaac Ewer came with him. He had the distinct impression that he was being shadowed.

'Perhaps you would like to rest somewhere?' he suggested.

'There is no need. We should leave soon or we will miss the tide.'

Robert wanted to seek out Dublin. He desperately needed to

make his peace with her, but he could think of no way of doing so with his constant companion at his elbow. He comforted himself with the thought that he would be back within two days and then he would sort things out.

He set off in the company of a troop of soldiers led by Isaac Ewer. He was desperately tired. For the next few hours he could give himself up to the journey, let Ewer make the decisions.

Stepping from the boat and onto the mainland soil, he had the strange feeling of waking from a long and disturbing dream. He looked back across the Solent but the Island was barely visible, a dream Island, and in some ways, a nightmare.

'We should be moving.' Ewer brought him back to the present. With a nod of his head, Robert accepted the horse provided for the journey and set out at a trot behind his fellow Colonel. The company formed a protective circle about them. Their destination was Windsor.

Troop movements were commonplace. They passed several other companies travelling south. As evening began to draw in and they were thinking of accommodation for the night, they were accosted by a single officer with two escorts, travelling in the opposite direction. Robert recognised Major Oliver Cromwell, son of his now-famous father.

Cromwell was clearly surprised to meet them. 'Colonel Hammond? What do you here?'

Robert explained the summons, looking to Ewer for confirmation. His companion looked uncomfortable. To Robert he said: 'Perhaps we should not delay but ride through the night.'

Cromwell turned to the governor. 'I fear you have made a grave error in leaving your post. I have with me orders from the Parliament, expressly commanding you to stay on the Island.'

With trembling hands, Robert read the written confirmation. Folding it carefully, he looked from Cromwell to Ewer. To the latter he said: 'I must go back.'

Ewer shook his head. 'I am afraid I cannot allow that. My orders are to take you to headquarters, no matter what.'

Robert looked to Cromwell. In the face of the superior number of troops facing him, Cromwell bowed his head in defeat.

'What of the King?' For a moment, Robert thought with relief that Rolph would hold the Island until he could get back, but in Ewer's expression, he saw his worst fears confirmed.

'It's out of your hands now. The army are in control. The time has come for the King to pay for his actions.'

'No. I have to go back!' Robert began to struggle.

'Robin, please calm yourself, there is nothing that you can do.'

Held by two of the accompanying guard, he looked into the serious eyes of Isaac Ewer, willing him to change his mind.

'I must get back,' he repeated.

Ewer sighed, his gesture fatalistic, saying everything. Aloud he said: 'I fear, dear friend, that there is nothing you can do. The King is to be escorted from the Island. Major Rolph will take charge of him. Even now he will be on his way. His Majesty has had all the chances that will come to him. You must face the fact that he is as good as dead.'

Chapter 60

Caleb did not go to the Hiring. Following his instinct, on leaving the Castle he installed himself back in his old bothy. He had a wonderful sense of coming home, and the memory of those past summers, guarding his sheep on the so-familiar hills, filled him with swirling waves of nostalgia.

Yet he could not stay. There was another shepherd at Caulbourne now; this was his hut. One day, that man would be coming up to check on things, to make his own preparations for the following year. Caleb had no right to be here, only an overwhelming longing to pick up the threads of his past life.

He was also faced with the question of survival. Apart from the few belongings he had carried with him from the Castle, he had no means of support. Food was the major factor. In part, he could live off the land, keep himself warm, but that would not be enough. The worst of the winter was yet to come, and the disastrous summer meant that there was little in the way of pickings to be found in fields or hedges.

Thinking of the difficulties, he almost weakened. It made sense to go back to the village and seek out his mother and Annie, except for that stubborn streak in him, that pride which complicated his life so often, which would not permit it. He would not be dependent upon his mother. His sensible voice told him that Mam would love to have him back and that on the contrary, instead of her supporting him, he would be able to look after her, fetch and carry for her, keep her safe. As for Annie – the memory of the little girl's arms about his neck, the unconditional love which she poured upon him, scared him. He dared not open his heart to such tender, honest love. If he did, he would be lost. Better to be as he was, forewarned, in control, responsible only for – and to – himself.

After a couple of days exploring the downs for nuts and seeds and berries, he wandered down towards Brixton Village. Perhaps in return for some work, he would be able to get a meal. He knocked at several doors, but was turned away. People looked at him with suspicion. He knew that look well enough, the fear that he was in some way Devil-touched. Tyke's constant presence, the dog's obedience that did not even call for a verbal command, underlined that this was no ordinary man and beast.

'Get away from here or I'll send for the Justice!'

He was beginning to despair, to wonder if he should go home after all, when he came upon a substantial cottage up near Gaggerhill. As he walked across the yard, a black bitch came bounding out, barking and wagging her tail. She and Tyke indulged in a canine greeting, sniffing, circling, bounding up and licking each other. It seemed like a good omen.

Before Caleb reached the door, a woman came out to see what was causing the commotion. She was well-made, perhaps in her thirties, good-looking in a full, sensual way. Her thick brown hair and dark eyes gave her the look of a Romany. As she waited for Caleb to come near, he felt the force of her gaze, a slow, deliberate look that seemed to be sizing him up.

The woman pulled her shawl tighter across her chest, folding her arms about her. Her full breasts rested on the encircling arms.

'What are you wanting?'

'Work. Anything in return for a meal.'

'Can you cut wood?'

'Of course.'

Without speaking, she nodded towards a pile of felled timber in the yard, then indicated an axe, lying abandoned near the door.

Caleb went across and picked it up, then he began to work. The woman stood watching, still appraising him. Her hands now rested on her hips, and he had the odd feeling that she was viewing him like some prospective purchase.

The cutting was thirsty work. 'Have you no ale?' he asked after a while. 'I'm fair parched.'

With a slight shrug, she went into the cottage and returned moments later with a jug. 'Here. Drink.'

416

Again she stood watching him. 'What's the matter with your shoulder?'

'I was born like that.'

She pulled a face. Taking the empty jug from him she asked: 'You wed?'

'What is it to you?'

She did not reply. His tone did not appear to offend her. Going back to work, he chopped solidly for another half-hour. By now his shoulders ached and he stopped to give himself a breather. Already it was growing dark.

'You can leave the rest,' she said, 'for now.'

He threw the axe aside and gathered up some of the timber. 'Where do you want this?'

She indicated the door into the cottage, and ducking under the lintel, he took it into the room. The woman followed close behind.

Inside, a fire burned in a makeshift grate, below a brick chimney. The room was permeated with the mouthwatering smell of cooking meat. Caleb realised how hungry he was. He looked round at the woman, waiting now, awkwardly, to be fed.

She took a trencher from the table and spooned a large helping of stew from the skillet over the fire.

'Sit you there.'

He sank down and began to spoon the meat into his mouth. It was succulent, tender, flavoured with herbs and for a few minutes he had no thought but the pleasure of filling his belly.

As he finished, he sat back and looked at the woman. She was still regarding him, with the same lazy, searching look.

'Will you come again?'

'If you wish.' He congratulated himself on having found a means of getting food.

Standing up, he went towards the door, suddenly remembering Tyke. He wondered whether to ask if the woman had a bone to spare.

As he went to step through the doorway, he almost had to squeeze past her as she leaned against the frame. His arm touched her breast and he drew back, but she did not move. She said: 'I'm a widowwoman.' She glanced out into the yard. 'Look at your dog.'

Caleb gazed into the gloom. The black bitch was crouched out in the yard, her hind legs splayed. Tyke was mounted across her,

417

pushing away. There was something vital and frenzied about Tyke's rhythm, something secret and self-satisfied about the bitch. Caleb glanced quickly at the woman, wondering if he should apologise for his dog. She raised her eyebrows, the message in her eyes clear.

It was a long while since Caleb had touched a woman. 'You asking me?' he said huskily.

'I'm not asking. But I'm offering.'

With a grunt, he turned and took her arm, pulling her to him. Already she was untying the strings of his breeches, feeling inside, exciting him to the point where he could hardly hold back.

Quickly, aggressively, he took her, straddling her across the rough oak table from which he had so recently taken his fill. In response to his thrusts, she moaned and gripped hard to his arms, her nails biting into his skin. 'Don't stop. Don't stop!'

He held back as long as he could, but when he came, he knew that she was unsatisfied. With his knee still pushing up between her legs, he prolonged her pleasure with his hand.

'Oh, oh, that was good.' She was panting, stretching herself like a cat. He felt a passing amusement at her wholehearted devotion to her pleasure.

'Does that earn me another mug of ale?'

'I'll give you a brandy.'

For a while they sat in silence, then she began to talk of her husband who had been an Excise man, but whose life had been cut short by a swift blow from a smuggler's dagger.

'He left me well provided for, but it gets lonely.'

'You should remarry.'

Her expression warned him off. 'Don't go getting ideas.'

Caleb stood up. 'Not me. I'm not in the marriage market.'

As he looked around for his jerkin, she said: 'Will you take off your shirt?'

'What for?'

'I'd like to see you.'

His throat tightened. 'I'm not a peepshow.'

'I never said you was. I just wondered . . .'

Evenly he said: 'I don't know you. I don't even know your name – and I don't want to.'

She shrugged. 'Will you come again?'

'To cut more wood?'

418

'And to drink a brandy.'

He relaxed, his own sexual release leaving him feeling better about the future.

Picking up his hat and settling it on his head, he said: 'I'll be back.'

During November, Caleb came several times to the widow's cottage. In return for odd jobs, he received a good meal and a good humping. In between times, he gave her no thought. He wondered how long this could go on. Cynically he thought that at least it took away the edge to his appetite, or should he say, appetites? His stomach was filled, and the couplings eased the longing, the empty void that against all reason, could only be healed by Dublin O'Neill. But common sense told him that it could not last.

As he approached the cottage on the last Tuesday of November, he knew immediately that something was different. Before he reached the door, it opened and a man came out. In his hand he carried a pistol. He was big, burly, aggressive. Above an almost violently thick belt, his shirt strained across his belly, thick black hair protruding between the gaping thongs at his neck.

To Caleb he said: 'That's far enough. What you doing here?'

Caleb hesitated. 'I – I do odd jobs for the lady of the house.'

'Oh, you do?' The man came closer and began to circle Caleb. 'What sort of odd jobs would they be, then?'

'Cutting wood, fetching water, digging a drainage ditch. Who are you?'

The man threw his head back. 'Me? I'm her husband.'

Caleb's eyebrows shot up in surprise. 'She said she . . .'

He did not finish the sentence. Slowly, deliberately, the man raised the pistol. 'I'll count to three,' he said. 'One, two . . .'

Caleb went.

The weather turned harsher. The ice on ponds and streams was inches thick. The ground was iron hard and try as he might, Caleb could not glean anything from the unwilling soil. Frost killed the remaining berries and late fruit froze on the branch.

His experience with the woman made him loath to risk any more such sorties. With each passing day he felt more and more isolated. There was no news. Sometimes he agonised about what might be going on at the Castle. Among everything else, he missed the comradeship, the gossip, the daily bustle of communal life. He missed his conversations with Polly Cranford who had given him precious morsels of information about Dublin. Most of all, he missed seeing Dublin herself. Whenever he thought of her now, it was with the mental vision of their last encounter, her standing alone and forlorn at the Castle gate, watching him walk away.

'Let me come with you,' she had said. For the first time he wondered what she had truly meant, then thinking of the Governor, her blind love, he dismissed it as an empty offer.

He wondered if the King was still in residence, or if he had been carted off back to the mainland. He also wondered if there was anyone back at Foxton.

The thought of the house brought back bitter-sweet memories. For days he was locked in a chasm of gloom. Then, in an attempt to throw it off, he set out at first light and walked over the downs to the Manor, wanting to know, wanting to see again at first-hand the grounds he had planted, the work he had supervised, the livestock he had purchased, and most of all the places where he had walked with Dublin.

When he arrived, it was to find the place locked up and deserted. He wandered about, tidying the grounds as he went, pulling up dead plants, gathering fallen leaves. He picked up some chestnuts in the orchard, a few brown speckled apples which were just about edible, and found a sack of musty corn in the barn. A few handfuls were still worth the taking. It was better than nothing.

Then he walked across to his own small cottage. It looked forlorn, unloved. He thought painfully of Annie.

After a while he realised that he had not seen Tyke for some time. He began to call the dog, first by name, then whistled for him. He did not come. Cursing him, Caleb retraced his steps around the estate, seeking Tyke out. Already it was growing dark. Surely the dog would find his way home when he was ready – if not, Caleb thought with growing despair, then he would be truly alone. As he trudged back to the bothy, he made up his mind. Tomorrow, he would go home.

Chapter 61

'Missed!' The report of a musket-shot followed by a swift oath drifted across the courtyard of Carisbrooke Castle.

Dublin was on her way to the guardroom. She hesitated as the shot reverberated around the ancient walls. For once the gates stood open, but there was no chance of escape.

As she approached the gate-tower, Edmund Rolph and a guard crossed back over the bridge and into the guardroom. Rolph rubbed his hands briskly and gave Dublin a wink, which she ignored. The men were about to have their meal.

'Mistress O'Neill.' Rolph bowed with exaggerated courtesy. 'I trust that you are well, not missing the Governor too much?'

Dublin had heard the rumours, suggestions that Robert would not be back. She did not believe them, confident that no one would leave the likes of Rolph in charge of the Island.

Rolph turned to the guard. 'You go.' He proceeded to dish himself out a large helping of stew. 'See if it's still there. You'll not eat till you've shot it. I'll lay odds that you can't hit it. It's Devil-touched, that beast, like its owner.'

With a sigh the guard went back outside and Dublin followed close behind, not wishing to be left alone with the Major.

'What do you shoot?' She accompanied the man to the gate and peered into the semi-darkness. It was the first time that she had stepped beyond the Castle walls for an eternity.

'That cur, there.' He indicated with his head a hazy shape out on the bank.

Dublin followed his direction, screwing her eyes up the better to see. When she made out the creature, her pulse quickened. 'That's Caleb's dog!'

'S'right. We're sure it's possessed. For all you know, it's the traitor come back to put a spell on us. The Major says to kill it.'

'No!' Dublin pulled up her skirts and ran across the bridge, calling as she went. 'Tyke! Come here, boy, come to me.'

The dog ducked down, cowed, the tip of his tail offering an appeasing wag. 'Come along, boy.' She held out her hand and with lowered head, the animal crept closer. Finally, when it was near enough, it licked her hand. Beneath her fingers, she could feel how thin he was, his coat stiff and dull, his eyes too large in his head. Her first thought was: Where is your master?

As she turned back towards the Castle, it was to find Major Rolph blocking the entrance, a musket aimed towards her and the dog. 'Stand aside, girl.'

'No!' She could not believe that he would shoot it. 'It's Caleb's dog,' she said, 'come to find him.'

'Well, he isn't here and it's no more than vermin, or an evil spirit. Traitor's dogs should suffer the same fate as their masters.'

'Please don't!' She stood her ground, holding the dog by the scruff of the neck. 'I'll take care of him.'

'Get out of the way, girl. There's scarce enough food now, without feeding a mangy cur like that.'

'I'll not let you shoot him!'

'You think you can stop me?'

'Please! I'll ask the Governor.'

He gave a low, unpleasant laugh. 'A lot of good that will do you.'

'What do you mean?'

'He isn't likely to be back.' He pushed out his chest. 'I'm in charge now.'

Dublin thought of Robert being lured away – to what? The reality of his danger shook her. 'Surely they won't –'

'He'll be safe enough,' said Rolph, for once taking pity upon her fears. 'But he won't be back.'

'What's going on here?'

In the heat of argument, no one had noticed Captain Bowerman come to the gate. He looked at all three of them, turning finally to Rolph for an explanation.

'Little lady's worried about her Governor. Then there's that dog. It's a scavenger, left behind by the humpty groom. I've given orders to kill it.'

As he was talking, Dublin shook her head, looking to Bowerman for help, pleading for Tyke's life. His response seemed to hang in the balance, then, with a shrug he said to Rolph. 'Go on, Edmund, let the dog go.'

Her adversary hesitated a moment, then lowered his musket. 'Pretty faces always win the day,' he said, with an ill-concealed attempt at humour.

Dublin's relief was total. She scurried back into the Castle courtyard, Tyke following close behind. No effort was made to close the Castle gate.

Going to her room, she pushed a minimum of clothing into a sack. She felt drained, exhausted. Today her courses had started and for the first time since she and Robert had become lovers, she felt relief. With something approaching grief, she realised that she no longer wanted his child.

For a while she gazed into emptiness, then Tyke nudged her hand, his wet nose making her jump. Picking up the sack, she left the room and descended to the courtyard. She crossed to the kitchen with Tyke close at heel. The first person that she saw as she went in, was Polly.

'Dublin.' Polly continued to slice turnips, giving a brief nod.

'I'm leaving here.'

The words caused Polly to falter. Before she could ask any questions, Dublin said: 'Have you any scraps of meat?'

Polly saw the dog and her expression changed from shock to compassion. Going to a cupboard, she brought out a mutton joint on a large, wooden board. The act of feeding the needy beast broke the tension between them. 'That's Caleb's dog.'

'Polly, please tell me where he is.' She willed her friend to be honest with her.

Polly put her knife aside and dried her hands on her skirts. 'I don't know where he is,' she said. 'Why do you think that I should?'

Dublin challenged her to stop the pretence. 'You and he are close.'

'Well, he talked to me sometimes.'

'When we were at Wolverton, you were always finding reasons to visit him.'

Polly gave a short laugh, shaking her head. 'I didn't go to see Caleb, not really.' She fed scraps of mutton to Tyke, the silence regulated by the hungry way he wolfed each chunk. Finally she found him a shinbone which he took to a corner and began to gnaw.

Polly glanced at her, shamefaced. 'I thought you'd guessed. I went to Foxton so that I could be with Isham Carter. How else was I to find a chance to see him?' Her cheeks flushed becomingly.

'*Isham*? Are you saying that you and *Isham* have been meeting?'

'Hardly at all since I came here. There's been no chance to get out and see him, and he rarely comes here, except to escort your Aunt Jane when she visits Mistress Hammond, but we're more or less promised . . .'

Dublin's heartbeat quickened. 'I'm truly pleased for you, but she's not my Aunt Jane. I'm a serving girl, the same as you.'

Polly forced Dublin to meet her eyes. 'Something has happened.'

In the face of her friend's shrewd look, Dublin could not hold anything back. 'Robert has gone to the mainland – Major Rolph says he won't be back.'

'I'm sure that he will return safely to you.'

Dublin paused. 'I don't want him back.' She thought for a long while, trying to piece all the strands together. Half to herself she said: 'He never really loved me; not enough. He's a brave soldier, but in other ways he lacks courage. He'll be happier with Mary.' She looked at Polly realising that her friend had known this all along.

Polly asked: 'Can you find happiness?'

Dublin shrugged. 'I've treated you badly,' she said.

'Nonsense.'

'Oh, but I have. I thought that you and Caleb . . .'

The astute Polly raised an eyebrow. 'Did you mind?'

'No.' The denial was automatic, but now she was faced with the truth. Of course she had minded! Ever since she had first encountered Caleb, she couldn't bear to see him close to another woman. A sudden, tidal-wave of longing engulfed her.

Polly reached out and put her arms about her. 'Dublin, you foolish girl. You've been so blinded by loyalty to one man that you never stopped to admit what you really felt for another.'

'I—'

Polly shook her head. 'Don't say anything. Let's get you some

424

sack, then you can decide what to do next.' As she poured out the drink, she added: 'The only reason that Caleb used to talk to me was to find out everything I knew about you. Didn't you realise?'

'Why didn't you tell me?'

'I didn't think you wanted to know.' Polly smiled. 'What will you do now?'

'Find him. Take his dog back. After that . . .' She made a helpless gesture.

Polly hugged her. 'Find him.'

Chapter 62

As the moon glimpsed its way through a bank of cloud, Dublin slipped across the bridge of Carisbrooke Castle with Tyke at her heels. As soon as they were over the moat, Tyke began to bound ahead. The mutton bones so ravenously gnawed earlier, seemed to have given him a new lease of life. Every now and then, he stopped and looked back, wagging his tail, waiting for her to catch up before moving ahead again.

Dublin did not question where she was going. Wherever it was, Tyke knew the way. She did not question what would happen when they got there. She had a strange feeling of giving herself up to her destiny. Resolutely, she refused to dwell on the choices that lay ahead, for they were not hers to make. Only Caleb could decide. With irony, she realised that once again her future was at the mercy of a man.

They walked for about half an hour, travelling west. Tyke had no doubt about where he was heading. As he sniffed his way along the banks, he seemed to find clues that set him off again until he reached the next scenting post.

They must have covered some two miles when it started to rain, silent, gentle drizzle that first caressed, then funnelled its way into her clothing. Before long she was immersed in a watery cocoon. The temperature dropped, and although her blood pounded from the effort of keeping up, she became increasingly cold. It was difficult to think. Only one task concerned her, not to lose sight of her four-legged companion.

The further they went, the more fatigued she became, and the more her confidence waned. With sinking heart she recalled how, the last time she had seen Caleb, he had been consumed with anger, thinking that she had betrayed him. As a result, he had been banished, his very livelihood taken away. It was obvious that he would not welcome her now. She dragged to a halt. Ahead Tyke stopped, looking back. When she did not move, he barked impatiently, bounding forward then stopping again. Eventually he came back and nudged her with his nose. She looked into his glistening eyes. His ears were alert and expectant. If he could have spoken she knew what he would say: 'Come on.' In the absence of any alternative, she did so.

As they neared Caulbourne, her spirits plummeted, thinking that they were heading for Caleb's cottage. This was his mother's home, the place where Sara had been his wife and his boychild had been born. Then, at the thought of Annie's wide, probing stares, and the memory of Lizzie's suspicion, the way she had left without explanation, her courage failed her. She could not go there.

Before they reached the sheepwash however, Tyke set off along a narrow track, loping easily, the regular whoosh of his panting keeping time with her footfalls. Suddenly, any tiredness vanished. Dublin knew with certainty where they were going. It was November. The shepherd's bothy would be empty. If Caleb had not gone home to his daughter, then where else would he choose to be?

As the incline steepened, she half-ran, wanting to get there as soon as possible. Tyke lolloped ahead, keeping always the same distance in front, checking now and then to make sure that she was following.

It was well after midnight. Her limbs tingled with her exertion and her eyes stung with the rain and the wind, but already the black silhouette of the bothy was in sight. Panting, she slowed to a halt, suddenly afraid again. The dog too stopped, looking at her with eyes that shone in the rain-soaked moonlight. When she made no move, he seemed to make up his own mind, and ignoring her too-late call, he ran on and ducked into the bothy.

Slowly, Dublin moved closer, ashamed, afraid, out of her depth. She could hear Tyke barking, then making that strange mock-growling sound that denoted he was tugging at his master's clothing, wrestling with him to drag him outside.

'In heaven's name, dog, where have you been? What do you want?'

The flap of the door lifted as Tyke came out tail-first, still pulling his master with him. Caleb came out half on his knees, struggling to get to his feet, pushing the dog aside.

He stood for a moment, brushing his clothing down, peering about him, then he saw her.

'I – I've brought your dog back.' The foolishness of the remark was such that she gave a little shrug of helplessness. Still he stared at her.

'I'll not disturb you.' In the face of his silence, she could think only of leaving, but for an eternity she still stood there, waiting for him to pronounce sentence. When he did not, she turned away.

'What are you doing here?'

She turned back. 'I . . .'

He came towards her, his brow furrowed with confusion. 'What in God's name are you doing here?'

She shook her head, having no words to explain.

'Look at you, you're soaked.' He squeezed the rain from her sleeve and it formed a cataract, splashing onto the shiny grass.

In silence he led her by the wrist to the bothy, ducking inside and pulling her with him. Within moments he had lit a candle, holding it high to look at her, his own face obscured in the shadows.

Embarrassed, confused, her only thought was to explain. She said: 'After you left I was confined to the Castle. I tried to get away, to go to the Hiring, so that I could find you and explain.'

'Then you'd have been unsuccessful. I didn't go.'

There was no encouragement in his voice, no sign that he understood, or wanted to do so. She tried again. 'Today is the first chance I have had to get away.'

He raised his eyebrows a fraction and she added, 'The Governor's been dismissed.'

'Is that why you come here now?'

'No! I wanted to leave when you did, to go with you, but you wouldn't take me.'

He brushed her remark aside and she still had no idea what he was thinking.

'Get those wet things off.'

As she watched, he drove the candle into the ground and it guttered and flickered until he secured the flap of the door. Numbed, no longer able to think, she began, childlike, to take off her wet clothes. Clad only in her shift, she looked to him for some direction. He reached out and felt the damp cloth. 'That too.'

Lowering her eyes, she stepped out of the crumpled garment. She let her hands drop to her sides, giving herself up to him, at his mercy.

With brisk, workman-like movements, he began to massage her arms and shoulders and back, drying her skin with a piece of fleece. The friction stirred her flagging energy.

'Rub some warmth into you' he said.

A distant, half-formed memory of another time came back to her, her mother brusque, efficient, rubbing her so, then it was gone.

She stood inert, too tired, too lost to do more than accept his ministrations. She did not know what she had expected, but it had not been this. After a while he stopped. He was gazing at her, his own expression taut, considering, then with slow deliberation, he pulled the shirt from his back and slipped it over her head.

Raising her arms, she let the garment tumble over her. She felt the heat of the cloth, the sense of his warmth being wrapped around her. For a moment she closed her eyes to absorb the comfort, then when she looked up, it was to find him still staring at her. She realised then the enormity of what he had done.

He stood before her, his shoulders naked, exposed to her view. She saw his jaw tighten, his eyes search her face for a response.

It was a moment that would stay with her for ever. The sight of his body, the broad left shoulder, the twisted hunch of his right, the vulnerability in his eyes, filled her heart with such tenderness that she gasped out her emotion.

'Caleb.' Hesitantly, she held out her arms and after a moment's uncertainty, he took a step towards her. She moved close to him, feeling his breath against her cheek. For a moment, she let her face rest against the crook of his neck. 'Oh, Caleb. Please, please don't send me away.'

He stood very still and after a moment she put her arms about him, wanting to hold him close. As her fingers touched the skin of his back, she stiffened. Long, deep welts criss-crossed his torso, across the fine manly shoulder, over the imperfect shape that tormented him. She stared at him, aghast.

His expression hardened and he drew back. 'Does it disgust you so much?'

'I – they did this to you?'

'I should have remembered my place.' His lips curled down in derision.

'No! You spoke up for me!'

'I did it for myself.'

For a moment, she could not believe that men could be so cruel, then, remembering the injured man cast into the river at Reading; the finger severed from the wounded soldier at Newbury; she knew that they could.

She reached out and laid her hand upon his arm, needing to keep him close, afraid that he would slip away from her again. When she spoke, her words were a jumble. 'Caleb. I don't know what to think. I don't know what *you* think. I never have. Most of the time you seem to hate me, and yet – I don't hate you.' Her words trailed inconclusively.

'I don't hate you,' he said evenly. 'But you destroy my peace. You make me feel things.'

'What things?'

By way of reply, he said: 'Why have you come here?'

'I –'

'Why? Be honest.'

'To bring your dog back.' Seeing his expression harden, she quickly added, 'Because I want to be here.'

He did not respond. Her voice little more than a whisper, she stated: 'I want to be with you.'

In silence, he turned his back to her. When he spoke, his voice was harsh. 'Then this is what you'll be getting – *this*! Look hard. Feel it.' He thrust his back at her, defying her to move away.

'Caleb.' She looked at the punishing scars, the irregular shape. Her mind searched for the right words, then her tongue seemed to run away with her.

'I thought there was more to you than that. I thought you were a man who had courage, and compassion; one who spoke out for what he believed. I thought you were a man who listened to the wind in the trees.' She faltered. 'I thought you were capable of love, but instead, I see someone eaten up by self-pity. And bitterness. Is that all that you are – a bitter tongue, someone so consumed by anger that he doesn't see anything else?' Then, unable to stop herself, she leaned forward, resting her lips against the skin

430

of his shoulder. 'You insult me when you talk as you do. Don't you know that I love you?'

In silence he turned. His eyes searched her face as if still he did not believe her.

'I'm sorry,' she said.

'For what?'

'For the King, for everything. I've been such a fool. I always seem to cause you pain.'

Still he looked at her, frowning, as if he did not understand her motives. Desperately she said: 'If you don't want me, then I'll go away. I swear that I'll never bother you again.'

He was a long time answering and when he did, he did not address her directly. 'You ask if I want you, but what do you want? Why have you come here now? What could you want with me?'

'I –' She could not tell him what she felt. There were no words to explain the tidal-wave of longing that immersed her.

Into her silence, he said: 'You'd find this life hard after what you've been used to.'

She hardly dared to believe what he was saying. 'That doesn't matter.' She held her breath; waiting.

'I love Annie. If you can't, then you'd best go now.'

'I – I'll learn to love her.' It would come in time. She still did not know what he was offering. She looked at his handsome head, the guarded expression. She said, 'I want a child of my own.'

He looked away and she said, 'I want you,' then hungry for this proud, distant man who belonged to no one, she whispered: 'I love you.'

Suddenly, it seemed that he could hold back no longer. With an exhalation of breath, he cupped her face, lifting her hair.

'Are you sure this is what you feel? Not gratitude? Not pity?'

'Never.'

He lifted her and carried her to his bed, laying her down among the reeds and bracken. She was trembling with cold, but even more, with emotion. He lay down beside her and she craved his warmth. For an age he was very still, holding her to him as he might have done Annie, a child in need of love. Tentatively she placed her hand on his arm, edging closer to him. She felt as if her whole life was poised to begin. Then, slowly, gently, he slipped his hand inside her shirt and cupped her breast.

431

The feel of his palm, gently squeezing her, filled her with an exquisite sensation. She moaned out her need and pressed herself to him. He began to love her.

He was wild, abandoned, and she found herself tumbling in a whirlwind of raw feeling, holding nothing back. His compact body, driven by his own sense of pride, delighted her in a way she had never imagined possible. It was wonderful, profound, the rainbow she had chased all her life.

At last he lay heavy and damp upon her, panting. She curled her fingers into his black locks and drank in the pleasure that settled upon her. She could not stop kissing him, hugging him close. Finally, sleepily, she snuggled against him, bathed in wellbeing, moulding her body to his, her lips brushing his skin.

The next thing she heard was a tentative scratching at the door-flap. Beside her, Caleb raised his head. 'Tyke.'

He scrambled up, now naked, and she looked with love on him as he bent to untie the flaps. The dog came inside, licked his master's arm and pattered across to push his nose against her cheek.

'He looks pleased with himself,' she said. 'Why do you think he came back to the Castle?'

Caleb scrambled back under the cover. 'To fetch a lost lamb.' He hugged her.

In reply she kissed him for the first time that morning, still not quite believing that he was hers. Aloud, she said: 'What do we do next?'

'If you mean to stay, we'll go and visit my mother, and Annie.'

'Of course I mean to stay!' She looked at him with affront, but he wiped her misgivings away with a teasing grin.

Thinking of his family, she felt a moment of unease, but pushed it aside. This was his mother, his child, both flesh of his flesh. There could be nothing to fear here. For a moment she thought of Mistress Elizabeth and her hostility, then of Robert.

As if tuning into her thoughts, he said: 'What about your master – Have you forgotten him so easily?'

She chose her words carefully, knowing that she had to be honest. Still holding him close, she said: 'He was good to me. He saved my life. He was my first love, but always there was something wrong. I could never admit it, most of all to myself. It's been a long time since I really loved him, but it had become a habit.' For a while she was lost in thought, then she said: 'I reached for

432

the moon, but I found that it was cold and distant. I need the warmth of the sun.' With an embarrassed smile, she added, 'But I'll always feel – gratitude towards him.'

'C'mon.' He flung the cover back and pulled her up. Seeking out the sack that she had dropped inside the door the night before, he threw it onto the bed. 'Have you got a change of clothes?'

As she nodded, he added: 'Good. Then give me back my shirt, woman, and I'll take you home.'

As they drew near to the sheepwash, the reality of returning to the cottage began to weigh heavy upon her. In Lizzie Gosden's eyes, she might well seem no better than a whore.

'What's wrong?' Caleb slowed his pace and turned to face her.

'I'm wondering what your mother will say.'

'What should she say? I'm bringing my bride to meet her.'

'I'm not your bride. What will she think if she knows I've come with you from the bothy?' She lowered her eyes. 'She'll think I'm a whore.'

Caleb shrugged. 'You want to be wed?' he said. 'Right. C'mon then. We'll go across to the green now. See, there's people present. We'll make our vows this minute.'

'We can't!'

'We can – unless you don't wish to wed with a penniless hunch—'

'Don't say it!' She shook his arm angrily. 'Don't ever say that again. You know I want to wed with you. Are you sure you want to marry *me*?'

'My foolish girl!' He bent forwards and kissed her. There was tenderness in his eyes, a calm acceptance she had never seen before. He repeated: 'Come on.'

He pulled her across the Green to the gateway that led up to the vilage church, and there, holding her by the hand, he cried out: 'To all those present here this day, take note that I, Caleb Gosden, shepherd of this Parish, do plight my troth to …' He hesitated.

Dublin looked at him, then without thinking, she whispered, 'Sorcha. My name's Sorcha.'

'To Sorcha O'Neill. Will you all bear witness?'

Two matrons came closer, their cheeks pink with emotion. 'We will,' the eldest answered. She plucked a sprig of myrtle, still green, from the hedge and held it out to the bride. 'God bless you, my dear.'

'Sorcha.' Caleb repeated the name, his eyes searching her face as if he had just discovered who she really was.

In her turn, she felt as if she had rediscovered herself. Her given name had been forgotten, along with that of her parents, Dervla and Ciaran. She mouthed their names, trying to recapture her own history.

'Sorcha,' said one of the matrons. 'That's a rare name.'

'A rare name for a rare girl.' Caleb kissed her in front of the small assembly, adding: 'As from this moment, you are looking upon my wife.'

Several people clapped their hands in approval.

'What day is it?' asked Caleb. 'A man needs to know the day upon which he tied the knot of love.'

'It is Wednesday, twenty-ninth November.'

Sorcha started. A year to this very day, Robert had been wed in his absence to Mary.

Caleb took her hand and led her back towards the sheepwash. They passed in front of the lean-to which had served as Sara's childhood home and he felt suddenly desolate at the memory of his dead wife, so good, so loyal. He did not deserve to be loved a second time.

'Now you look sad, what is it?' Sorcha hugged his arm to her side.

Remembering Sara's kindness, he knew that she would have wished him well. He shook off the ghost of the past. ''Tis nothing. Come along, say hello to your new mother, your new child.'

Banging upon the door, Caleb lifted the latch and stepped inside. Lizzie heaved herself painfully from a stool set near the fire. Her brow furrowed with the strain of trying to see clearly. At the same time, Annie retreated behind her grandmother's skirts and peered out at them.

Lizzie said, 'Annie, kiss your father,' and to Caleb himself, 'Where, in the Lord's name, have you been?'

The child looked up at him, then she ran to him, squealing as he held her high.

'Annie, your father is wed. Bow to your new mother, promise to serve her well.'

Annie eyed Sorcha with suspicion. Sorcha thought, She has not forgiven me for going away as I did. Bending forward, she held

434

out her hands. 'Annie, come and kiss me. I hope that you will not find me wanting.'

Looking from under darkened brows, the child pouted, then with a dash forwards, hurled herself against the caller. Sorcha just managed to keep her balance, sweeping the girl off her feet, hugging her close. She felt a great wave of relief.

Lizzie Gosden's expression softened and Sorcha realised that Lizzie too had forgiven her.

Sorcha said, 'Forgive me for leaving as I did. I was discovered and did not want to bring trouble to your door.'

Lizzie bowed her head. When she spoke, her voice was unsteady with emotion. She said: 'There is nothing to forgive. Any woman who can make my son smile, lighten his heart, is welcome here.'

Her words were the final gift that Sorcha needed. Taking her new mother-in-law's hands, she replied: 'Then, ma'am, I hope that I shall always be welcome.'

Chapter 63

For Robert, the winter months were difficult. As soon as he was released from the ordeal of his governorship, he succumbed to a series of agues and fevers. Stoically he endured them, knowing that they were the price of his honest service in impossible conditions. In time, he would recover. He had done his best and no man could do more. Rest and care would heal him and he had plenty of both.

In the meantime, he made plans for the future. Seated at the desk in his private study, he settled down to write a letter. It had burned in his brain for weeks, but ill-health and uncertainty had prevented him from giving it life. Now, he knew just what he must say. He wrote:

Reading
27 January, 1649

My dear Dublin,
Although I have been absent from Carisbrooke for nigh on two months, I have received constant news of events taking place therein.

I learn that you have chosen to absent yourself from there but not to Foxton. It seems that you were serious when you said that you no longer wished to live there. When I left the Island, I did not foresee that I should never return – perhaps you knew something that I did not.

In the meantime, it seems that destiny dictates that I shall stay here. Parliament have been generous to me. If you are in need of anything at all, you must write and tell me.

I write to inform you that I have found a property near to hand. As soon as this letter comes into your possession, I trust that you will make ready to travel here.

436

I miss you greatly. I know how much you have suffered on my account. It is my earnest wish to make it up to you. I long for us to find the promise and fulfilment that was always destined to be ours, and yet so far has been denied full expression.

Seeing that you no longer wish to live at Foxton, I have sold the house. By the time this letter finds you out, in all probability, the new owner will be installed.

Do not be sad that Foxton has gone. The place that I have selected here is far superior . . .

Robert's train of thought was interrupted as his study door opened. He did not look round, but smoothly pushed the letter beneath other correspondence. A moment later, slim, loving arms clasped him around the neck.

'Mary, my love, what do you do?'

'Robert, could we not go out riding, or perhaps for a walk? It is a fair day. Fresh air would do you good.'

Mary kissed him and Robert nuzzled his cheek against her head, enchanted by his young wife.

'If you wish it, my dear. Give me a few more minutes to complete my business.'

As soon as she had gone, he hastily finished the letter. Sending for his groom, he ordered him to deliver it for onward transmission. Soon, he would have Dublin back, then his life would be complete.

For Charles, the winter months were difficult. When news of Governor Hammond's departure reached him, he knew that only bad could come of it and on 1 December, his worst fears were confirmed. Under close guard, he was taken from the Isle of Wight, bundled across the Solent and secured in the dank void of Hurst Castle.

Yet all was not lost. The Parliament, if not the army, were still willing to negotiate with him. Nightly he prayed for common sense to prevail.

But worse news was to come. On 6 December, the army, either by arrest or intimidation, restrained all those members in favour of negotiation from entering the House of Commons. Those who remained, agreed that the King should face charges. The whole thing was a nonsense! There were no laws in the land that permitted a king to be put on trial. Surely God, in His wisdom, would show them the error of their ways? Charles sought within himself for some inner strength.

Once again he was removed, this time to Windsor Castle. With sinking heart, he found that any pretence at respect for his person was abandoned. None of his friends or advisers remained. Overnight, every vestige of court ceremony was stripped away. His food arrived untasted, and with each mouthful, he feared that he might be poisoned. Day and night an officer stood guard over him and all the while, the malicious Parliament and the demon army plotted against him.

On 19 January 1649, he was taken to London. Sadly he reflected how often he had longed to be back in his capital. Installed in his own dear Palace of St James's, he knew that he had returned to an empty shell. In his absence, the Parliament had desecrated his sacred rooms, tarnished the very nest where once he had been so happy in the bosom of his family.

There was little time to reflect on these evils, for the following day, Charles was taken by boat up the Thames and into Westminster Hall. There, he listened with disbelief as John Cook, the Parliament's stooge, pronounced that: '*Charles Stewart shall be impeached as a Tyrant, Traitor and Murderer and a public and implacable Enemy to the Commonwealth of England.*' At these words, Charles laughed.

He refused to recognise the court. He refused to recognise the charges. With only Juxon, Bishop of London for spiritual guidance, he stood alone against the evil that was being perpetrated against him. There was no one to help draft or read his speeches, but God, in His infinite goodness, gave him the words, held back the troublesome stammer. Charles spoke out, proud and unbowed, denying the right of this rabble to try him. He knew where his duty lay. Silence him how they might, he resolutely refused to bow to their illegal proceedings. God was on his side.

On 27 January, they announced their intention to sentence him.

'Do you wish to speak in your defence?' Cook asked one final time.

'Only before the Lords and Commons.'

The plea was denied. The commissioners withdrew and when they returned, Charles listened with disbelief. Calmly they announced their intention to end his life by the removal of his head from his body. It could not be so! Angrily he tried to speak out in his own defence, but they would not listen.

'You refused to recognise this court and now, this court does not recognise you. It is too late to plead once sentence has been pronounced.'

Still, Charles tried to make himself heard. 'I am not suffered to speak,' he shouted but even as he did so, he was hustled away by soldiers.

For Caleb, the winter months were difficult. With four mouths to feed, he was hard-pressed to make ends meet. In spite of this, his heart was alive with love. Sometimes he remembered the days when he had lived in this same cottage with Lizzie and Sara. Then, his overwhelming need had been to get away from that cloying, female world. Now, nightly, he returned home to the ministrations of three women, and he gloried in their undivided love.

In January, he heard about a job at Buccombe. A house was being constructed for one of the officers from the Castle. The man had met a local woman and decided to settle nearby.

'It's worth a chance,' he said. 'I'll go and enquire, see if there's any work.'

Sorcha felt saddened that he should nurse such a burden for all of them. With the little flour that remained, she baked him bread for his journey.

'Take good care of yourself.'

'Don't fuss, woman,' he scolded her, but his voice was tender.

Lovingly she put her arms about him. All her fears were soothed when he held her close. Yet one anxiety remained. She had not told him yet, not warned him that since their coming together, her courses had ceased. She hoped, feared that she was with child. This precious gift would add a further burden to his already weighty problems. She felt guilty but her joy could not be denied.

'Hurry back.'

While he was away, she felt anxious, afraid that he would be snatched from her. She did not deserve him. When she finally saw him coming down the slope towards the sheepwash, she could not stop herself from running out to meet him. She got there seconds before Annie and had to restrain herself from pushing the child aside.

Sweeping Annie into his arms, Caleb leaned across and pecked his wife on the cheek. In spite of the long day, the arduous journey, his eyes were alight with excitement.

'What has happened? You found work?'

He shook his head, but could not hide his elation. 'It is too much to take in. Here –' He held out a document to her. 'First of all, you had best read this. I'll tell you the other news afterwards.'

Sorcha took the package from him with questioning eyes. As she broke the seal, she felt her face colour, realising from whom it came. She read, and Caleb watched her.

When she had finished, she went to hold it out to him then remembered, just in time, that he did not have his letters. She said: 'It is from Robert. He has sold Foxton. He – he enquires about my welfare.'

Before he could comment, she pressed her mouth against his, willing him to know that Robert Hammond could never intrude upon their happiness.

Caleb grinned, untouched by Robert's letter. He showed no suspicion, no doubts. She thanked God for his confidence in her.

He said: 'That's just it. The house at Foxton – it's been bought by Tristram Fortunatus.'

Sorcha stared at his grinning face, waiting for some explanation. Shaking his head, hugging himself with undisguised excitement, Caleb said: 'I dragged him from the battlefield, at Newbury. As soon as they told me at the Castle, I went straight there. He's given me work, my old job back.' He stuck out his chest. 'You're now looking at the bailiff of Foxton.'

She laughed aloud and flung her arms about him, about Annie. 'This is wonderful.'

'It's no more than we deserve.' Taking Sorcha by the hand he added: 'It looks as if our future might not be so hard after all.'

She thought about the lodge-house at Foxton, the simple, warm, clean room where she had watched Caleb and Annie eat their bread so long ago. They could be happy there, and in addition, they would still have the pleasure of the beautiful gardens. Their beautiful gardens.

'Did you see Polly?' she asked, linking her arm through his.

440

'Aye. Polly's getting wed, to Isham Carter. They've both got a place at Wolverton.'

She felt a surge of undiluted pleasure. 'And Fortune?'

'The mare is well. Once we're installed at Foxton, you should be able to have her back.'

Sorcha laughed again. The horse was the only legacy she wanted from her long association with Robert. For a moment she thought about him, wondering. She earnestly hoped that his future would be more to his liking. Poor Robert, a slave to honour. She wondered if his letter was not so much an act of love as of duty.

That night, as they lay cuddled together, she said: 'I have something to tell you.'

'What?'

'I think I am with child.'

'I know.'

'How?' She raised her head and gazed into the darkness where his face was.

'You've had a strange look about you – as if you were poised for something.'

She relaxed and rubbed her cheek against his shoulder. 'You don't mind?'

'Foolish girl.' He kissed her and his hand came to rest on her belly. She felt that he was blessing the babe inside.

As she settled down to sleep, full of wellbeing, she allowed her thoughts to wander. Next to her, Caleb wriggled, fashioning himself a hollow in the bedding. She pressed her body close to him, loving him.

For the first time in as long as she could remember, she thought confidently about the years ahead. They stretched bright, comforting, full of possibilities.

Caleb. Robert. The King. For a wild moment she remembered that she might have been the King's mistress, had she so chosen. In the sanctuary of their chamber, that life at the Castle was hard to imagine. She wondered if she had dreamed it all. Remembering the King's slender face, she then wondered how he fared and hoped he had found a way of bringing peace to his kingdom. In her own way she was fond of him.

Then there was Caleb and Robert. How different they were. Fancifully she thought that Caleb was the sort of man who lit fires, while Robert was the sort to put them out. Caleb, strong, fierce, a man burning with passion. Robert, cool, upright, a man bowed by duty.

She turned over and in response, Caleb moved with her. She smiled into the darkness, fulfilled, at peace. When it came to choosing, she had picked the richest of them all, the man who knew his own worth, the man who would never put her second. As her eyes closed, she whispered into the darkness, 'Caleb, I love you.'

Historical Footnote

– On 30 January, 1649, only three days after the passing of sentence, Charles Stuart was executed by beheading at Whitehall. He faced his end with dignity, confident in the rightness of his cause. He was forty-nine years of age. His grieving widow, Henrietta, remained in her native France and he left behind three sons and three daughters.

– After a year on the centre-stage of English politics, Robert Hammond returned to relative obscurity. He became MP for Reading, and in 1653, he purchased the Manor of Willen, near Newport Pagnell.

In August 1654, appointed by Cromwell to the Irish Council, Hammond set sail for Dublin. There, two months after his arrival, he succumbed to a fever and died. He was thirty-three years old. He left behind a grieving widow and two daughters, Elizabeth and Mary. A third daughter, Lettice, was born some months after his demise.

– In the seventeenth century, most poor people lived and died with no written record of their passing. However, the Parish Register of All Saints Church, in Calbourne on the Isle of Wight, records that William 'Caleb' Gosden died in his native village in 1664. Twice married, he left behind three sons and three daughters.

– There is no historical record to show that Sorcha O'Neill ever existed – except within the imagination of the writer.